Charming DECEPTION

TITLES BY JAINE DIAMOND

CONTEMPORARY ROMANCE

Dirty Like Me (Dirty #1)
Dirty Like Brody (Dirty #2)
2 Dirty Wedding Nights (Dirty #2.5)
Dirty Like Seth (Dirty #3)
Dirty Like Dylan (Dirty #4)
Dirty Like Jude (Dirty #5)
Dirty Like Zane (Dirty #6)
Hot Mess (Players #1)
Filthy Beautiful (Players #2)
Sweet Temptation (Players #3)
Lovely Madness (Players #4)
Flames and Flowers (Players Novella)
Handsome Devil (Vancity Villains #1)
Rebel Heir (Vancity Villains #2)
Wicked Angel (Vancity Villains #3)
Irresistible Rogue (Vancity Villains #4)
Charming Deception (Bayshore Billionaires #1)

EROTIC ROMANCE

DEEP (DEEP #1)
DEEPER (DEEP #2)

Charming DECEPTION

BAYSHORE BILLIONAIRES

JAINE DIAMOND

DREAM WARP PUBLISHING LTD

Jameson

I stroll into the luxurious living room of the owner's suite at the Vance Bayshore resort to find my siblings seated around the coffee table, awaiting me.

Firelight from the hearth flickers across the walls and rain pummels the floor-to-ceiling windows, the waters of Coal Harbour churning beyond, black in the night. "Who died?" I make my way behind the bar. "It's literally gothic in here."

"You're about to," Harlan growls as I start fixing myself a drink, "if you don't come sit your ass down."

"What? I had a thing that ran late."

Harlan grunts. He reclines in a wingback chair with his feet up on the coffee table, dress shoes and all. In theory, I have three brothers and a sister, but in actuality I have two brothers, a sister, and what appears to be a male human sibling but is probably some sort of demon. "Lemme guess," Harlan drawls. "The blow job took longer than you expected."

"It did, actually."

"I'm right here," our sister, Savannah, says irritably as I sit down between her and Damian on the curved sofa. The vibe in the room is tense as hell. All my brothers and I wear dark suits, and Savannah wears a black dress.

I'm not even sure what we're doing here tonight. I just got a call from our grandfather's attorney, who told me attendance was "mandatory" and that it was "will-related business." But the last couple of times the five of us met like this had left us all on edge.

One week ago, we'd gathered to celebrate our grandfather's life and legacy at his funeral, and yesterday, we'd gathered for the reading of his will. Not only had we lost our beloved grandfather and patriarch sooner than we'd hoped, but he'd left us with a surprise in his will: a beneficiary we didn't even realize was so important to him.

If there was one thing Stoddard Vance taught his grandchildren, it was that you never lay all your cards on the table at once.

Which means... maybe he still has a hand to play.

"Why do I feel like old Stodd's still playing with us?" Damian muses, voicing my thoughts as Graysen gets to his feet.

"Let's just get started," Graysen announces. Even he doesn't seem thrilled to be here, and he lives here.

"How?" I inquire.

He draws an envelope from inside his jacket. "We have a letter from Granddad."

"Valerie dropped it off just before you got here," Savannah fills me in.

Valerie was our grandfather's longtime secretary and, as we discovered when he was on his deathbed, his lover. Turned out they'd been having a passionate affair for decades. Even before Grandma died.

Granddad's life was one giant plot twist, even when he was dying. And apparently, Valerie's still doing his bidding, even from beyond the grave. Just like the rest of us are.

"Valerie said we should read it together, so." Graysen tears open the envelope, unfolds the letter and reads: *"You're here to play a game."*

Damian smirks and shakes his head. Savannah laughs under her breath. Harlan growls.

But we can't really be surprised.

Our grandfather was a game master. Lover of sports, competition, fine liquor (and women who organized his calendar for him, evidently). He'd made his first millions off a chain of upscale sports bars, spawning a property development empire that evolved into what Vance Industries is today.

Which is a multi-industry, multibillion-dollar family of companies.

"*If you're reading this letter, I'm dead,*" Graysen reads on, kind of sighing at Granddad's bluntness. "*Earlier this year, aware that my remaining time was running short, I met with each of you privately. And I asked you a very important question.*" Graysen glances up, his gray eyes sweeping over the rest of us.

Well, *shit.* I remember that conversation.

"*I asked you,*" he reads on, "*if you could handpick a challenge for one of your siblings, something that would really test what they're made of, push them to grow, to better themselves, what would it be? Out of those conversations, as you may now be gleaning, such a challenge was devised for each of you by someone else in this room.*"

My gaze snags with Harlan's, and he lazily flips me the finger.

"*I asked you to keep that conversation a secret, just between us,*" Graysen continues. "*I trust that you all did that. And I entrusted my dear Valerie to write down the challenges for me and keep them safe. The five challenges you devised are now contained in five envelopes, one for each of you, located inside the box in front of you.*"

I now notice the wooden box on the coffee table between us: one of Granddad's antique cigar boxes.

"*One by one, each of you will attempt to complete your challenge. To get things started, my lovely granddaughter, Savannah, will draw an envelope from the box.*" I glance at Savi, and she shrugs. "*The name on the selected envelope will be the first of you to attempt his or her challenge. When the first person completes their challenge, you will meet again for the next name to be drawn, and so on.*"

"So, Savannah gets first pick because she's the only woman?" Harlan interjects.

"Picking first doesn't mean anything," she says.

"To be clear," Graysen reads on, *"this is not a business challenge. You have all earned your current positions within Vance Industries. However..."*

Graysen glances at us as he flips to the second and final page of the letter.

"... in order to receive your full inheritance, including your portion of ownership in the family business, you must successfully complete your challenge."

"And there it is," Harlan mutters.

I watch Graysen closely. As the oldest, he's always been our collective leader, personally and professionally. Second in command only to Granddad. I wonder what he's thinking right now.

"You have one year from the reading of this letter, collectively, to complete the game," he continues. *"Should you fail to complete your challenge for any reason, you lose the game. This means you lose your full inheritance. All moneys and assets left to you, including your ownership portion of the family business, will be redistributed among the winning players: your siblings."*

Harlan drops his head back against his chair.

"Of course, I love each and every one of you, and I would not wish to see you destitute and penniless. If you lose the game, those who win the game will have the option of retaining you in their employment, so that you will continue to have a place at Vance Industries."

"In other words," Harlan says, "lose the game, lose everything. But don't worry, the others can hire you back as a janitor."

"You have to admire the mastery," Savannah marvels. "It forces us to rely on each other in our darkest hour. Should that hour come to pass."

Yeah. This is definitely game-master shit of the highest level. Granddad's probably howling in his grave right now.

"Just the way he wanted it," Damian muses. "Life... the endless game." He tips his glass to the portrait of Granddad and Grandma over the fire, their wedding photo.

"Let's just agree," Savannah says dryly, but with affection, "that this won't be the game that turns us all against each other."

"Which is a hint at how bad my challenge is," Harlan says.

"Everything isn't about you, Harlan," Graysen mutters.

"Said the oldest sibling and the one with the least to lose."

"Least to lose?" Graysen frowns. "If I fail my challenge, I lose my position as CEO."

"You heard the rules," Harlan counters. "We can still employ you. And none of us are about to step into your shoes and run the entire fucking empire."

"He is right," Damian says lightly.

"Let's just agree that we all have equal risk here. We all stand to win or lose." Savannah raises her glass. "To the game."

"To the game," we all chorus grudgingly and clink glasses.

"To Granddad," Graysen adds.

"May the best man, or woman, win." Damian smirks.

"We're not playing against each other," I point out.

"Sure we are." Damian's eyes spark at me, the sly fucker.

"There's more."

We all look up at Graysen, who's still standing, holding the letter.

"To begin, none of you will know who devised your challenge. It is up to the person who devised your challenge to divulge this information if and when he or she so chooses. It is my hope that you will play this game the same as you live your lives: as a team, rather than as opponents. For in the end, it will be up to your siblings to decide if you successfully completed your challenge and won the game."

"Fuuuck," Harlan groans.

"Additionally, may I remind you that the Vance family's privacy should remain paramount at all times. Aside from the people in this room—and this part is underlined—you cannot discuss the game with anyone or tell anyone about the challenges."

Since I have no idea what my challenge is, it's hard to know how that might play out.

However, I know what one challenge is. The one I devised.

Harlan's eyes meet mine and I glance away, sipping my whiskey.

Graysen sets the letter down next to the cigar box. "Well, Savannah. I guess you're up."

Savannah gets to her feet, smoothing her fitted dress. "All right. Let's get this done."

Graysen picks up the cigar box and lifts the lid for her.

"What do you see?" I ask her.

"Envelopes," she says dryly.

Graysen, who can also see into the box, says, "They're upside down. She can't see the names written on them."

"Whatever you do," Harlan says, "don't pick mine first."

"Maybe there's an advantage to being picked first," Savannah says. "You get it over with."

"I'd rather be picked first." Damian sits back, perusing his "competition." "Imagine the pressure if you're last, if everyone else already completed their challenge and time is running out."

"Or maybe worse..." Savanna says. "What if we all fucked up?"

"Just pick a name already," I growl.

Savannah takes a deep breath and reaches into the box. She pulls out a small gold envelope, sealed with a wax seal.

She turns it over and reads the name on the front.

"*Jameson.*"

Everyone looks at me.

Harlan laughs his demonic laugh.

I groan and drag a hand through my hair. The idea that one of my older brothers or my older sister has devised a personal challenge for me, to test what I'm made of? It's the stuff of nightmares.

I'm definitely no saint.

"We seriously can't contest this shit?" I complain as Damian pats me on the back. I know this challenge will be hard. That's why it was chosen for me. And I do *not* want to lose my inheritance—hell, my birthright—over a fucking game.

"Just play the game, Jamie." Savannah hands me the envelope; my name is handwritten on it, probably by Valerie. "It's what

Granddad wanted." She goes to top up her drink, probably relieved to be off the hook.

"Easy for you to say," I mutter. "Your name wasn't drawn first."

"Savannah will take her turn, just like the rest of us," Graysen reminds me.

"Not like any of us have a choice," Damian says.

"Just man the fuck up and open your envelope," Harlan growls.

I can feel them all watching me.

There's no way around it; whatever it says in this envelope, I have to complete the challenge. It's what Granddad wanted.

No matter how difficult or fucking ridiculous it might be.

I have to win the game.

I break Granddad's wax seal, stamped with an elaborate V for Vance, then tear open the envelope. There's a card inside. I pull it out and read my challenge.

Just five words.

I read it again. And again.

I take a deep breath in the stretched-silent room, feeling everyone's eyes on me. Then I stand up calmly and toss the envelope and the card onto the coffee table. They all lean in to read it.

"You can all go fuck yourselves," I tell them and walk out, Harlan's dark laughter grating at my spine.

No sex for ninety days

CHAPTER 1

Jameson

Y ou really don't realize how many times a day/hour/minute you think about sex until you're trying not to think about sex because you can't actually *have* any sex.

"Stop the car."

I growl the words before I even know I'm going to, and the Bentley rolls to a stop in the middle of the street. Sex has invaded my brain like a thought-numbing toxin.

A woman stands in the street, bent over.

There's a rolling suitcase at her feet, split wide open. The contents have dumped out onto the pavement, but that's not what I'm staring at. She's wearing a soft terra-cotta-colored sundress, the ruffled skirt fluttering around her smooth, bare thighs in the breeze.

"I figured I'd go around, take the next street..." Locke's gruff voice from the front seat interrupts my staring and I meet his eyes in the rear-view mirror. The woman and her suitcase are blocking the street to the right, where we'd normally turn to reach the street where I live. "But you're right. We should offer her help."

It didn't occur to me to offer her help. The only thing that occurred to me was her bare legs and her drifting hemline.

He's right, though. And he's already opening his door.

"Stay here."

Locke stops as I clear my throat of whatever's clogging it—lust?—and get out, fastening a button on my suit jacket as I walk over to her. I hear Locke shut his door.

She's crouched down and has managed to stuff most of her things back into her flimsy-looking suitcase. She's now tugging on the zipper, which isn't budging. Maybe she hears my crisp, agitated footsteps on the pavement, because she looks up.

The early-evening sun flashes in her amber eyes. Her long brown hair dances across her face and she tucks the soft waves behind one ear as she gazes up at me, eyes widening.

My jaw clenches.

Irritating. That's the only word I'll acknowledge to describe the feeling in my body right now.

"Uh, hi." Her voice is soft and sexy, which just irritates me more.

"You need help." I mean it as an offer, but it comes out as a rude observation.

"I'm fine." She stuffs her things, which are spilling into the street again, back into the broken suitcase. She seems harried, her smile forced, but it still lights up her pretty face.

I try not to look directly at her eyes.

Or her breasts.

The sundress has little white flowers on it. The short skirt flows loose, but the waist is cinched, the bodice fitted, and I have a direct view down her mouthwatering cleavage.

I clear my throat again. "Okay. But you're kind of blocking traffic." Again, I sound like a rude, impatient asshole.

I guess I am.

She glances past me, at the dead-quiet residential street where the only sound is the purr of my idling Bentayga. There's no other car around, no other humans other than the ones tucked into their mansions.

"Uh... I'm sorry? I'll just get this fixed real quick and get out of your way." She laughs under her breath and tingles actually run down my spine, like she's swept her fingertip along it. "That high curb murdered my suitcase. The zipper split when I rolled it over, and once it started, I couldn't get it to stop."

"Why don't I help you."

"Oh, thanks, but I don't need any help." Her tone is fake cheerful, a wary edge beneath.

My gaze slides to the lacy bits of what has to be lingerie peeking out of the suitcase. And the white lace bra on the pavement that she snatches up.

She stuffs it out of sight.

"See, I knew this might happen..." She digs in her other bag, a well-worn hiking backpack that in no way suits her current outfit, and pulls out... bungee cords.

I watch, my irritation/fascination growing as she stuffs her remaining personal effects into her split suitcase, slams it together and wraps the whole thing in red bungee cords, all while trying to keep smiling. "No problem."

"You carry bungee cords around?"

"You have to be prepared for anything," she says brightly, really forcing the *I've got this* vibe. She rights the rolling suitcase. It resembles a sloppily made sandwich, bits of her lacy clothes poking out like wilted lettuce in the summer heat.

My eyebrow creeps up. "Large chance that's falling apart on you again."

"I'm not going far." She gets to her feet and brushes off her dress, her flushed skin coated in a fine sweat that makes me think of luxurious summer sex.

"We can give you a ride." Even as I offer, I mentally punch myself in the balls.

Getting in a backseat with this woman will hardly make my day any better.

"Oh. Um..." She glances at the SUV, where she can clearly see Locke behind the wheel, neck tattoos and all, and probably weighs the risks of getting into a car with two men she doesn't know, one of whom looks like a well-dressed felon. "I really don't need a ride. But thank you."

Good. See? You're not driving her anywhere.

We stare at each other.

She looks so... vulnerable... standing there with her sad little suitcase, the ruffled edge of her sundress fluttering limply.

No. She looks irritating.

Just walk away. She'll be fine.

It's a safe neighborhood.

"Well, good luck," I force out.

Why am I still standing here?

"Thank you."

"Nice meeting you." Why I throw that in before I walk away, I'll never know. It wasn't nice. We didn't meet. We didn't exchange names or shake hands.

We'll never see each other again.

I stalk back to the car with blood pumping to my cock. I'm half-hard, my pants are too hot, and I'm itching to get home and change out of this suit. I yank at my tie, loosening it, and I swear Locke smirks at me.

I feel way more agitated than I already did before we stopped.

I climb back into the Bentley and growl, "Take me home," half wondering if one of my brothers planted that woman in the street just to fuck with me. A little *welcome home* gift.

Harlan.

Harlan would totally do such a thing. If he could.

As we turn the corner and drive past, though, I doubt very much that a woman like that would ever be bought or bribed by a man like Harlan Vance, for any price. She's standing on the curb, wearing her backpack and holding the handle of her ridiculous bungeed suitcase.

I know she can't see me through the tinted window, but her eyes seem to meet mine as she gives the car a little salute, like royalty's driving by. Then she rolls her eyes like she's mentally kicking herself.

I almost smile.

Then she's gone from view.

Nope; way too sweet, not to mention human, to be on Harlan's payroll.

I almost want to turn so I can see her out the back window, but I don't.

Maybe instead of "Good luck," I should've said, "Have dinner with me."

Maybe I would've, if not for the game.

This fucking challenge.

I never actually thought my siblings hated me, even Harlan, but I'm seriously starting to wonder.

I'm also half sure they all expect me to fail.

Which is a huge question mark.

Do my siblings really want me out of the family business? Cut off from my inheritance? I can't believe that, no matter how much we piss each other off. At the end of the day, we've always had each other's backs.

One of them definitely wanted me to suffer through this no-sex dry spell, though.

Why?

We already lost a one-*billion*-dollar portion of Granddad's estate to his now-not-so-secret lover, thanks to the little surprise in his will. Valerie isn't even related by blood or marriage.

What next, I lose my entire inheritance to my siblings and lose my job to whatever greedy peon they promote to replace me, all over some ridiculous personal challenge gone too far?

No.

No way I'm going through this for nothing.

I'm almost halfway through this challenge; I just need to stay away from attractive women and stop thinking about sex every thirty seconds.

Like right now.

The hem of her little sundress fluttering as that sweet ass bounces in my lap...

And those plump tits bounce in my face.

I rearrange my package and decide to send a text to my—I assume—most sexually active brother. The one who owns a sex club.

Me: You're an asshole.

I've sent him a text along these lines once a day for forty-three days straight.

He gets back to me remarkably quick; maybe he's not having sex right this second.

Damian: Love you too little brother.

Then he sends me a kissy-face emoji. So fucking smug atop his high horse at the club, where he can have sex at the snap of his fingers.

Any kind of sex he wants.

I grimace as the woman in the street flashes in my head. In my mind, the breeze lifts her dress a little higher, and I glimpse her panties. They're white and lacy, like that bra.

I tried not to mentally undress her when she was right in front of me, literally on her knees...

But she was fucking gorgeous.

Her soft hair.

Her bright amber eyes.

The swell of her tits in that little dress...

Me: We'll just see who's laughing when you get your challenge.

If only I knew what it was.

Locke parks the Bentley in my garage and comes around to open my door, but I'm already stepping out. I leave him to collect my bags.

Clara's waiting to greet me as I stalk into the house, shucking off my suit jacket and handing it to her.

"Welcome back, Mr. Vance." She follows me as I grunt a response and make my way up the back hall to the living room, her high heels clipping along as I tear off my tie. "How was Las Vegas?"

"Vegas was Vegas. So, a shitshow."

"I'm sorry to hear it," she says politely, following me straight to the bar, where I pour myself a drink.

I snort. "No, you're not."

She gives me a small, professional smile. Clara is my live-in personal assistant and house manager. She's fifty-one, infinitely patient and well-mannered, and probably deserves a raise for dealing with my mood swings over the last forty-three days alone.

Don't be an asshole. Last thing you need is Clara quitting.

She doesn't know the personal hell you're in right now.

I slug back the whiskey and grimace. She watches me, probably mentally updating her résumé as I pour myself another.

"Before I forget," I tell her, "have Annabeth set up another meeting with the distillery. The whiskey's not where it should be." I slug back another mouthful and swish it around, trying to put my finger on what's wrong with it.

My latest brainchild is another celebrity alcohol brand, and who better to sell whiskey than a rock star? I might think it's just my bitter mood souring things, but the taste still isn't quite there. Jesse Mayes himself, the aforementioned rock star and my neighbor, told me as much over the phone while I was in Vegas.

"I see you're still drinking it," Clara notes dryly.

"It's not perfect. But it's not bad."

"Annabeth called from the office, actually, just now. Your brother wants to see you as soon as you get back—"

"Which one?"

"The nefarious one."

Harlan, then.

"No."

"That's your entire response?"

"Yes."

"I'll pass that along." She hurries to follow me as I cross the living room. "There's more. Mr. Hudson is here—"

"Ten minutes." I hold up my hand, silencing her. It's quiet in the house, which is just the way I want it right now, but my best friend is the only person I actually want to see. "Just tell him to hang tight and we'll have dinner. Give me ten minutes for a shower, then meet me in my office for a debriefing. I need some of my travel plans adjusted." *Cancelled, actually.*

I need my entire fucking life cancelled for the next forty-seven days, before the limitations imposed upon me by this fucking challenge make me lose my mind.

"Of course. And by ten minutes, you mean twenty?"

"I might mean an hour, and I'll expect you there, waiting, whenever I show up." I hold up my drink. "And bring me a refill."

"Perhaps I should bring the whole bottle?"

"You should, if you want a raise next quarter."

"Ten minutes it is."

Clara's high heels clip away as I stalk down the long hall toward my private wing, unbuttoning my shirt as I go. It's humid this evening. I can smell the scent of the freshly cut lawn drifting in, sticky and sweet.

Just as I'm starting up my private staircase to the second floor, my head of security creeps up in that ninja-silent way of his. I feel Locke before I hear him, and I turn to find him standing at the bottom of the stairs, hulking and stone-faced.

He says nothing—just holds out his phone to me.

"What is it?"

"You best see for yourself, boss."

I take the phone. On the screen, a web browser is open to a celebrity gossip site—showing a photo of me, holding hands with A-list actress Geneviève Blaise.

I scroll, finding three more photos, all similar to the first. Stalker-style paparazzi shots of me and Geneviève, walking out of one of my family's hotels together.

Pulling out my silenced phone, I scroll through messages from Annabeth and the rest of my team at the office, which I ignored in the car. They're all trying to reach me, to alert me to this breaking scandal.

It's all over the internet already.

Apparently, just moments ago, while I was standing in the street watching a stranger bungee-wrap her broken suitcase, these photos hit the web and the whole online world decided that I'm fucking a movie star.

My family included, I'm sure.

I swear and shove the phone back at Locke. "I'm going for a shower."

As I stalk up the stairs and into my bedroom, I wonder if Mr. Hudson—my best friend, Cole—is out by the pool. Or in the games room. Or the basketball court.

Or fucking someone in his guest room, because he doesn't have some overbearing older sibling who's banned him from sex because they've decided his cock is a scandal magnet.

It's in moments like these that I can't totally say that I blame them.

CHAPTER 2

Maybe white knights really do exist.

M I stand at the foot of the driveway, gazing up at the black iron gate, closed, with the imposing stone pillars on either side. The one closest to me has a security pad with an intercom on it, and I press the button to ring the house.

All with that man in my head.

The handsome stranger whose help I refused in the street.

My god. Do they really make men like that?

Not in my hometown.

A face like that, with a body like that, in a suit like that?

Triple threat.

He was so well-dressed, with the shiny shoes and the designer watch, to say nothing of the bespoke suit that clung to his tall, masculine frame. His expensive haircut was obvious even with his light-brown waves beautifully askew in the breeze. His car was a shiny black SUV, like the kind celebrities roll up to red carpets in. And clearly, he'd stopped for one reason.

Because I looked like a damsel in distress.

He'd towered over me like some gorgeous, manly angel, and I was so out of sorts with my situation, I'd barely found the words to communicate with him.

As I watched him walk away, I'd felt a vicious stab of regret.

What if he was an actual gentleman, just being courteous, and I wouldn't accept his help because of all the baggage I'd brought with me—the invisible kind?

I press the back of my hand to my forehead, wiping away the sticky sweat and the hair that's sticking to me. It's humid here on the West Coast, but in a different way than it is in the prairies. Much fresher. Lighter. The evening air seems to kiss my skin.

It might be pleasant if I didn't feel so gross from living in this dress while riding on public buses for two days straight.

Finally, a woman's voice greets me through the intercom. When I tell her my name, she asks me to wait.

I wonder what's taking so long. Cole promised me he'd be here when I arrived.

Beneath the security camera, the address is on a plaque. I check my map app; this is definitely it. The address my brother gave me.

I also wonder if the woman on the intercom can see me through that camera. I glance down, and cringe at the sight of my sad suitcase.

I can't believe my life just exploded at my feet like that.

The cheap zipper burst as I rolled it over the curb, and just as my clothes were hitting the pavement, I heard the car pulling up.

So embarrassing.

Yet so weirdly appropriate, I almost had to laugh. It was a perfect snapshot of the state of my life right now; packed up and dragged to the big city, yet the whole plan is flimsy at best.

No matter how much my friends keep telling me I'm so strong to do this, so courageous, and that I'm doing the right thing—the hard thing—I feel weirdly powerless.

I don't feel brave.

I just feel kind of numb. And tired and sweaty.

The iron gate in front of me makes a clicking noise and finally drifts open. I hoist my backpack a little higher onto my back and grip the handle of my suitcase as my heart starts to thud. I already feel so out of place in this ritzy neighborhood, but I hardly expected otherwise. Certain parts of my brother's world always make me nervous.

This part. The successful, wealthy part.

Though I seriously didn't know Cole was *this* wealthy.

I make my way through the gate and start up the curved drive. It's lined on both sides with flowering trees and shrubs that keep the house hidden from the street. I glimpse a man in black, standing beneath a tree, wearing an earpiece and a scowl. And black sunglasses, through which he's watching me.

Obviously, he's security.

I smile at him tentatively and continue on. One of the wheels on the suitcase is now giving me grief as I tug it along, but I try to make it appear effortless.

I can't even see the house yet, but the yard is nicer than any place I've ever dreamed of living.

Then I see the house.

The drive sweeps in a loop in front of the mansion. It's ivory stone, a sprawling two stories, with a massive set of black front doors.

I hesitate, confused. Cole is wealthy, but this is clearly another level.

It's the kind of estate a man like the one in that big SUV would live in.

I take a deep breath and push on. Why do I keep thinking about him?

Because you haven't had a sweet, juicy O with a man in way too long. And imagine what it would be like to peel him out of that suit, feel his pulse under his hot skin...

Really not what I should be thinking about right now. But I'm still kind of kicking myself for saying no when he offered me help. And I realize, Troy did that to me.

Of all the things he ruined for me, honestly, eroding my faith in humanity—stress the *man* part—was the worst.

Maybe I should've said *yes*. It's the Summer of Yes, after all. So declared by my friend Nicole when I told her I was leaving Troy. She'd been so thrilled about the new life I was going to have now that I was free of him, she'd made me swear to her that this would be the Year of Yes.

But that just seemed too daunting. So I'm starting with summer.

Yes to all the things I used to say no to, the things I put aside for the wrong man, the wrong town, the wrong life.

Yes to the big city.

Yes to my crazy big brother.

Yes to opportunities and risk and the unknown.

"Fucking yes," I say under my breath.

"Hello?"

I startle as a man's voice floats out of the foliage beside me. I peer over the lush hydrangea bushes. "Hello?"

A man in the garden gets to his feet. He wears a loose, soil-streaked T-shirt, and squints in the evening sunlight, the lines in his sunbaked face telling me he's in his fifties or sixties. "I thought I heard a voice."

"Sorry if I startled you. I don't usually talk to myself out loud."

"I do it all the time." He smiles. "The plants don't talk back. It's very peaceful."

"I know. I work in a garden center."

Worked. I worked in a garden center. Before I ran out of town.

"Oh? You know plants?"

"I know as much as I can." I glance around. "We can't grow a lot of this in Manitoba. I can't wait to see what all grows here."

"Well, I'll take you on a tour, anytime." His kind eyes crinkle. "They're my pride and joy. Don't tell my kids."

"You planted all this?"

"Some of it. Some was here long before I came along. Gardening... They say it's cheaper than therapy." He winks at me. "If someone's paying you to do it, even better."

I smile at him, the first real smile I've felt in days. The way he gazes at the roses, so lovingly... "I'd love a tour sometime." I offer him my hand. "I'm Megan."

"Romeo." He offers me the tips of his gloved fingers with an apologetic smile. "I'd take off the glove, but my hands are even dirtier."

"Romeo," I muse. "What a romantic name."

"Ah, my mother was the romantic. My father was just in love. She got to pick the name. He had no choice."

I smile again. *See? There are good men in the world.*

"Megan!"

I turn at the unmistakable sound of my brother's voice. Cole strides toward me, his arms outstretched in welcome.

"Cole!" A sweet relief I did not expect to feel so hard hits me at the sight of my big brother.

"Get your ass over here, girl."

I go straight for his open arms and let him crush me in a hug. He lifts me right off my feet. "Man, it's good to see you."

I wheeze a little, laughing as he squishes the air out of me. "Ouch. Let me take off my backpack. Wow." He's shirtless and all sweaty, and I already felt grimy enough.

He drops me on my feet and tousles my hair like I'm some twelve-year-old boy instead of a twenty-seven-year-old woman. "You look pretty."

"Seriously, could you never do that again?" I rake a hand through my hair, which isn't winning any hairstyling competitions at the moment anyway, but come on. My brother is such a jock, he's like a hyperactive golden retriever, always expecting you to play with him. "Go fetch a ball or something."

He just laughs.

When I glance toward the bushes, Romeo has slipped away, vanishing into the lush foliage and flowers.

"What is this place?" I ask my brother. "You could've warned me you'd bought a palace."

Cole snorts. "How much money do you think I have?"

"Enough... to buy this?"

"I wish. This is my best friend's place."

Best friend?

My curiosity is piqued, and not in a good way.

Cole's "best friends" are always people he's just met. They come and go from his life as fast as the women do. And usually, in my opinion, they're nothing but fanboys. Guys who glom on to my brother because of his fame, just like the women do.

As a professional hockey player and a very handsome one at that, Cole has celebrity status, and every wannabe VIP, influencer, and socialite who crosses his path seems to want to plant a foot on his back on their climb to the top.

And unfortunately, he has a habit of letting them.

"My new place is undergoing a full reno," he explains. "So I'm staying here until it's ready to move in. It's not far from here. I'll take you over to see it sometime."

"Okay. I'd like that." I know he bought a new house. I'm relieved, in a way, to hear that this isn't it. If he can afford this, there's definitely something he's not telling me. I know what his contracts are worth.

Even the millions Cole makes playing hockey wouldn't cover this place.

"Come on, let's get you settled. And I'll introduce you to Jamie. I think he's in the shower."

"Um. Okay..."

Cole chuckles at my general confusion and awe. He bounds up the sweeping stairs with my suitcase, and I follow him into the house. As my eyes adjust, I set down my purse and backpack with a sigh of relief. My shoulders are aching.

We're standing in a grand, two-story marble foyer with a modern glass chandelier soaring above us. But even that can't pull my attention from my need to inspect my brother.

The hockey season just ended and he's in prime shape, toned and tanned. He has a nice haircut, a bit edgy and skater boy for his thirty years, but with his tattoos and the dazzling playboy smile, Cole pulls it off.

He seems happy as he drapes an arm around my shoulders, and I let him steer me across the foyer. Ahead of us, there's a step down into a massive living room. Across the luxurious room, through the soaring glass walls along the back, is the most gorgeous, lush green backyard I've ever seen.

The living room itself is like something I've only seen in movies and magazines.

The gleaming white floors marbled with caramel lead to three separate, elegant seating areas, clusters of designer furniture in calming off-whites and earth tones. What has to be painfully expensive art, both paintings and sculptures, adorn the walls and the tabletops, and multiple minimalist glass chandeliers drip from the double-height ceiling.

I glimpse a couple of long hallways that lead deeper into the house, one to each side of the living room. Huge paintings line both hallways.

Paintings of hockey players.

I eye my brother again.

He eyes me back. "Seriously, you look great, Megz. Considering." Maybe he's trying to lighten my load with humor.

It doesn't work. "Thanks." I poke his ribs lightly. "How are you more handsome than I want to remember? I'm a mess right now."

Cole winks effortlessly. "How was your travel here?"

"Long."

He frowns. "You should've let me help you out. I would've arranged a flight."

"Honestly, I needed the time to decompress. It's fine."

He glances over my shoulder, at the suitcase he deposited next to my backpack and purse. The scowling man in black I saw lurking in the bushes has followed us into the foyer. "Where's all your stuff?"

"Sadly, that's it."

My brother's expression sobers as the truth of that hits hard. I really am starting over, and I had to give up a lot to be standing where I am right now.

Free.

Cole nods at the man in black, who takes my things, carrying them away into the house.

"Uh—" I start to protest, but he's already gone.

"You did the right thing, Megan." My brother's eyes meet mine again, a little hazy with emotion.

He's right.

But leaving my ex behind, my job, my whole entire life in Crooks Creek, Manitoba, the tiny town where we grew up, wasn't easy. It was incredibly fucking hard.

I can't even handle talking about it right now. I'm way too worn out from the journey here and all the hours on buses. My ass is still numb.

"I know."

Right now, though, I still can't quite feel it.

"You'll be happier here."

I blink at him for a long moment as that sinks in.

I must be *really* tired, because I swear he just said...

"Here?"

Like *here* here?

He expects me to stay *here?*

"Where else would you go?" His eyebrow spikes. "Of course you'll stay here, with me. Right?"

Well... my things have been whisked away to who-knows-where, so it looks like I am staying. For now. So I force myself to say the one thing I promised myself I would say. "Okay. Yes."

"Jamie and I are great friends," he assures me, maybe picking up on my concern. "He's really been there for me."

"That's nice," I say cautiously.

My brother chuckles. "You'll like him, Megz, I promise. He's a lot like me."

"Yeah." I swallow a groan. "That's what I'm afraid of."

CHAPTER 3

Megan

"I won't be long," I promise Cole. I figure it's the only way I can reassure him that I'm okay.

When I turned down his offer of dinner and a dip in the pool, opting to shower first, his eyebrows twisted with big-brother worry.

Priorities, though. I haven't showered in two days.

So, he shows me up one of the long hallways lined with paintings of hockey players and up a flight of stairs to one of the guest bedrooms. As it turns out, his best friend's mansion has an entire wing for guests. But Cole tells me no one else is staying here right now.

Just us.

He hesitates to leave me, though. "You sure?"

"I'm okay, Cole. Really."

"All right. We'll do dinner when you come down, with Jamie."

"Okay."

"I'm glad you're here, Megz."

I try to smile. "Me, too."

He gives me another hug, and finally he leaves me there, closing the door gently behind himself like I'm in mourning.

Maybe I am.

I exhale as it hits me how badly I just want to be alone right now. But that's probably a bad idea. If I'm alone, I might just curl up and feel sorry for myself.

I can't let Troy do that to me.

I've given him enough of my past. He doesn't get my present or my future anymore.

I look around the guest room, which Cole said was right next to his, and a swell of gratitude for my brother lodges in my throat.

My suitcase, backpack, and purse have all been left for me by the foot of the bed.

It's a queen-sized four-poster bed with luxurious white bedding. There's also a cozy sitting area and an adjoining bathroom. Like the rest of the house, this room is elegant, a mix of classic and contemporary, white and airy, with earthy, warm tones, and there's something about it that feels very coastal-chic. All the wood and the natural colors, maybe, along with the subtle seaside vibe of the stones around the fireplace.

It's so nice, I could weep.

But I've held it together this long, I'm not about to cry now over luxurious bedding.

I wonder what the man who lives here is like—this "best friend" of Cole's—besides having great taste in decor. And why Cole never told me much about him. I'm pretty sure he vaguely mentioned a Jamie he'd been hanging out with a while back, but that was it.

I wander over to the curtains. Soft and white, they cover one whole wall, the muted light of evening glowing through. I draw them open and find tall glass doors that open to a balcony over the lush backyard.

Below, several stone paths meander through the gardens, connecting the patio that wraps around the pool to what appears to be a private path down to the beach. Beyond, I can see the dark waters of Burrard Inlet. And along the far shore, at the base and a little way up the mountains that erupt to the north of the whole Vancouver area, homes glitter as the sun begins to set over the water.

Wow.

I step onto the balcony for a better view of the pool I glimpsed below. My brother is there, settling onto a lounge chair on the poolside patio, talking on his phone. I can barely hear his voice, he's so far away, but I can tell he's laughing.

I just hope he's doing as well as he seems to be. Trusting men is sort of a sore spot, and unfortunately, my brother helped form that wound.

I pull out my phone and take a photo of the view, shirtless athlete included. Then I post it to my Instagram with the vague caption: *Room with a view.*

I know Troy will be looking at my account, somehow, even though I blocked him, and asking around to try to figure out where I went. But I'm not about to live in fear of him.

This is *my* life, starting today. It's not *ours* anymore.

. In truth, it never really was.

Cole's back is to me, and he's small in the photo, so you can't tell who he is. I never post about him. No one who follows my account knows that I'm the little sister of a famous hockey player.

They just know me—or at least my pseudonym—as what I am: a fledgling author who knows a lot of random stuff about plants, voyeuristic sex, and how to survive an apocalypse.

Most of my readers are women who, according to their emails, read me for the sultry postapocalyptic world I created, the gripping survival-struggle story arc, and the hot sex scenes. They'll eat up that photo, for sure.

Then I text the photo to my friend Nicole, the only other person I know here in Vancouver.

Me: Home sweet home? Temporarily.

I know she's waiting to hear from me as soon as I arrive. Her response comes in like lightning.

Nicole: Fuck yes! Where the heck are you? Are you okay?? And who's the hottie?

Me: I'm okay. And there's no hottie. It's just Cole. LOL. How are you?

Nicole: Oof. He's looking good. Call me when you can! I'm on my way to work :(

Me: I will. Let's chat tomorrow. Enjoy your night!

Nicole: You too! Can't wait :)

It occurs to me that I could go see her, right now, though I'm relieved she doesn't ask. I know she's waitressing at a hot nightclub tonight, out there somewhere in the sparkling city. But I'm emotionally drained, probably still halfway in shock, and sticky with two days' travel sweat. I'm in no way ready for a night out on the town.

I go find a large towel in the bathroom, and lay it out on the bed, then heft my suitcase onto it. I don't want the wheels to get dirt on the lovely bedding. I unhook the bungee cords and spread the whole, broken thing open.

Even in my hurry to leave town, the leaving itself was so deliberate, so final, I'd lovingly selected the few things I felt I couldn't live without and packed them with care.

But I'd jammed them back in so haphazardly after they tumbled out into the street, mostly because that sophisticated, drop-dead-gorgeous man in the expensive suit was watching the whole thing. My life had poured out in front of him, and I'd felt naked, exposed. Pathetic and sad.

I pick through my things now, taking inventory. I'll have to make the few outfits I brought last awhile. I didn't bring a swimsuit; it didn't really seem like a dire necessity when I was trying to fit my entire life into a suitcase and split town.

I find a tank top and shorts I can wear poolside and lay them out on the bed for after my shower. I figure I'll feel a lot better after I wash up and put on fresh clothes.

But as soon as I strip down and get into the shower, something shifts. I let go of all the composure I've gripped so tightly since saying goodbye to Mom yesterday—for her and for my brother and for me—and I break down in tears.

Under the stream of hot water, in total privacy, I let it all out.

I left my apartment, the apartment I shared with my on-and-off-again boyfriend of eleven years, in the night, while he was out. I hid at my coworker's house until I could get a ride with my mom to the bus station. I left town without Troy knowing, so he couldn't try to stop me.

I wasn't scared of him. Not physically. But I was broken down by his endless manipulations, his selfish orchestration of my life, and his bottomless black hole of need and insecurity that he expected *me* to fill for him.

And I was scared to leave my hometown. The only home I've ever known.

But Crooks Creek is small, and Troy is all up in it. Everyone knows him there.

Though not everyone loves him as much as he wants them to. Far from it.

My online therapist explained it to me, many times. But now that I've put distance between myself and Troy, I feel like I can safely acknowledge the truth to myself: that Troy Duchamp is a pathological narcissist who almost sucked the life out of me.

The man is an energy vampire and I'm drained.

The only good part of having nothing left to give to someone because they've taken way more than their fair share from you is coming to the realization that your feelings for them have eroded to the point that they're completely gone.

It's the only reason I was able to leave.

I'll miss living so close to Mom. I'll miss some of my old friends.

But I just knew I had to start over, somewhere else.

I haven't seen Cole in person in two years, but running to my brother was really my only option. I know I can count on him for at least a few days respite. My brother isn't a narcissist. But he has issues, too, that will make living with him long-term a bad idea.

The racking sobs fade into silent tears. My eyes just don't seem to want to stop leaking.

But finally, they do.

I wash my hair, then step out of the shower and dry off with one of the big, plush towels, hiccuping a little in the aftermath of all that crying, and letting my frayed nerves settle.

I just need a day or two to recoup, regroup, and see what Cole can do to help me get settled. That's why I came to him.

After that, I need to take care of myself like I've always done, because that's what survivors do.

I know it won't be easy. I've never even visited Vancouver before.

I need a job and an apartment, maybe some fun girl roommates. I need friends. I need dishes and furniture and so many things.

Most of all, I need my own life back.

The one Troy Duchamp stole from me, piece by piece, from the time I was seventeen.

I swipe the fog from the mirror with the side of my hand and look into my pink-rimmed eyes, and I remind myself that my heart is safe now.

But there's a terrible fear that's accompanied me all the way here, warning me that I'll never be free of him.

Because he's an energy vampire, and vampires need to feed.

CHAPTER 4

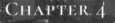

Jameson

W hen I step out of the shower, I make the mistake of checking my phone again, where I find more texts from my team at the office.

Those photos and the accompanying salacious speculation are already trending as #geneson, some lame celebrity couple nickname for Geneviève + Jameson.

Obviously, this well-timed photo leak is meant to bolster Geneviève's movie opening. Her new blockbuster opens tonight.

It's so obvious, it's almost boring in its predicability. She really needs new PR people.

I don't care about that.

What I care about is that she's one of Vance Industries' brand ambassadors. She's scheduled to attend the grand opening gala of the all-important Vance Bayshore resort next spring, and we need her there. We need her everywhere, like on the red carpet at her opening tonight, endorsing our brands. Not fielding rumors that she's fucking me.

Graysen is going to be pissed.

But I've been aboard this roller coaster before. It'll run its course.

I need to talk to my team about this, but fuck it. That can wait until tomorrow.

In my walk-in closet, I pull on a pair of loose linen pants. The sun's going down, but it's still warm. Tonight, I'll have a quick chat with Clara; she'll have Annabeth talk to PR, set up a meeting for tomorrow morning, while I spend the evening with Cole by the pool, a steak dinner, and maybe that bottle of whiskey.

I head downstairs and into the living room. No one's around, so I continue along the hall on the other side, to the guest wing and up to the second floor.

Cole's door is ajar, so I knock, then nudge it open. "Cole, you here?" The room is empty, so I send him a text.

Me: Where are you? Let's do BBQ by the pool. I'm hungry.

I text Clara to get Chef on it.

Then I notice the flowers mounted on the bedroom door next to Cole's. Fresh flowers on the door means *occupied*.

Someone's staying in the room next to Cole's.

I fucking told him no guests.

Last thing I need right now are the usual kinds of houseguests and parties that I have in my house. For ninety days, while I'm in no-sex hell, this is a no-party zone.

Annoyed, I stash my phone in my pocket and go back downstairs, heading for my poolside patio. But on my way up the hall to the living room, Clara approaches. She opens her mouth, but I cut her off as she hurries to fall in step.

"Why the hell is there someone in one of my guest rooms and no one told me?"

"I thought you knew by now. Mr. Hudson implored me not to tell you. He said he wanted to tell you himself."

I slow down. "Why? Who is it?"

"His sister. I'm sorry, I should've told you. He just seemed so..." Clara seems to agonize over the right words. "Broken up about her, when she called the other night."

I consider that. I need more information, but I need it from Cole. "Where is he?"

"He's waiting for you out on the patio. But I wanted to alert you, you've got another visitor. He's at the bar."

She doesn't need to say more. I feel the distinct chill in the air at the same moment I notice the dark figure lurking at the bar in my living room.

As I approach, trying to scrape my head together to deal with this, he turns to me, and Clara wisely disappears.

"There he is," Harlan drawls, leaning back on a bar stool and scrutinizing me. "The Vance family prince, back from his travels abroad. Sin City, was it?"

"Harlan. Come all the way down from your cave on the mountainside? I'm flattered." I head behind the bar and pluck a couple of glasses from the shelf. "I didn't know you could travel by daylight anymore."

"And this is the warm welcome I get?" He pretends to be offended as he smooths his shirt. It's a warm summer evening, and he's wearing a suit, black on black, no tie. Pretty much what he sleeps in, as far as I can tell. "Your house girl didn't even offer me a drink while I waited."

"Maybe because she's a professional, old enough to be your mother, and you call her 'house girl.'" I mix us both a Manhattan, his drink of choice. "You've been a demon since, what, puberty? It can't shock you anymore if the villagers toss holy water on you when you walk by."

He ignores that as I slide his drink in front of him. "So how was Vegas?"

I know what he's doing. Sniffing around to find out if I failed my challenge in Sin City. He doesn't even try to finesse it into the conversation. Harlan doesn't know how to finesse a conversation.

Maybe because he spends so much alone time in his crypt.

"How do you think it was? It fucking sucked."

"I find that hard to believe."

"Maybe because you're such an expert liar, you expect lies."

"You're telling me there was no fun to be had?"

"There was fun to be had. I didn't have any."

"Now, if you're me, do you believe you?"

"I don't care what you believe. I kept my hands to myself."

"How about your dick?"

"Same."

"How about your mouth?"

"Are you planning to list every body part? I'm winning this game. I'm not lying, and I'm not cheating."

Harlan scowls, skeptical. He knows me well enough to know I wouldn't just breezily lie to his face. I have a major aversion to that kind of dishonesty.

But he also knows celibacy isn't exactly my lifestyle of choice.

Through the wall of windows to the backyard, behind his back, Clara bustles into view. She's escorting a woman across my patio.

A brunette woman, wearing a tank top and shorts, her long hair damp. Heat floods my chest at the sight of her, and my breath lodges in my throat.

It's her.

It's fucking *her.*

The woman from the street, with the bungeed suitcase.

Cole's sister??

What the fuck.

I cough and shift to my left, away from the windows, and Harlan regards me with suspicion. I probably look guilty... about something.

I don't want him to see her. I'm not even sure why. The challenge?

The fact that I don't even know what to make of this sudden discovery that that gorgeous woman is in my house? Last thing I need is Harlan getting any ideas about it. Or about her.

Fortunately, Clara guides her out of sight.

"It's been forty-three days," my brother points out. I'm sure he's tracking it on a calendar. "Have you ever gone forty-three days?"

"Why would I?" I mutter.

"And now one of us has made it so you can't enjoy your favorite pastime," he muses, sounding borderline pleased. Harlan doesn't really do pleased, but he's practically glowing right now.

"Yeah. For your own fucking shits and giggles."

"It's called personal growth, Jamie. You're supposed to be learning something about yourself."

"As if you give a shit about my personal growth. You just want to watch me suffer, because you're a goddamn sadist."

"Hey, I'm just checking in for the family, making sure you're okay." He gives me a smile that doesn't reach his eyes. Kinda like the Grinch.

God, he's a liar.

No one would send Harlan to "check in" on me, much less make sure I was toeing the line.

If this family has a black sheep, Harlan is the monster who ate it alive.

And if Harlan is the beast of this family—he is; we literally call him that—then like he said, I'm the prince.

Would anyone really care if the fifth in line for the family treasure lost his share? Would it make any difference?

This is the kind of thinking a visit from Harlan brings about.

I hate that he's making me sweat.

I need to get rid of him.

I need to go outside and see what the fuck is going on, and why Cole didn't tell me his sister was coming.

And get a look at her again.

"Well, I'm fine. And I'm telling you the truth. You know I couldn't lie to a master of deception like yourself. You'd know."

"Probably. Just depends how bad you want to have your cake and eat it, too. 'Cake' being pussy and 'too' being your inheritance, in case that wasn't clear."

"I'm not having any cake, okay?"

The truth is, I'm not even licking any icing.

I don't need the tease, or the risk.

The night I opened that gold envelop and read my challenge, I'd walked out, angry.

The next day, I'd gone right back to Graysen's, had him gather the rest of our siblings on a conference call so they could decide what the hell "no sex" even meant.

And decide they had. With great amusement, on Harlan's and Damian's parts. Savannah had hung up on us as we debated the finer points.

Obviously, fucking in any form is out of the question. But what about blow jobs?

Ha. No.

Hand jobs?

Try again.

Happy endings of any kind?

Nope.

And I definitely won't be finding any loopholes—getting a woman off, using an object between us to buffer actual touching, touching over clothes. Absolutely anything that's sexually gratifying or results in an orgasm in a woman's company—hers or mine—is a no-go.

Can I kiss and touch a woman? Sure. As long as I keep my naked sex parts off hers and no one comes.

Fun times.

Can I jack off? Absolutely. If I'm alone. The challenge isn't about deprivation. It's about not having sex with women.

So it's me, myself, and I for ninety days.

Which means that I've masturbated daily to try to make it not bother me that my sex life has been put on a time-out.

Unfortunately, it hasn't made me any less angry.

It's not that I can't have sex. This is the part my siblings don't seem to get.

It's that *one of them has forbidden me* from having sex. Probably the one who's sitting in front of me right now.

Harlan tips his chin up, assessing me. "I guess it really is an honor system, isn't it?"

"Good thing I have some honor left."

He downs the drink that he's ignored until now. "I guess we'll see." And with that, the lord of darkness seems satisfied that I'm sufficiently suffering and gets up to leave.

Good riddance.

I follow him to the foyer. I know he won't be the first of my siblings to "check in" on me in the wake of those photos hitting the web. I don't even know if he saw them. He didn't mention them, and Harlan tends to ignore his phone.

Just knowing I went to Vegas was enough to raise his suspicions, probably.

"So, tell me." He pauses at the door. "Will my challenge be an honor system situation too?"

"Yeah, right. How stupid do you think we are?"

"You really want me to answer that?"

"Be honest for once in your life, okay? It was your idea to make me give up sex for ninety days, right?"

My brother's smile is feral. "I would've stipulated six months. At least. But I'm sure there are some of us who think even ninety days is an unreasonable amount of time."

"Let me guess. Damian is taking bets against me."

Damian is probably the one person in this family who'd just let us disown him in favor of reserving the right to fuck.

"I would never want to profit from your failures, brother."

"Uh-huh."

Weirdly, I know he kind of means that.

One of the strangest things about Harlan is that he doesn't care that much about money, exactly. He just cares about maintaining his privacy, and nothing can afford impenetrable walls like wealth can.

"I'll see you on the other side of forty-seven days, Jamie. In the meantime, have fun with your hand."

"Yeah. Have fun with your hollowed-out graveyard bones or whatever it is you fuck."

I slam the door in his face. *Fucking brothers.*

Who needs them, really.

CHAPTER 5

Megan

I've barely gotten dressed after my shower when a woman knocks on the bedroom door, introduces herself to me as Clara, the "house manager," and urges me to come down to the patio where my brother is waiting for me. She escorts me downstairs and out to the backyard, where she hands me off to Cole.

He takes me into the outdoor kitchen and introduces me to the "house chef," whom he simply calls Chef, a friendly man in a white coat who's prepping our dinner. I offer to help, but my brother steers me back out to the patio and puts a drink in my hand.

He then starts needlessly sales pitching me on the wonders of living in Vancouver, which I struggle to absorb. I'm so mentally exhausted, the steamy afterglow of my shower is almost putting me to sleep.

I'm halfway through my second Campari and soda, and Cole is still talking, when the big glass walls to the living room slide open and a man steps out.

As he strides in our direction, the world suddenly does this strange stopping-in-its-tracks thing.

It's like he's walking in slow motion, and my stomach squeezes, reminding me that I haven't eaten enough today. I feel strangely weightless, and I must be doing something weird with my face because I feel Cole's eyes on me. But I can't take mine off the man strolling toward us.

It's the man I met in the street.

He's shirtless now. Tanned and muscular and athletic, with a gleaming eight-pack. A few artful tattoos, mostly etched in black, wind up the side of his sculpted torso and both gym-toned arms, including a dagger tattoo featured prominently on his perfectly sculpted chest, above his heart.

It literally takes me *that* long to drag my eyes up to his face. And by then, my cheeks and several other parts of me are warm.

He has stunning light-blue eyes, blondish stubble along his strong jaw, sun-kissed hair with a bit of wayward curl in it, and an air of *bad boy* about him that's somehow more prominent now that most of his clothes are gone.

Wearing nothing but a pair of low-riding white linen pants, he stands in front of us, staring at me.

No, devouring me with his eyes.

Cole greets him. They hug, and still, he doesn't take his eyes off me. I don't even hear whatever they say to each other.

"Megan, this is Jameson," Cole says, somewhere far away.

I feel warm all over now, tingly, and breathless. My brother is miles away. My feet no longer touch the ground. There's nothing but the man in front of me, as everything else falls away like a dream I'm waking up from.

Is this what love at first sight feels like?

No. If it was love at first sight, you would've felt this in the street.

All I felt in the street was embarrassed, and like I wanted to sink through the pavement and disappear.

But I've never felt half as floored with the adrenaline rush of being introduced to a man in my life. My entire nervous system trembles with euphoria while outwardly, a strange paralysis overtakes my limbs.

"Nice to meet you, Megan." His voice is a low rumble, and just as guarded as it sounded in the street. He doesn't smile, and I realize belatedly that he's offering me his hand.

I take it, hoping my fingers aren't shaking. My heart seems to think I'm on the brink of death, and pumps blood through my system so hard, I might black out.

"Jameson." My voice is gooey. It's like I'm liquefying under his gaze.

He's the sun, and everything around us is just a watercolor world, melting under the force of his heat.

"Cole has told me such nice things about you," he says. And I love my brother so much right now, I could grab him and kiss him.

I don't.

I just hold onto his best friend's hand for an awkward beat—or two—longer than a handshake requires, staring.

For several of the most awkward minutes of my life, under the guise of "getting a drink"—even though both of them already have a drink in hand—Cole and his bestie relocate themselves to the far end of the patio, by the bar adjacent to the outdoor kitchen.

To talk about me.

I mean, I'm assuming they're talking about me. Because my brother just deposited me on a lounge chair like a pet and told me to stay.

I finish my Campari, try to overhear them, fail, and try to look anywhere but at Jameson.

Lord of all that's good and holy, though, he's hot. Or maybe it's lord of all that's bad and dripping in temptation?

Does he have to be so shirtless?

Cole's shirtless too, but who cares.

Men who aren't related to me shouldn't be that naked in front of me unless I'm allowed to stare.

Cole will definitely disapprove if I stare.

I can't help it, though. The arrow of groin muscle leading down into the front of his best friend's low-slung pants keeps magnetizing my attention.

At least when they come back, they bring a fresh round for all three of us. Cole sets the tray of drinks on the table between us and hands one to me.

"So, Cole tells me you're new in Vancouver." Jameson stiffly starts the conversation, like Cole told him to be nice to me or something.

"Yeah. New." I wonder what Cole really told him about me. Not Troy, I hope. "I hope he told you I was coming."

A small smile twitches on Jameson's mouth before he buries it. "He didn't."

"Man. I did," Cole protests. "I texted you while you were in Vegas."

Jameson raises an eyebrow. "You did?"

"You never got back to me."

"Well, hey," I interject, "if you know Cole like I do, he's always full of surprises."

"That's true."

"He, um, definitely never told me that his best friend is a billionaire."

Cole scratches his neck, which I take to be his idea of an apology.

I've put it together myself by now—that my brother's best friend is none other than *that* Jameson.

Jameson Vance.

The Vances are the wealthiest family in Vancouver and one of the wealthiest in Canada, but I only know this because they own the Vancouver Northmen hockey team, and my brother has been playing for the Northmen for three seasons. That's why he settled in Vancouver.

I can't believe I didn't make the connection when I first saw him in the street. Maybe if I hadn't been so self-conscious about my broken suitcase and my intimates pouring out, I would have.

I know I've definitely seen that gorgeous face somewhere before, like in a newspaper photo. The sports section.

And maybe the front page.

"Yeah, maybe I should've warned you," Cole says. *Why? Do I look that stricken?* "I know meeting a billionaire can be... intimidating." *Especially for a girl from Crooks Creek,* the sparkle in his eyes seems to say. "But I told you about Jamie, that we've gotten tight. Didn't I?"

"You didn't." Honestly, Cole never has been all that reliable with staying in touch and keeping me updated about his life.

Although... I haven't been all that good about sharing the details of my life with him either. He had no idea how bad things were between Troy and me, and that was entirely my doing.

"How did you guys become so close?" I inquire. I'm still trying to adjust my initial assumption that Cole's new best friend is a fanboy, because members of the Vance family are not wannabes. They're the ones the wannabes aspire to brush shoulders with. And surely they can hang out with any hockey player anytime they want to.

"Well, I've known Jamie casually for years. But we crossed paths at some parties when I landed in Vancouver, started hanging out a lot. He was going through some shit personally, and so was I, and we were there for each other. One of those things. We just clicked."

I take that in. Jameson says nothing, just sips his drink.

"That's nice, then."

Cole leans in. "You can relax, Megan, I promise. You're so on guard."

I take a breath, and glance around the beautiful yard, trying to process this whole strange situation. It's not the one I expected to find when I got here. I thought I'd be staying with Cole in his renovation-zone of a new house, maybe dealing with the awkwardness of having breakfast with his latest fuck buddy on the odd morning. But not this. "You really bought a place in this neighborhood?"

"Yup. It's not nearly this big, though."

I eye him. "Is there something I should know?"

He kind of laughs. "Nothing bad. I promise."

"Cole."

"Come on. You really doubt me that much?" My brother frowns, but I'm not about to dance around my distrust of him like it's not there.

I'm never doing that again. Even for a man I love.

"Well, let's see." I broach the subject as gently as I can. "You partied and gambled away actual millions you made playing hockey, years ago. Then you lost the money you made *illegally* gambling. Then you got arrested."

If he and Jameson really are best friends, this won't be news.

I can tell it's not, by the way neither of them flinches.

My brother even subtly rolls his eyes. "That was over three years ago, Megan. And it's all been cleared up."

"Yes. Ancient history."

He stares me down. "How long ago did you go back to a guy you'd already broken up with because he emotionally abused you for years?"

A lump forms in my throat, leaving me speechless. There's really nothing I can say to argue that, because he's right. I did do that.

And yes, it was a giant mistake. Every damn time I did it.

Jameson softly clears his throat, and I try not to look at him. This is humiliating enough.

"I seriously can't take any more man drama right now, Cole."

"No drama. I promise." He reaches over and takes my hand. I let him. "Come on, Megan. I'm sorry I brought that up. Just let me help you. Maybe I wasn't in a position to do that before. You know, mentally. But I am now."

That tugs at my heart. It gives me a sense of hope I'm not sure I'm ready for.

My brother sighs. "It's been a long, shitty two days on a bunch of buses, right? Let's just eat and talk, and you can get comfortable here. If you end up wanting to go somewhere else, I can help with that, too."

"Okay."

"You have a home here. As long as you need it."

"Thank you."

When I finally look at Jameson, who hasn't said another word, he doesn't seem particularly happy about that.

Actually, if I'm not mistaken, he looks like he wants me gone.

CHAPTER 6

Megan

As the evening sky grows dark and the patio lights come up around us, my brother carries the bulk of our three-way conversation over drinks, catching me up on the highlights and shenanigans of the recently completed hockey season. Wherein the Northmen made it to the playoffs but not to the final round.

Occasionally, Jameson adds to the conversation, mostly prompting Cole to tell another story, and I do the same.

I have no idea why Jameson is so short on words—surely my hyperactive, talkative brother's best friend isn't always this quiet? But I'm too tired and self-conscious to say much myself, and it's easy to get swept up in Cole's stories, entertained.

Then the three of us sit down to dinner at the outdoor dining table. The meal is served by Jameson's staff. Cole sits at the head of the table, between Jameson and me. And while we eat, Cole peppers me with questions about my job in Crooks Creek—which I get the weird feeling is for Jameson's benefit.

My very uninteresting job at the general store and seasonal garden center, which Cole knows I held for years.

While Jameson, seated across from me, says little more than nothing.

It's so fucking awkward.

It feels like I'm on a first date with a guy who doesn't want to be on the date. And my brother is on the date, too, chaperoning or something.

No, worse. It's like Cole is trying to fix us up. But not so we can date. So I can *work* for the man sitting across from me.

It's a job interview.

I realize this when we reach dessert. No one really touches it except me. My brother the professional hockey player definitely doesn't touch it. Jameson tastes it, like he wants to be polite to Chef. I enjoy every bite of it. Why not? It's not every day that a billionaire's personal chef cooks for me.

But then Cole does a very Cole-like thing and blurts out something that makes perfect sense to him, probably, but none to me, kind of killing my appetite. My brother has been communicationally challenged like this forever.

It goes something like this...

Cole: "You can have a job here. Gardening. If you want it."

Me (almost choking as ganache slides down my throat and I forget how to swallow completely): "What?"

Cole: "Gardening. You love gardening, right?"

Me (still swallowing ganache and clearing my throat): "I do. Yes."

Cole: "Jameson needs a gardener."

At this point, I look at Jameson, but Cole speaks for him. "The job is yours if you want it."

Jameson glances at Cole, but he doesn't say anything. And I figure with that one look I get the picture. This job offer is Cole's idea.

Doesn't Jameson already have a gardener?

"Really?"

"Really," Cole says.

Then he nudges Jameson, who remembers how to speak. "You come highly recommended."

I can't tell if he's being sarcastic or what.

"I..."

"Whadya say, Megz?" Cole prompts when I get stuck. "You like the gardening shed."

Yeah. I do.

Cole took me to see it before we sat down to dinner, while Jameson went into the house for a meeting with Clara.

Though "shed" is not really the word for it.

It's a small greenhouse at the back corner of the yard that's lush with plants, many of them tropical varieties that wouldn't survive the harsh winters where I come from. There's an array of gardening tools, and a cozy sitting area with cushioned chairs arranged in front of a wood-burning stove.

It's a gardener's dream.

I glance at Jameson, who helpfully says nothing.

"Couldn't you see yourself happy in a place like this?" Cole presses.

"Uh, sure." *If it were mine.* "I mean... *wow.*" I'm shocked, that's all. This yard is a gardener's paradise. It's my idea of paradise, anyway, and Cole knows it.

He winks at me.

But Jameson is so stiff. Different from my first impression of him in the street, when I could've sworn he was undressing me with his eyes.

Now he seems so closed off. Cold, even.

Because now that he knows who I am, he's no longer interested in the view?

"Thank you. It's really generous of you." I direct that at Jameson. Because bottom line, I need this job.

He replies with a gruff, "No thanks necessary."

"It's just temporary, though," I assure him. "Until I get on my feet, find a job, save up some money and get my own place to live." I know, whatever Cole says, his best friend doesn't need me as a gardener.

I'm the only one in need here.

I swallow my wounded pride about it, though. Sitting here, fatigued from the last two brutal days, with these two successful men, I'm aware that they're trying to help.

"It's no rush," Cole says. "And you can always come live at my place, when it's ready. For as long as you want."

Well, shit. What do I say to that?

I don't think I could live with my brother, certainly not longterm. Does he really want to live with me?

"When will it be ready?"

"Six months. Maybe less."

Jameson's eyes are fixed on the water glass in his hand. There's been a slight frown on his face all through dinner, like there's some problem he's trying to solve.

I have the feeling I'm the problem.

I can't live in this man's house for six months. Even if I'm earning my keep as his gardener.

Besides the fact that I doubt very much he'd want me here that long, I'm not ready to be thrust into the proximity of a man I find so attractive for months on end. His nearness muddies my thoughts and does crazy shit to my body.

His light-blue eyes lift to mine, and suddenly, it's hard to breathe.

I try to smile at him.

He doesn't smile back.

We pour a celebratory glass of champagne to toast my new job. Cole's idea. I'm still trying to mentally adjust to the fact that my new employer is the most fuckable man I've ever met, when Cole's phone buzzes.

He pulls it out, and gets to his feet. "It's my agent, about tomorrow. I need to take this. You guys hang out."

"Oh. Uh..." I don't really have anything else to say as Cole strides away and disappears into the house, leaving me alone with Jameson.

Silence falls.

I take a gulp of my champagne, swallowing loudly.

"He didn't tell you about tomorrow, did he?" Jameson's voice is somehow soft and rough at the same time. Like velvet when you rub it the wrong way.

"No. What's tomorrow?"

His eyes pinch, like maybe he wants to punch Cole in the face, just a little bit. "He's leaving for LA in the morning."

"What?"

"He has a commercial shoot for one of his endorsement deals. And meetings. And women. You know."

Yeah. Unfortunately, I know.

But Cole didn't tell me.

He told me over the phone to come stay with him in Vancouver, but he didn't tell me we'd be living with his best friend, much less that he'd be flying out the next day. He gave me a whirlwind introduction to his best friend, a job, and tried to make me feel welcome.

And now he's leaving me here.

That's so like Cole, I actually laugh out loud.

Although, if he'd told me... I might've hesitated to come, right?

I can see why he didn't.

Something unreadable passes over Jameson's face in the wake of my laughter. Then he tops up my champagne in silence, as maybe it sinks in for both of us.

He's stuck with me, more or less.

And I'm just... stuck.

What can I say except... "Thank you." I take another deep swallow of champagne. Might as well get drunk?

Jameson's blue eyes burn into me as he settles back in his chair. The word *penetrating* was invented for this man. I've never been eye fucked so casually in my life.

I swear, it's the same look he gave me in the street.

I didn't imagine it...

I try not to return the look, but it's hard. I'm not even sure what my face is doing, he's got my wires so tangled.

"Your yard is incredible." I try to make conversation; the only thing I can think to offer is a compliment or three. "I don't just mean the gardens. And you have private beach access?"

"The beach is public. But, yes. You can walk straight down there. There's a locked security gate at the bottom of the stairs. Clara can give you a fob so you can go in and out."

"Oh. Thank you. Um, is that North Vancouver?" I point at the glittering homes on the mountainside across the water.

"That's West Vancouver. North Vancouver is more to the east."

"That's... confusing."

"Well, North Vancouver is north of Vancouver. But so is West Vancouver, really. It's northwest."

"Okay. And what is that line of lights floating in the dark, above the houses?" It looks like it's partway up the mountains, but I can't tell. It's getting so dark, the mountains are becoming indistinguishable from the sky.

"That's one of the ski hills. Black Mountain. My family owns the resort, actually."

I try not to look at him. It's so much more awkward sitting so close to him without my brother here as a buffer. "You own the ski hill?"

"Just the resort at the top. It's more of a chalet, with a restaurant and bar, shops."

"I see." I sip my champagne, considering that. "Can we see anything else you own from here?"

I'm joking. But he points in the direction of the sparkling stretch of downtown, over to the far right of the view. "Vance Tower. My sister lives there. The big one with the red lights on top."

You're kidding. It has to be one of the tallest buildings downtown.

I don't know what to say. I'm miles out of my depth here. The people I know, besides my brother, own, you know, clothes and books and maybe a nice car. Maybe a home of their own, if they're lucky. Maybe a little cabin out at the lake, too, if they're really lucky.

That's in small town Manitoba.

I can't imagine the price tag on a skyscraper in downtown Vancouver, or a mountaintop ski chalet. Or, for that matter, a professional hockey team.

I dare a look at him. He put on a beachy button-up shirt for dinner, linen, with the sleeves casually rolled up and the front wide open, so I can still see the dagger tattoo on his chest. I notice the two tattooed drops of blood that drip from the tip of the blade. The second one looks a bit pink and raw, like the tattoo is new.

I want to ask him about it, but it seems too personal.

I can't think of a thing else to say to him that wouldn't be awkward.

So, you're rich and gorgeous, that's cool. What movies do you like?

"So." He breaks the silence this time. "Is that really what you came to the big city for? To be a gardener?"

His tone is neutral. Not accusatory or judgmental or anything. But he's probably asking because my discomfort with the whole situation is so obvious.

"No." My face flushes as I speak; I've never been so embarrassed about my general position in life as I have been today, in this man's company. "But I'm grateful for the job."

"Why don't you have any money?"

"Um..."

Blunt much?

I take another swig of my champagne. It's not a question I have an easy answer for, if I'm being honest.

I'm not even sure why I want to be honest.

Self-respect? I don't like the idea that maybe he thinks I'm hiding something from my brother. That's the furthest thing from the truth. Cole knows how I ended up here.

Maybe it's just the champagne.

"Okay, the thing is..." I take a deep breath and tell him what I've told so few people in this world. "I'm an author."

Jameson's expression is slow to shift, but something like curiosity hones his features. "Really?"

"Well, I'm writing a series of books. I've published the first three already, under a pen name. It's just novels I write for fun." I hiss out an annoyed-with-myself breath. "Okay, that was a small lie." I put my glass down on the table and kind of wring my hands, feeling the faint ache of all the hours at my keyboard. "It's my passion. I'm just not used to talking about it."

"Okay. But why are you going to work in my garden if you're an author?"

"Well, um, I didn't say I was successful."

He doesn't smile at my self-deprecating jab.

"I just love storytelling. I love plotting and world building."

Now a faint, heart-stopping smile drifts across his lips. "Cole never mentioned you were such a nerd."

It takes me a long moment to compute that he's teasing me.

"Maybe I am," I admit. "I just love getting lost in this fictional world I created. I think I developed such a knack for it because of living in a place I didn't want to be. Wanting another life? I created my own escape, especially during the endless winters when I was stuck in the apartment so damn much." It really hits me as I say it out loud: how much I resented living in Crooks Creek.

Yeah, this is definitely the champagne loosening my tongue.

But he seems to be waiting for me to continue, so I venture on. "It's so personal for me, writing. I'm still uncomfortable sharing it. That's why I use a pen name."

"That's understandable. Plenty of celebrities use pseudonyms. It's not just a marketing tool. It can be a layer of separation for your private self."

"Yeah. I like my privacy. People back home don't even know about my books. Cole knows and our mom knows, but they're sworn to secrecy. And... Troy knew. My ex-boyfriend."

I hesitate there, not really wanting to talk about him at all. But I do want to be honest with Jameson.

Maybe because I think he deserves to know why I'm here invading his life. And why, like he pointed out, I have no money.

"The thing is, I've made a small amount of money off the books. Very small. I send them out to book reviewers and social media influencers and I've steadily grown a little following. The first few months after I published the first book, I made like five hundred dollars, and I told myself if I could make a thousand dollars a month off my books, then I could grow it from there to two thousand a month and so on." I hesitate. "Well, when I finally reached the one-thousand-a-month mark, on top of what I was making at the store, I was able to really start saving. Troy and I were going to buy a house. We were renting."

I hesitate again, wondering if I should really keep talking or just keep drinking, as Jameson waits for me to go on.

"Troy saved more money than I did because he made more, but I saved all the book money, besides what I put back into promoting the books. We had this joint account for our house fund."

I stop there, because it's really hard to say the rest.

But maybe I want the billionaire sitting in front of me to know that I have dreams, and I am trying to better my life. So I take a fortifying sip of champagne and forge on.

"Anyway... My portion was only fifteen thousand dollars. That was all I'd saved up so far. I know it's such a tiny amount to someone like you. But it would've been enough to cover my rent and expenses for a while here, until I got on my feet."

"Would've?" Jameson's tone is cool and lethal, and it startles me.

I realize I've been staring into my hands when I meet the jagged look in his blue eyes.

Well, fuck. You got this far.

Might as well hit bottom.

"Troy took it all. Right before I left. We had a big fight and I told him I thought we should break up, that things weren't working. And the next day, all the money was gone from the joint account. He'd used it to buy a new truck, so I couldn't do anything about it. And two nights later, I left town."

The line of Jameson's jaw hardens. "Cole knows about this?"

"He knows. And yes, he insisted on murdering Troy for me, but I won't let him. Even if Troy deserves it." I try to laugh, but fail.

Jameson appears entirely unamused.

"Look, if you want to revoke your offer, I totally understand. You didn't know your new gardener came with all this baggage. I just wanted you to know that I haven't always been penniless, and I do have aspirations—"

"I'm not revoking anything." He cuts me off in a low voice that welcomes no negotiating. "You can be a gardener if that's what you want, but for what it's worth, I think you should tell more people about your books. Passions should be celebrated, not kept secret. Be proud of yourself for what you've accomplished."

I take that in with a deep, inaudible breath like it's the freshest air, floored by this strange, euphoric feeling that's expanding in my chest.

His words seem so genuine.

I told him about my books, and he said I should be *proud*. *Him*, the billionaire marketing genius.

Cole told me, while we were in the greenhouse, what Jameson does for his family's business. VP of Brand Marketing. I don't know exactly what that entails, but now that I know his "family business" is that of the illustrious Vance family, it's definitely a bigger deal than sort of author or gardener by pity vote.

I glance around for any sign of my brother. Where the hell is he?

"He might not be back for a while," Jameson says.

Shit. Is that his way of hinting that he doesn't want to be stuck sitting out here with me all night?

"That's okay. I should get some sleep anyway." I push to my feet, pick up my dessert plate, and reach for his.

But his hand lands on my wrist, warm and gentle. "You can leave that."

Oh god. He's touching me.

"Are you sure?"

"I have staff for that."

Right. That'll take some getting used to. If I actually stay here for any length of time.

I put the plate down, mainly so I can slide out of his gentle grasp.

"Sit."

The word is so evenly commanding, so ruggedly warm in his rough-velvet voice, my butt is back in my seat before I can think about it.

CHAPTER 7

Megan

"Tell me more about your books."

Holy fuck. This man has the bossy-alpha thing nailed. Jameson's tone is so irresistibly commanding, it strikes me what a bad idea it is to get hired by a boss this hot. I pick up my unfinished champagne and take another swallow, knowing I'm probably going to tell him anything he asks.

Imagine if he told you to drop your shorts.

"What would you like to know?"

"What's your pen name?"

I sigh under my breath, feeling silly. "Jessica Rivers. Are you gonna look me up now?"

"What are your books about?"

I notice he didn't answer my question.

"Well... They all follow the same story. So it starts in book one and continues on."

"And what's the story?"

I put my glass down, wondering if I can really sum it up. I'm not used to pitching the story verbally to someone. And it's not finished yet. I don't even know how the series ends.

In the silence, insects chirp beyond the glow of the patio lights, and I notice: no mosquitos. If this were Manitoba, we'd be eaten alive out here. The night's so peaceful around us, and distantly, I think I hear my brother talking on the phone, the low lull of his voice.

It's so comforting.

I could really get used to this.

Except for the intimidating man sitting across from me, regarding me in demanding silence.

Waiting.

"Well, it's about a girl named Rowan and a guy named Wolf." I play with my hands while I speak, a nervous tic that always shows itself when I talk about my writing. "It's set in the future, in a postapocalyptic wasteland. Rowan's family are aristocracy, and Wolf is one of the nomadic outsiders known to Rowan's people as savages."

He hasn't told me to shut up because he's sorry he asked yet, so I tentatively keep going.

"When the first book opens, Rowan's parents are long dead and her oldest brothers have just returned from battle with an enemy tribe, victorious. Now it's Rowan's turn to do what she can to protect her family. She's the only girl, and she's been raised to be a Lady. Which means to be married off to the ruler of another tribe as a sort of peace bond between them."

I bite my lip, pausing to give Jameson a moment to steer the conversation elsewhere if he's not interested.

His eyes drift to my lip as I twist it between my teeth. "Sounds barbaric."

I laugh a little. "That's what Wolf says. But it's a common custom among her people. So, as the first book gets going, Rowan is heading off on what they call her bridal march, where some of her brother's trusted guards and hired mercenaries form a caravan and literally walk her to the foreign territory of her intended husband. Wolf and his little brother are two of those mercenaries." I pause to take a breath and gather my thoughts. "But there are many dangers in the open wastelands, and very soon, the bridal march is attacked by roaming bandits. A battle breaks out, many men are killed, including Wolf's little brother, and Wolf ends up fleeing into the woods with Rowan. She's his paycheck, you see. If he can success-fully deliver her to her intended husband, he gets rewarded. So, uh..." I hesitate again, fearing that he might be getting bored. "The books follow their adventure."

Silence falls, and my mind reels as I try to make sense of what's happening right now.

Then it hits me.

He's listening.

Troy never listened.

As that sinks in, I want to hate my ex-boyfriend so much in this dark, violent little place in the depths of my gut. But I don't even care enough about him anymore to hate him.

I thought I'd be spending my life with him. With a man who didn't have the slightest interest in the things that made me happy. For years, I thought that.

Shit, was I wrong.

Thank god.

If anyone ever told me I'd be explaining my nerdy books to a super-hot billionaire who looks like he and his abs belong on a movie poster for the next comic-book action blockbuster, I'd tell them they needed to lay off the mind-altering drugs.

But here we are.

Not only is he listening, he appears to be thinking about every-thing I've said.

"How many more books are there to write?"

"Two more, I think." I'm practically salivating. Vibrating, like a lonely puppy who's just found a playmate. "I have the general story arc planned out."

He waits. Like, *Tell me more.*

"So they're, um, just over halfway through their journey now, and they've encountered all kinds of dangers along the way." *Calm down. You're talking too fast.* "Other men try to take Rowan from Wolf. Early on, he makes her ditch her fancy dress for men's clothing so she doesn't stand out so much. She's been raised in a keep, very sheltered, so she's a total fish out of water trying to survive in the wild. She's, um, also a virgin. That's part of the deal, that her intended husband gets her delivered to him, ah, 'fresh,' as they call it. Wolf knows it. And he knows how to keep them both alive. He's skilled, he grew up in the wastelands, but it's not easy. And along the way..." I hesitate again. "Well... there's lots of sex."

My face burns as Jameson stares at me.

Wow. Who knew writing explicit sex scenes was so much easier than mentioning them in passing to a ridiculously hot man?

He clears his throat, but the words still come out low and gravelly. "He fucks her?"

"Uh-huh." Hopefully, it's dark enough out here that he can't tell how badly I'm blushing. He just said the word *fuck* to me and I'm dying.

Why did I need to bring that up?

Because it's a major thrust of the story.

And he asked.

"But she's supposed to stay a virgin?"

"Yup. But she gives it up to Wolf."

I pick up my champagne and bury my face in it. At some point while I babbled, he filled it up again.

My pulse is thudding. My pussy is starting to throb just talking with my brother's best friend about this imaginary sex that I've dreamed up between these fictional characters.

"And how does she feel about all this arranged-marriage stuff?"

I'm not even sure if he's purposely steering the conversation away from sex or if he's actually curious, but it's an interesting question for a man to ask.

"Well, she's scared. She feels like it's her duty to protect her brothers. She's not a warrior, she's a bride. It's her destiny. But... she falls in love with Wolf. Badly."

He seems to consider that for a moment. "Well, that's shitty."

"Is it?"

He sips his champagne. He's barely drunk a single glass.

I'm on at least my third.

"Does he love her back?"

"Yes. He falls in love with her, too. He knows when he takes her virginity that he's basically signed his own death warrant. Even if he delivers her, if her new husband finds out..." I shrug. "But he takes the risk for her."

"How does it happen?"

Oh, sweet Jesus.

I'm pretty sure I won't be able to look away from Jameson's suddenly half-lidded eyes if my brother walks right into the middle of this. Or live monkeys fall from the sky.

The words spill right out of my mouth.

"On a cold night, in a cave by a fire, wrapped in animal fur. She's very curious. Like I said, she was sheltered. And Wolf opens up the world for her without meaning to. He's her guide on this dangerous journey, and she grows to trust him. And she drills him with questions about sex. He tries to resist her, but it's sort of futile. She's pretty charming."

Jameson doesn't even blink as he drinks that in. "So, it's a romance?"

I shrug uneasily.

"It's part fantasy and part steampunk and part epic journey of survival. It's a mash-up of genres, which I find really fun to write. Romance, though..." I stare at my champagne, avoiding those light-blue eyes. "I don't know. I haven't decided yet if it has a happy ending."

"I'll walk you inside."

It's getting late, and as we head into the house, Jameson unnecessarily moves a chair out of my way.

I'm warm from all the liquor and good food, and his attention. He falls into step behind me, and I'm hyperaware of his presence, even though I can't see him.

Why do I feel, again, like I'm on some bizarre first date?

He's so quiet as we walk across the living room. I can't hear my brother. The house is silent.

"Well, thank you for everything." I don't know what else to say. I need sleep. I'll be thinking more clearly in the morning.

Maybe he isn't even *that* hot.

I glance at him.

Fuck. *He's beautiful.*

Does he routinely go shirtless in his house?

Am I gonna get fired for licking him without meaning to?

"Last chance, okay? If you're uncomfortable with me taking the gardening job, or regretting the offer—"

"The job is yours." His firm tone tells me there'll be no swaying that decision.

"Okay. I can't really tell you how much it means to me. It's been a long day. Maybe I'll find the words tomorrow."

"You don't have to say anything. It's for Cole. He asked, I'm happy to say yes."

He doesn't seem happy, though.

Whatever wisp of rapport I'd sensed while we talked about my books has been replaced by the same cool formality as before. But at least he's admitted what I guessed: the job was Cole's idea. And now that he knows why I'm broke, he probably pities me.

We've wandered all the way to the grand entrance of the living room, where the two halls spread out in either direction. I have no idea where he sleeps, but obviously, not in the guest wing.

I pause, and so does he, his hands jammed in his pants pockets.

"I guess this is where I leave you." I fill the silence, feeling awkward when he says nothing. It makes me squirm.

No. It makes me hot. Like everything else he does.

Yeah, there's no way he'll be less hot in the morning.

Just a few hours ago, he was the billionaire in the luxury SUV and fine suit, and I was the train wreck in the street, blocking traffic with my cheap, broken suitcase. My broken life.

It's inconceivable that we're standing here together right now.

And yet we are.

The odd moment stretches out, like we're now at the *end* of the bizarre first date. And we're both contemplating whether or not we're going to kiss.

But that's ridiculous. He isn't thinking about kissing me.

"Have a good sleep, Megan." His voice is low and brushes across my senses like velvet. It makes me want to pet him.

"Good night, Jameson." I almost thank him again, but that's just getting sad.

For all I know, he's been judging me and my life choices—harshly—this entire time. When it comes to his private thoughts, the man is giving nothing away.

I turn and head toward the guest wing. All the way up the hall, I feel the lingering warmth of his attention, like he's watching me. But when I reach the end of the hall and glance back, Jameson is gone.

It strikes me that he'd make one hell of a character in a book.

I just have no idea yet if he'd be the hero or the villain.

CHAPTER 8

"I'm a lot tougher than you seem to think," Rowan says stubbornly. "You know, I grew up with four brothers."

"Right, I almost forgot. Four brothers who were probably tit fed until they were twelve and had their asses wiped for them with daisies."

I smirk, because I was raised with older brothers like that. And my sister has four brothers, just like Rowan.

I can already relate to this book.

This Jessica Rivers is a decent author.

I put my feet up on the lounger, settling back into the deeper shade where I can read the screen on my tablet better. It's sunny this morning, the sky a vibrant, clear blue overhead.

"If we run into someone out here," I tell her, digging through the ratty clothes in the abandoned shack we've come across, "it's not gonna be one of your precious brothers, so spare me the 'I can handle anything that you can' act." I toss some clothes on the table. "Put these on."

"I will not." She looks scandalized. "They're dirty and they're men's."

"And I told you, that dress will get you killed. You can't even run in that thing."

"How will it get me killed? It shows I have value."

I scowl at her embroidered corset. "You really have no idea what would happen to you. What a Lady's worth out in the wide world, to other tribes beyond the Westlands. You'd be lucky if they killed you." I flick my knife in the air. "Now take it off."

She doesn't.

"Or you can stay like that. But if you fall and break an ankle, I'm leaving you behind."

I turn away as she finally starts moving. I hear the rustle of her skirts. I hear her boots clunk on the floor. I give her a moment to pull on the leggings, then turn. They fit well enough. They're too short, meant for a boy, but once she puts her boots back on and tucks them in, you wouldn't know.

The fancy corset now looks even more ridiculous.

"The rest of it. Come on."

She seems distraught. "You have to help me. My dressing girl used to do it."

Bloody hell. She can't even dress herself?

I jam the tip of my knife blade into the tabletop and spin her around. I unhook the many hooks on the back of the corset, exposing her naked back. Then I rip the corset off.

She turns around, holding her slender arms over her chest. Her breasts are larger than I would've thought. You couldn't tell a thing about her tits through that corset, which is not the least of what's wrong with it. I toss the thing on the floor, where it belongs.

"Is there a bra?"

"You don't need a bloody bra. Just put this on." I shove the boys' undershirt at her.

We stare at each other like we're from two different planets. I'm starting to think we are.

"Savage girls don't wear bras?"

"Why on earth would they?"

She takes the undershirt like it's diseased, but she turns around and slips it on. She tucks the shirt into her leggings, and when she turns back around, the thin fabric is stretched over her breasts. I can see her nipples through it.

I toss the other shirt at her. She pulls it on. It's long sleeved and fitted, and I can still see her nipples. It's not even cold in here.

I hand her the vest, and she pulls it on. There. Now she looks like a human being instead of some fairy-tale nightmare.

"And no more fancy hairdos."

"Fancy?" She touches her mussed hair. "What's fancy about it?"

"No one besides some stuck-up Lady would wear her hair like that. Take it out."

She starts taking it out. "But I don't know any other way to wear it. How do savage girls wear their hair?"

"Just do a plain braid."

"I don't know how to do a braid."

What girl doesn't know how to do a braid? What person doesn't know how to do a braid?

I really hope she's a fantastic fuck, for her future husband's sake, or the man's getting nothing out of this deal.

I grab her hair, pull it forward over one shoulder. I split it into three sections and braid it so she can see. "Just pull each section over the one in the middle, back and forth. Left, right, left, right." I get to the bottom and grab the strip of leather she pulled from her fancy do.

"Have you braided a lot of savage girls' hair?" she asks as I tie the leather around the bottom of the braid in a little bow.

"Horsehair." I drop the braid. "Same damn thing. Now keep up, or you get left behind."

I head outside, and she hurries to follow me into the forest. "Stop making idle threats. You're not going to leave me here alone."

"So what if I do? With your newfound braiding skills you can weave yourself a raft and float on home down the river."

Her face reddens with anger. "Look. We both know if you leave me out here, I'll probably die."

Yeah. Don't tempt me.

"Let's just agree on that," she huffs, "and you can stop throwing it *in my face. You're not going to abandon me, and we both know that, too."*

"And how do we know that?"

"Because you love my brothers."

I don't refute it, but I don't like letting her win. "Love is a strong word between men. They're not cunts, though, I'll give them that. Your little brother, Forest, now there's a cunt." I start heading up the hill in front of us, forcing myself not to think about my little brother, or I might just leave her behind for real.

I hear her struggling to keep up with my long strides, and when I glance over my shoulder, she doesn't appear pleased. "Will you stop saying that?"

"What? Cunt?" I stop short, and she bumps into me. "Cunt, cock, shit, fuck. What's the problem?" She gapes at me. "Look, princess—"

"It's Lady Rowan," she insists.

"It's not Lady anything to me. And you might get used to the way I speak, because I'm not changing it."

Then I stride on up the hill.

"Huh." I lower my tablet to the patio table in front of me. I'm sitting out on the balcony off my bedroom, and I can see my new gardener in the backyard below. Over at the far corner, where that kid from the landscaping service who trims the hedges is showing her around.

I pull out my phone and send her a text; Locke procured her phone number for me. Security, of course.

Me: Wolf is an asshole.

I observe her reaction as she tugs her phone from the back pocket of her little khaki shorts and reads the message, then taps out a reply.

Megan: You're reading my book???

Me: I started the first one last night. He just made Rowan give up her lovely dress. He's quite a dick. The story's good, though.

Her response, again, is quick.

Megan: His little brother was just killed right in front of him!

Me: Still.

I wait while she types, then shoves her phone back into her pocket. My phone chimes.

Megan: I'll have you know that Wolf is hot.

I jolt when a hulking man with neck tattoos looms over me out of nowhere, blocking out the sun. Locke shoves his phone at me.
This, again.
I know my head of security wouldn't barge into my bedroom unless it's important. However, his sudden presence makes me uncomfortably aware that I have a hard-on.
"Jesus. Since when do you not knock?"
"I knocked. You didn't answer."
I take the phone and glare at him, and he leaves.
On the screen is yet another celeb gossip site, showing a photo of me—with another female celebrity.
I swallow a groan and scroll, finding several more photos. But it's the first one that's the most damning.
"Fuck me."
There's really nothing else to say, as my morning goes to shit.

When Clara announces a visitor midafternoon, I head into my home office and settle behind the desk in time to glimpse, through the front windows, the distinctive Rolls-Royce Black Badge Cullinan SUV rolling up my driveway.

I'd wondered why he didn't call yet today. Now I know.

I thumb away from the web page where I found one of the rare online photos of Cole with his sister and set my phone aside, making myself look busy at the home computer I never really use. My oldest brother and boss, Graysen, is big on appearances, and as far as he knows, I work from my home office most of the time.

I literally never work in any office. What's the point of being a billionaire if you're tied to a desk all day?

Anyway, I haven't wasted my *whole* day stalking Cole's sister. There's not much to be found about her online anyway. No other press besides the few photos taken when she's attended some hockey game or fundraiser with Cole over the years. No gossip.

Her life couldn't be more different from mine that way.

I can't even find any social media profiles except an Instagram account in her pen name. Her page is all quotes from her books and random photos of things she must think her readers will like. Most of them feature flowers. She has fewer than two thousand followers.

All the world seems to know about Megan Hudson is that she shows up every now and then at a hockey game with her brother, seems to prefer plants to people, and gets flush faced, adorable, and unbelievably sexy all at once when she talks about her writing.

That last part is my own personal observation.

I should've said no when Cole asked me if she could stay here with him. And again when he asked me to give her a job.

But I just couldn't.

Cole is that kind of friend. He has this roguish charisma that endears him to people, including me. You just want him at your party and at your back.

But more than that, I owe Cole so much more than a place to stay while his house is being renovated and a temporary home and a job for his sister.

I promised myself, after he told me the hard truth that no one else would: *Anything he asks.* Because when your friend has your back like that, you have his, too.

Cole has never asked me for anything. He has his own money, his hockey career. It was a given he'd crash here while his house was being finished. That's what best friends are for. But this... this is the only thing he's ever outright asked me for, and I can tell it's important to him.

She's important to him.

But wealth builds walls, right? That's practically the Vance family motto. I don't have to let her in.

She doesn't have to be important to *me*.

I'm only reading her book because I'm curious. It's not every day you meet an author.

I probably won't even finish it.

She might say it's not a romance, but it's starting to feel like one, and what guy reads romance?

I've got more important things to do with my time.

I've actually spent the bulk of my day so far on and off the phone with my team at Vance Industries and our PR department as they work on dousing the flames of today's fresh, new scandal, which is spreading like wildfire in a drought. People are, as always, weirdly ravenous for this shit.

When I met up with pop star Nina Joy in Vegas, we hadn't seen each other in a while, and she'd come on strong—as can be seen in the photos that went viral as soon as they were posted this morning. Like Geneviève, Nina is one of Vance Industries' brand ambassadors. She's the face of Sea Salt citrus gin and their trendy bottled gin cocktails, one of our leading product lines, she's performing at the Vance Bayshore resort opening gala in the spring, and Graysen is probably fit to blow. Or bury me.

"Come in," I growl, when Clara taps on my office door.

"Mr. Vance is here," she announces from the doorway.

"By all means, show him in."

She does, then shuts the door behind him.

Graysen strides into the middle of my office and frowns as he looks around. He hasn't been here in a while; usually, we all go to him. He lives in the house that we all grew up in, which still feels like home base to the rest of us. Or at least he did before Granddad died and he moved into his suite at the resort to oversee its completion to an obsessive-compulsive degree.

Besides that, Graysen Vance is notoriously "too busy" for such things as hanging out with other humans, even ones he's related to.

His thick, dark-brown hair is compulsively neat, his jaw set, and the ability to smile, if he ever had one, seems to have been decommissioned due to its irrelevance. He wears a dark suit and a stiff-collared shirt with a silk tie. As he does every day of his life.

I like to picture Graysen as a baby, in a diaper and tie, holding a briefcase. It makes it easier to deal with him when he gets all holier-than about my life choices.

Which he's definitely about to do.

"Day forty-four," he remarks, his storm-cloud-gray eyes meeting mine.

"This is how you greet me now?"

"That's what it is. Day forty-four of the most important challenge of your life. Or is it?"

"Get to the point, Graysen. You can't pull off coy. You just look constipated."

He frowns deeper, which just makes him look more constipated. "Let's start here. As of last night, there are photos all over the internet of you and Geneviève Blaise."

"Was that a question?"

"Does it need to be?"

"They're paparazzi photos, Gray."

"You're holding hands, Jamie."

I stretch back in my chair. "How new are you to this game?"

"You sound like Granddad," he notes, and there's some affection in it. "You're way more like him than you know. Grandma always said so."

"So?" Seriously, the last thing I want to chat about right now is the man responsible for this actual fucking "game" we've been forced to play. "Don't believe everything you think you see."

"I will when I see it with my own eyes."

"Jesus, you're getting paranoid. You're sounding more like Mom every day." It's not a compliment, and he knows it.

He makes a grumbly noise. "So you aren't fucking Geneviève?"

I hate to admit it, because it's really not his business or the wide world's. But I won't lie to him. "I was."

He sighs.

"But not during the challenge. That photo is months old. Someone held it back, timed this little gossip frenzy to coincide with her movie opening. PR knows the truth, and they're on it."

"And I'm just supposed to believe that you're no longer involved with her?"

"You're supposed to believe a brother who's never lied to you. I'm not the lying kind. I think we can agree that Harlan got all those genes."

"The challenge is only part of the problem here. Geneviève is also one of our brand ambassadors," he reminds me. "Which means it's unethical."

"My job is to oversee our brands, and the celebrities who endorse them, is it not? I don't need you micromanaging me."

"It's not your job to fuck the celebrities in question. You know how many of our companies have a no-fraternization policy?"

I look out the window. Unfortunately, at that exact moment, Megan Hudson wanders into view.

"Every single one of them." My brother answers his own question. "Because it's one of the policies we mandate when we create or acquire them..." As he continues his lecture, my eyes trace Megan's curves in her tight tank top and little shorts. "... and it was important to this company's founder. So it's important to us."

I drag my attention away from Megan when I realize he's stopped talking. "Excuse me? Founder?" I cup my hand behind my ear like I must've heard him wrong. "You mean Stoddard Vance?

Granddad? The man who was fucking his secretary *for decades?* *While* he was married?"

Graysen looks constipated again. "Let's not repeat the mistakes of the past."

I get up and stroll to the window, but Megan's vanished. "I'm not making any mistakes, Gray." Does he really think I'd be that careless?

Just forty-six more days.

Then it's his fucking turn, or someone else's. I know every one of my siblings is dying to know what their own challenge will be. I didn't devise Graysen's challenge, and I have no idea who did or what it is. But I can't wait to find out.

I turn to face him. "I'm doing just fine. Honestly, at this point, the drive to complete this challenge so I can watch you all sweat through yours is almost worth the suffering."

"I don't care how much 'suffering' it causes you." I know he means it; Graysen could probably easily give up sex for ninety days. It would just give him more time to micromanage the rest of us. "I'm fucking tired of your playboy ways, Jamie. All this never-ending gossip just fuels the fire. It's threatening our reputation. There's a reason we put such a premium on maintaining our privacy."

"Uh-huh. You know what your problem is?"

"I'm sure you'll enlighten me."

"You don't see any difference between gossip and true bad press."

"There *is* no difference when it negatively impacts us. The result is the same."

"I disagree. The truth matters. Facts are worth defending."

"Well, the fact is, if you can't keep yourself out of these salacious headlines, I'll have to remove you from your position as VP of Brand Marketing. At least for a while."

I stride back to my desk and face him across it, weighing his seriousness on this. "You won't. You need me."

"Not as badly as I need our company image, our *family* image, to remain intact. The completion of Granddad's resort is contingent on so many details, so many relationships, so many damn regulations... Since losing him, we're under extreme pressure to prove that we can deliver without him. I need you all to keep your heads down, even more than usual. And trust me, I've got enough issues with your brothers to deal with. I don't need another black sheep."

"Which is why you need *me*. The resort isn't the only asset that we need to prove we can deliver on without Granddad. What about the hockey team? What are you going to do if the Northmen's new president attends his first board meeting with the National Hockey Organization and shits the bed? You might need me on that board, and you need *someone* in the family smiling for the cameras next to the team captain on the sports page. You're not gonna do it."

"Don't push it."

"Just admit how much you need me."

"Not that badly."

Bullshit.

"I may not know hockey like you do," he says, "but I know business. And I will learn about hockey, damn fast, if that's what it takes."

I drop into my seat and recline back.

He's bluffing. Trying to scare me.

The fact is, we all need each other.

Granddad knew it.

He'd handed his successor at the Northmen organization a lot of power right before he passed, because he was making a final power play. The hockey team was his childhood dream. When he bought the Vancouver Northmen and the arena where they play, it was one of his greatest life achievements.

Passing his role as president of Northmen Sports and Entertainment to someone outside the family, instead of one of his grandchildren, was a warning to us, maybe. That nothing should ever come easy.

And like Savannah said, this game he's left us to play forces us to rely on each other if things go to shit.

Ultimately, I'm pretty sure Graysen doesn't want me to lose the game any more than I want to lose it.

"Then, by all means." I call his bluff. "Do what you have to do. Hand my job over to Harlan and let him represent us in the media."

I fucking dare you.

The constipated look is back. "Harlan isn't... palatable... as a public face of this company."

I snort. "Understatement."

"And Damian is best left an enigma."

"You mean a dirty secret that hides in plain sight."

Graysen's jaw twitches.

"I've given you my word. What more do you want me to do to prove I'm trustworthy on this? Wear a chastity belt?"

"I want you to put your money where your mouth is. Remove yourself from the immediate handling of all female talent. Hand them off to your team. Stick to the men. You've got this whiskey deal with Jesse Mayes, all the hockey endorsement deals with the Northmen. Focus on those."

"You're kidding me."

"Do I look like I'm kidding?"

"From where I'm sitting, you look eternally constipated."

"You'd have trouble taking a shit too if you knew your entire family, your thousands of employees and your dead grandparents were all watching your every move, every moment of every day."

Yeah, I have to admit that sounds exhausting. At least I only have him breathing down my neck.

"So, in summary, I'm an out-of-control playboy who's destroying the family reputation. Damian owns a sex club, but I can't have a sex life?"

"Damian is discreet. You're not secretly banging your secretary or privately indulging in a kink. Your sex life gets smeared across the internet at least once a week—"

"That's an exaggeration."

"And we haven't even gotten to Nina Joy yet. You were photographed with her in Vegas two days ago."

And here we go.

"She's been all over the web for months dating a famous soccer player," Graysen grits out, "and there she is, two fucking days ago, in *your* arms, kissing *you.*" He's actually getting mad, a flush of red creeping up his neck.

It's not like Graysen to get mad at me.

As the oldest, eight years my senior, he became like a parental figure to me after Dad died when I was only eleven, and Mom remarried and lost interest in motherhood.

Maybe he really thinks I'm lying to him.

What can I do but keep telling him the truth?

"Yes, I saw Nina in Vegas two days ago. And yes, she kissed me. *She* kissed *me.* Someone caught it on camera, and now it's online. But that kiss was not reciprocated. I didn't touch her except to remove her from my body, which she was trying to climb. End of story."

"So you're telling me nothing happened?"

"I'm telling you what happened. And that was it. She tried. I turned her down."

My brother's jaw is twitching again.

"You don't believe me."

"It's hard to believe."

"Why?"

"Because you used to date her, before we partnered with her."

"So, you think I can't control myself?"

I want to tell him how fucking wrong he is about that.

Like the fact that this morning, I jerked off thinking about my new gardener wearing nothing but gloves as she knelt in the flowerbeds, weeding. I got myself off in the shower before I dared risk running into her today. And I did it slow.

While I came, I pictured my best friend's little sister gasping my name while *she* came, her pussy juice dripping down her thighs.

In my mind, I've already fucked her.

But in reality, I have reasons not to touch her. The challenge.

Cole. The fact that I'm not the out-of-control sex monkey my siblings seem to think I am.

Really, none of this is any of his fucking business, though.

My word should be enough.

"You think I'm a sex addict or something? Is that it? I can't possibly resist a woman just because I find her attractive?"

Graysen swipes a hand over his face, looking weary and so much older than his thirty-eight years. He looks like a dad, actually. Like a guy who has no children of his own yet, but has worried about his younger siblings all his life.

"No, Jamie. I think you just never have a reason to keep it in your pants. So I chose this challenge for you, to give you a reason."

CHAPTER 9

I stare at my brother, too shocked to respond for a long-ass moment as the meaning of his words weighs down on me like an anvil with the words *fuck you* etched into it.

"*You* chose this challenge for me?"

"Yes," Graysen says with distaste. "I did."

I'm stunned. I would've seriously put every dollar I had on Harlan being the one. Or maybe Damian.

But it was Graysen.

Which means it wasn't meant to make me suffer. It's much worse than that.

Maybe he really doesn't trust me.

Maybe he really believes I'm a liability.

And if that's true, then my inheritance and my job and literally everything I have is really on the line here.

If Graysen tells the others I failed...

They'll believe him over me. Even if they don't want to, even if they want to trust me, they'll take his side.

Graysen is the boss.

Every pack, even a pack of alphas always snapping at one another's necks, needs an ultimate alpha. And Graysen has always been ours.

Which means that if I can't convince him that I've won the game, I've failed anyway.

Fuck. Time to just lay all my cards on the table.

"Look, I'm not allowed to tell anyone about this challenge, right? I can't tell women *why* I can't hook up with them, which makes it extra fucking difficult."

He says nothing, just frowns.

"Also, I make it a policy not to lie to people I care about. And Nina has always been good to me. But I lied through my teeth to her in Vegas, because of the fucking challenge. The only thing I could think to tell her that wouldn't piss her off was that I *can't* hook up with her because I'm in a relationship."

Graysen's eyebrow lifts with interest. "You told her you have a girlfriend?"

Yeah. That was the plan. But me being an inexperienced liar, it kind of spiraled out of control. "I told her I have a fiancée."

"And that worked?"

"It worked. She was actually happy for me. Threw me an impromptu dinner with her band."

He shakes his head. "And how long do you think that lie's going to hold?"

I exhale, rubbing my face. "Maybe a few weeks until she wonders why I haven't publicly announced my engagement?"

"You have another lie locked and loaded to deal with that?"

"No," I growl. "And I really hope you're happy that this challenge is killing me slowly."

My brother goes quiet in a way I know I'm not going to like as he stands there, hands on his hips, thinking.

"I just realized you haven't sat down since you got here," I say uneasily.

"I'm thinking."

"That's what I'm afraid of."

"Your sex life is a magnet for gossip," he mutters, the gears turning in his head.

"*Speculation* about my sex life," I correct him.

"I tried to make it stop by making you give up sex," he goes on like I haven't spoken. "But that didn't work. So, if we can't stop it, we need to counteract it. Bury the gossip under something bigger."

"Such as the truth?" I say dryly.

Graysen scowls at me like I'm an idiot. "No one cares about the truth."

"I do."

He starts pacing, ignoring that. "What's the one thing that could effectively bury these never-ending gossip pieces? What could outshine the rumors of a playboy lifestyle?"

Damn. How did this spiral so out of control? The media is my domain. That "playboy lifestyle" is usually an asset for us, whether my brother wants to admit it or not.

Suddenly, it's become a liability.

When I realize maybe he's waiting on an actual answer, I grimace. "I told you. The truth. I'm already talking to PR—"

"A fairy-tale romance." Graysen answers his own question. "With one woman. That's the only thing that gets more attention than this shit. Nina Joy bought into it, right?"

"Uh—"

"What makes the covers of magazines and featured articles and goes viral every damn minute? *Celebrity love stories.*"

A vein starts throbbing in my forehead as we stare each other down.

I hate that he's making sense right now. Marketing is *my* thing, not his.

"That means *you*," he adds grimly, "plus someone the family approves of. Which means no gold diggers and no bimbos, Jamie."

I'm gradually absorbing how serious he is about this. "You know I'm not in a relationship."

"Then get in one." *Yup. He's serious.* "And it needs to be grand. Yet believable."

Believable. Because it won't be real, but he'll want me to sell it like it is. Is that what he's saying?

"So now celibacy isn't enough? Now you want me to ask

someone to marry me, but not have sex with her, or, what? You'll choose to believe I failed the game and lock me out of my inheritance?" I keep my voice calm, but that vein in my forehead is ready to explode. "Because of some fucking online gossip?"

My brother just looks annoyed. "You can have sex with her. Eventually. You've only got a few more weeks on the challenge."

"And where am I supposed to find a woman worthy of your 'approval' out of nowhere? She's just supposed to appear out of thin fucking air—"

The door bursts open and a small, disheveled whirlwind Tasmanian-devils into the room, spraying soil. "You fired Romeo?" Megan pants at me in her little tank top, her sweaty cleavage heaving.

Her nipples are hard.

"I'm so sorry." Clara's right behind her, huffing and puffing. "She outran me."

I sit back, not sure how to process that Megan Hudson just sprinted into my office. "It's all right, Clara. You can leave us."

Clara nods, smoothing her mussed hair as she shuts the door.

"You fired Romeo?" Megan repeats, whipping her gardening trowel in the air for effect. And flinging mud across my office.

"Is that mud?"

"What?" She wipes her sweaty forehead with the back of her wrist, smearing mud across it.

Graysen crosses his arms over his chest, glancing from my mud-sprayed sofa to Megan to me. I ignore him, trying to look unfazed, but mud on my sofa from Brianza is a hard no. I don't even have sex on that sofa.

"What are you, auditioning for some Shakespeare-in-the-Park thing?" I demand, fucking irritated in five different directions.

"Huh?" Megan looks from me to my brother and back, suddenly self-conscious, like she's just realized she exploded into a meeting spraying mud and shouting at me about Romeo.

"Who's Romeo?"

She blinks at me. "Uh, Romeo is the very sweet, kind man who's been making your gardens beautiful for the last *four years* and he has three kids he's trying to put through college and his wife is going blind and you just fired him from the job he loves!" She stares at me, panting, waiting for me to respond to that.

Oh. *That Romeo.* I thought his name was Raymond or something.

"We'll talk about this later," I tell her. "I'm in a meeting."

She glances at Graysen again.

I grind my teeth. Her nipples are still hard, and he's looking at her.

"This is my brother, Graysen," I force out.

In a much more polite tone, she says, "Nice to meet you."

"Likewise."

"I'm sorry to interrupt. But this is important."

"Please, don't let me stop you," Graysen says.

Thanks, bro.

Megan's eyes cut back to me. "I can't believe you fired him."

"So I could hire you," I point out, my voice low.

My brother raises an eyebrow at me.

I do not want to continue this conversation in front of him. Not when my blood is boiling like it is. It's not anger. I want to explain to her that I'm not always an asshole. She's just caught me at a very, very bad time. "I was trying to help you—"

"Because Cole asked you to. And I do appreciate it, but—"

"This is you being appreciative?"

"This is you helping?"

"This is how you talk to your employer?"

"Not usually." She glances at Graysen, looking embarrassed and frustrated. "You have to hire him back," she tells me.

She's trying to tell me what to do. In front of my brother.

Heat spreads through my chest. My fingers twitch, and I have to clamp them down on the arms of my chair.

"I can't do that." It's amazing how calm my tone is, considering I'd like to drag her across my lap and spank her round little ass right now. Teach her some manners. Without witnesses.

"Why not?"

"Because I gave you the job. How many gardeners do you think I need on salary?"

She takes a deep, silent breath. "Okay. I understand. And I quit."

What?

"Wait." I get to my feet.

Megan looks at Graysen again, who's standing back like he's watching an enjoyable rom-com. "Again, I'm sorry for the interruption," she says—to my brother. "Have a nice day." Then she walks out.

"Megan—" I growl, but the door shuts behind her.

Graysen smirks, which is terrifying, since Graysen never smirks.

"Do not say it," I bark.

"Say what?"

"Whatever the hell you're thinking right now. She's not available."

"Too bad. She might make a great Mrs. Vance. Who is she?"

"I thought you already had your future Mrs. Vance picked out," I mutter.

"I didn't mean for me."

"Ha." I snarl as I drop back into my chair, and Graysen's brow furrows in a way I don't like. I can feel his brain running calculations again. It's goddamn creepy.

Then he pronounces, "She'd do."

"And you know this, because...?"

"Because she's not afraid to get dirty, or to stand up to you. You think any of the discardable bimbos you screw is going to make a good wife?"

"You don't know who I screw," I say calmly. Which is mostly true. I don't alert him when I get laid; the internet does that, apparently, and the internet is an unreliable source. "But at least I didn't let Mommy pick a wife for me."

The constipated look returns in full force.

"Anyway," I deflect, "she's Cole Hudson's sister. And she works for me. Remember that whole lecture you just gave me about our fraternization policy?"

"She just quit."

"She didn't quit. That won't hold." It can't, unless I want Cole to be very pissed at me.

"So, fire her."

"Because that'll make her want to marry me. You really missed your calling as a matchmaker, Gray."

"You don't have to love each other, you know. Look at Granddad and Grandma."

"Ah, yes. The blueprint for wedded bliss."

"I didn't say it was bliss. But it worked."

"Did it?"

"Getting engaged will keep women away from you while you finish your challenge," he grinds out, "and it will drown all this playboy crap in the media. Which means it should be your top priority as of right now."

"So you really want me to conjure a fake fiancée just for appearances? I'm not you, Graysen."

He scrapes a hand through his hair. I rarely see Graysen lose his cool, but this whole conversation is getting under his skin.

He abhors public exposure of any kind. He probably hates having to get engaged at all, just because it's what's expected of him, though he'd never admit it.

Asking me to create positive press to bury the bad is like a worst-case scenario for him.

Desperate times.

"Fake or real," he growls, like a man who has way more important shit to deal with than standing here arguing with me about my sex life, "I give less than zero fucks, Jamie, okay? Just make sure it's convincing. You're Prince Charming and she's your Cinderella."

With that, he stalks out of my office, probably wishing he were an only child.

The feeling is mutual.

I watch his black SUV roll down my driveway through the window, the vein still throbbing in my head.

At least Cole left for the airport already. Call that a win. I'll just have to smooth things over with his sister before he hears anything.

Hopefully she didn't already call him to complain about me.

I don't see her in the garden from my office windows, so I go looking for her. I'm not about to go near her room, and I don't see her out by the pool or anywhere else, so I go to Clara's office. "Where's Miss Hudson?"

"She left."

"What?"

"I believe... she's gone." Clara rises to her feet when she realizes I don't like that answer. "I sent you a text."

I pat my pockets, realizing I left my phone on the desk in my office. "What text?"

"I thought you'd want to know. While you were in your meeting with Mr. Vance, she left with her little suitcase."

I stand there, heart pounding, as I process this. The feeling that rises up in me, setting fire to my senses and stopping my breath, is unnamable.

It's as confusing as it is unexpected.

Later, I'll be able to look back and understand what I felt when I first heard that Megan was gone.

In the moment, it feels like a sudden and all-consuming madness, which isn't far off.

CHAPTER 10

Megan

I knock on Nicole's apartment door, my sad suitcase, once again held together by bungee cords and a prayer, at my feet.

She just buzzed me into the building, which is, as she'd described it, just off South Granville's "Art Gallery Row," near the Granville Street Bridge, where a steady stream of Friday night traffic glides in and out of downtown. Nicole's street is surprisingly quiet, just one block off the main drag. Her building isn't the newest on the block, but it has security, and the glass lobby looks renovated.

The elevator brings me up to her floor, and when she throws her door open, I hear the comforting voices of women inside, the throb of music, and the hiss of something cooking, like vegetables sizzling in a wok.

"Yes!" My old friend lights up at the sight of me and practically shouts the greeting, and I have to laugh. Nicole was the one who dubbed this my Summer of Yes, after all.

Minutes after I quit my gardening job today, I called to tell her that I needed a new place to stay; she immediately invited me to come stay with her. I said *yes*, and here we are.

She throws her arms around me. "I can't believe it's been so long since I saw you!"

"I know!" Nicole and I grew up together in Crooks Creek, right next door. We've kept in touch over the years, and I've seen her every few years when she comes home for Christmas or a wedding or a funeral. But it's been a while. "It never feels like any time has passed at all when I see you, though," I marvel.

"Girl, same." She grabs my suitcase without a comment on its sorry state and whisks it inside. "Come in!"

Inside the apartment, I'm immediately greeted by the comfy chaos of too many people living together in a small space. Personal belongings are strewn everywhere. The living room features an unmade futon bed, and the open kitchen is a sea of groceries and dishes.

Two twenty-something women are in the living room, one painting her toenails, the other one lacing up her tall Doc Martens boots. Another one is in the kitchen, making a stir fry that I can now smell: oil, hoisin, and broccoli. That hip-hop song "Stir Fry" thumps through the apartment, kinda loud, but not so loud it'll annoy the neighbors, maybe.

They all wave at me when Nicole introduces us, rattling off their names. I already know all three of them live here with her.

I do the math. Nicole said there were two bedrooms. She's in one; that means one roommate on the futon and the other two in the second bedroom?

"Welcome to big-city living, my friend," she says, maybe reading my overwhelm.

"Are you sure it's okay if I stay for a bit?" I follow her as she rolls my suitcase up the short hall to her bedroom. "Your roommates won't mind?"

"Nope." She pushes open the door to her room, which is at least a lot tidier than the shared space beyond, though it's smallish. There's only one bed, a double. "My name is one of the two on the lease. We have more people than we're supposed to in here, but it makes the rent cheap. They wanna charge three grand, to start, for a decent apartment around here? The modern girl makes it work."

I blanch as she shuts the door behind us, and the music fades out a bit. *Three grand...?*

"We're all busy girls, so everyone just comes and goes. We're rarely all here at once." She takes my backpack and purse from me and puts them on her bed.

"This is so generous of you, really. I'm sure you don't need one more to add to the chaos."

"It's no problem. I'm undaunted by chaos." She smiles at me.

I remember that about her. Love that about her, really.

With her wild brown hair and good-time vibes, Nicole Lalonde is the energy I want to become. Where I'm careful and overly cautious, she never lets anything get in her way. When we were kids, I'd be hovering on the edge of the river, weighing the dangers of jumping in, and Nicole would already have dived right in, without pause or regret.

And our whole lives have rolled out just like that.

Sadly, as cautious as I've been, it hasn't saved me from getting hurt. Nicole went to the big city to expand her life. I stayed put, stayed safe—in theory—and suffered for it.

She slides open a drawer in her dresser. "I cleared out two drawers for you, and I'll make room in the closet."

"Nicole..." I sigh. "You're amazing. I'm sorry this is happening."

"Hey." She catches my arm and gives it a squeeze. "It's all good. You're welcome here. As long as you need."

"Thank you. I really appreciate it." It's not ideal. As I look around, I know that. I'm not Nicole. Living like this will be stressful for me. I need a bit of my own space, to think, to write, but I can't afford that yet. "And I'm happy to sleep on the floor. I don't want to bother you."

"Don't be ridiculous. You're sleeping right in the bed with me. It's way more comfy, there's room for both of us, and I won't snuggle or snore, I promise."

I smile because she's trying to cheer me up.

"I know you won't be here long anyway. You've always taken care of yourself. You'll find a way. And who knows." She shrugs. "Maybe you stay more permanently, we get bunk beds."

I laugh a little. "You're not serious."

"Hey, I'm not here forever either. Only until I meet my Prince Charming and he sweeps me away from all this." She swoons her way into the en suite bathroom, flicks on a light and rummages around. "I'm making room for you in here too!"

"Thank you!"

I find a spot on the floor to untie my suitcase and lay it open. I open my backpack, too, and start gathering my toiletries and cosmetics. The least I can do is unpack and get my things stowed out of her way. Settle in.

Commit to this.

Not just for her, but for me, too.

It cost me a lot to take the taxi here. I'm terrified by the minuscule remaining balance in my bank account. But I know this is for the best.

My first few impressions of my brother's best friend, overall, did not bode well. Besides his overwhelming good looks, which are a whole problem of another kind... I'm not sure I like him much.

I threw myself into gardening today, optimistic. But then I found out from a couple of the other staff that Jameson had fired Romeo. I couldn't live with that; I couldn't take that man's job from him. He needs it more than I do, and he definitely earned it more than I did.

"So, what happened at your brother's?" Nicole eyes me as I bring my things into the bathroom, to put in the drawer she's cleared out for me. She places a folded towel on the counter for me, too. "You guys weren't bonding? Enjoying catching up? You were always so close."

We were. When we were younger. Nicole was Cole's age, but she was always closer to me. We were Team Girl.

"Would've loved to, but there was this growly homeowner in the way." I shut the drawer and head back into the bedroom. "Because get this. Cole is living with his billionaire best friend while his new house is renovated."

Nicole leans in the bathroom doorway. "Billionaire?"

"Yup."

"And he's not over fifty?"

"His name is Jameson Vance. He's the youngest sibling of the Vance family. You can look him up." *I know I did.* "You know, *that* Vance family? The one who owns the hockey team?"

Nicole doesn't answer because she's suddenly nose-down in her phone. "The hockey team, and the arena... Black Mountain ski resort..." She scrolls, reading the same list of properties owned by Vance Industries that I'd found online.

I start organizing my clothes into the dresser as she rattles them off.

"There's an endless list of upscale bars here. Liquor companies, wineries, high-end restaurants, luxury hotels. They own, like, everything on Bayshore Drive downtown, in Coal Harbour. The whole several-block waterfront. Including the posh new resort hotel, which they're calling the Vance Bayshore resort. And endless surrounding properties."

"I know."

She goes silent for a moment, then: "*Holy shit.* He's beautiful."

"I know."

She laughs. "You sound disgusted."

I grimace. "It's been a crazy week. I'm not really in the head-space to admire any man's beauty right now or, you know, think of him that way." *Bullshit.* My eyes have admired him plenty.

So did my dreams last night.

"Okay. Sure. But how often do you meet *that*." She shoves the phone in my face, where a shirtless photo of Jameson accosts my eyeballs. He's ripped to hell and goddamn stunning.

I try to downplay it.

"Um, often enough, actually. My brother plays hockey. They're all ripped like that." *Though they aren't all that pretty.*

I try to focus on Nicole instead of the pecs in my face.

She blinks at me. "I am hating you right now, just a small amount. It'll pass."

I laugh under my breath. "Believe me. Most of them aren't half as charming as they look. In my limited experience, hockey players are bratty jocks, total sluts, and/or players. And the ones who are actually a great catch, because yes, they do exist, are already married."

"Okay, clearly, you're not in your right mind right now. When you're feeling more optimistic about life in general, we'll circle back to the idea of you introducing me to Cole's hot hockey friends."

I sigh again, but smile. "You have a way, Nikki. I'm sure I can introduce you to some hockey players if you really want."

"Oh, I want." Her eyes go big and round. She reminds me of a meme I once saw of a cartoon cat with huge eyes that simply said *WANTY*.

I snicker and gesture at her phone. "Where did you find that anyway?"

"It's on his Instagram."

"Jameson Vance, billionaire, has an Instagram?"

"Yup. Blue check mark and all. It's all charity gala red carpets and thirst traps. He's at the gym or the beach or by a pool, half-naked. With friends, but still. He's in a suit or his birthday suit and nothing in between."

"Can you imagine the DMs he gets?" My mind wanders, trying to picture even a glimpse of the life he leads. Kinda like my brother's, but just... more. "I wonder what it would be like to be that... eligible."

"Is he seriously single?"

"I believe so. No one introduced me to Mrs. Vance during my brief stay at his palace."

Nicole swallows, looking like that hungry cartoon cat again. "Palace?"

I laugh. I haven't laughed this much in... ages. "Are we *that* into a man's net worth?"

She shakes her head as if trying to come back to her senses. "Maybe?" She flashes me another photo—Jameson with sweat pouring down his naked chest, holding a basketball and smiling a smile that could melt the freaking sun. "Either way, how can you not want to climb that?"

"Well. First of all, I just broke up with—*no*. I just *fled* from a man who has serious psychological issues. I might need a little detoxing period. Also, he's kind of—"

"Lickable? Suckable? Fuckable? Do you need more adjectives?"

"I was going to say aloof or something. Stuck up? I don't know." I think about the way I melted when he shook my hand. The way everything else washed out around me and I found it so hard just to breathe. The man is beautiful, for sure. But. "He's also overbearing. Bossy, in the worst way. He fired his gardener to give me the job."

Nicole looks confused. "And that's bad?"

"Yes. It's very bad. The man worked for him for years. And then the little sister of his best friend shows up and boom, goodbye, Romeo."

"Who's Romeo?"

"The gardener."

"So, you're his gardener now?"

"Hell to the fucking no. I quit. That's why I couldn't stay there anymore. I don't want his charity. Not if it's evil."

"Evil might be a stretch," she suggests. "He gave you a job. He wanted to help his best friend's sister. I consider myself fortunate that I only work two waitressing jobs these days to stay afloat. If I had a brother and he had a rich best friend, I'd suck his cock for a job. On the regular."

I give her a disapproving look, really trying *not* to laugh. She shrugs and pokes her fingers into my open backpack. "And by the way, why do you have so many bungee cords?"

"Survival. You never know when your cheap-ass suitcase is gonna fall apart. Like right in front of a billionaire." I cringe. "I hate to be caught unprepared. It's a thing."

"Ah." Nicole sits on the edge of her bed, near me. "Look. If Cole is that close to this guy, maybe he's a great guy. You just caught him on a bad day or something."

I groan. "Why do I get the feeling you're already mentally picking out your bridesmaid dress and flirting with his groomsmen?"

"Because I envision my girlfriends marrying every potential husband they meet. It's a side effect of being a hopeless romantic and a pathological optimist. Honestly, though, I was envisioning you screwing him."

I laugh abruptly, which was maybe why she said that last bit. "You seriously want to picture that?"

"Uh-huh. But *now* I'm picturing you marrying him."

I shake my head as I toss underwear into the drawer.

Nicole snatches up a red lace thong that I ordered online for too much money last Christmas as a surprise for Troy that he obviously didn't deserve. I don't even know why I brought it with me. It was just such a waste of money otherwise.

"You would look great in this," she says seriously.

"Thanks for noticing. Troy didn't."

She gives me a *well-he's-a-dick* look, hands me the panties, and announces, "We're going out tonight."

"We are?"

"Yes. You get a proper ladies' night to welcome you to Vancouver. I've already alerted the troops. And by troops, I mean Dani."

"The sister-in-law to the hot rock stars?" I've heard of this girl, a lot, from Nicole, and I'm not sure I'm ready for Nicole's version of a "proper ladies' night." Apparently, this Dani girl's twin sister has *two* rock star husbands (though only one legally), and Nicole seems eternally in awe of what she imagines to be the "absolute kinkfest" of their three-way marriage. "Is this some scheme to introduce me to hot, sexually adventurous men?"

"Quite definitely. And may I remind you, you can't say no."

"I will live to regret the day I let you dub this the Summer of Yes, won't I."

"Probably."

"Maybe we should preagree on the fact that every guy who crosses my path does not get a yes, though."

"If they look like *this* and they're a billionaire..." She flashes me another photo of Jameson—this time wearing a sharp suit—that I don't need to see. "They most definitely do. Tell me you have anything higher on your wish list."

"Hot and has money? Yeah, I can think of a few more important characteristics that I might want in a man."

"Such as?"

"Let's see. Warm. Generous. Fun. Smart. Handy with tools. But at this point, I'd settle for not emotionally abusive."

Nicole softens with sympathy. "You left him behind, babe," she reminds me gently. "That chapter is done. The book is firmly closed. Time to write yourself a new beginning."

"Yeah."

"And we know what a good writer you are."

"Thank you." Nicole is one of the very few people I've told, besides Mom and my brother, about my books.

Well, and Jameson.

"Also, you left out good in bed from your checklist," she says.

"Great in bed would be better."

She grins. "Now there's the girl I know and love." She hops to her feet and opens the closet. "Put on that thong, and let's find something *hot* for you to wear tonight. The sexually adventurous men of Vancouver are just waiting to meet you."

I give in—Summer of Yes and all—and admit, "There's a matching bra," and pluck it from the drawer.

"Perfect." She's rifling through her clothes, tugging out pieces and tossing them on the bed. "One question. What if it turns out that this Jameson guy checks off *all* the boxes on your list?"

I roll my eyes to the ceiling. "Can I just focus on getting a job, some plates, and a way to pay rent, and then we'll see about a guy fitting into the picture?"

"Sure, sure. I'm just saying, a man like that won't be on the market forever. Don't move too slowly if you see something you like."

"Oh, Nikki."

That evening, when Nicole's friend Dani rolls up in an Uber to pick us up, we rally down to the lobby and push through the heavy glass doors, laughing.

It's strange; I haven't heard myself laugh like this in so long.

As we got ready for ladies' night, we drank a couple of shots of Nicole's favorite alcohol, Sambuca, while she told me all about the rock stars she's met by now, because I asked. The list included the ones who own the nightclub she works at, the ones who come into the nightclub, and of course, Dani's connections. Though, despite her best efforts, Nicole's only ever managed to hook up with one of them.

A few years back, through Dani and her twin sister, Nicole met drummer Xander Rush, and screwed him, twice. But then, according to her, he ghosted her because she asked him to put her over his knee and spank her and he said, "I don't know you well enough for that."

For some reason we thought that was crazy funny, and I demanded, "How can a rock star be such a prude?" Because the two (giant) shots were already going to my head and I was getting lippy.

And I thought, *This is what I never had.*

I never, ever had this period in my life when I lived wild and free with my girlfriends, got dressed in sexy clothes and put loud music on and did shots and went barhopping and flirted with men I'd never see again.

Or hooked up with them for the night.

I lived in a town where everyone knew everyone, and there was only one bar, and anyway, I hadn't been truly single since I was seventeen, but still.

When I told Nicole about this sad lack in my life, she said soberly, "You just described every night of my life," and I laughed my way right out her front door.

When Dani's Uber honks at us from the street, Nicole heads toward it along the sidewalk, but I stop in my tracks. I stumble a little as my attention is seized by the view across the street.

The laughter dies in my throat.

Parked at the curb directly across from Nicole's building is a gleaming black limo, and a man stands next to it, staring at me.

A tall, strikingly gorgeous man with wavy, sun-kissed hair and light-blue eyes. He wears tight, deep-blue dress pants that showcase his long, muscular legs and a fitted button-up shirt the same color as his eyes. And a tie.

His clothes look like they might split open if he flexes.

Jameson Vance has the body of a superhero and the face of an angel, and how the hell he's single, I'll never know. There are stunningly beautiful women out there, too, and there's no way they aren't all over this man every time he leaves his house.

And there he is, staring at *me*.

I suddenly feel ridiculously sex-forward in the black velvet leggings, glittery, sleeveless T-shirt, and heels that Nicole talked me into. I grip my purse tight to my ribs and try to remember how to breathe as his eyes move over me.

"Megan?" Nicole calls to me from the open back door of the Uber.

I barely hear her.

I'm in that tunnel again, where the world turns blurry and unreal around me, like a watercolor painting, leaving nothing but the man in front of me.

"Um... just a minute," I say hoarsely.

Nicole must see what I'm seeing, because she doesn't say another word as I wander to the curb and dangle there, uncertain.

Jameson crosses the street, strolling toward me. He slides his hands into his pockets and stops a couple of feet in front of me.

"Megan," he says in that low, rough-velvet voice.

"Jameson," I breathe. It's nonsensical the way my heartbeat speeds up when he's near. My body responds to his presence in a way that is, in a word, unnerving.

I'm supposed to be taking care of myself right now. Which means putting myself first for once. Which definitely means staying away from toxic men. And despite the fact that my brother is friends with him... What he did to Romeo, how cold he was to me when I confronted him about it, and how he acted like I was an unwelcome imposition in his giant, empty house... none of it bodes well.

For all I know, he's just another selfish, careless narcissist.

But whatever he's come here to say, I should hear him out. I tell myself I'll do it for my brother's sake.

It's not for me.

I don't really need this man's mansion or his pity job. Or this distracting inability to breathe normally whenever his attention is focused on me.

"You left."

"I quit," I remind him, my voice soft and breathless, even as I try to give it substance. He's caught me off guard. What is he doing here?

"I heard you. You flung mud on my sofa."

Did I? Shit. "I'll pay for that. I'm sure it can be cleaned—"

"I didn't come here about that. I'd never accept your money, Megan."

"Then what do you want?"

He studies me, a crease forming between his brows. "I want you to come back."

Yes.

The word flits through the back of my mind. I can hear Nicole's voice in there. *It's the Summer of Yes, Megan.*

But fear paralyzes me.

Memories of Troy and his self-serving manipulations hold me hostage, and I can't seem to force the word from my mouth.

CHAPTER 11

Jameson

Megan's wary amber eyes glow, enhanced by her smoky eye makeup, as she gazes up at me.

It's brutal how relieved I am to see her again.

"I'm sorry you wasted your time coming here." Her voice is soft but firm, her arms wrapped protectively around her waist. "But I'm not coming back."

I'm not surprised when she resists.

She left my place without a word to me or her brother, so we couldn't try to stop her. Cole is already in LA, and when I spoke to him on the phone a while ago, I didn't mention she'd left, but he didn't either, which meant that he had no idea.

He did suggest that maybe I check in on her tonight, though. It's Friday night, after all. He wants her happy but mostly safe right now, tucked in at my place, yet he didn't seem to like the idea of her sitting all alone in her room at my house.

He'd like it even less, I'm sure, if he knew she was going out clubbing in the big city her second night in town, without anyone looking out for her.

That makes two of us.

"Have dinner with me."

She blinks at me, surprised.

I'm determined to start this over right, though.

And get what I want.

I probably should've asked her to have dinner with me in the first place, when I met her in the street, but I'd been caught off guard.

I had no idea I'd ever be seeing her again, and get another chance, but here we are.

Things have changed.

For starters, there's no way she's going out tonight without me. She's too vulnerable to having some rebound fling with the first asshole who makes a move, and I can't have that.

It's counterproductive to my goal.

"Have you eaten?" I prompt when she seems low on words.

"I... No, I haven't. We were going to eat out."

"I know a great place."

"Why? Why are you asking me to dinner?"

"Because your brother and I are tight. And I want to apologize for what happened this afternoon."

"You mean, firing a very nice man so you could give me his job, and not telling me?"

There it is again. That subtle fire of hers.

The one that makes my fingers twitch with the need to tangle themselves into her hair and squeeze until she gasps, opening her mouth for my—

"Yes. That. I didn't think it through. Cole wanted you to have the job, so I gave it to you."

She softens, her shoulders relaxing a little. "I do appreciate that."

"Then have dinner with me. Give me a chance to start over."

She considers, with a glance over her shoulder at her friends. Her ride. She takes an excruciating moment to decide, but I can feel it, the moment she decides to give me another chance.

"Okay. I mean, yes. Just let me go tell them."

"Of course."

She goes over and leans into the open back window, saying

something to her friends that I can't hear. Her black velvet leggings hug her perfect ass, and my cock swells.

I take a deep breath, stuffing down the sexual attraction by sheer force of will.

I can't believe how drawn to her I am. I know it's the challenge. She's beautiful, but it's the abstinence from sex that's fucking with me.

I need to keep it under control. Even if I didn't have the challenge to deal with... there's still Cole to think of.

His little sister is dear to him, and she's clearly off-limits.

When she comes back over to me, her cheeks are flushed, and I wonder what her friends said to her.

"I do have one condition," she announces, eyes flashing with challenge. "You have to give Romeo his job back."

She means it.

I kind of like that; she's negotiating.

But fuck, there's a part of me that wants to put her over my knee for talking to me like that, spank her until she gasps out a *please.*

My hands fist in my pockets, squelching the urge. *Not happening.*

"Of course I'll hire him back," I say smoothly. "I need a gardener. And my new one just quit."

Locke sweeps the door open for us, and I guide Megan into the restaurant, my hand on her lower back when she hesitates, surprised by what she sees inside. We step into the expansive room with its curved wall of windows, the panoramic view of Coal Harbour and the mountains beyond.

It's breathtaking, but we're the only ones who'll be enjoying it tonight.

Not only is the restaurant empty, it's unfinished. Scaffolding and equipment from the painters and other tradesmen who work here during the day are scattered around the edges of the room, the recently constructed bar covered in sheets of plastic.

Only one table has been set up, with two chairs in front of the windowed wall, right in the center. It'll be the prime table when the restaurant opens.

Right now, it's all ours.

As Locke stands watch by the door, the manager greets us and leads us to our seats. The restaurant will have its grand opening with the rest of the Vance Bayshore resort nine months from now, but a small team is already working to perfect the menu and table service.

Tonight, they're here for me. For us.

"Perhaps your guest would like the northwest view, Mr. Vance?" the manager offers, drawing out the chair on the right for Megan.

"Thank you, Sylvie." I pull out my own chair and wait to seat myself once Megan takes the seat she's been offered, the one with the best view: the sparkling Lions Gate Bridge stretched across the water, the dark ridge of the mountains, and the strip of lights on the ski hill, twinkling along the spine of Black Mountain.

Sylvie makes recommendations for wine that will pair with the chef's creations this evening, and once I've selected a bottle, she leaves us.

Megan's gazing out at the view in awe. "You own all this?"

"My family owns this resort and all the real estate along this drive. My siblings and I. I hope you don't mind the unfinished state of the restaurant. I promise the food is incredible."

"When does it open?"

"In April."

"And you already have staff and incredible food?"

"When you want things done right, it takes time."

She takes that in.

"On the other hand... sometimes you need to move quickly, or you miss an opportunity."

"That is true." Her voice softens with a tinge of what I take to be regret.

We're interrupted briefly as a waiter arrives to present me with the wine I've selected, offering a taste and then pouring us each a glass. As soon as he leaves us alone, I ask her, "Who were those girls you were going out with?"

"My friend Nicole and her friends. That was her apartment you found me at."

"And that's where you were planning to stay tonight?"

"I am staying there tonight."

She won't be, if I have a say. She seems to believe otherwise, but the night is young.

"Is it a nice apartment?"

"Well, it's kind of hard to tell under all the stuff." She breathes a slightly exhausted-sounding laugh. "She lives with three roommates."

"I see. And that seems like a reasonable place to call home?"

"As reasonable as any option I've got." Her amber eyes flash; that spark of challenge again. "How did you find me, by the way?"

I'd love to watch that defiant look melt into ecstasy as I shove my cock into her.

Christ. The sex thoughts are rampant tonight. Every time she looks away, I'm mentally groping her. Undressing her.

Bending her over and fisting her hair, wrapping my hand around her throat...

It takes me a moment to understand what she's asking.

I clear my throat. "It wasn't difficult. Your taxi driver was very vocal, at a certain price."

Her eyes widen. "That's unethical."

"Ethics often fall low on the priority list when money is involved."

"And that's sad."

"Is it? If you ask me, a lot of people have a toxic view of money in the other direction."

She considers that. I notice she hasn't touched her wine. "How so?"

"Money itself shouldn't be resented or feared or misconstrued as evil. Especially not when it's a means to most things in life."

"Most?"

"Everything except those few things that money can't buy," I clarify.

"And what are those things?" she asks, like she's checking to see if I know what they are.

She wouldn't be the first.

"Freedom, to a certain point. Life, to a certain point. Immortality, certainly. And, of course, love. Or any true emotion." I lift my wineglass and nod toward hers.

She lifts it for a sip, and her face lights up.

It's fucking magical.

"Wow." She moans a bit, licks her lip, and my cock hardens. "That is so much better than the shots."

My mouth quirks in an unexpected smile. "You did shots?"

"Oh, yeah." She cringes adorably, her lips plump and wet as she takes another sip.

I stare at her, oddly perplexed, as my cock throbs. How can one woman be so effortlessly cute and fucking sexy at the same time?

It disarms me. I'm not sure I like it.

I glance at my watch. "It's not even seven thirty."

"Is there a proper time to do shots?"

That has me thinking. "I suppose it depends on the shots. And why you're drinking them."

"We drink them before we go out on the town, to make the boys cuter."

My jaw clenches as I bite back my response to that.

The corner of her mouth twitches. "I'm kidding. Actually..." She takes another sip. "We probably drink them to make it easier to talk to the really cute ones."

My molars grind. The thought of her flirting with random guys at the bar...

Fuck, no.

I can't have that.

Cole won't have it either. Not right now, when she's so vulnerable.

And besides that, Megan Hudson is clearly not a woman who needs some "cute boy" in her life.

What she needs is a man.

Doesn't she realize that?

I inform her, "I have a question for you, Megan."

"Okay..."

"What if we got engaged?"

CHAPTER 12

Jameson

Megan's wineglass is halfway to her lips when she freezes. "Engaged? *We?*"

I'm not sure which word confuses her more.

"Yes. You and me."

"What...? What are you talking about?"

"I realize this might be a shock—"

"Might be?"

"—but I need a fiancée. You also need something. Right?"

She sets her wineglass down, and nervously licks her lip. I take a sip of my wine while she struggles to digest what's happening. Then she drags her teeth over her lip, tugging on it. Heat floods my chest like I just pounded my whole glass.

Our stare-down doesn't seem to be ending anytime soon, so I prompt, "You need a fresh start to your life. Am I wrong?"

"You need a fiancée?" she says, clearly confused.

"Yes."

"Why?"

"It's a family obligation," I summarize. "An expectation."

I don't particularly want to tell her that this obligation material-ized during an argument with my oldest brother today, because he believes my sex life is such a public blight on our family's reputation that he needs to aggressively intervene. And obviously, I can't tell her about the game.

The game I'm afraid of losing.

But since the horn locking with Graysen this afternoon, it's really sunk in that he has no way of knowing if I fail the challenge or not.

It *is* an honor system.

And the engagement will be a public affair. As soon as the media stops circulating gossip about my sex life in favor of swooning over my fairy-tale romance with my fiancée, Graysen will have what he wants. Then he can accept the truth—that I'm taking Granddad's game seriously—and get off my back, start stressing about our siblings' challenges instead.

How to explain this to her, though, when I'm not allowed to explain it?

I've decided to keep it simple.

"So, this would be an arrangement that would benefit us both."

She looks like she can't decide if I've lost my mind or if she's being punked. "Um..."

"You're surprised."

"That's a very mild word that doesn't quite explain the numbness in my fingers right now."

I consider that. "You're upset?"

"No. Maybe. I'm not sure yet. Does Cole know about this?"

"Not yet."

She gives me a look that says she knows as well as I do that he's going to be pissed. But I've been trying not to focus on that part.

"So far, no one knows. But that would change quickly, once you say yes."

I can practically see the shock moving through her system. Or maybe it's terror that's turning her cheeks pink and her skin damp.

"So... you want me to act like your fiancée, in public? To please your family?"

"You'd *be* my fiancée. You won't need to act."

She picks up her wine and... *gobble* would be the right word for what she does to it. "Except to pretend I'm suddenly in love with you?"

I choose my words carefully. "I won't ask you to behave any differently from whatever feels natural to you. Except to behave like we're engaged." I try to add a dry note to my voice, but it comes out strangely growly. "If you can put across that you're pleased to be engaged to me, it would help."

Did that sound bitter?

Why is this making me sweat?

It seemed so much more natural in my head, where I envisioned her saying *yes*.

But she's not saying yes.

"So we'd be... dating?"

"Yes."

"And living together?"

"Well, yes. That would be the plan."

"And we'd be... a couple?" Her eyes on me don't waver, but the words come out a little huskier than the rest.

My cock throbs.

I have no idea when these pants became three sizes too small, but it's definitely getting hot under the table.

I shift uncomfortably.

That shaky note in her voice...

Is she turned on? Or about to bolt?

"You mean, will we have sex? No. Your brother made it clear you're recovering from a bad breakup. You're off-limits." *Conveniently*. "This isn't about sex." *Unfortunately*.

Megan stares at me, maybe weighing the likelihood that any man would actually mean that while asking her to be his fiancée.

"You are very loyal to my brother."

"Yes. I am."

"You want me to get engaged to you and date you, publicly, and live with you," she repeats back to me. "But not have sex with you."

"Correct."

"For how long?"

"The engagement would be for a year. Then we'd go our separate ways."

She stares at me for a long, tense moment.

"So it would just be an engagement? No wedding?"

"No wedding. I'm not looking for a wife. I wouldn't even be getting engaged if my family wasn't pressing the issue. I won't be marrying anyone, for any reason." I'm being as honest as I can be. I thought that would make her feel better, but as soon as it's out of my mouth, I hear how it sounds. And it sounds damn cold.

Am I just convincing her to say no?

"I see..." She definitely looks part flustered, part *I'm talking to a crazy man.*

I don't want her to feel insulted. Used. A woman like her, she deserves to be appreciated by her man. Adored. Lavished with attention and affection. Praise and devotion.

If it wasn't for Cole, I'd lavish her with all the sexual affection she deserves—maybe put her on her knees and teach her some manners, too; show her what it's like to be with a real man, maybe help her get over her shithead ex and whatever other little boys are in her past. As soon as possible. Which is in exactly forty-six days. But telling her so would just invite questions I can't answer.

I'll be honest with her about everything I can, but that means everything but the game.

"I'll treat you with respect," I tell her. "The way your brother would want me to treat you."

She stares at me, her cheeks flushed, but doesn't respond to that.

Our appetizers come, three different locally sourced dishes, and the distraction seems to ease the tension a bit. We taste the food, avoiding the elephant that's just sat its ass right down between us.

I ask her what she thinks of the food. The presentation, the aromas, the textures, and, of course, the flavors.

When the empty dishes are cleared away, and we sit back with refilled wineglasses to await the entrées, I say, "You're taking this all very calmly."

She'd seemed uncomfortable with the conversation, sure. But she hasn't said no to my proposal.

She hasn't said yes yet either.

"I'm getting the feeling this is normal to you," she says carefully. "So I'm trying not to freak out."

"Normal." I consider that. "What about it seems normal?"

"Just calmly asking a woman you barely know to get engaged to you as if you're offering her a job."

"It's not a job."

"You showed as much emotion when you hired me to be your gardener."

That gives me pause. "I'm trying not to make it emotional. It doesn't have to be."

The conversation is interrupted again as our entrées are served. Thick, tender slabs of Pacific halibut, the white fish drizzled with Sea Salt citrus gin-infused sauce and layered atop a crab cake, paired with grilled vegetables. Simple West Coast fare, but impeccably prepared.

I give Megan some time to enjoy it before pressing her for an answer.

"Tell me, honestly, what you think of my proposal."

"I don't know what I think." She dabs her mouth with a linen napkin. "I'm sorry. This just doesn't make any sense to me."

"What part of it?"

"All of it." She looks at me uneasily, like she's still waiting for the hidden film crew to leap from the shadows as I shout *Gotcha!* "It's just odd to me that you're suggesting an engagement like it's some business deal."

"Well, we're negotiating a serious contract."

"Contract?"

"Just verbally. I'm not asking you to sign anything. I just want to make my expectations clear."

She kind of chews her lip. "Yeah. Nothing more romantic than expectations."

That throws me.

I wasn't trying to make it romantic. I brought her for a nice dinner out of respect. And maybe I wanted to give her a glimpse of the life I can offer her for the next year. "I could be more romantic, if you want."

She sits back in her chair and studies me. "You're serious."

"Getting engaged is very serious for me."

It is. It's not something I thought I'd ever do, so there's that.

"I mean... you'd be romantic if I wanted you to?"

"Yes. Of course."

"Fake romantic."

"You'd be my fiancée. That part would be real. There would be a ring. And money you'd have access to."

"Money?" she echoes softly.

"Yes. Two million seems reasonable. Unless you think it doesn't."

I think I've floored her. I'm starting to understand that look on her face.

It's not terror. It's utter shock.

"You'd give me money?"

"I'd give you whatever you want."

She swallows more wine. "This is... weird."

"I guess I can see how it would be."

I know she didn't expect this proposal. But it's an easy decision, isn't it? Whatever worries she might have, I can take care of them.

I can take care of *her*.

Maybe I failed to make that part clear. "You'll have a home, access to any funds you need to get back on your feet. Without having to ask your brother for it or share an apartment with a bunch of people." Wasn't that what she wanted, ultimately?

She just keeps staring at me. "Right. So that's what's in it for me. What's really in it for you?"

"Well... you. As my fiancée. Which, as I mentioned, I'm in need of."

"And how do you know I'm trustworthy?"

"Cole trusts you."

"But you must know other women. You just met me."

I consider how to put it. "You've made a good impression."

"How is that possible? I threw mud on your couch and made a scene and quit the job you gave me."

"And in doing so, you impressed my brother." I hate to say it, because it sounds so damn lame. But. Honesty. "Graysen is my oldest sibling and he's my boss. He has a lot of say over what happens in our business. And in our grandfather's estate. Granddad just passed."

"Oh. I'm sorry. Were you close?"

"Yes. Very. But even so, when a person leaves such wealth behind, it's not always straightforward what happens with it. There was a will, of course, but there were certain..." I struggle with how to put it without breaking the rules. "My brother has high expectations of me. If I don't meet them... let's just say I'll lose his respect, and lose power and position in my family, much like my uncle did with my father. Eventually, my uncle got disinherited. Or more precisely, paid to go away. There were only the two of them. I have four siblings in line before me." There. Now she knows there are big stakes on the line for me, without actually getting into the details about Granddad's will or the game.

She still looks uncertain, though. "But wouldn't your family prefer that you get engaged to some wealthy socialite or celebrity?"

"No. Because that won't solve my problem."

"What problem, exactly?"

I realize I'm being a bit opaque. But fuck.

Do we really need to go there?

I look at my wineglass, twirling it by the stem. "Graysen is tired of the drama he thinks I cause. Or my public image causes. My dating life, I mean. I'm bad for his blood pressure."

"I know what that's like," she says softly. "My brother's blood pressure probably hasn't been great lately, thanks to me."

I meet her eyes. "Then we have that in common."

She takes another sip of her wine, studying me. "I don't know you, Jameson," she concludes.

"Your brother knows me."

"That's not the ringing endorsement you seem to think it is."

"You'll get to know me."

"What if I don't like you? Or you don't like me? Couples usually need to like each other for things to work out. God. I can't even believe I'm entertaining this..."

"Okay, first, I'm fairly certain we'll like each other enough to make this work. Second, relationships aren't always based on affection. Third, I'm not asking for an ongoing relationship, just a one-year engagement. After that, the will is settled, and I won't..." *Need you anymore.*

That sounds... fucking bad.

So instead, I say, "After that, I won't be so worried about my brother's opinion of my love life anymore."

"I see. But we're not really talking about love. Are we."

We aren't, yet the whole time we've sat here talking, I've barely eaten the amazing food.

Neither has she.

I'm focused only on her, and my heart is beating harder than it should in any mere business negotiation. I'm tense, hyperaware of her every reaction.

"No. We aren't," I agree. "I'll tell you upfront that I'm not going to fall in love. It's not what I do."

She stares at me, and it unnerves me.

"Come home with me tonight," I practically growl. "Then decide." The words fall out of my mouth, hot with all the lust I feel for her.

Her gorgeous amber eyes go wide in the candlelight, and I know I should've worded that differently.

Really need to tamp that down.

Cole wants her home with us. I need to bring her home. Graysen wants this engagement.

I'm just trying to focus on those facts.

But I realize there's a slight possibility I'm not thinking straight.

I haven't had *that* much wine.

But there's something about Megan that makes me question my own motives. And I don't do that.

It's highly confusing. Disorienting.

Maybe I'm slightly intoxicated from staring at her all night?

Is that a thing? Because it sure as fuck feels like it.

"No." She shakes her head slowly. "I can't."

"Can't or won't?"

"Won't." She tips her chin up a little, flashing that defiant look that makes me want to drag her over my knee. "You're a terrible distraction, Jameson Vance. But I have some pride. And I'll be okay."

"You deserve better than okay," I growl.

We stare at each other for long moments as my heart pounds.

A terrible distraction.

What, exactly, does that mean?

I'm not totally sure, and it's making my dick hard.

Finally, she sighs almost under her breath. "I should probably say yes." She sounds strangely sad about it when she adds, "But my answer is no."

She says it like this is some kind of ending.

But she just doesn't know me well enough to know that this isn't over yet.

CHAPTER 13

Megan

You'd think telling him no three times in one day would mean something.

I quit. I'm not coming back. My answer is no.

But Jameson just studies me across the table, with that look on his face like I'm some problem yet to solve. He even waves the waiter away with a brush of his hand when he tries to check on us.

I don't mean to offend him. Or seem ungrateful or foolish or untrusting. But maybe I am all those things.

I'm just not ready to forge ahead into some new relationship—any type of relationship—with a man I've just met.

Even if he is my brother's best friend.

And even if he's ridiculously hot.

But what did he really expect?

He "proposed" to me, if you could call this a proposal, to please his family. What he's proposing is a *fake* engagement—never to turn real. Because, clearly, men like Jameson Vance don't fall in love with women like me.

What they do is offer them business proposals, apparently.

First the room in his guest wing, then the gardening job, now this. What next, he offers to impregnate me with his firstborn, just to make his brother happy?

Maybe he can't know it because he doesn't know *me*, but this is hardly the proposal scenario of my dreams.

Dinner with a sophisticated, gorgeous man? Sure. That's dream-worthy. But a proposal for a fake engagement where we pretend to be in love, for money?

I don't even know where to start explaining how wrong that is for me and my hopes of future happiness.

"You don't mean that" is his growly response to my rejection.

Good lord, he's bossy.

"I assure you, I do. And I'm not into games. I won't mislead you. I won't mislead the whole world about a fake engagement either."

A muscle slides along his jaw. "I'm not one to back down from something I want, Megan."

Oh, boy. I tell myself not to get tingles over those words. *I want.*

He doesn't want *me*. Just a fake fiancée.

But too late.

The tingles are rising, spreading across my skin as he informs me, "I'm looking at what I want right now. And, fair warning, I will try to get it."

"Well, fair warning... You might fail."

"Maybe I will," he concedes, but his eyes burn with the challenge, making my core tingle with heat.

This whole conversation is suddenly feeling less and less like a business negotiation, and more like a proposition for filthy, possibly incredible sex. Or maybe it's just me.

"Tell me why," he demands.

It really shouldn't turn me on like it does when he talks to me like that.

"Because it would never work. We're complete opposites."

He calmly counters, "We're not that different."

"Honestly, we are. No one would even believe we're a couple."

"Why not? You're my best friend's sister. We're close in age. We're both single and attractive."

I clear my throat as my response to that catches. *Yeah, okay. I'm attractive. Sure. But you're...*

Is there an adjective that means "so hot, I didn't even know it existed in a fantasy sense"?

He's hotter than the hero in my books. And Wolf is *hot*. He's made up, for god's sake.

"We'd both make a good partner," he presses.

"How do you know what kind of partner I'd make?"

The heat of challenge in his eyes hones to a fine point as he studies me, and I struggle not to squirm. "Your brother filled me in last night, after you went to bed, about your ex."

"Great. So he told you I'm a doormat and you decided I was an easy target?" The words come out quiet and more wounded than I want them to.

Jameson leans on the table, closing the space between us. The sleeves of his elegant shirt are casually rolled up, and the arm porn alone, along with his forearm tattoos, are enough to break me.

God, I'm so thirsty.

Be strong, Megan.

Just because it looks delicious doesn't mean it's safe to eat.

"No," he says. "That's not what I meant. The way Cole spoke about you... It sounds like you went through a lot to try to make it work. He didn't get into details. But he made it clear that your ex didn't deserve your efforts. Or you."

I take a breath.

"And you know what I thought?" he goes on. "I thought you must have a really big heart to try that hard and that long without giving up on someone. It's not your fault you chose the wrong someone. You were young when you met him, right?"

I really don't want to talk about Troy, so I don't. "And now you're asking me to choose a virtual stranger. For money."

"Not for money. Money is just a means to an end. Do it to set up your future. You deserve it, after what you've sacrificed this far."

"We're too different," I hedge.

"How? How are we different? Do you want financial security and a nice home to live in?"

"Most people want those things. And your house is beyond nice. I have no money. The power balance is deeply disturbing to me."

"I was born into a wealthy family. You weren't. That's circumstance. It hardly matters. And once you're with me, you will have money. There's no need to feel like I have the upper hand."

I almost laugh.

Truly, I'm still shocked by how casually he offered me such a large amount of his money.

Two million freaking dollars.

But it's sinking in that he's deadly serious about this.

So am I.

We aren't a match, even if we fake it.

Judging by the absolute deluge of Google hits Nicole scrolled through today while narrating the headlines to me and shoving the accompanying photos in my face as we got all done up for ladies' night, Jameson Vance is a people person. A marketing exec who works with celebrities, parties with celebrities, and dates them, too. He must thrive on the attention he gets dating all those famous women.

Otherwise, why would he keep doing it, so often and so publicly?

I've dated one man in my entire life. That man is a carpenter who grew up in the same small town I did.

Just the thought of trying to navigate the world of Jameson Vance, billionaire, a world of red carpets, cameras, moguls and celebrities, makes me sweat. I'm shy and introverted. I make up people in my head because I often find them better company than actual people. Not to mention less harmful.

The last few years, I've spent as much time as I possibly can writing and hanging out with plants, to *avoid* people.

"I just haven't had a chance to earn your trust yet," he says, in that bossy way of his. "Give me some time."

"I'm sorry, but like I said, my answer is no. Thank you, but no."

His beautiful, kissable mouth presses into a hard, dissatisfied line. Maybe this doesn't happen to him very often. Getting turned down. Being unable to convince a woman to give him what he wants.

He sits back, giving me a look that seems to say: *You're making a mistake, Megan Hudson.*

I realize there's no reason to finish this dinner. I don't want there to be any expectation of anything more. My answer is no, and it's final.

That, and the longer I sit here looking at him, the more I'm in danger of letting him change my mind.

I lay my napkin on my plate. I'm about to get up when he says, "Does Cole even know you left?"

"I'll call him and explain that I just wanted my own space."

"So you're really going to live with four other girls?"

"Women," I correct him. "Independent women. Cole will understand. I've always been stubborn."

"You can stay at the house," he says firmly. "You'll be in the guest wing with Cole."

Does he still think this is a negotiation?

I said no, like twenty freaking times.

"He's gone," I remind him. "Knowing Cole, he'll be gone most of the summer. And then he'll be in training camp."

"Not that soon."

"He'll be in and out all the time. I know how his life is. Cole has never been one to sit still. It's not like he's ever really home."

And I can't be alone there with you.

"It can be your home," he presses. "Just like he said. Until you're on your feet."

I push my chair back and stand. "I'm on my feet, okay?"

He pushes his chair back and gets up as soon as I do. Like a gentleman.

I have to look away from him to avoid the pull. The truth is, he's a hard man to say no to.

It's not just his looks or the magnetic attraction I feel that makes me want to linger. Or the soft spot he has for my brother.

It's so many things.

Like the way he pursued me to Nicole's.

And the way he focuses on me when I speak. And listened when I told him about my books.

And the things he says. Lord, the things he says. I can hear them replaying in my head even as I walk away.

I'm not one to back down from something I want, Megan.

I'm looking at what I want right now.

I probably wanted to say no before the appetizers came, but I let us draw this out. Maybe I liked the way he kept pressing me to say yes.

I mean, it was flattering, in a warped way.

"Megan."

I stop at the sound of my name on his low voice. I'm drawn to that voice, too. I feel this hot and sticky pull to turn around, sit my ass back down, and stay. Just let myself melt into him, do whatever he tells me to do.

"Come back to the house. Please."

Fuck me. And now he's asking nicely.

I turn to face him again. *Stay strong.* "I think I've been clear that I'm not doing that."

"Cole really wants you to."

"Cole doesn't get everything he wants."

He stares at me for a long beat. "If you leave, it means I've failed him."

I'm not even sure why that's *so* important to him.

"I'm sorry. I'm sure you're not used to it."

I continue across the vast room, but his voice follows me. "Wait."

I take a breath. His hulking security guy stands in front of the door, hands clasped casually in front of him, making no move to step aside and open the door for me.

I turn back.

Jameson is crossing the room toward me, his jaw set. Clearly I've ruined whatever plans he had for this evening.

He stops directly in front of me and I feel desperate to get out of this room. It was hard enough to say no to him as many times as I already have.

Standing, he's so much more imposing. I forgot how tall he is. And how hard his body is. He's like a wall of manly and gorgeous towering over me.

He smells incredible, too.

Did I actually tell him he was a distraction?

Yeah. Pretty sure I did.

"Please call Cole like you said you would." His voice is low and gentle now. "Let him know where you're staying. It should come from you."

"Of course I will."

He glances at the security guy and nods. "Locke will arrange a car to take you where you're going."

"Oh. Thank you." Since it will save me cab fare, I decide I'm not in a position to refuse this kindness. "I'd really appreciate that."

As I hesitate to actually leave, Jameson's blue eyes hold mine, burning into me one last time.

When will I see him again?

I hear the door open behind me, and force myself to turn and leave the restaurant.

Locke leads the way, and my pulse races when I realize Jameson is following me in silence, along the hall that will take us to the elevator and down to the lobby. And even though my stupid pounding heart kinda wants me to throw caution to the wind and just say yes... I can't.

Because my heart has been so very wrong before.

In the elevator, he stands next to me and slightly behind, and all the way down, my stomach feels weightless and tight, gripped with this terrible foreboding that I'm making a mistake.

That I'll never receive such a grand offer, such an opportunity to say *yes* to anything so life-changing, ever again.

CHAPTER 14

She said no.

And I'm still reeling from it.

Late into the night, I'm awake when I should be sleeping, reading more of Megan's book.

And thinking about her.

I thought about her, and about our conversation in the restaurant, while I sat in the limo, alone, outside the nightclub she met her friends at. Waiting for updates from Rurik, one of my bodyguards, who drove her there, then followed her inside.

I didn't bother going into the club. No-sex challenge and all. Last thing I needed was to spend my night watching Megan Hudson dance in her shimmery little top and velvet leggings after she told me *no*.

I thought about how she told me no all the way home, after Locke and I tailed her back to her friend's apartment and made sure she was all tucked in for the night.

Not the most exciting Friday night I've ever spent. But at least I've managed to read a bit more of Megan's book. The truth is I've been sneaking in pages all damn day. It's becoming a problem.

Especially if this story is turning out to be the romance I suspect it is.

So far, it's definitely a survival story, featuring several near brushes with death and a lot of bickering between the two main characters. The scenes switch back and forth between Wolf's point of view and Rowan's, and I'm still reserving judgment on which one I'm going to sympathize with more.

Wolf lost his little brother, sure.

But he's still being a dick to Rowan, who's basically on a death march to sell herself off to some stranger who might turn out to be a fucking psychopath for all we know.

Only Megan knows for sure.

Even though it's subtle, I'm pretty sure Rowan is starting to like Wolf, though. She's been calling him *savage* the whole time, and when she finally asks him his name, several chapters in, he gives her such shit about her manners, I somehow want to high-five him.

I pick up my phone and type.

Me: You know what, I changed my mind. Wolf is charming.

Moments later, as I'm reading, my phone chimes in the dark. It's the middle of the night. Why is she still up?

Did I wake her?

Megan: You're reading my book again??

Me: I never stopped.

She texts me five "mind blown" emojis in a row.

It's not a yes, though.

I bury the brief thrill of victory that courses through my veins like a drug and resist the urge to text her back. *You haven't won her over yet. Relax.*

In truth, Megan's mind is becoming a trickier web to unweave the more I read.

She's written two characters into a pretty dangerous scenario where, according to her, they're going to fall in love, she's three books in, and she doesn't even know if they're going to get to a happily ever after.

In real life, she stayed with a guy for a decade, in hopes of that happy ending, probably, even when it didn't get there.

Yet she said no to my proposal, when I really wasn't asking much of her in return for a hell of a lot of security. Because, presumably, she'd rather be in a real relationship or no relationship at all than a fake one.

Have I ever met a woman who'd say no to the offer I made to her tonight, fake or real?

Plenty of women from my past would balk at the idea of being hired to be my gardener, sure. I can't see a one of them doing it. But being my fiancée, especially with so few strings attached? I can think of more than a few women who would jump at that chance.

Even the ones who have their own money. Some of the wealthiest women I know would happily find a way to relieve me of that two million, given the chance.

Clearly, Megan Hudson is not like the other women I've known.

But, interestingly, Graysen never told me I should get engaged to any of those women.

The more I think about it, the more interesting it gets.

Megan impressed Graysen, without even trying. Without even being aware of it. And that's not an easy feat.

Graysen Vance is not easily impressed or won over. He's not warm and fuzzy. And he's definitely not trusting of outsiders.

But he liked Megan.

Hell, *I* have a hard time impressing my brother. If I show up with her on my arm, and a ring on her finger, it will go a hell of a long way to winning his vote right now.

I need her to say yes to me.

To meet Graysen's expectations, for sure. But also, if I'm being honest with myself, for my ego. If she won Graysen's stamp of approval that fast and I can't win his *or* hers, what the hell does that say about me and the state of my life right now?

I just need to figure out how to convince her.

I told her at dinner that I'd give her anything she wants, but maybe that was too vague.

Maybe she didn't even believe me?

As I read, I've been trying to find hints about her in Rowan's character, but I really don't know her well enough to know if it's all fiction or if there are bits she's pulled from her own reality.

But then I get to the trust-fall scene, and I'm pretty sure I feel Megan speaking right through the page.

It's been bothering me all morning.

Wolf doesn't seem bothered at all, which just bothers me more. All he does is walk and walk and walk and expect me to keep up.

But I know it bothers him.

"Why does it bother you being called a savage?" I ask him.

He frowns at me.

"What else should I call you? You have no tribe."

"My people are nomads," he says, like I'm stupid. "We live in tribes. We just don't give our tribes fancy names that are supposed to mean something to anyone else. We know who we are. When I was born, my grandfather said I had the blood of a thousand men in me."

"You say that like it's something to be proud of."

"Why not? My people are from all over the Eastlands and beyond. We mix with other tribes to keep our bloodline diverse. We take the best of all qualities and pass them down to our children."

He does look like he's a bit of all over. There's something wildly exotic about his green eyes. His skin is tanned but not quite brown, and his hair is unruly and thick. He looks exactly like the epitome of the savage Aunt Rose warned me about.

He shakes his head. "You Westlanders give away your Ladies as brides and you think it's noble, but it's barbaric, sending a girl away from her home to marry a man she's never met."

"And I suppose you have a better way?"

"We trade, so it's mutual, and both males and females leave for other tribes. And not without their choice."

"It was my choice to leave my homeland."

"No, it wasn't."

And now he's arguing with me. Again.

"And by the way, you called me savage, not *a* savage," he says. "There's a difference, you know."

"I don't think so."

"It's the way you say it, like I disgust you."

"You don't disgust me."

He stops walking. His expression is sore as he comes over to me, and I back up. "But I scare you."

"I'm not scared of you." *I don't want to tell him the truth, that pretty much any man I didn't know who was left alone with me in the woods would scare me.*

His lips curl in a cruel smile. "No? Let's see you prove it." He takes me by my shoulders and turns me around. "Fall back, straight back, and let me catch you."

I huff, trying to glimpse him over my shoulder. "This is stupid." *He's already saved my life, and we both know it. What will this prove?*

That he doesn't want me dead? I know that already.

"Don't look back, just fall."

"Are you going to catch me?"

"That's the point."

"Fine. One, two—"

"Don't count, just do it."

I fall back, straight back, and he catches me in his arms. He stands me up again, and I pull away, turning to keep an eye on him.

"Now kiss me," he says, "if you're not afraid."

"No way."

"So. You trust me not to let you get hurt, but you won't kiss me."

"This is a stupid test you just made up so you could kiss me."

"So to you, kissing me seems a greater danger than falling on your ass and hitting your head on a rock." He starts walking again. "Now that's interesting."

I hurry to keep up with him. "It's not interesting! It's not really anything at all. It's just something you made up."

I lower the tablet to my lap in bed as it strikes me: that Megan doesn't trust me.

She's just left a man who treated her badly. She was with him for years, and according to what she and Cole told me about him, he was a real piece of shit to her, in the end.

He even *stole* from her.

How can she trust me, a man she just met, no matter what I say or what her brother says about me?

How can she know if I'm being honest with her or not?

And maybe cash in the bank isn't enough to win her trust.

Maybe I just made her the wrong offer.

Maybe I need to make her the *right* offer... whatever that is.

Something she can't say no to.

Something she wants so badly, she'd be crazy not to say yes.

CHAPTER 15

Megan

"Something's wrong with me." I slump across the high-top bar table, sucking mango margarita through a straw. "Maybe I'm crazy or something."

"You may be right about that." Nicole leans on her elbows against the table, wearing the cleavage-revealing black tank top worn by every female staff member in Champagne nightclub. "What did he offer you this time? The Pink Star diamond ring?"

I laugh uneasily, not even knowing what that is. Though it does sound outrageously expensive.

It's been a week since Jameson Vance "proposed" to me, and I've been questioning my answer ever since. Maybe especially so since I'm ninety-nine-percent sure most single women, and many men, would've said yes to him.

Nicole included.

"Well, last night he sent me this." I pull up his texts to read it to her. "*What if I bought a garden center like the one you worked at in Crooks Creek and you could manage it for me?*"

Nicole gapes. "Well, what did you say?"

"I didn't say anything. Do you think he's serious?"

"He asked you to be his fiancée, right? That seems pretty serious. Did you even ask to see a ring?"

"Of course not. And I could never agree to the garden center thing. I can't be indebted to a man I barely know over something like that. What if it doesn't work out? Would I owe him money? I mean, I can't even afford a lawyer to review a contract for me." My voice is getting squeaky. "I'm not a businesswoman."

"So, talk to your brother about it. He'll make sure you're protected. Cole must have a lawyer. And also, just so you know, I don't think he wants you to owe him *money*, if you know what I mean."

I frown. "Then he's trying to buy my loyalty?"

"No, Megz. He's trying to warm up your coochie by being nice to you."

"I don't think it's like that." I didn't actually tell her this part yet; I lean toward her for more privacy, but it's loud in the nightclub, and we're alone at this table. "He said we wouldn't have sex."

She snorts. "Yeah, right. He's coming on way too strong for you to believe that. He's just trying not to scare you away by telling you whatever he thinks you need to hear."

"You think?"

"What does he need to do, show up with a glass slipper?"

"I... I don't think he's trying to charm me."

"*Billions*, Megan. The man has billions of dollars. He doesn't even have to charm women. He's rich and motherfucking beautiful and you're cockblocking him. Look around you. This is the big city. There are beautiful women all over the place. Beautiful, hungry women who would be quick to get naked with that man and try to lock him down. And yet he's laser focused on *you*."

"Because of my brother."

"Honey. No guy cares that much about his best friend's sister unless he wants to rail her."

My eyes go wide, and she just shrugs.

Does Jameson Vance want to rail me?

She's not wrong about the beautiful women. It's not as if they're streaming down the streets, but Vancouverites are decidedly more appearance conscious than people are in Crooks Creek, that's for sure. The women here at Champagne are all dressed to the nines, and the women employed here are invariably beautiful and/or voluptuous.

"Speaking of beautiful women..." I cringe. "I hope I didn't embarrass you in front of your boss. I don't think she'll be calling me. She literally glazed over when I described my work experience."

"Maybe when someone quits, she'll call you," Nicole says easily. "We're so busy in summer, but we just did all our extra hiring for the season. It's bad timing."

"I know. I totally appreciate you putting my name in."

"Anytime." She pushes off the table. "I'm off in a few. Just have one more tab to clear up." She tips her head at a group of well-dressed men who've gotten louder with each round she's served them. "Wish me a big, juicy tip," she says, then saunters over there.

I watch her go, in awe of her ease working in this massive, glamorous nightclub. She told me this was her favorite hangout, so getting a job here just seemed natural. Of course to her, it would.

I'm really not here to beg her boss for a job, though. I just want to get out of the apartment for an evening. I've put in so many hours this week staring at my laptop, scouring job postings and tweaking my résumé.

Searching for a job has become a full-time job in itself.

But I don't have enough money to cover next month's share of the rent and utilities, a work wardrobe and transportation, much less going-out-on-the-town money, so this will have to be a rare treat.

My phone lights up with a text, and I check it with an awful feeling in my stomach, like worms writhing. It still happens every time a message or a call comes in: dread that it will be Troy. And usually, it is. He's more persistent than Jameson, more overbearing, and in a much less enjoyable way.

And, yup. It's him.

The energy vampire strikes again.

Troy's text begins with the word *I*, and I swipe it away into oblivion, feeling exhausted without even reading it. His texts and his voicemails always start with I. *I want... I need... I think...*

It's always about him.

As a grade-A narcissist, he doesn't have any capacity to see me as an individual human. In his warped mind, I'm just an extension of himself. As is everyone who comes into his life.

It's sad, really.

All I can do is keep reminding myself that his interest will fade. When it gets through to him that I'm not coming back, that he really can't squeeze anything more out of me, he'll move on.

Like I have.

I set my phone aside, and as I people watch from my high table, absorbing this budding new life of mine, the sights and sounds thrill me. The music is loud and pumping, sexy, and people keep bumping into my table. Maybe it's strange that I'm sitting here alone in a busy nightclub, because four different guys—and a girl—have tried to talk to me and buy me a drink. I probably should've just said yes, but I always say no. I'm not ready to date someone new, and I don't want to lead anyone on.

I just want to enjoy the spectacle as people flirt and celebrate their Friday night all around me. The lone bar in Crooks Creek is nothing like this, and this place is just one of many upscale hangouts in downtown Vancouver. The sheer volume of well-dressed people, the energy... Other than the one time my brother flew me to New York City to watch him in a playoff game, then wined and dined me in the Big Apple, I've never experienced anything like this.

I've been getting to know the city as well as I can on foot, walking from Nicole's place to Granville Island, along the beautiful Seawall and over the Granville bridge into downtown, and I've been falling in love with Vancouver. The fresh, saltwater breeze off False Creek. The majestic mountains that frame downtown. The hustle of big city life, the fast pace and the crowds.

People call Vancouver a "laid-back" city, but to me, it's pumping and vibrant and thrilling.

I love it all.

I can even see myself hanging out with my brother at his new house, having dinner together and watching hockey games. Both of us living our own lives, but getting to spend more time together.

To his credit, Cole has backed off. He wasn't thrilled when I told him I'd moved over to Nicole's apartment, but he's stopped calling from LA to check on me every day. At first, I thought maybe he'd gotten it through his head that I wanted to do this my way, on my own.

But then I realized Jameson had just taken over the task of butting into my life.

Since I quit the gardening job and moved out of his house, my brother's best friend has offered me four more jobs, an apartment of my own that he'd pay for, and this morning, he offered me straight-up cash to cover my rent—for the next six months. I haven't even mentioned those last two to Nicole; if I told her I turned those offers down, she'd drive me straight to the nearest psychiatric ward and ask them to run a full diagnostic check.

I just don't want my big brother swooping in to save me, no matter how he goes about it. But I do feel guilty about saying no to Jameson's offers. I know Nicole probably wouldn't, which just makes me feel worse for freeloading off her right now.

I watch her as she approaches, a smile on her face and a frosty mango margarita in her hand.

"Juicy tip?"

"So juicy. The girls are on their way. I just need to grab my things from the back, then I'll join you." She sets the margarita in front of me. "Thought you'd like another before I clock out."

"Yes, please. But two's my limit tonight. I'm on a budget."

"Don't worry about it. This one's on me."

"Ugh. You're too good to me."

Really, I shouldn't be drinking eighteen-dollar margaritas at all. But they're delicious and I've been such a good girl. I've done everything I could do this week to get hired somewhere—other than anywhere owned by Jameson Vance.

My prospects going forward are not looking good. If none of the places I've applied at this week come through, I'll have to start widening the search.

"Have you ever heard of a professional cuddler?" I ask Nicole before she can walk away.

She wrinkles her nose. "What is that? Some kind of code for escort?"

"I'm not sure. I'm scared to click on the ad."

"Don't get desperate," she warns me. "You are far too gorgeous to get desperate."

"Unfortunately, 'gorgeous' isn't a qualification on any of the job postings I've seen."

"Of course it is. You just need to read between the lines." She leans in. "Speaking of your ravishing good looks. That guy keeps staring at you." She hooks her eyebrow, and I glance past her shoulder at the man in the plain black suit who's been loitering by the bouncers at the front entrance.

"I know."

Jameson's security guys have been following me around ever since I said no to his proposal. It's not always the same guy, but they always drive a shiny black SUV and dress head to toe in dress blacks, and while I catch them watching me, none of them ever smile or approach me.

Tonight, it's the guy I saw in Jameson's front yard that first day. The one with the permanent scowl. He tailed me to and from Granville Island yesterday, and to a job interview and back a couple of days before.

I've let it slide. For now.

"I'm pretty sure he's being paid to look at me," I explain to Nicole. "He works for Jameson. They follow me around everywhere I go."

"Really?" She glances over.

"Yup. I'd be upset about it, but I know this is just Cole's way of stalking me to make sure I'm okay in the big city, and really, it's the least of all evils. He hasn't come to drag me back by my hair like a caveman, and I know it's hard for him. When I called him to tell him

I was leaving Troy, he threatened to come get me and tear Troy a new asshole—with a pitchfork—while he was at it. He meant it. I'm just doing what I can to keep him out of jail at this point."

Nicole regards me with sympathy and maybe a little envy. "He cares about you."

"Yeah."

"So does Jameson," she purrs.

"Not this again."

"It's so obvious he's into you! He's got muscle following you around!"

"He doesn't know me."

"Well, he saw something he likes."

"He's just being loyal to my brother."

"Uh-huh. Did he text you yet today?"

I sigh. "He's basically offered me everything but his left kidney to come back."

"Megan. Open your eyes. The man is *guarding* you."

I blink at her. "No he's not." I mean, I know he has a security guy literally following me around, but that's just for general safety and spying purposes. "He's just being nice. For Cole..."

"God, I love you." Nicole shakes her head in wonderment. "But you are one crazy blind bitch, Megan Hudson. *Go* already. Run into the arms of that beautiful billionaire. Do it for every woman who's ever found herself on a date with a total frog. Kiss the prince. *Please.*"

I laugh softly and Nicole kind of rolls her eyes, because of course, she's serious. She turns on her heel to go get her things. "I'll be back," she says, in a tone that tells me I'm hopeless.

Maybe I really am.

CHAPTER 16

"One day, if I'm broke," I muse aloud, "will we still hang out?"

Cole cocks an eyebrow at me. If that alarmed him, he doesn't show it. "Brother. I've been broke. The food's not as good and the women aren't as fancy, but they fuck just the same."

I swallow a groan.

When Cole got home from LA yesterday, I didn't bother telling him that I asked his sister to be my fiancée, more or less on order from my brother. Though Cole's family is nothing like mine, he knows mine now, so maybe he'd even understand. Even he calls Graysen "the boss."

Not to mention that he was disappointed as hell to hear she'd moved out. Maybe if he knew I'd gone as far as to propose to win her back, he'd forgive me for not talking to him about it first?

One can hope.

But there's nothing to tell, really.

She said no.

And that answer clearly isn't changing anytime soon.

He slaps my shoulder and gets up, stretching. We've been lying out by the pool after eating dinner and shooting a few hoops, but it's getting late.

"See you at breakfast?"

"Yeah," he says. "We can eat before I leave for the airport."

He's heading out of town again, just like that.

"Okay. Good night."

"G'night," he says.

I watch him cross the patio and disappear into the house. I usually travel more myself. Right now, though, I'm feeling pretty damn antisocial.

Without that fairy-tale engagement to splash across the internet, I don't want to risk igniting any gossip because I'm seen in public in the vicinity of a female and someone takes a photo of it. Graysen's way too worked up about the whole thing right now.

I just need to lay low and work this out. I'm still convinced I can win Megan over, somehow, but maybe that's just my stubborn pride talking.

She's already shot me down an embarrassing number of times.

Is this my life now?

I drop my head back on the cushioned chair with a groan. The bruised purplish sky in the west fades to black as I sip my still-not-quite-there whiskey and slowly absorb how much my life has changed since Granddad died.

I didn't want it to.

I've tried to pretend it didn't.

Just like when Dad died.

But pretending doesn't alter reality. It just delays the inevitable truth: that sometimes terrible shit happens and you just have to let your heart break so it can go about healing.

When Granddad died, we knew it was coming. Just not so soon. His health was failing, but he had the best care a man could get. We thought we'd have more time with him.

The tragedy was that we didn't.

I never even got to say goodbye to him in the end, it was so sudden.

Or thank him.

Fuck, I should've said *thank you* more.

Before it was too late.

Everything was just rolling along... and then it felt like everything derailed, so unexpectedly.

I've only been derailed like that two other times in my life. But those were major fucking derailments.

When Dad died in the helicopter crash.

And when Mom remarried.

No. Not when she remarried.

When she abandoned me for another life. Another family.

But if there was one thing I learned from losing my dad so young, life is short. And it's never a good idea to let a good thing slip away. Any more than it's a good idea to hang on to the bad.

I finally head up to bed, feeling stuck in a way that I hate.

I keep trying to come up with some other approach, some way to win Megan over. But I'm running out of ideas.

Clearly, dinner and drinks, money and all the job offers I can conjure just don't do it for her.

She likes plants, right? Flowers? I could send her a ton of them, but then maybe she'll think I'm in love with her or something.

Too romantic.

There has to be something else she wants, something I haven't offered her yet. Something I can do for her.

Something *only* I can do for her?

As I'm stepping into the shower, an idea occurs to me, and I pause to send her a text.

Me: What if I help you deal with your ex?

She doesn't answer.

Me: You arrived here with that one little suitcase. But you must've owned more than that when you left him. I can get you a good lawyer. Send someone to collect your things.

Again, she doesn't answer, so I get in under the water and let the heat pound down on me.

I know, in these moments, alone and without any distractions, when my thoughts converge on nothing but her, that I'm far more interested in her than I've let myself believe.

I feel oddly off-kilter.

It's like some corner I didn't see coming has been turned, but when I look back to see where it happened, it's all murky.

All that's clear to me is that every time she says no to me, it fuels me.

My motivation has shifted, from my loyalty to Cole to my personal desire to win her back. To win her over. Even the pressure from Graysen is starting to take a backseat to just winning one with this girl.

When I get out of the shower, a thrill runs through me when I discover she's texted me back.

Megan: That's a really generous offer. And I appreciate it. But it's not necessary. I don't want anything from him.

I think about those words as I lie in bed, and I hear the unspoken message.

I don't want anything from you.

I stay up for hours, plowing through book two.

Rowan is still a virgin.

Wolf is still a dick, in a way, but he's saved her life so many damn times, *I'm* falling in love with him.

Rowan seems to be struggling on the issue.

Megan hasn't said another word to me about her books or asked if I'm still reading them. I keep hoping she'll bring it up so I can ask her more questions.

But when she doesn't, it just reinforces the truth of what she told me. She extended trust to me when she told me about her books, because I asked, but she never brought it up again, because writing is deeply personal for her.

And I keep trying to glean her secrets through the pages.

But I still haven't figured them out, and it's been a book and a half already.

"Turn the other way," Rowan says, *trying to order me around, as usual. "Don't look."*

"Whatever you like, princess."

"I don't want you to see."

"Why not? Do you think your cunt is so much more special than every other girl's cunt?"

"Stop saying that word."

"Vagina. Is that better?"

She just fumes and stomps around.

"I'm sorry, you're right. I shouldn't call it a cunt. That's too fierce. I bet you have a lovely little pussy. Pink and demure. Like a flower bud that hasn't opened. Like a little pink kiss."

She throws the food pot at me. The pot. She misses because I dodge in time, but really. "Those are some manners for a Lady."

Oh, she hates it when I critique her manners.

"Manners! You don't know the first thing about manners."

"Really? Seems to me I've been traveling for weeks, alone, with a young Lady, who we've established has a fresh pink pussy, and I haven't even tried to rape her once. What more manners do you want from a savage like me?"

"Stop looking at me like that!"

"How am I supposed to look at you?"

"Like a gentleman! Like a man my brothers entrusted with my life!"

I pick up my phone and send Megan a text, despite the late hour. She doesn't have a job to get up for early in the morning, right?

Me: These two fight a lot. Are they ever just going to fuck already? Obviously, they want to.

I keep reading, combing for hints into her psyche, but I'm not sure it's getting me anywhere. Even when something seems to resonate, I'm not sure why.

She's still too much of a mystery and it's driving me a bit crazy.

I don't like not getting what I want, that's all.

Maybe I'm like Wolf that way. Because he sure as shit wants to fuck Rowan by now. How could he not? He's been traveling with her, one moment from death at almost all times, for weeks now.

My phone chimes.

Megan: I know. It's delicious.

I keep reading, skimming hungrily through the next few pages.

Wherein Rowan catches Wolf with his dick in his hand, in the woods.

I almost laugh out loud.

Especially when he tries to play it off so cool.

"Was that about me?" Rowan demands.

If it was or it wasn't, it doesn't help me for her to know. "Don't flatter yourself."

She seems unconvinced. "I'm the only person around."

"It doesn't have to be about anyone specific, you know. Sometimes it's just taking care of an urge."

"How many... urges... do you have?"

"What do you mean, how many?"

"Well... have you been doing that every time you say you're going off to piss?"

"Not every time."

My phone chimes again.

Megan: Okay what's happening? What part are you at?

Well, shit. She finally asked.

Me: You wrote it, Jessica.

I let that hang for a minute as I almost get sucked back into the scene and forget to answer.

Me: Rowan just caught Wolf masturbating. I thought she was going to watch. But she freaked out and ran away. And now they're arguing again.

Megan: If I'm not mistaken... I think you're enjoying my book.

Me: Books.

She doesn't reply, and I keep reading.

"So, you're nineteen? And you're still fresh?"

She glares at me. "That's really none of your business."

"How's that possible? No one ever slipped you a finger? Nothing?"

"You're just being crude to get a rise out of me." She nibbles at her drumstick, tearing the meat off in little strips and licking her fingers.

"But how do you manage your urges? Don't you have them? I knew a girl who used to play with carrots when she went too long without cock." She stops eating and just stares at me like I've grown a repulsive second head. "You do anything like that?"

Her face is so pink, she could be broiling in the fire. "My 'urges' are also none of your business."

"So you do have them, then. How do you go through years of urges and not do a thing about it?"

She keeps eating and kind of rolls her eyes.

"That doesn't sound very healthy to me." While I eat, I decide to regale her with the way we do it in my tribe. "In my tribe, we become adults at sixteen. It's a rite of passage having sex on your birthday. You do it in a tent while the whole tribe dances outside."

She tosses her bones into the fire with a lot of fat and gristled meat still on them. The stuff I would've gladly eaten. "Sounds perfectly savage to me."

"It's so you understand sex is a part of life, and your body isn't something to fear. And you don't have to be afraid to express your sexual desires. It's natural to have one lifelong lover, or as many as you want. There aren't any rules about it."

"Sounds to me like you just can't control yourselves."

I laugh. "Serious?"

"That's what I heard."

"Right. I'm gonna turn into an animal right before your eyes and savage you." My grin fades when I see how she's staring into the fire.

She is serious.

"If I was planning to savage you, Lady Rowan, wouldn't I have done it by now?"

She glares at me, her cheeks flaming red now, hot with anger. "My Aunt Rose says savages are always in heat."

"Sounds like a woman who knows." I stretch out on my back. The stars are bright in a clear, black sky above.

"What does that mean?"

I hear her gasp over the crackle of the fire when I say, "It means, maybe a nasty savage broke Aunt Rose's heart."

I check my phone even though I don't hear a chime. Megan hasn't texted me again.

It's almost two in the morning.

I should be sleeping.

The chapter ends with Rowan pissed off at Wolf again, and I start another.

We walk the next day in endless silence, tension sharp in the air between us.

At dusk, Wolf makes a fire in the mouth of one the largest caves we've come across, and we settle in to take our supper there. While Wolf prepares his now-infamous rabbit stew, I clear some stones out of the back of the cave and arrange the furs for sleep, giving us each half of them and hoping the fire will warm them before we go to sleep. The temperature has steadily plummeted all day and it smells of rain outside, though not a drop has fallen.

Over supper, we still don't speak.

I still haven't forgiven him for what he said about Aunt Rose, and he doesn't seem to mind the silence like I do. He never does.

I'm still entirely grateful for his company, for the knife in his boot and his capable hands and the food he provides without complaint, but I don't know how to tell him so without making myself seem weak.

I'd die before I'd admit how much I need him.

After supper, I wash the one pot and two spoons and lay them out on a rock to dry while Wolf pokes at the fire. I strip down in the cave, behind his back, and wrap myself in a fur. Then I go outside to take care of nature between the trees while I chew on a mint leaf.

When I return to the cave, Wolf is already lying down in the back, his leathers and his clothes slung over a rock. He's doused the fire with dirt, and only a few embers are left glowing, making just enough light for me to stumble to my furs. When I wrap myself in them, I realize he's given me one of his, but I don't say anything.

I don't want to thank him for this or anything else.

Thanking him will just make him think he's in the right, that all his rudeness has been forgotten.

We lie head to head, stretched out in opposite directions, and I can hear him breathing. I can smell his warm smell, too, the scent of his leathers and the fire smoke in his hair and his male musk beneath.

I inhale deeply, savoring it, trying to do it without making a sound.

I stop and set the tablet down. I'm pretty sure it's about to get smoking hot in that cave.

I decide I need to quit reading. Now.

And possibly delete this book from my tablet.

I pick it up again and skip ahead a few pages, just checking.

"Talk to me," I practically beg. "Keep talking." I want him here with me, and it's fierce, this wanting.

"Keep touching yourself," Wolf says. "Don't stop. Imagine... imagine someone's kissing you down there. Imagine their mouth—"

"Who?"

I listen to his hastened breathing in the dark. "Whoever you want."

"Tell me who." My voice sounds awfully desperate as I stroke furiously between my legs. "Tell me who's kissing me."

I want him to say it. Please say it.

"I am," he whispers. It's so quiet, I almost miss it under the ripples of thunder outside. The rainstorm is growing stronger. I shudder with the thought of his mouth on my flesh, the pleasure surging through me. *"I'm kissing you. I'm trying to... but you won't let me."*

"Oh..." The groan escapes me without thought.

"I want to kiss you and lick you between your legs, but you keep stopping me," Wolf says. "I'm on my knees and I'm begging you. Just one taste. Then I'm kissing you. I'm licking you, and you taste so good. But you tell me to stop. You're being cruel. I lick you again, but you tell me I'm a dirty, filthy savage. I keep licking you anyway. I love how you taste. I can't get enough. I taste you all over my lips, you're so wet, and I keep licking you—"

I cry out, my body exploding, arching, my flesh spasming beneath my hand. I gasp and groan and writhe, unable to stop myself. I keep rubbing, keep squeezing as my body quakes, as the thunder rumbles through the night.

Spasms ripple between my legs, my tender flesh throbbing, my heart pounding in my chest. I'm so wet, all over my thighs, my hand.

I can smell my arousal, and at the back of my mind, I wonder if Wolf can, too.

I slam the cover on the tablet shut.

Yup. I'm going to sleep.

I toss the tablet on my bedside table along with my reading glasses, turn off the lamp, and roll over.

Then I get up and go jerk off in my bathroom because there's no way I'll be able to fall asleep with this hard-on if I don't.

As I stroke myself to climax, I'm weirdly twisted up inside.

Part of me still can't believe I proposed to Cole's sister behind his back.

Another part is pretty sure I've got a crush on Megan Hudson that doesn't really fit anywhere in my life.

And there's a tiny, possibly insane part that wonders, in the heart-pounding silence just after I ejaculate, if fucking her would be worth losing everything anyway.

If it would be worth trading every dollar I have just to touch her.

CHAPTER 17

Megan

"I'm unhirable," I moan.

"Oh, please. It hasn't even been two weeks." Nicole doesn't spare me a glance. She's getting ready for another night shift at Champagne while I wallow over my laptop and my empty email inbox.

"Actually, it has. And besides the interview you got me at Champagne, I've had two crappy interviews for jobs I desperately need, but don't particularly want, and I didn't even get any offers. And no one else is contacting me."

"Something will come through. It just might take a while. You don't have to kick in rent this month, okay? I can cover you."

"Oh god, this sucks." I fall back on the bed. "Maybe I should just go back to Crooks Creek."

"What?! You did not just say that. What the hell is there in Crooks Creek for you?"

"My old job back? And a place to live?"

She turns to me. "You wouldn't seriously go back to him."

"Not to him. But at least I could afford a place of my own." I catch the foot in my mouth and choke on it. "Not that I'm not totally grateful for what you're doing for me, letting me stay here with you all—"

"Megan. It's okay. I know it's not the Shangri-La." She returns to doing her makeup. "Just stop putting so much pressure on yourself. It'll all work out." Her phone buzzes. "It's the front door," she says, picking up. "Hello?" She listens, then says, "Just a minute," and covers the microphone hole with her finger. "Some guy named Roderick? He has a package for you."

I frown, thinking. "Rurik?"

"Maybe that was it."

She buzzes whoever it is into the building and I jog down the hall to catch the elevator. I hear it coming up, and when the door opens, Jameson's grouchiest security guy is standing there, wearing that faint permascowl.

His name is Rurik, he's originally from Russia, his English is flawless, but he doesn't talk much. I learned all this when I bought him an iced coffee while he was following me around the other day. He looked thirsty. It was hot out, and he was in his suit.

At his feet, there's a suitcase.

I back up as he rolls it out and parks it at my feet. Then he hands me the envelope he's carrying. "For you," is all he says.

My name is handwritten on the front.

By the time I open my mouth to ask what it is, the elevator has swallowed him and starts to descend.

The suitcase he's left looks expensive. It smells new. It's all black, leather with metal trim, and has double G symbols stamped all over the leather.

I open the envelope, my heart thumping, and slip out the hand-written letter. I read it right there in the hallway, with my fingers faintly shaking and a strange lump forming in my throat.

Dear Megan,

I want to let you know that Romeo returned to work the day after you left. I should've mentioned that before, to alleviate your worries about him, but somehow in my single-minded pursuit of you, it didn't occur to me that it might ease your mind to know that.

Also, I'm getting his wife appropriate care for her vision loss. Thank you for bringing the issue to my attention.

I also want to apologize for the hasty proposal. I realize now that I went into it overconfident and failed to give it the proper care it was due. I've had more time to think about it, and I hope you've been thinking about it as well.

If your answer is still no, there will be no hard feelings on my part.

However, I can't promise you that I won't ask again.

Sincerely yours,

Jameson Vance

My pulse is thudding too loudly in my ears and my breathing is shallow and fast. The man floors me. He isn't even here and I'm shaking with nerves.

No, excitement. I'm shaking with a heady excitement.

I take a few deep breaths that do nothing to calm me as I grasp the handle of the heavy suitcase, and roll it back to the apartment, then into Nicole's room.

She pauses as she's putting on mascara. "Wow. Nice suitcase. From Cole?"

"No," I say weakly, "not from Cole."

"Oh, shit." Her eyes widen. "The beautiful billionaire strikes again. Now he's giving you Gucci?"

I go sit on the bed. My legs feel weak. I'm getting a sick adrenaline rush off all his attention.

Nicole goes to check out the suitcase that's clearly worth more than everything I brought with me to the city. She turns over the stylish luggage tag. "There's a note here." She reads it out loud: "*In case you want to come back.*"

I squeeze out an uncomfortable noise.

"Well, aren't you gonna open it? What if there's stuff inside?"

"I'm pretty sure there is."

"Want me to open it?"

"Sure." I scan the letter again, not really seeing it. Certain words just keep floating around my brain.

Romeo returned to work...

I'm getting his wife appropriate care for her vision loss.

My single-minded pursuit of you...

"Oh, it's heavy!" Nicole spreads the suitcase open on the floor, delighted.

It's *packed.*

She carefully turns over another tag that's been attached to the inside and reads another note: "*In case you don't come back.*" Her eyes meet mine, her pupils blown wide. The *Wanty* cat is back. "Oh, baby. I'm swooning inside."

"Thank you for containing yourself," I say dryly.

"I'm trying."

I watch as she pores over the items in the suitcase.

"It's all things you might need, you know, for starting your new life! There's a set of cutlery and plates and linen napkins and luxury soap and toiletries and... oh! Seed starter packs for herbs and flowers, and some little pots to plant them in! There's a gift card here for Gardenworks. And a cute little pack of bungee cords!"

She picks it up. Mini ones in bright colors.

"There's a note on it. It says... *You have to be prepared for anything.*"

I swallow. That was exactly what I said to him when we first met, in the street, when I pulled out my bungee cords.

"And there's a little toolbox..." She lifts it out. "This is so cute! And it's so... you."

"It is," I say faintly.

"How does he know you so well?" Nicole marvels. "This is incredibly thoughtful."

I clear my throat, trying to find words. "Or incredibly creepy, considering he's been spying on me."

"Spying?"

"The guy who brought this, Rurik, is one of his security guys. I told you, they've been following me around."

I don't want to acknowledge that Jameson could've learned so much about me simply by paying attention.

And, you know, being interested.

"I don't care what you say, Miss Jaded. This is romantic!" Nicole continues pawing through the items in the suitcase. "There's a lovely towel set in here! And dish towels. He thought of everything."

"Or one of his assistants did."

She makes a face. "Don't try to devalue it just so you can keep pretending he's not fabulous."

"If you think he's so fabulous... maybe you should get engaged to him," I offer weakly.

Nicole drops the towels she's feeling up. "Now *there's* an interesting idea. Look me in the eye, Megan Hudson," she demands, "and tell me you'd actually let me do that."

I look away.

"HA! I knew it. You think he's fabulous, too."

I sigh.

There's no way I'll admit to her how right she is.

CHAPTER 18

Megan

"Hello." My voice shakes slightly.

I stand in the middle of Jameson's grand foyer, feeling small as I try to discreetly wipe my damp palms on my dress.

Jameson is walking toward me, backlit by the evening sun that pours through the open living room walls to his backyard. He's come in from the back patio, after his big bodyguard with the neck tattoos and the iron jaw went to tell him that I'm here.

He's tousling his wet hair with a towel, his sleek, muscled body damp. He wears nothing but a pair of light-blue swim trunks that match his striking eyes and cling to him wetly.

I'm not sure what to do with my eyes, which are desperately trying to fuck him.

"Megan." His gaze slides from my face to my chest, to the back-pack and two suitcases by my feet. One secured with red bungees, one with the Gucci logo all over it.

"I'm sorry to interrupt your evening. I should've called first."

I'm not sure why I didn't.

Maybe I was just too nervous, too uncomfortable with the idea of him knowing I was on my way over, and having time to prepare.

To prepare what?

Maybe I just wanted us to be on slightly more even ground.

But standing here, staring at him with his thin swim trunks glued to his obviously more-than-ample package, it hits me that there's really nothing I can do to even the playing field with this man. Jameson Vance has the entire upper hand in pretty much everything, from his beauty to his wealth. He could show up wearing a garbage bag and I'd still feel intimidated.

"It's okay. I'm glad you're here." He brushes the towel up and down his arms, then swipes it across his chest and down his abs as I try not to gawk. Jesus, though, the man is eye candy. "Do you mind if I have a quick shower? I feel underdressed." His gaze wanders down my sundress again.

It's the cutest one I own, a pale terra-cotta color that goes well with my eyes, with a fitted bodice and a ruffled skirt. The one I was wearing when I met him.

I realize belatedly that he's complimented me.

"Oh. Of course. I'm so sorry. I really should've—"

"It's fine. Just wait here. Don't go anywhere. I'll have Clara get you a drink."

"Uh, I really can't go anywhere." While we've been talking, his tattooed bodyguard whisked my bags away. Maybe he has standing orders to seize them on sight. "One of your ninjas kinda took my bags, so..."

It's not like I can't go get them; I know where my guest room is.

But I came here for a reason, and I'm not planning to go anywhere.

Clara ushers me along the hallway that leads into what she calls "Mr. Vance's private wing." At the end of the long hall, there's a foyer, smaller than the house's main foyer, with a grand staircase leading up.

On the far side of the foyer, beyond the staircase, is a set of wide double doors.

Jameson's office.

I've only been here once. When I tossed mud around and quit the job he'd hired me to do.

I cringe a little at the memory of how Clara had to chase me in here because I was so upset about Romeo being fired that I ignored her when she asked me to stop.

Now, Clara shows no sign of holding a grudge. She simply opens the doors to the office and leads me through to a sitting room that's off to the right side, through a grand archway. I politely decline her offer of a beverage, and she leaves me there to wait for Jameson.

While I wait, I pace around the room, peeking at the few framed photographs on the mantel over the fireplace. Jameson and his family. There are a few of him and his siblings, casual photos taken at black-tie events. And there's one of all five of them as children, with a couple who must be their parents. Their father in the photograph looks a lot like Jameson's brother Graysen does now.

Jameson looks more like their mom, with similar light-brown, almost blondish, hair.

"I should probably update those."

I startle a little when Jameson enters the room. I didn't hear him coming. His hair is still damp, but he's dressed in linen lounge pants and a white T-shirt, both of which showcase his strong, muscled body. His feet are bare. "Those photos are all a few years old," he explains.

He does look younger in the images. He's smiling broadly in all of them.

I wonder if he smiled more back then or if it's just that he doesn't smile much around me.

"I hope this is okay." He gestures at his casual clothes. "I was trying to match your vibe."

"Oh, god. Are we matching already?" I try to make light of the whole situation to calm my nerves. "Doesn't that come at least a few years into a relationship?"

His eyes burn into me. "I didn't realize we were in a relationship."

I take a deep breath. "I'm here to accept your proposal."

I'm not sure what I expected, but after the way he pursued me, maybe I thought he'd seem happier?

But all he says is "Have a seat," and indicates one of the beautifully upholstered chairs.

I take a seat, and he takes the one facing me.

He studies me. "I was beginning to think I'd never win you over."

"Honestly, everything you've done since I quit and walked out of here has won me over." I pick at the hem of my dress, feeling even more nervous than I expected I would. "I didn't think I wanted your help. I didn't want my brother's money, or yours, or your pity. The truth is I was embarrassed about the way I left Crooks Creek. I ran out in the night and never even told my ex I was going." I blow out a breath, realizing how tightly I've been holding on to that truth.

"You did what you needed to do."

"Yeah. I needed to start over. And I know I can do this on my own. But the thing is... The more you reached out to me and tried to convince me to give your offer a chance, the more I realized that I really have no good reason to say no."

"You want a choice," he says simply, "and you want to feel safe in the choice you make."

I nod, feeling exposed and raw.

"It's understandable that you wanted time to think it over."

"Thank you."

"So, your answer is yes?"

"Yes."

"Then let's have a drink."

I laugh nervously as he gets up and pours us both a glass of something over ice at the small bar in the corner. He hands me a glass and touches his to mine. "To our engagement."

Shit. That really brings it home. This is getting very real.

Even though it's fake.

"Yeah. To us," I force out, and sip the drink. "Is this rye?"

"It is." He settles back into his seat again, appearing totally comfortable with the situation, while I'm perched on the edge of my seat, tense as hell. "Do you like it?"

"I'm not sure. I've never been a whiskey drinker."

"We just acquired the distillery. This is a new product." He sips his, watching me over the rim of his glass. "I think there's some room for improvement. But it might be nice to have my fiancée's opinion on these things."

I have no idea what to say to that. Or to him, now that it's all settled. What the hell do I know about whiskey, or any of his business endeavors?

"So... that's it? A one-year engagement, starting now?"

"That's it. All I ask of you, other than playing the part of my devoted fiancée, is that you respect my family's desire for privacy."

"Oh. Of course. I'm not a gossip."

"Good. My brother wants our happy relationship to be highly publicized. But other than that and the work I do with celebrities and the hockey team, my family prefers to stay completely out of the media."

"I understand."

"And what about you? Do you have any requests of me?"

Oh god. *I can think of a few.*

Most of them involve a lot less clothing than we're currently wearing.

"Well... I guess it's the same for me. I'm pretty introverted, and I value my privacy. But I'm not worried. I believe that you want me safe and secure. You know... like Cole does."

I don't know why I slip that in.

Maybe I'm taking his temperature.

He nods and sips his drink. "Well, the best way for me to ensure that you're safe and secure is to keep you here, engaged to me."

Yeah. A small, hot bubble within me bursts.

I brought it up. But maybe I'd hoped his response would be different.

Different, how?

He's doing this for my brother, and for his.

It's not personal.

I need to remember that, and make sure it doesn't get personal for me. No catching feelings or romanticizing him, or getting swept away by all his Prince-Charming-to-the-rescue vibes. My heart needs to remain intact at the end of the year. He's not looking for a wife, and I'm not looking for another broken heart.

For him, this is about his family's expectations and his public image. For me, it's about getting my new life on track.

That's all.

However, I don't want to lie to him. And I won't lie to myself either. I won't try to convince myself that things I know to be true are false.

I did that with Troy for so many years, and maybe it was a survival mechanism. But I don't need to survive him anymore. I learned a long and painful lesson from those mistakes, but I learned.

I'd considered not bringing this up at all, but I don't want this hot, unsettling thing in the room between us, unacknowledged. That seems not only dishonest but dangerous. I've definitely never experienced this kind of molten, magnetic attraction to a man I barely know. And now I'm about to suddenly be living with him, and fake dating him. Honesty, not to mention mutual respect, should be part of the arrangement.

So I scrape my courage together. "There is one thing that I'm fairly concerned about."

"Then let's talk about it. I want you be comfortable here, Megan. This is your home now."

I struggle to swallow that. It's still hard to digest.

"I find you very attractive," I blurt. And then I just keep rambling. "That's very weird to say out loud since you're not my boyfriend, I'm not trying to pick you up or anything, you're my brother's best friend, and we just agreed to get engaged with no strings attached. But it's the truth. And I thought you should know. Also, I have no game. I haven't been single since I was seventeen. I've been with one guy in my whole life. He's the only guy I've ever kissed, had sex with, lived with. This is going to be a steep learning curve for me. And I'm aware that you could've asked another woman who's at least had more experience with relationships than I have to pretend to be your girl. You're asking me to act like we're dating and we're in love, when I don't even know what that is. It was so long ago that I felt... that I experienced..." I press my hands to my flushed, hot face. "God. I'm so uncool. Are you sure you want to tell everyone I'm your fiancée?"

I have no idea what he's thinking, and it's just making me more nervous. But at least he doesn't seem revolted by everything I just said.

His blue eyes burn steadily into mine when he says, "Megan. Did it ever occur to you that's why I chose you?"

I frown, confused. "You knew when you asked me to be your fiancée that I've only been with one guy?"

"Not exactly. Cole mentioned that you met him when you were seventeen. But that's not what I'm talking about."

"Then what are you talking about?"

"That," he says gently, nodding at me. "That sweetness in you. That honesty. You're a good person, and anyone can see that."

"Oh. Well, thank you. *Wait.* But I thought your brother chose me."

He sips his drink, then goes silent for a long, heated moment, as the muscle along his jaw dances.

Then he says, "He did," with such distaste, it's pretty clear he resents his brother telling him what to do.

And yet, he did it.

So maybe in a way... he did choose me?

We stare at each other.

As usual, I can feel his raw, potent male energy, his masculine ease and command of everything around him, his dominance choking out the air until I'm almost forgetting how to breathe. He's elegant and alpha, so exquisitely male, my whole body hums when he's near.

I feel way out of my depth, just sitting here, alone with him in this room.

No guy cares that much about his best friend's sister unless he wants to rail her.

Damn. Nicole's in my head, and I know there's one more thing I have to ask.

"Um, about that other thing," I say breathlessly. "You said we wouldn't be having sex...?"

His eyes darken as he regards me. Is that his pupils enlarging? Like a predator sinking into the shadows on a hunt?

"We won't be." His voice is low and smoldering, or maybe it's just my neglected lady parts hearing things. "For now."

Okay, I heard that for sure. With my ears. "For now?"

"Why don't we get to know each other a bit first?"

"That's a good idea," I choke out.

Wow. *He really is a gentleman.*

He reaches to set his empty glass on the table between us.

I sip my whiskey, my thoughts flying in so many directions at once, I can't grab hold of a single one of them. My heart is racing and my core is warm. This is at once the most perplexing, thrilling, and unbelievable conversation I've ever had in my life.

"Something is still bothering you," he points out, in that annoyingly delicious, bossy way of his. "What is it?"

I take a breath, and ask. "Are you being honest with me?"

"Of course."

"That's important to me."

"It is for me, too. Relationships, of any kind, should be built on trust. It's absolutely essential."

"I'm glad you feel that way," I say hesitantly. "Because the last man I trusted really betrayed that trust, and it's a big deal for me to go out on a limb here with you."

"I'll do everything I can to ensure that you feel the ground is solid beneath your feet. I'm a stable man. I won't be throwing you any curveballs."

I swirl the liquid in my glass, the melting ice. "He cheated on me," I confess.

In the ensuing silence, I force myself to meet Jameson's eyes. I should've done that when I said it, to gauge his reaction. How else will I know what kind of man he is when it comes to the subject of being unfaithful?

The eyes that meet mine burn with a restrained fury that takes my breath away. He leans toward me. "Is that what you're afraid of? That I would do something like that to you?"

The tension in my chest loosens somewhat. The fact that he put it that way, acknowledged that to cheat on me is to do something *to me*, gives me hope that he understands. That Troy's infidelity wasn't just an act of betrayal and disloyalty, but aggression. He did it to hurt me as much as he did it to make himself feel good.

"I don't want to be cheated on," I confess. "I know this is a fake relationship, but that's unfair. It would still humiliate me. It would still... hurt me."

"I respect you too much for that. I know you have no way of knowing this is true, but I'm a man of my word. I've never cheated on a woman in my life, and I have no reason to do that to you." His words feel sincere.

"Even though we're not having sex?"

"Yes."

"Which means... you won't be having sex... at all."

He clears his throat. "Yes. For now."

Those two words again.

I down the last of my drink, then place the glass on the table next to his.

"You're nervous," he says. Reading me, once again.

"It's not the engagement that makes me nervous, exactly. It's just... having to fake it."

"I understand. I don't like lying either. Just think of it as a private arrangement between us. A lot of marketing is an illusion, but what's true, what matters, is what's in private, between us. If we're both committed to this arrangement, invested, honest with each other... We won't have to fake much."

My throat pulls tight. It's like he's still talking business, on the surface, but there's undeniable heat coming off him that makes the conversation feel overtly sexual.

Maybe this is just his natural vibe at all times? And I'll have to get used to it?

"We'll be a couple," he goes on. "No cheating, and no need for lies. If we decide to have sex with each other, or have sex with other people, we'll discuss it first. Come to an agreement about it."

He studies me until I know I'm blushing as I absorb those words. So clear, so fair, so sensible, given our arrangement.

I don't even know why the mention of "other people" doesn't bother me more. Maybe because he also mentioned having sex with me, and honesty, in the same breath?

Whatever the reason, there's a meteor shower going off in my chest, and my panties are wet.

When did my panties get so wet?

"Right," I say faintly.

"It's getting late," he points out as my mind reels like a kaleidoscope; a thousand pretty pictures, and Jameson stars in every one of them. "What time do you usually go to bed?"

"Oh." I blink. "Now?"

He chuckles softly, though I'm serious. "I'll walk you there."

He gets to his feet and escorts me out of his office. Which is good, because I'm keen to get some alone time after that whole revelation about us possibly having sex. So I can breathe.

And maybe touch myself while trying to recall his exact expression when he said those words.

If we decide to have sex with each other...

I really thought he meant we were never having sex, ever. This revelation is a lot to swallow.

As I imagine his cock would be.

I see the way he bounces around in those linen pants. Whether he's wearing underwear or not, clearly whatever he's packing is too heavy to be conservatively contained by mere fabric.

We stop at the foot of the grand staircase outside his office, and I manage a hoarse "Thank you, for, you know, talking it through with me."

"Anytime, Megan." His low, velvety voice brushes over my senses. "Come on. I'll show you the way."

Then he starts up the stairs.

I stare at his fantastic backside. Those linen pants aren't so loose when he's climbing the stairs, his muscled ass flexing, the taut globes defined through the thin fabric. "Uh, what way?" I ask, dazed.

He pauses. "The way to my bedroom. Well, our bedroom, now."

CHAPTER 19

Megan

Hold the phone.

Jameson wants me to sleep in his bedroom?

With *him*?

"But, what about my things?"

Weak protest.

I picture my suitcases in my guest bedroom, and myself fleeing there to get them. And maybe hide from my new fiancé. I'm sweating.

But I don't move.

"They're all settled in our room. I had Clara get it ready for us."

Our room.

Ready for us.

Oh god.

"When... when did you do that?"

"When I got out of the shower. While you were waiting for me in my office."

"You knew I was here to say yes?"

I mean, I brought all my things with me, but still.

"I had some time to think about it. In the shower."

"Well, that was... presumptuous."

"Optimistic," he corrects me.

I stare at him in a mild panic.

He stares back at me calmly, with that hot-as-hell commanding look in his eyes. The one that makes me want to lift my skirt.

In lieu of that, I start to move, climbing the stairs. I mean, I could at least go get my stuff, right? Then explain to him politely that there's no ever-loving way I'm sleeping in his bed next to his glorious body and not licking him all over.

Does he seriously expect me to do that?

I follow him in silence to the second floor, where he gestures vaguely at a couple of doors we pass. "That's an unused bedroom. And that's another one. For kids, I guess."

I smile nervously when he glances at me over his shoulder.

"This one's ours." He opens the grand double doors, and I follow him in.

A luxurious king bed in the middle of the room dominates the huge space, with a sitting area clustered around a fireplace off to the left side. Huge windows all along the back have layered drapes across them. It's a lot like my room in the guest wing, just much bigger.

"It's very nice." I don't even look at the bed, and I try not to think about how many gorgeous women he's probably screwed on it. "I don't see my bags."

"They're in the closet."

"Oh. Well, I'm sorry your staff went to the trouble of bringing them up here. I can move them myself. I think it's probably best if I stay in the guest wing, like I did before."

Jameson stares at me.

Then he shuts the doors and says abruptly, "I'm no virgin, Megan. Are you telling me you are?"

"Uh... no."

"It would make zero sense for my fiancée to sleep in the guest wing."

"I mean, who would know?" I hedge nervously.

He studies me, maybe reading how tense I am. He seems very good at reading me, like I'm some smutty open book.

"This will go much more smoothly," he says, "if my staff actually believes the engagement is real."

I find myself looking at the neatly made bed. The corners of the covers are turned back. Both sides.

"I just didn't think of it that way. This is a lot more than I thought I was signing on for."

"What did you think?"

"I guess I didn't really think about this part. When I pictured coming back here, I just pictured staying in the same room as before. And hanging out with you and Cole."

"Cole is away for the next two weeks."

"Right. But when he comes back."

"Megan."

I look at him.

"I don't want you to feel like you're not safe here when your brother's not around. I'm your fiancé now. We have an agreement. Any woman of mine is a woman I protect."

Any response I might have to *that* gets jammed up in my throat.

Any woman of mine...

"Okay. It's just... when you said we wouldn't be having sex, I didn't picture us sleeping together."

His eyes darken a shade before he looks away. "No one will be in that bed but us. All they need to know is that we're sharing the bed."

I take a breath. He's right, probably.

And I said yes to this engagement.

Am I afraid of him doing something out of line? No.

But am I afraid of what might happen if I sleep next to him?

Fuck, yes.

What if I do something stupid? Read his signals wrong?

Lose my shit and jump on him, and he turns me down?

What if I make him change his mind and kick me out?

I've never been in a situation like this, so vulnerable to a man I barely know. It feels intensely intimate just standing here in his room with him. I can't imagine being in his bed while he sleeps next to me and I can't touch him.

The first date I went on with Troy, he kissed me. The second date, he kissed me and then we made out. And the second time we made out, he tried to go much further than that.

It was me who'd held the brake firmly in place until I was ready to let go and plunge into my first sexual relationship.

And I have literally no other experience to go on.

I've never had the first date or first kiss or first make-out scenario with any other man. I've definitely never done anything as strange as share a bed with a man who's drawn a no-sex line between us before we even touch.

I know sleeping next to him will blur the line for me. Just being near him blurs the line.

And he's still waiting for my response. "I need you to be okay with this," he says.

I'm not even sure how to respond to that. It's more of a command than a question.

But maybe sleeping next to him won't be as awkward as I fear it will be? He seems calm and collected.

"Okay," I say softly. "Yes."

"Let me show you the rest."

He leads me through one of the two open archways on the wall to the right, both of which open into a single, massive walk-in closet. It's almost as big as the bedroom.

I move through the room, my pulse thudding, every cell in my body hyperaware of Jameson's nearness as he stands back, watching me.

It's like a private boutique in here. There's cleverly recessed lighting, built-in drawers and shelves, velvety ottomans for sitting on or draping clothing.

His on one side, hers on the other.

"Has this side always been empty?" I ask him. The woman's side has nothing in it except my bags. He hasn't mentioned much about his relationship history to me, but if I'm standing in some ex's closet, I'd like to know.

He slips his hands into his pockets. "Yes, it has. I told you I'm not looking to get married. I've had girlfriends, but never a live-in girlfriend." His eyes meet mine, and I look away.

I drift my fingers along the display case atop the island in the center of the room. The sleek glass top reveals velvet trays within for housing jewelry. It's empty, too.

I circle the island, until I face the twin entrances into the bedroom; his and hers. Through his, there's a clear view of the head of the bed.

And there are no doors to close for privacy.

Which means that if he was lying in the bed, he'd have a partial view into the closet.

The thought of him lying there, watching some former girlfriend get undressed, makes me slightly queasy.

Jealousy.

Which is weird since that imaginary woman isn't here. She's not his girlfriend anymore.

I'm not either.

"There are no doors," I point out.

"We each have our own bathroom. Mine's over there." He tips his chin toward the far corner, at the back of his side of the closet, where there's an open doorway. "Yours is through there." He nods at the identical doorway at the back corner of my side.

"Can I go look?"

"Of course."

I go through the doorway, which also has no door, and find a short hall to the left. It turns right, then left again, and opens into the large, airy bathroom. The top third of the walls have frosted windows letting in soft moonlight. As soon as I step onto the white tile, the lights come on, a soft, warm glow.

There's a large glassed-in shower and a freestanding bathtub, and a sitting area.

Anyone could wander in from the bedroom, no doors to imply

privacy, no sound made by footsteps at all. And watch whoever's in that glass shower.

Maybe that's the point.

Jameson has followed me into the room and watches me as I take it all in. Maybe he has a thing for watching?

My heart is beating so hard, I feel like he can see it.

I turn to him and try to sound calm. "You have something against doors?"

His tone remains neutral when he says, "If you need privacy, the toilet is through there." He indicates the lone actual door in the far corner. "There's enough room in there to get changed. And I won't come in here. This is your space."

"Okay."

"I'll let you get ready for bed. If there's anything you need, just let me know. It should be fully stocked. And feel free to put away your things. I would've had Clara unpack for you, but I thought you'd prefer if I checked with you first."

"I appreciate that. I'll unpack myself."

He nods. "I'll be in bed." He delivers those words in a low, soft voice, and heat flashes through my body.

I look away, feeling downright dizzy. "Good night."

There's the slightest pause. "Good night, Megan."

He slips out.

Goose bumps spread across my skin in the wake of his voice, and I stare at the open doorway where he disappeared.

I exhale.

Shit. This man.

Have I ever met anyone so freaking magnetic in all my life?

Nope.

My life has been spent in Crooks Creek, so no wonder. But still. No offense to Cole and Troy; they both come from where I do, and they're both attractive men. Hot men. I can admit that, even when one is my brother and the other hurt me immeasurably.

But Jameson Vance is a whole other conundrum.

It's ridiculous how little I actually breathe around the man. And now I've agreed to sleep in his bed.

Brilliant.

Maybe I'll die at the age of twenty-seven from lust-induced lack of oxygen.

I move around the bathroom, acquainting myself with the amenities. I poke my head into the room with the toilet, and he wasn't kidding. It's bigger than Nicole's whole bathroom. Plenty of room to change in privacy.

When I go back into the walk-in closet, I stay tucked into my side, out of the line of sight from the bed. I open my bags and unpack my cosmetics, and put them in the bathroom. Then I return to my suitcase to find a fresh pair of panties and my nightshirt. While doing so, I unpack all my clothes, hanging a few things on hangers and tucking the rest into drawers.

It doesn't take long.

In the bathroom, I turn on the shower. I wish I could close a door. But by the time the water is nice and warm, I've gotten over it.

He said he wouldn't come in here, that he'd be in bed. I have to believe him if this whole arrangement is going to work.

I slip the straps of my sundress over my shoulders and slide the whole thing down. Then I unclasp my bra and peel it off, and slip off my panties. All the while, I watch myself in the full-length mirror on the wall.

Wondering if Jameson would like what he sees.

If he walked in, to watch me in the shower...

There's nothing wrong with my body. Men's eyes tell me so, without their words even having to.

But Jameson is so... powerful. Not only is he physically outstanding himself, he's a wealthy man, and that gives him the opportunity to have his pick of women. According to Nicole, he's been with some famous beauties.

It's so hard to face the mirror and not just see Megan from Crooks Creek. I've only ever been loved by one man, a man who, in truth, didn't actually love me. And that man did so many numbers on my self-esteem, I'm still trying to rewrite the script that he etched into my heart with his hurtful words.

In the end, he told me he wasn't attracted to me anymore.

It would've hurt so much more if I hadn't fallen so out of love with him by then, so out of trust, that I didn't even know if I could believe him.

My gaze wanders down, to the soft flesh between my legs. It's so strange to think of a new man looking at me there, touching me, when only Troy had ever done that.

What would Jameson's touch feel like?

Would he be slow and careful? Fast and hungry? Would he be bossy, aggressive and alpha, taking what he wanted in a way that satisfied me so completely that I didn't even care? Or would he be tender, seeking out all the ways to drive me wild, before he took his fill?

Maybe he'd be all those things, depending on the mood, the situation. And the woman. How attracted to her he was. How impatient he was to have her.

How much he wanted to please her.

I'm dying to touch myself just to pretend it's him, exploring my body for the first time with his fingers...

Shit. Stop thinking about that.

Thinking about that, knowing Jameson is lying in his bed and I'm about to go lie in that bed with him, is making my core ache, and sucking all my attention to it.

God. *I'm horny.*

It's been so damn long since anyone touched me there.

Besides, well, me.

I tie my hair up into a loose bun and force myself into the shower, turning the temperature down to a cooler setting when the penetrating warmth only makes me internally hotter, my pulse throbbing insistently in my clit. I wash quickly with the bodywash on offer, leaving my hair dry.

I keep glancing at the open doorway, checking to see if I'm being watched. But Jameson doesn't appear.

When I finish in the shower, I dry off and slip into my fresh panties, then my nightshirt. I've never thought of it as sexy. It's a comfort item, soft cotton, ending halfway down my thighs. But when I turn in front of the mirror now, my breasts are pretty jiggly through the thin fabric. My nipples stick out.

I'm still horny.

I turn sideways to my reflection. I cut the sleeves out long ago, and the enlarged armholes show some side boob. I never really thought about that before. I've only ever worn it to sleep in front of Troy, and now Nicole.

Well, fuck. I don't want to be a tease.

Or worse, seem desperate, like I'm trying to seduce him or something.

Maybe he'll be asleep by now anyway. And if he isn't, I'll just be careful to keep the shirt in place so a boob doesn't pop out in his face.

I press my arms down at my sides and head into the bedroom.

As it turns out, Jameson is awake. He's lying on the side of the bed closest to the walk-in, the small lamp on his night table glowing over him.

He's on his back, the thin covers tucked up around his ribs, which means that his strong, gorgeous arms, his muscular, tattooed chest, and his ruddy-pink, lickable nipples are all bare.

He turns his head on his pillow to face me, and his eyes trace the jutting shape of my breasts through my shirt, his pupils big and dark in the dimly lit room. "Dirty," he says, almost to himself.

I tug self-consciously at the hem of the nightshirt, which is actually an old band shirt, trying to cover more of me. "Yeah. They're my favorite band."

He watches as I round the bed to my side and peel back the covers, carefully, so as not to expose more of him than is already exposed. But I'm dying to know what he's wearing under there.

"If only I'd known," he says dryly. "I could've introduced you to Jesse on day one, won you over right there."

I slip into the bed as he speaks, and now I'm trying to slide down under the covers without the boob on his side falling out. "What?"

"Jesse Mayes." He nods at my shirt. "I know him."

I drop my head on the pillow with a thud. My eyes go wide, the way I've seen Nicole's do at the mention of something she wants badly. "You know heartthrob Jesse Mayes? Dirty's lead guitarist and one of the sexiest men on planet Earth? Can I rethink this whole engagement?"

He half rolls his eyes.

"I'm kidding." I kill the cartoon-cat eyes. "It's not a big deal. Cole has introduced me to famous people."

"Glad to know you won't get too swept away," he mutters, "when you find out he's my neighbor."

"Really?" Honestly, I'm intrigued. Who wouldn't be? "On which side?"

"Not right next door. And hell if I'm telling you now." He reaches to turn off the lamp and the covers slip farther down his muscled rib cage. Before I can really enjoy the view, the light goes out.

"Hmm. Too bad. I am a bit of a voyeur."

Silence.

When he doesn't respond, heat creeps up my face as I mentally kick myself. It sounded funny, innocent in my head, but the fact that it's true—and maybe he can tell I meant it, even though it was a joke?—makes me deeply regret opening my mouth.

"Um. Did I mention I have no game?"

"You mentioned." His voice is low and rough. If I'm not wrong, there's a note of pain in it.

Am I making him uncomfortable?

Wait. Does talking about sex things make him uncomfortable?

Thinking back, it kinda seems so. Not that we've talked about much sex stuff.

Though maybe that was because he was uncomfortable...

"I was kidding," I clarify.

"Okay."

"I mean, I like to look at men. Attractive men. You know what I mean."

"You don't have to explain." The pained note is still there.

"He's attractive. It was a joke. I know he's married."

Silence.

But I just can't keep my mouth shut.

"I guess that was bad form. Telling my new fiancé, on our first night in our shared bed, that his neighbor is attractive and I want to spy on him. You know, sexually."

"It's okay, Megan," he grits out, which probably means *Shut up, Megan.*

Unfortunately, Megan isn't so good at shutting up when she feels like she just put her foot in her mouth. "I'm not gonna spy on him."

"You don't know where he lives."

"Yet."

He groans quietly.

"It just didn't occur to me that you might feel... bothered," I offer.

Silence again.

"I mean, since we're not even having sex. We don't have a sexual relationship. You know. For now."

More silence.

"But... I know I'm supposed to act like it's real, in public. At least, in terms of that kind of thing."

Just stop talking, Megan.

"Other guys, I mean. That's the thing I was referring to."

Stop digging this grave. You're way too uncool to make it better.

Somehow, I seem to think I can.

"I'm not... I'm not looking at other guys."

He sighs softly. "I didn't think you were. Until you said it."

Oh. *Oops.*

I can almost hear him thinking about it now.

I'm afraid to say anything else stupid, so I finally shut up.

"Megan?"

"Yes, Jameson?"

"Can we agree that checking out other guys in public is not cool? You're with me. My fiancée. *You're mine.* We're newly engaged and other guys are off the menu. You're in love with me, remember?"

"Right." I swallow, because every word he just semigrowled at me is making saliva flood my mouth and something else flood my panties. "I'll just look at you."

He shifts, kinda growling low in his throat. It's so sexy, I hold my breath to listen, savoring it.

"Good night, Megan."

"Good night."

I'm silent for maybe five seconds. But when I try to roll onto my side, my preferred sleeping position, my boob almost falls out of that damn gaping hole. What if he wakes up in the morning to find my boob out?

"You're very intimidating," I blurt in the dark. "How do I relax enough to fall asleep?"

"You're very honest." His words are underscored by a soft sigh.

"Is it too much?"

"No. It's good."

I've rolled to face him, and in the dim moonlight that slips in through a small gap in the curtains, I can see that he's facing me, too.

He runs a hand over his face, and I can feel his inaudible sigh. "Look, I'd never want to hurt someone Cole loves. And he loves you. I'd be good to you for his sake, even if I didn't like you."

I understand what he's saying. He's trying to reassure me that I don't need to worry so much. That I can relax here, because I'm safe with him.

And I try. I really do.

But it's not so much him I'm worried about.

Cole's best friend.

Business deal.

You're not going to grope him. Or flash your boob.

Just go to sleep.

"Shit." He swears under his breath. "That sounded really bad. I didn't mean to imply..." He fades out.

"Imply what?"

I hear him breathing softly in the dark, and it may be the hottest thing I've ever heard.

Is he feeling the same tension I am, lying here so close?

"I like you," he breathes.

"I like you, too," I say instantly.

No game.

Silence stretches between us.

"Um... so, if you change your mind about that thing you said... about us not having sex, for now..." I take a breath, letting that dangle in the dark between us for a long moment. In case he feels the need to interject.

He doesn't.

"That's okay with me," I continue. "I just want you to know that. I guess what I'm saying is I'd like first dibs, please. If you decide to have sex with someone. You know, me or someone else. You said we'd discuss it first. So, I'm discussing it. And I'd like first dibs." I take another breath and let the words flow that I just need to put out there. "You can touch me if you decide you want to."

He doesn't respond right away.

Then he swears again.

"Jesus Christ, Megan. You really need to stop saying exactly what you're thinking."

"I didn't. I was thinking much more than that."

"Holy fuck." He mutters the words under his breath and rolls onto his back, then tosses his arms over his eyes and lies still.

I blink at him in the dark, watching his chest slowly rise and fall. I can still hear him breathing.

I heard the strain in his voice, the way it changed, taking on that pained note again. This is uncomfortable for him, too. He's trying to be a gentleman for Cole. I'm certain of it.

It's not that he doesn't want me.

He's just not going to fuck his best friend's sister the first chance he gets.

Knowing it just makes me like him more.

I try not to say that, so instead, I say, "This whole fake engagement might turn out to be the stupidest thing we've ever done. You realize that, right?"

He huffs out a soft laugh. "Yeah. I'm starting to get that." He adds roughly, "You still in?"

I can hear the grudging smile on his voice.

"Yes." I sigh sleepily, finally relaxing as a strange, nameless current of warmth spreads through my body. "I'm in."

I realize as I drift into sleep that it's happiness.

CHAPTER 20

Jameson

Sleeping next to Megan without being able to touch her? Stupid isn't even the word for it.

This is much, much worse than stupid.

I can't sleep.

My cock throbs, half-hard, teased by the constraint of my boxer briefs, the cool weight of the light summer sheets, the awareness of her lush body so close to mine.

Even with a careful space between us, I can smell her soft feminine smell, and it's driving me wild. It's a hint of the same bodywash I use, which she obviously showered with, and her own natural scent. It makes my mouth water.

I want to devour her whole.

My cock wants to plunge deep inside her warmth and stay all night.

I stir, agitated. I'm not used to sleeping with underwear on. It's snug and annoying.

My whole body thuds with the urge to release all this tension. I can't believe how loud my heartbeat is in the dark.

She's been silent a long while. The clock on my nightstand says it's after midnight. I haven't slept a second since we got into bed.

I just keep thinking about everything she said tonight.

How cute she is.

And how fucking brave.

I'd like first dibs.

You can touch me if you decide you want to.

Fuck me. Why the hell did she have to say that shit?

I like an honest woman.

Actually, there's probably nothing I value more in a relationship with a woman than mutual trust.

But shit.

She's so sweet and earnest. So kind and considerate.

She also has a lack of ego that's fucking refreshing given the people I usually spend time with.

And no list of Megan Hudson's finest qualities would ever be complete without mention of her petite but luscious body. Those high, bouncy tits jiggling under that thin shirt. That plump, round ass. Those goddamn creamy thighs.

And I'm starting to realize that those aren't even the most beautiful things about her.

Though she's here for the money, at the end of the day, she's not really here for the money. She clearly has morals and values that even staggering amounts of cash couldn't sway.

She's here because she imagines a better future for herself, one year from now, even though her past hasn't been all that good to her.

I admire the hell out of that.

That unshakable optimism.

He cheated on me.

I realize I'm grinding my teeth as I replay what she told me about her ex. Not only did he steal from her, he cheated on her, too. She could be bitter and broken, guarded as hell from the shit she's been through.

Like me.

But she's not.

It doesn't help matters that she's got the most beautiful eyes I've ever fucking seen, those light-amber eyes that just get more beautiful every time she stares at me like she's melting from the heat between us.

Thoughts like these are not helping the erection situation.

Every time I think about that look, and her soft, supple body under the sheets, her warm pussy so fucking close to me, my cock grows hard, aching, and hungry.

Like it is right now.

I breathe through it, trying to think about something else.

Harlan.

He emailed me about some bullshit today. On a fucking Saturday. He wants receipts for the last party I threw on the yacht. As if the CFO of a multibillion-dollar company chases anyone for receipts. He has minions for that.

He just likes crawling up my ass any chance he can get.

There. The hard-on has definitely softened.

Then Megan stirs in her sleep, and my cock throbs again.

I can't go on like this.

I'll get no sleep.

That, or I'll fall asleep, get hard again and maybe come all over the sheets in the night. I haven't had a wet dream since puberty, but I wouldn't put it outside the realm of possibility under the circumstances.

An image of Megan pops into my head—my come dripping down her naked tits.

It's stunningly easy to picture.

My cock throbs with want.

I roll onto my side, away from her, and grab the tablet from my nightstand, along with my glasses. I crank the screen brightness way down so I won't bother her and start reading as a distraction.

It rains that day, and our trek is slow.

Late morning, I find a cave to wait out the rain. Neither of us wants to be inside or wants to sit.

So we stand, restless, at the mouth of the cave beneath an over-

hang of rock, where we're dry. Her to one side of the cave and me to the other.

We don't look at each other.

There's an urgency building to get to our destination, maybe because we both know we're almost halfway there. And something's changing between us, the balance tipping so fast, if we just keep going, maybe we think we can somehow outrun the inevitable.

It's been different since I talked to her like I did the other night. Since she touched herself while I talked her through it.

Since she came as I guided her there.

"How is it you know nothing about sex?" I sound irritable and angry, which is exactly how I feel. I'm getting shittier at hiding it. The miserable weather isn't helping.

"I never said I know nothing about it."

"The other night, I was afraid I was gonna have to draw you a map."

"Well, we don't exactly get a sex tent for our sixteenth birthday in my tribe," she snaps. "My mother died when I was six years old. My father died when I was eleven, and he always treated me like some angel who was too good for every boy in the world. He was hardly going to tell me about sex. My brothers only ever talk about themselves. And my Aunt Rose left when I was twelve. All she ever told me was to stay away from savages."

"And did you?"

She just keeps staring out into the woods, avoiding my eyes. "Until now."

"You don't need to be embarrassed about what happened."

"I'm not."

"Then why won't you look at me?"

Finally, she looks at me.

"What you did, people do it all the time," I tell her.

"It just... feels weird."

"What does?"

"Taking pleasure from myself. Using my body that way."

"You talk about it like your cunt's not part of you. Like it's not you." My gaze skims down her body and back up to her pretty face.

The longer we're out here... the wilder she gets, her uncombed golden hair falling loose from the terrible braids she still struggles to make... the prettier she becomes.

"I know it's me," she says softly.

"Then you should touch it more. You should look at it. Get used to it."

"What do you mean, look at it?"

"Have you ever really looked at what's between your legs?" Her silence is my answer. *"Because you should. You should touch yourself and watch, over and over again."*

"Why would I do that?"

"Because you should know what you like, before someone else decides for you."

I shut the cover on the tablet.

I glance over my shoulder at Megan, lying asleep next to me.

I'm really starting to like this Wolf guy. Not only has he saved Rowan's life like a dozen times already, he gives solid sex advice.

And the way Megan's mind works...

I slip off my glasses and rub my eyes. They're sore from reading in the dark, and I'm hard as hell.

Fuck it.

I have to end this torture.

As quietly as I can, I slip out of the bed, careful not to wake her. I don't want to wake her when I walk across the hard floor, so I take a moment to make sure she's sleeping soundly before I go.

I turn to the window, taking a deep, quiet breath.

In the stillness of the night, here with her, I know this whole thing is going to be way harder than I thought.

Having her near me is too much temptation.

And I never would've thought she'd be so willing, so damn fast. I thought telling her we wouldn't have sex would put her at ease, and put her off. She didn't seem like the kind of girl to jump into such things, or to push for them.

Eleven years with one man, for Christ's sake. One man who turned out to be a cheating, abusive dipshit.

And now she wants "first dibs" on being my next lover.

I wonder if he took care of her in bed. If he was good to her that way. Or if their sex life fizzled out long ago.

And why she's so damn willing to let me touch her.

The possible reasons for that don't help.

Maybe he was a terrible lover. Maybe he wasn't even having sex with her anymore, just cheating with other people.

Maybe she hasn't had good sex, or any sex, in way too long.

Thinking about it just makes me want to fuck her even more than I already do, to show her how good it should be.

If I'm not fucking careful...

Thirty-one days.

I glance at her again. I can see her face in the moonlight, snuggled into her pillow. Her eyes are closed.

I ease into the walk-in, then on into my bathroom, emerging into the cool moonlit space as the automatic lights come up. The nighttime setting is a soft glow that doesn't quite reach the corners of the room.

It insulates me, makes me feel an aspect of privacy that isn't really there.

But I can be quiet.

I blow out the breath I've been holding. What the fuck am I doing?

If I run the shower, I might wake her. And she knows I already had a shower tonight, when she got me out of the pool.

Sitting on the toilet to jerk off in hiding just seems fucking lame.

But my cock is not going to let me put the idea aside.

I turn to the mirror over the sink.

I've really fucked myself over here.

I thought the whole engagement idea checked off so many boxes. That it was brilliant, on so many levels. Maybe I let Graysen convince me of that.

But Graysen isn't the one who has to share a bed with Megan while not having sex with her.

Fucking ridiculous.

If I knew she was coming here tonight, maybe I would've relieved myself of this tension in preparation.

But maybe I didn't fully realize, or want to acknowledge, how much tension there would actually be, until she got into my bed.

I hook my fingers into my boxer briefs and tug them down.

CHAPTER 21

Megan

I wake to something moving. A shuffle of fabric, whisper-soft, and the sensation of nearness. A body in the dark, somewhere next to me.

I open my eyes to a soft haze of moonlight filtering through the slit in the curtains.

Jameson stands next to the bed, one arm stretched above his head as he leans against the window, like he's looking out.

He doesn't have a shirt on.

His side is to me. I can see his beautifully muscled body, down to his trim waist and hips, and the boxer briefs he's wearing.

The bulge in front looks thick.

His head turns my way, and I shut my eyes. I'm not even sure why I don't want him to catch me watching him. But I keep them closed as his soft footsteps pad across the room and fade away.

I open my eyes. I'm sure he went into the walk-in closet.

I listen, hearing nothing but the pounding of my own heart.

What is he doing?

The glowing clock on his night table tells me it's the middle of the night. If he got up to use the bathroom, why was he just standing there at the window?

And looking at me?

I peel back the covers in silence, with the buzzing awareness that something's happening. I feel his restless energy in his wake, like a ripple of heat in the night.

Why isn't he sleeping?

I creep toward the walk-in and listen, but I still don't hear anything. If he was getting dressed in there, I'd hear it, right?

I move quietly, trying to think up some excuse in case I smash right into him. I heard him get up and came to see if he's okay, that's all. There's nothing wrong with that.

So why do I feel guilty as I steal through the closet?

Because he's not in here.

Which means he continued on, into his bathroom or mine, and I'm about to follow him.

I go for his, and tiptoe along the twisting hall, still hearing nothing. If he's using the toilet, he'll be in that room with the door shut, and I'll just run back to bed.

But my heart is pounding because somehow, I know he's not using the toilet.

And I'm about to spy on him.

He won't be showering. He showered when I arrived tonight. If he turns on the shower, he's definitely masturbating.

But no water turns on.

I hear something. Like the soft sound of feet shifting on the tile, from within the bathroom.

I creep to the edge of the wall and peek around the corner. His bathroom is large and pristine, a mirror image of mine.

And standing in the middle of it is Jameson.

As I watch, he hooks his thumbs into his boxer briefs and tugs them down. His swollen cock and balls bounce free, and I hear his rough, pleasured breath.

Anticipation.

My heart lodges in my throat as the same feeling rises in me, on a wave of heat.

He drops the underwear and steps out of it.

With a panther's grace, he stalks silently to the wide marble counter, his side to me as I cling to the edge of the wall, hidden from view, out of reach of the lights. His long, strong body is completely bare, and I stare.

He's *big*. Bigger than what I'm used to.

I've never seen any man's naked cock in the flesh except Troy's.

Jameson is taller than Troy, more muscular, and his cock is thicker, longer. It's partially erect, swollen, the plump head bobbing with each step. His balls bounce heavily against the fronts of his thighs, fat and full.

I'm instantly intoxicated by the sight of him, as the sexual response floods my system with chemicals, making me shaky, needy, hungry.

I shouldn't be spying on him. He didn't spy on me. But I stare, and I can't stop myself.

He stands directly in front of the sink. There's a large mirror above, and he seems to be looking down, with heavily lidded eyes, at his cock in the reflection. He spreads his feet, stabilizing himself, his thighs pressed to the marble counter, his cock over the sink.

I know what he's about to do, and I still can't look away. I'm too transfixed by his naked body, his virility, his obvious arousal.

And the overwhelming desire I feel for him.

His hand goes to his balls. He huffs softly, a gruff sound of relief, as his fingers slide over the swollen sac. That sound he makes goes straight between my legs, and my core pulses in response. I can feel myself growing swollen, wet, as I watch him swell.

He squeezes his balls, and his cock bounces, straining. The thick length flexes, stiffening, and he hasn't even touched it yet.

I know I shouldn't be watching this.

I can't stop.

He pulls on his heavy sac, stretching it and squeezing. Then he runs his other hand up the length of his thick shaft, all the way to the head, and back down, a groan lodging in his throat, the sound sending a shiver down my spine.

He's pleasuring himself.

After he told me we wouldn't have sex.

Clearly, something stirred him to arousal. But he didn't try anything with me.

I told him he could touch me. And considering how uncomfortable he'd seemed sharing a bed, I'm starting to think he finds me attractive. Maybe very attractive?

Which means... he's doing this out of respect for me?

I watch his hands expertly work his own body, sliding along his shaft, squeezing his balls, as his cock grows stiffer, angrier. He's breathing heavily, his chest rising and falling, his entire body tensed, his muscles tight, as he teases himself.

As his fingers slide up and down, his cock responds, standing up tall, his hips flexing restlessly, his swollen sac tightening. He looks every inch the virile man he is, primed, aroused, and probably aching to ejaculate.

And here he is, alone.

I'm utterly fascinated by this.

Troy never put my comfort, my feelings of safety and security, much less happiness, before his own pleasure. I knew that was wrong. Eventually, I admitted it to myself.

But I've still never experienced anything different.

It's eye-opening.

Moving, in a way I can't explain.

There's a part of me that knows I should go back to bed, stop watching this. But there's no way I can tear myself away as my heartbeat thuds in my throat.

I wasn't joking that I'm a voyeur. I love to watch.

It was one of my favorite things, watching Troy masturbate.

Of course, Troy always knew I was there, watching. He liked putting on a show for me.

Right up until the day he put on his final show—not solo—and I walked away.

Guilt trips through me; I don't want to think about that now.

I also don't want to betray Jameson's trust.

But still, I can't back away.

He knows there's no door. And I try to convince myself that

there's some small part of him that knows I could walk in on this, that I might watch. That in that knowledge, he's wordlessly consenting to let me watch.

If he wanted total privacy, he'd go into the room with the toilet, right?

But he doesn't.

And I've never watched a guy touch himself like that before.

Drawing it out. Stroking so deliberately, so slowly, reveling in the feel of his own fingers sliding from root to tip and back again.

A groan rumbles in his throat, and his cock jerks. He wraps his hand around his shaft and slows way down.

And I wonder what he's thinking.

I try to imagine how that thick shaft with the fat, blunt head would feel, shoving into me instead of his hand. Forcing me open, stretching me. Pummeling into me, over and over, as those heavy balls slap against me.

His breath catches on another stifled groan as he squeezes the wide base of his shaft in his fist. The hard length jerks again, and my core contracts with longing.

His hips buck, grinding his thighs against the counter... like he's imagining grinding into something else.

CHAPTER 22

Jameson

I fuck my cock into my fist, imagining it's Megan I'm thrusting into.

Megan's pussy, tight and hot.

There's so much precome, my hand is slick with it. Slick, like her pussy would be.

My strokes grow brutal, tight and fast, my eyes closed as I imagine fucking her against this sink, her creamy thighs spread high and wide, her fingers spreading her tight little pussy open to take all of me.

I tug on my sac, imagining her playing with it, loving the warm weight of it in her small, soft hands.

Then I let it drop and tip my head back as I jack myself greedily, hammering my hips forward as I fuck that tight little pussy in my mind.

My ball sac slaps heavily against my thighs, and now I imagine it slapping against Megan's sensitive little clit as I fuck her from behind.

I pull on my cock, slowing my hands and trying to catch my breath. I'm about to blow, and I don't want it to end yet. I'm too lost in the ecstasy of fucking her in my head.

One more tentative squeeze of my fist, and I almost go over. My hips buck, my ass clenches, and I swallow the growl that rumbles up my throat.

I have to be quiet enough that she won't hear me. I don't want to wake her with the obscene sounds of me fucking myself like an animal while she sleeps, and terrify her on night one.

I squeeze my cock again, trying to force the urgency back now, but my whole body shakes with the effort.

Too late.

I lock my hips, tensing.

I picture her beneath me in bed, that thin shirt riding up over her hips. She's moaning in pleasure, urging me to come, her pussy spread for me as I pump into her and let go...

I come, choking on what would've been a shout if I didn't swallow it. The climax is so intense, my whole body jerks as my balls contract. My cock strains in my hand, spasming.

I feel the hot jets of release lashing over my knuckles, dribbling down my thighs, the spasms gripping me again and again.

As I empty myself into the air, I test out her name. *Megan.* It rolls around in my head.

But I won't let myself utter it between the choked-off grunts of pleasure.

CHAPTER 23

Megan

Jameson's ass flexes as he ruts his swollen cock into his fist, and a choked groan of pleasure escapes his throat as he ejaculates.

A thick rope of semen lashes the air, then another, splattering the mirror, the sink. He chokes back soft, pleasured grunts, milking himself with long, luscious pulls that make his tense, muscled arm shake.

His eyes remain closed.

His hand slows, squeezing out another spurt of cream and the accompanying grunt of pleasure. Then a few more strokes, slower now, as a shudder runs through his body.

His muscled ass finally relaxes, and the taut muscles along his arm do, too.

He huffs out a breath and releases his cock, a gruff, masculine sound of satisfaction. His cock bobs heavily, still swollen and half-hard as he leans, pressing his hands to the sink. He's breathing hard, his head pitched forward.

I don't dare move or make a sound as I stare.

He's so beautiful. Perfect. His muscled body moist with sweat, his cock heavy, sated, a sticky coating of semen gleaming wetly on the flushed crown.

I want to suckle it. Lick up every drop.

A man like that should be taken care of, every drop of semen savored, not wasted.

But it's hot as hell that his ejaculate is all over the sink and mirror, all over his body. It's primal.

He chose a place where he thought he was alone and wouldn't bother me. He could've used something, come into a tissue or his hand. But because he's alpha, he just stood there naked and let himself shoot freely, releasing all over what's in front of him.

My lips are swollen; I've been rubbing them with my teeth, and I drag my tongue across them. I breathe as quietly as I can, soft, fast, shallow breaths.

My panties are soaked.

It's so hard to tear my attention away, but I'm terrified he'll see me.

I need to go.

I turn and hurry back to the bed, my pulse flying. I would've died if he caught me there, watching him.

And yet nothing could've torn me away while I watched, soaking up every pleasured breath, every twitch of his muscles, every pulse of his cock.

That was the hottest thing I've ever seen, by miles.

My core pulses with need, but I slip back into bed before it occurs to me that maybe I should go into my own bathroom and make myself come.

My pulse thuds loudly through my body, and I hear nothing from his bathroom. I'm afraid to move. To have him return to find me gone, to know that I'm up.

And even more afraid that if I try to slip out of the bed, he'll walk in right at that moment, and I'll have to face him.

So I remain still, lying under the covers on my side of the bed with my heart thumping.

Long minutes pass while I barely breathe.

The ache between my legs only grows worse as everything I just witnessed replays, again and again. I see him in my mind, naked, so expertly pleasuring himself, bringing himself to orgasm.

I can hardly believe I watched him come.

And if I don't stop thinking about it, this is going to be a very long and painful sleepless night.

I hear the soft padding of his feet on the smooth floor, and I know he's trying to be quiet as he slips back into the room. I don't dare peek to see if he's still naked.

He moves slowly, carefully into the bed, obviously trying not to disturb me.

I wait, breathless, until he settles.

Then I wait some more.

The entire time, my clit throbs. My pussy is swollen and wet.

There's no way I can sleep like this.

Carefully, my fingers steal to my clit and stroke through the thin cotton of my panties, unable to stop themselves. Just trying to ease the ache.

But it's not enough.

My other hand steals quietly to the rescue and tugs down my panties, baring my clit for my trembling fingers.

As my fingertips drift over my clit, a featherlight touch is all I dare.

But I must make a sound or something.

His low, rough whisper makes me freeze. "You okay?"

"Fine," I whisper back. My voice is thick with desire, but it probably sounds sleepy.

"Sorry if I woke you," he breathes.

"Mm."

The covers slide over me as he shifts, relaxing into the bed with a soft, rugged sigh, and the fabric brushes my clit, sending tingles of pleasure and awareness through my body. He touched the fabric, which touched me, and it's enough to send me tumbling down the rabbit hole.

There's no way I can resist this.

My fingers drift over my clit, the swollen softness and the sensitive bud within. I tease it with my fingertips, tentatively, gently, making no noise or movement that disturbs the bed or the covers.

My core, deep inside, clenches in response.

I'm going to come. I need to. Badly.

I need relief from this terrible, throbbing ache, and I can do it quickly, quietly.

I've learned how.

In bed, next to Troy, in those long, dark periods when he refused to touch me. When he shut me out.

Don't think about him.

I picture Jameson vividly. I see his cock in his hand, so distinctly his. Long, thick, virile. Straining with arousal, with the need to come. Precome beading wetly on the lush head, his balls swollen and full, more than ready to fill a girl to overflowing.

I imagine him guiding himself toward my opening and then the flex of those strong hips, the clench of that muscular ass, as he shoves himself deep inside me. The heat of him and the weight. His heavy balls slapping wetly against my drenched, dripping pussy.

That wonderful, pleasured grunt of his when he discovers how wet for him I am...

I lock my hips tight as pleasure explodes between my legs. I hold my breath and I'm flying. I'm coming silently in the bed, right next to him, my body outwardly still while my core clenches with deep, shuddering spasms, one after another... the muscles inside me clutching, wanting the fullness of his rigid cock... my intense emptiness aching right through the pleasure.

I think of how he came, those luscious jets of semen.

I imagine him emptying himself inside me like that, in long, hot pulses that make him shake.

Would he grunt with each spurt like he did in the bathroom, restrained, fighting the ecstasy?

Or would he let go, releasing with a full-throated growl, shouting his pleasure, purring my name?

As I tease my clit through the contractions that rack my core and leave my panties a slick, drenched mess, I don't dare make a sound.

I don't move or jerk the bed. I don't disturb him.

I don't let on that I'm coming long and hard, my head spinning with pleasure, right next to him.

After I've teased out every twinge of pleasure I can with featherlight caresses, I slip my panties into place and push my nightshirt down. I roll onto my side, away from him, to cover the movement.

But my heart pounds so hard, I'm afraid he'll feel the bed trembling with the force of it, and know how badly I want him.

CHAPTER 24

Megan

I jerk awake, startled, and blink in the faint morning light.

There's a man standing over me.

Jameson.

"Hey." His husky, velvet voice, low and soothing, caresses my senses. "Good morning, Miss Rivers."

He seems to be speaking to me.

I look around groggily. There's no one else in the room. "Who's Miss Rivers?"

"You are. Jessica Rivers. Future bestselling author."

Oh. Right. My pen name.

No one calls me Jessica, much less Miss Rivers.

Just him.

I blink at him. He stands by his side of the bed, diffused sunlight playing across his flexing abs as he pulls on a T-shirt. My gaze follows his hands as he smooths the shirt down, covering the generous package in the front of his boxer briefs.

Is he covering up for my benefit?

Well, little does he know that I've already seen it all, and have zero problem with any of it. Guilt creeps through me, but I try to swallow it down. How can I not admire him?

Every solid inch of the man is delectable.

His wavy hair is mussed, and he looks sleepy, incredibly sexy.

I instantly wonder if I have bedhead. And morning breath.

I push myself up on my hands, trying to function as I suck in a deep breath of the morning air that breezes in through the stirring curtains. "My gosh. That air. Is this paradise? This is the most comfortable bed I've ever slept in."

The smile that flickers across Jameson's face is devastating.

Holy Christ, he needs to smile more. Even if it kills me. Swooning to death seems like a decent way to go.

"I'm going to get dressed and shave. Meet me on the balcony for coffee in fifteen?"

"Okay."

When he turns away, I stare at his firm, toned butt. Which I can now picture naked, vividly. Flexing as he chased his release. Clenching as he ejaculated long and hard...

God.

Everything that happened in the night returns to me in a hot rush.

He disappears into the walk-in, and I collapse back on the bed with a *maybe-I've-died-and-gone-to-heaven* moan. The sheets smell of lavender and *him*. Sexy alpha male. I didn't even notice in my nervousness last night.

Waking up to him, and feeling so damn good about it, peels back another layer of my uncertainty. I can feel it falling away like so much useless resistance.

We slept side by side, in the same bed, and we survived.

I mean, I came my brains out and he didn't know that I knew that he did the same thing, and I watched.

But hey, we survived.

Which means we're getting comfortable with each other, bit by bit.

Maybe it's not that big a deal to him, but it is to me. I've never shared a bed with any man but Troy, and the last few years, I didn't feel very safe, relaxed, or happy in that bed.

Right now, I'm relaxed. I slept like a baby.

I try to tell myself it's the incredibly soft sheets and the lavender. And of course, the deep, intense, rolling orgasm in the middle of the night.

But Jameson put me at ease. He gets credit for that.

Which just makes me more uneasy that I spied on him last night, watched him in that intimate, private act. I'd kidded myself in the heat of the moment that maybe he was okay with it. Because, no doors.

But that was just a desperate excuse from a horny woman.

There's no excuse for keeping something like that from him. It doesn't even matter if he minds that I watched or not. It's dishonest not to tell him.

But hell if I want to confess.

What if he gets mad? Embarrassed?

Asks me to leave?

All I know is he said he's not having sex with me. *Yet.* I have no idea how he'd feel about me perving on him while he jerked off.

But I know I don't want to leave. I'd be downright sad if he asked me to go, and pissed at myself for ruining this.

As I start to slide out of bed, I barely register the bedroom door opening before Clara strides in.

I startle, covering myself with the sheet as I do a quick side-boob check. Luckily, I'm covered, because she's followed by a man.

He wears a white coat similar to Chef's, and pushes a rolling food service cart in front of him, but he doesn't look my way. Dishes rattle as he swiftly maneuvers the cart to the balcony. He opens the doors wide, letting in more fresh air and sunlight, and rolls it right outside.

"Good morning, Miss Hudson," Clara says professionally. "I trust you had a nice sleep?"

"Uh, yes. Thank you."

"If there's anything at all I can do to make your nights more comfortable, please let me know."

"I-I will."

"Shall I get the shower running for you or draw you a bath?"

When I just stare at her, she prompts, "I can select an outfit for you and have it accessorized and ready for you when you step out."

"Um." I struggle with this information. "I don't really have any accessories. I'm fine getting dressed on my own. But thank you."

In the back of my mind, all I can think is *Jameson cleaned up his mess last night, right? He wouldn't leave that for his staff to deal with?*

We stare at each other for a moment as my face flushes.

"I'll get that shower running." Clara turns on her heel and disappears into my bathroom, and a moment later, I hear the shower water distantly flowing.

When she emerges to find me still clutching the sheet to my collarbone, she suggests, "How about this? There's a dressing gown in the bathroom for you. If you require any assistance or have any questions or concerns, simply pick up that phone." She indicates the one on my night table. "Dial six and you'll get my office. Or you can simply text me. That's Mr. Vance's preferred way of reaching me. I'll send you my number right now."

She pulls out a phone and taps out a text.

"I... thank you." I'm not sure what else to say. I've never had a woman I barely know bustle into my room the moment I wake to offer to help bathe and dress me.

Jameson must've given her my phone number. And asked her to come help me get my day started?

"My pleasure." Clara departs, along with the food guy, shutting the door behind them, and I exhale. Then I force myself out of the luxurious bed.

I had a shower last night, but that was before I watched Jameson make himself come, gushed in my panties, and masturbated. A quick rinse and fresh panties are definitely on the agenda before that coffee.

And just maybe... some kind of outfit that'll make Jameson want to play with his dick again would be grand.

The multiple showerheads pound down on my muscles, warming my skin and massaging me to buttery contentment. By the time I dry off and head out to the balcony clean and refreshed, light makeup on, I feel reborn.

Billionaire life is working for me, so far.

Especially the billionaire himself.

I find Jameson alone on the balcony. My belly does a happy little flip at the sight of him, relaxed and waiting for me, lounging back on a cushioned outdoor dining chair. His sunglasses are pushed up onto his head, and the breeze licks at the waves of his hair.

Apparently, his idea of "shaving" is trimming his light layer of blondish stubble, and I am here for it. The man has the exact right amount of almost-beard for my liking.

I'm usually not a total morning person, but my eyes could die happy waking to a sight like this.

The balcony is in partial sun, and he squints a little in the bright morning light, his eyes following me as I settle into the chair opposite his at the table for two.

Then his gaze moves down, settling for a moment on my breasts.

I wore my most gravity-defying push-up bra with my most low-cut sundress. The one with the straps that always fall off my shoulders. Like they're already doing now, the top few buttons popped open so that my cleavage jiggles in his face when I sit down.

I dressed this way after a brief argument with myself in the walk-in, because I'm winging it here and I decided that being a tease might not be so bad after all. Not if it gets a reaction like what happened last night.

Because that was a hell of a reaction.

The man either hasn't come in ages, is naturally high yield when it comes to semen, or he was just that worked up about my presence in his bed.

I'm really hoping for that last thing, because at least that means we're suffering in the same boat.

"Enjoy your shower?" His eyes skip away, then land on my breasts again as if drawn by magnets as I lean forward to take a sip of water. There's no trace of anything he might be thinking or feeling in his tone.

He's very practiced that way.

But after last night, I feel like I got a glimpse behind the curtain.

He's used to being highly composed, in control, but I saw him lose that composure completely. I saw him helpless to the orgasm he'd unleashed, his body racked with pleasure, muscles clenched and gleaming with sweat as he came. Grunting with the over-whelming release as he struggled to keep quiet, and failed.

I realize he's staring at me, a good half minute too late.

What did he just say?

"Um, the shower is amazing. I hope I wasn't making weird noises in there. It was so luxurious. I wasn't touching myself or anything, I swear."

Holy Christ. Did I just say that?

My cheeks flush hot.

"I mean... not that I..."

Just stop, Megan.

The heat in his eyes as they graze over my cleavage, then my lips, hones into something hungrier before his gaze skips away to focus on the food.

"Glad you enjoyed it." His tone is still neutral.

Very practiced.

"This is amazing." I change the subject, admiring the spread before us. "Coffee," as it turns out, is nothing short of a gourmet breakfast for two, complete with omelets in little skillets, an array of meats, cheeses, fruits, and pastries.

"I had Chef roll out some things I thought you might like. Rurik noticed you went to the market for fresh food a lot."

"Yes. Spies are handy that way." I eye him sidelong.

He lets it pass.

"We've got fresh berries, jam, honey, ham, eggs, everything

sourced locally. I thought you might like a taste of what Vancouver has to offer."

"It looks fabulous, thank you. What more could a newly engaged woman ask for on her first morning as a fiancée?" I smile tentatively.

He smiles back, but it doesn't quite reach his eyes. It seems like something's troubling him.

It always seems that way, really.

I wonder if he's always stressed out because of the pressures he lives with. Financial pressures. Family pressures. Fame, or infamy, depending on how you look at the kind of media attention he seems to get.

Yet he suddenly seems concerned about me, his brows drawing together. "If there's anything you'd like, anything you want to be different, just let me know."

"Thank you. I will. This all might just take an adjustment period. I'm not used to being catered to at this level." *And by someone like you.*

"Well, you'll get used to it."

I doubt that.

With that, we dig in, and I make it my mission to sample everything on offer. Jameson watches me eat, his attention skipping between my face and my breasts.

Maybe I've overdone it with the open buttons. Without the straps holding it up, the dress is gradually slipping down and my bra is actually showing, along with the generous upper half of my boobs. But I just keep eating. I'm hungry.

Finally, I dab at my mouth with a napkin and sit back. "I can't eat any more. I'm sorry. I'm stuffed."

He says nothing, just sips his coffee, a strangely black expression in his light-blue eyes. It's confounding. I'm seriously not sure if he's irritated with me about something or wants to fuck me up against the wall.

Intense.

"So," I venture nervously. "It's Sunday. What do you do on a Sunday?"

"Whatever I want to do."

The weight of his gaze makes me want to squirm, but I try not to.

"There's nothing that needs your attention right now? Work? Billionaire stuff?"

"Maybe I just want to enjoy my fiancée." He hasn't taken his eyes off me. "Megan..." His voice is low and heated. "I can see your nipple and it's driving me crazy."

I look down. The perky demicups of my bra are indeed showing, my boobs spilling out of them. It might be a good vibe, seduction-wise, except the right one is spilling *over* and my nipple has popped out.

"Oh my god." I cover my breast with my hand.

Jameson tears his eyes away.

I try to keep my voice calm when I ask him, "How long has it been out?" I jiggle my boob back into place while he politely keeps his eyes averted.

"I'm sorry, that was rude of me." His voice is tight. "I don't mean to flirt."

So, a while, then.

Great.

Bra in place, I slip the straps of my dress back up onto my shoulders. *What am I doing?* I'm no seductress. "You couldn't have told me sooner?"

He swallows thickly. "It was distracting. My brain wasn't working."

I fasten the little buttons on the bodice of my dress and take a breath, confused by all his mixed signals.

No flirting. Okay.

But my boobs are killing his brain functioning. Okay?

He's attracted to me.

But he doesn't want to be?

Or something.

I clear my throat, grasping for something to say. Make a joke? Deflect? Apologize for my slutty breakfast attire?

I go with "I guess I'll need to be more careful. You know, when we're in public."

He finally looks at me again, like he's afraid I'll be sitting here naked. His gaze flicks down to my now-contained breasts and back up. "We won't be in public a lot. But when we are, yes, it'll be different from what you're used to."

"I'll try not to let a nipple pop out."

His jaw flexes. I suppose he didn't find that funny.

"People will come after you, try to get photos, ask you questions. That gets worse if you start showing off your... body." His eyes drop briefly to my cleavage again, like he can't help himself.

"And how do I deal with those people coming after me?"

"You don't," he says gruffly. "My security team will take care of it. Locke is the head of my team, and that kind of thing is now his concern, not yours. You don't have to worry about a thing."

"So, Clara and your security guys and Chef, they'll really all think we're engaged?"

"Of course." He searches my face. "Does that bother you?"

"No. I guess not. But I won't lie to Cole. Since his little sister is now engaged to his best friend, and he introduced us so recently, I feel like we both owe him the respect of telling him the truth."

"Of course. I already told Cole."

"What?" I almost choke on my coffee.

"Just now. While you were in the shower." He sips his coffee and seems to misinterpret my shock when he says, "Don't worry. Cole will honor our privacy. So will my staff. They all sign nondisclosures, so even if they gleaned that the engagement was fake, they wouldn't talk."

"Right. Okay. But we could've told Cole together."

His eyes sharpen as he studies me. I'm not sure if he's irritated by my tone or what. That black look is back, and it seems half hot and half cold.

But then he nods. "You're right. I apologize. Next time, we'll do that. But if we want this to work, I think it's best we keep the circle of people who know the details very small."

I consider that. "So, I shouldn't tell my friends or my mom?"

"I think it's best if you don't. But I'll leave that up to your discretion. What's the point of any relationship at all if we can't trust each other?"

I like that. "And what about your family? Your other friends? Will you tell them?"

"Friends, no. I won't lie to them outright, but they don't need to know the details. But family... it's just not in me to be dishonest with them. They deserve the truth on this." He takes another sip of coffee, and I can sense the tension there.

"I understand if you don't want to get into detail about your love life with your siblings," I offer.

"I usually don't."

"I don't either. The dirty details aren't really Cole's business."

"I agree. My family has been butting into my personal life lately, and I don't mind clarifying the boundaries for them."

"You're talking about your brother pushing you to get engaged."

"Yes. That's part of it."

"But you got engaged."

"Because he was right. I don't like the way he went about it, but he was right."

"Right about what?"

He studies me for a long moment in that way that makes me forget I'm supposed to be breathing over here. Then he says, "Maybe he understands me in ways I'd rather he didn't."

"I get it. Cole knows me better than I want him to, sometimes. It's a big-brother thing. They think they know what's best for us."

"Sometimes, they do." He smiles a little, and I can't help smiling back. "It's infuriating."

"It is." I laugh softly. "So, what does your brother have on you? Was this a blackmail thing? Be honest."

His smile fades. "No. But I've had some high-profile relationships that he disapproved of. Some of them attracted a lot of media attention. And it wasn't always good attention. The way Graysen saw it, I broke the long-standing rule to protect our family's privacy."

"You must've had reasons." I venture, "Strong feelings for those women."

"I did have reasons. But not feelings. If I'm in the media, it's generally because I choose to be. It's all part of the marketing machine. My brother doesn't understand that, or how necessary it is."

I consider that. "But he wants your engagement in the media. Instead of the other media attention?"

"Yes."

"Will that work? I mean, is it really one or the other?"

I hold his burning gaze as he takes way too long to answer that, and a trickle of sweat runs down my back. I tell myself it's the sun, but it's the man sitting across from me who's burning up the atmosphere.

Finally, he says, "Graysen seems to think so. And I have a feeling the media will love you. Us, I mean."

Yikes. The thought of myself *in the media* is not something I've warmed to yet. I just keep reminding myself I'll be on his arm, like that will make me feel better about it, but I'm not so sure.

What if all his gloriousness just makes me look like a cave troll in comparison?

What if people troll me, just because I'm on his arm and they think I shouldn't be?

They probably will.

And just like getting a scathing review on one of your books, you'll cry your face off, binge a bucket of ice cream, and move on.

"I still can't believe I made any kind of positive impression on Graysen," I tell him.

"Why not?"

"Well, I flung mud on your sofa. I made a scene, and quit my job in a very unprofessional way. I reamed you out in front of him."

The crooked smile he gives me is fucking adorable. "I believe that's the part he enjoyed the most."

"Shit. He thinks I'm trouble."

"Not at all. He'd never want to see me with 'trouble.'"

I struggle for a response to that. The implication being that I'm the opposite of trouble?

Like, Jameson's brother thinks I'm good for him?

I sip my coffee just for something to do, as this morning keeps growing hotter. Jameson just keeps looking at me, and somehow, I didn't know that would be the hardest part. It was almost easier lying next to him in bed, in the dark. Here, I have nowhere to hide.

I need sunscreen to deal with my new fiancé. I'm burning out here.

"Look, I don't mean to sound insecure or anything," I tell him. "I think I'm all right. But you'll have to excuse me if I just never saw myself as the kind of woman who'd attract the attention of a billionaire."

"Do you mean my brother or me?"

The corner of his mouth twitches. He's teasing me, maybe.

"I guess... both of you."

"Then maybe the way you see yourself is not the full picture." He adds casually, "Maybe, Megan Hudson, you don't know how rare you are."

Rare?

What does he mean by that?

I'm not special. Not like he is.

I decide to change the subject again. "So, you really just do whatever you want on Sundays?"

"I do whatever I want every day."

"Wow. Now that's freedom."

"Yes, but I do work. I like to keep busy, and I don't often sit still for long. Usually that means a lot of travel. Do you like to travel?"

"I don't know. I never have."

"Then we'll soon find out."

"We will?"

"I'm sure we will. Today, I'll be getting my team up to speed. I wasn't planning any travel for a few weeks, but that might change now. And everyone needs to know I've got a plus one now. You'll go where I go."

"Right." My heart pounds at the thought of being his plus one. Fancy galas and posh, private clubs attended by the world's elite flash through my mind, making my limbs feel shaky.

Good thing he's strong. He might have to hold me up while he drags me down all those red carpets he seems so fond of.

"And," he adds, "you'll have your own security detail. That part is necessary."

"Oh. Okay." I guess that won't be much different from the way things have been these last couple of weeks anyway, his guys shadowing me around.

Then he kills me with "You're part of the Vance family now, and our security is high at all times."

I think I squeak out a response to that.

"We can video call Cole later today, talk to him together, like you wanted," he continues, like I'm not almost fainting over here. "I'll get that arranged. And tonight, we'll have dinner with my family. We need to tell them in person. Then we'll make a public announcement."

Oh, Jesus. And Mary. My nerves are flipping out already. I'm not religious, but I'm thinking I'll start praying to every biblical figure I've ever heard of to help me get through this. Can't hurt, right?

I can't even decide if I'm more nervous about facing his family, acting as his fiancée in front of them and trying to convince them that Jameson made the right choice in me, or in front of the world.

"I'll make the dinner arrangements and let you know what time to be ready, once I know," he tells me. "I have a preexisting lunch meeting, so I'll be out of the house for a few hours. I want you to feel at home here, whether I'm here or not. The staff are now here for you as well. Don't hesitate to ask them for anything."

"Okay..."

"And Clara will coordinate with you today, everything you need."

"Need?"

I'm not even sure what I could possibly need that he hasn't already offered me.

But Jameson doesn't elaborate. He just gives me that rare, killer smile that makes me inwardly swoon.

CHAPTER 25

Megan

As it turns out, what I "need" is an engagement ring that features a diamond capable of being seen from outer space.

As soon as we finish our breakfast, Jameson receives a text from Clara, then informs me that we have an appointment downstairs. Then he leads me there, holding my hand, while I quietly freak out. Since we're now "engaged," I should really get used to the hand-holding and the killer smiles.

Quickly.

Lest I pass out in shock as all the blood rushes to my loins every time he does it.

All he tells me, or all I really hear, is "The jeweler will have security in the room. They're here to guard the rings—"

"Jeweler?" *Rings?*

I have so many questions.

They're all answered when I find myself in a meeting in Jameson's living room with a local jewelry designer and her assistant. Apparently, she's a friend of the Vance family, and her rings are, according to Jameson, "worn by many celebrities."

I can see why.

The one he helps me choose from the small selection on offer, after some low-key bickering, is stunning. The others all feature clear diamonds, other than one that's blue, in various shapes. This one has one large, round, slightly pinkish stone. It's a simple solitaire style, classic, and I love it.

I would've been content with a much smaller diamond, but this is the smallest one Jameson will allow me to get. The ones he suggests at first are way too intimidating. He tells me the fiancée of a billionaire would wear a more expensive diamond, I tell him I'd be scared to walk around wearing the ones he picked out without an armored cage around me, and he finally relents.

I'm told by the jeweler's assistant that this one is an Argyle Light Pink Champagne diamond from some famous Australian mine. Twenty carats.

I have no idea, really, what he just said. All I heard was *fucking expensive*.

The way the sunlight sparkles off it is nothing short of dazzling. It's the most gorgeous thing I've ever seen. Next to Jameson Vance, of course.

Somehow, that makes wearing it as his fiancée utterly perfect.

"It goes so well with your light eyes," he remarks, finally coming around to how awesome this ring is, when he slides it onto my finger.

I melt right there.

If I have to wear an attention-grabbing ring to sell this whole engagement-to-a-billionaire situation, it won't be a hardship to do it with Jameson looking at me like that.

Unfortunately, I don't get to wear it. The jeweler takes it with her when she leaves, to have it properly sized for me, along with Jameson's demand that it be returned "before five o'clock."

As soon as the jeweler's team clears out, we meet with a man from Jameson's bank who's come to his house *on a Sunday* to go over paperwork with me for the account Jameson is opening in my name.

With two million dollars in it.

My fiancé works fast.

Was he up at four in the morning setting up all these meetings?

After the man from the bank leaves, I don't follow much of what

Jameson says to me. It must be all the ringing in my ears. An allergic reaction to the close proximity of rare diamonds and multimillion-dollar bank statements.

I manage to catch something about how we'll want to close the joint account I still have with Troy. And how, if necessary, Jameson will fly the manager of *that* bank out to meet with me in person to take care of it.

Then he mercifully leaves me to reteach myself the ability to breathe for at least the dozenth time since meeting him, when he heads upstairs to get ready for his lunch meeting. He passes me off to Clara, and I gradually get the feeling back in my extremities as she goes over her lists with me. The woman has lists coming out of her ears.

First, she wants to know my "housekeeping preferences" and what I require in the way of personal items, toiletries and the like.

Then she wants to know if I'd like her to make me some appointments with Mr. Vance's personal trainer and masseuse, and with a hairstylist and manicurist. I say yes to all. Why not? "If it's okay with him," I tell her, because I have approximately zero dollars on hand for any of those things.

To which she says, "He'll be pleased."

She also wants to know if I need a dentist and a doctor referral in the city. To which I also say yes.

She then passes me along to Chef, who wants to know all my favorite foods, any dietary restrictions or concerns, and my meal preferences. As if I have any. Getting fed by a professional chef on a regular basis so I literally don't have to think about it sounds like paradise to me.

Then Locke—the behemoth with the neck tattoos—takes over. He wants to go over my schedule with me in detail, though I tell him I really don't have much of one. And he wants the names and numbers of all my "approved contacts," for his "security purposes."

I gather from this that he means to run some sort of security check on my friends and family.

When I ask him if he did a security check on me, he simply says, "Not so far."

I wonder what that means.

But Locke is clearly finished with me, and doesn't love questions. He hands me off to a sweaty man wearing work clothes and a tool belt, who introduces himself simply as "the handyman."

This man walks me down the long hall to Jameson's private wing, where I'm surprised to find men, some of them delivery guys, moving in and out of a side entrance in a steady stream. Like worker ants, they carry boxes in and pieces of furniture out, under the watchful eyes of two more security staff, one of them Rurik.

I follow the handyman into the sitting room off Jameson's office, where we toasted our engagement just last night, to find it completely altered.

The attached bar is still there in the corner, as is the fireplace, but the Vance family photos and the furniture have all been removed.

I gape as the workers move around me.

A sleek new desk has been set in the middle of the room, along with a comfy chair that looks like it has incredible lumbar support. A cushy, velvety chaise longue and an ottoman have been set up under the window that overlooks the garden.

Boxes from an office supply store and a bookstore form ever-growing stacks in one corner, and a couple of men are setting up a computer on the desk.

The handyman wants to know where I'd like my bookshelves set up.

They're in pieces, leaning against one wall.

He shows me the options of where they could go, and I must pick one, because he sets to work.

I watch, stunned, for a long moment.

Then I dip my fingers into one of the open bookstore boxes, peeling back the flap and peeking inside. I lift a few books, glimpsing the titles.

Books on writing and publishing.

Wilderness survival guides.

Postapocalyptic fiction.

Before I can pass out from sheer shock or maybe fall in love with my brother's best friend on the spot, Clara fetches me from the room that is obviously my new office and takes me back to the living room. I feel like I'm in a daze, a lovely, dreamlike nonreality wherein Prince Charming himself is trying to spoil me rotten.

Clara tells me there's a delivery of flowers—for me. It's a lovely exotic bouquet, and it's massive.

It's from Jameson.

The card simply says, *Enjoy your day*.

I'm reading it when he walks in, breathtakingly masculine, elegant and alpha all at once in a navy-blue three-piece suit. He comes straight for me across the living room, where I'm helping Clara put my flowers in a giant vase of water at the bar.

"You clean up decently. What a nice suit," I force out in panic, so I don't say something much worse. Like *Let's get married*. At no point have I ever seen him unclean, but damn; the man was made for a suit.

The smoldering look in his eyes makes me squeeze my thighs together as he leans in—and presses a soft kiss to my forehead.

It's the first time he's kissed me, and I'm paralyzed as warm honey pours through my veins.

His lips are on my skin.

"Be good," he says gruffly, his low voice a promise of sex.

But I must not be hearing well.

I want to thank him for everything, especially the office—and the books; *my heroin*—but the words stick in my throat as I watch him walk away with Locke, his ass like sculpted granite in that fine suit.

Greek gods would be envious of that artistry.

I swallow.

Wanty.

My pupils must be huge right now.

"The styling team is ready. I have them all set up in the guest wing for you." Clara interrupts my staring, and I blink at her.

"Pardon?"

"I got them set up while you were talking to Locke. They're ready and waiting."

I follow her as she heads up the hall to the guest wing, still unclear.

"Styling team?"

"Your wardrobe. Mr. Vance expressed his concern that you haven't brought a lot of clothes with you."

"Oh." *Of course he did.*

Is there a thing I could possibly need that he hasn't already thought of?

I almost giggle hysterically when I glance at my cell phone and realize it's not even eleven-thirty in the morning. I must make a weird sound, because Clara gives me an uncertain look.

"He mentioned that you'll need clothing for every occasion. From enjoying the pool to black-tie events. Is that correct?"

"Uh... well..." I stammer. *He's not wrong.* Even after unpacking my things, my side of the closet is utterly empty next to his. "Yes. I guess that's right."

"Oh, I *love* this one," I gush. I'm alone, talking to myself in my old room in the guest wing. Today, it's my dressing room.

I take a selfie, which I'm terrible at, trying to get the whole dress I'm wearing in the shot. I've been getting Nicole's opinion on the outfits I try on all afternoon. She's thrilled about my "life upgrade," as she calls it. When I told her yesterday I was going to accept Jameson's proposal, she practically shoved me out her apartment door.

When I send the pic of the dress to her, I find she's sent me one, too. Of Jameson at a restaurant table with a bunch of other handsome men in expensive suits. Three of the men I don't recognize, but one of them is Jameson's brother Damian.

I looked up his siblings' names after he left for lunch, in a panic about meeting them tonight.

In the photo, Jameson's wearing the same suit he left the house in today.

Me: Do you have eyes on my fiancé right now? You stalker.

Nicole: That dress is HOT.

Nicole: I'm not stalking him in person dummy. I have a Google alert for that. Here.

She sends me a link that takes me to some Instagram account about the Vancouver "scene," where I see the same image, with the caption: *Dane Davenport, Brandon Ellis and Trey Jones lunching with the Bayshore Billionaires at Nightingale. How do we get an invite?*
Weird.
At least it's late afternoon now, and the photo was posted only twenty minutes ago. He's probably not still at that restaurant.

Me: I wonder if he knows someone took a picture of him eating his steak and salad and now it's online.

Nicole: Of course he does. It's a power meeting. If it was meant to be private, it would be in private.

Right. He said that himself. That he's in the media because he wants to be. Marketing and all.

Me: Do you know who those men are?

Nicole: My girl Dani knows Brandon Ellis. He's not into me. I tried. (crying laughing emoji)

Nicole: But if Google tells me the other guys are single, your fiancé better hook a girl up.

Nicole: Also, you should set up an alert. Keep an eye on your man.

Me: Gross. I don't even want to look at his Instagram.

Nicole: That is the craziest shit I've ever heard.

I laugh under my breath.

Me: It's about trust, my friend.

Nicole: Oh? Days ago he's the big bad billionaire who can't be trusted and now he's golden? Please tell me he slammed some sense into you. Against his headboard.

She's right. I'm acting way too weird today—*happy*—but I don't want to get into it right now.

Me: I have to go.

I toss my phone aside, ignoring the alert as she responds, and take another look in the mirror.

I've been back and forth to the room across the hall constantly, where the two stylists Jameson brought in have racks of clothing set up for me to try on. It was weird for the first outfit or two, being the object of their attention, but over the course of the afternoon I've settled into the rhythm of it. And I've tried on so many items I've fallen in love with. Like this dress.

It's *the dress*; the one I'll be wearing to dinner with the Vances tonight. I know it as soon as I put it on. It's perfect for an elegant dinner with a table of billionaires and my new fake fiancé at my side.

It's a pale amber-ish color in a silky fabric that sparkles all over. Fitted, with long sleeves and a slight V neckline that gives an alluring hint of cleavage without being pushy about it. Like my new diamond ring, the color is similar to the lightest tone in my eyes.

It goes perfectly with the ring.

I wonder if Jameson will notice.

I intend to gush all over the stylists about how much I love it, but when I open the door, there's a big body in my way.

I stop in my tracks.

My brother stands in the hallway, fist raised like he was about to knock.

"Cole," I breathe, startled.

He drops his fist, his eyes raking over my new dress. His jaw is weirdly stiff, and there's a vein popping out in his neck. "Clara said you're getting a bunch of new clothes," he growls.

He's breathing way too hard, like he just sprinted here all the way from California.

I swallow. For some reason, I feel guilty. Maybe it's the way Cole is looking at me.

Like I've done something wrong.

"I am. It was Jameson's idea. Come in, okay?" I take his arm and draw him back into the room with me. "We should talk—"

"He's dressing you up? Why?" He scans the three different bras that I left on the bed with distaste. "I thought you were staying with Nicole."

I take a breath and plunge. "He asked me to be his fiancée."

"I know. He told me."

"I... *Shit.* Cole... we should've told you together. So you didn't have to worry about me..."

At that word, *together*, his eyes burn into mine. "*I fucking knew it*," he mutters, his voice low and tight. "I knew something was up. He's been acting strange as fuck. I fucking *knew* he was into you." He starts pacing as he talks, like a caged gorilla... and I flush hot with mingled anger and embarrassment as my brother jumps to all the wrong conclusions.

"So... you flew here from Santa Cruz? Right now?" He was supposed to be hanging out with one of his hockey player friends in California. For two weeks.

"Tell me right now," he demands, jaw rigid and muscles flexing, "if I need to intervene here. I will kick his ass if needed."

Damn. He meant that.

"He just asked me to be his fiancée," I repeat. "Very respectfully. And he's not into me. His brother Graysen wanted him to get engaged."

"Uh-huh. And since when do you want to get engaged to a guy you just met?"

I hesitate. There's no easy way to put it. But my brother's inner caveman is staring me down right now and it's making me irritable. "Since he made me an offer I can't refuse."

He chews on that for a long, dark moment, like he's trying to swallow broken glass. "When did this happen?"

"Like two weeks ago. I said no," I add, fiddling with the diamond bracelet I'm wearing, the one the stylist picked to go with this dress. "Then I said yes. Last night."

Cole stops pacing, absorbing that. He scowls at the dress. "And now you're, what, dressing up for him?"

"He's taking me to dinner with his family. And he mentioned some travel. I think he just wants to help me feel comfortable when he takes me out. You know I didn't bring much—"

"So this is how you get out of Crooks Creek? Hook up with my best friend so he'll pay your way?"

Oh, now I'm pissed. "It's not like that, Cole."

"It looks exactly like that to me."

"You don't need to come charging in here to protect me from myself, or from him, okay?"

He raises an eyebrow at the diamond earring I'm now fiddling with. "So you bought all this yourself?"

"Don't judge me," I grit out. "You got out of Crooks Creek because you played hockey. They weren't exactly handing out hockey scholarships to girls in our hometown, Cole."

"Mine didn't get handed to me either. I worked for it from the time I was old enough to put on skates."

"Yeah. Because Dad was a loser who never did anything with his life except pin all his hopes and dreams on his little boy becoming a hockey star. He put everything we had into you."

Cole huffs out a frustrated breath. "And I'm sorry about that. But it's not my fault. I was an innocent kid in that situation, just like you were. I didn't know how badly he neglected you."

"Because you weren't there."

He scrapes a hand through his hair, frustrated, and starts pacing again. "You want to punish me for things in the past that I can't change. Things that were never even my fault to begin with."

"I don't want to punish you."

"You do. Deep down, you do. And I don't blame you. Because you can't punish him."

Ugh. He's right about that.

You can't do anything to affect someone who just doesn't care, and our dad doesn't care about me. He doesn't even care about Cole.

Cody Hudson only cares about himself.

Narcissists are like that.

"He has no fucking conscience about any of it," he growls. "I know that. He doesn't give a shit, because he's not capable of it. He's a sick fuck. And that's not your fault or mine."

I take a deep breath, trying damn hard not to take my daddy issues out on my brother. Is that really what I'm doing?

"You've taken care of them both, I know," I tell him. He bought both Mom and Dad a house once he was making money playing hockey, and he always made sure Mom had what she needed, in a way that no one had ever done for her before. "And you know I appreciate what you've done for Mom. But I don't need you to take care of me."

He fires me a look. "So you're letting Jameson take care of you instead?"

"It's not like that. He's not just giving me a handout."

"No. You're putting out for it. Am I right?"

What the fuck.

"You just called me a whore, Cole. What do you think Mom

would think of that?" I adjust the dress self-consciously, trying to cover more of my cleavage.

He stops pacing and swipes a hand over his face. "I'm sorry. That was way out of line."

"He hasn't even touched me. If it makes you feel better."

"Megan." My brother's tone softens. "Fuck. It's not even my business. You're both adults. *Shit.* I'm sorry I assumed something bad was happening. I just don't want to see you get hurt anymore."

Yeah. I can see that. He flew here to intervene because he obviously thought he needed to.

And I love him for it.

But I *don't* need him to.

"You think that's all he could possibly want from me?" I ask in a small voice.

He chews on that for a minute. "I fucking hope not. You're worth way more than that."

"He asked me to be his fiancée. Not his fuck toy."

"Jesus, Megan."

"He's a good man." *Damn.* Here I am, defending my new fiancé now, when I barely know him.

Cole doesn't miss it. Maybe because I didn't exactly express any fond feelings toward the man when we'd all had dinner together that first night, which was the only time Cole has seen us together.

"You don't even know him," he challenges.

"So, what are you saying? You're telling me if I came to you and told you I was interested in him, you'd advise me against it?"

He rubs a hand over his mouth and down his neck, obviously deeply uncomfortable with this whole conversation.

Too bad. He started it. And we're finishing it.

"Are you asking?"

"No."

"I wouldn't do that," he admits. "Jamie's a good guy. I told you that already. And I know he'd never hurt my sister on purpose."

"You're right about that. Maybe I don't know him well yet, but I can tell, he has huge respect for you. He's treated me with respect. He gave me a choice and he won me over."

"How?" he asks, like he doesn't want to, but he's morbidly curious to know.

"Well, let's see. He asked several times. Nicely. He offered me jobs, a home, money. All of which I turned down. Until he gave me a new suitcase."

His eyebrow creeps up. "A suitcase?"

"Did you see that broken thing I arrived with?"

"Yeah. I saw."

"He's thoughtful. He pays attention. He asks my opinion on things. He's smart and he's courteous. And... he's gorgeous. I find him attractive, okay?"

Cole seems skeptical. "He was 'gorgeous' when you quit the gardening job and took off to Nicole's, too. What changed? Don't tell me it was just a suitcase and his blue eyes."

"Maybe it was."

He gives up a ragged sigh. "Megan. You said he's not into you. And he explained it to me like this was some business arrangement between you two. What are you telling me now? You like him?"

I swallow the painful reminder that this *is* a business arrangement with some difficulty.

Fuck, am I in trouble here or what?

"Of course I like him." *Too true.* "If I didn't, I wouldn't be playing along with this, no matter how badly I need rent money. I am not whoring myself out to your best friend, okay?"

My brother just stares at me, his hands resting on his hips. He shakes his head, apparently at a loss for words.

I'm just growing weary of this argument. "Look, you've really made something of yourself, Cole. But it wasn't always a smooth ride. You've had plenty of bumps in the road. How can you sit in judgment now of the path I'm taking?"

"I'm not judging."

"You are. When have I judged you, challenged you on your decisions like this?"

"Maybe you should've," he admits.

"Yeah. Maybe."

We stare at each other.

"It's just so damn fast, Megz. You were with Troy for almost eleven years, you ran out on him in the night, and like two weeks later you're engaged to my best friend?"

I can see how he'd be concerned. Of course I can.

"Yeah, I just went through a brutal breakup. And when I called you, in tears, so lost... I desperately needed a change. I needed to reset my whole life. And you didn't hesitate. You offered me a life-line. I need to thank you for that. But I don't owe you anything else."

"You're right. And you don't have to thank me. It's the least I can do." He goes over to the bed and sits down, tossing the bras aside. "I know I was never there for you, over the years..." His jaw flexes and that angry vein pulses in his neck as he seems to bite back what he really wants to say. "I should never have let you stay with Troy. I should've come, packed you up, and taken you away, long ago. I should've kicked his fucking ass."

"I love you for saying that. And I get that you're trying to make up for it now. That you're trying to protect me in ways you couldn't before. But no one could've made me leave Troy. My friends tried, believe me." I sigh. "Mom tried. But apparently I had to hit rock bottom myself, then sink through the mire under that, and fucking drown."

"No. I should've been there to protect you. I'm your big brother."

"You didn't do anything wrong. You had a life to live that didn't exist in that town. You got out, like everyone dreams of. You made it. You don't owe me anything either."

"Still. I should've protected you. If I knew it was that bad..."

"How could you know? I never told you." I sit down next to him. "I never really told anyone. I was his ride or die. That was what I thought. I would've done anything for him, at a certain point. Even stay, at the cost of my own happiness."

Cole gazes at me. "Because you're loyal. You're selfless and strong. You're everything Dad never was. I wish I were half as strong as you."

I laugh shortly. "I'm a mess, seriously."

"You'll be okay," he says, with conviction. "You're away from him now."

"You mean Troy or Dad?"

"Both," he says soberly.

"Yeah. So let's just move forward, okay? I've spent so much time regretting all the moments in the past I wish I could change. But I can't change them. The fact is, I fell in love with an extremely charming guy, too young, who turned out to be incredibly messed up. But I left him. It's done. I'm the last person who wants me to repeat the same mistakes all over again, believe me. I just want to move on. You need to let me. In whatever way I decide is best for me."

"Yeah. Okay." My brother sweeps me into a crushing hug. "I'm sorry, Megz. I just want you to be safe and happy."

"I know. Have you seen Jameson's security guys? I'm definitely safe."

He snickers grudgingly.

As for happy... the more time I spend with Jameson, and the more time passes without another word from Troy, the outlook just gets better and better on that.

The first week, Troy texted and called nonstop.

His attempts to get a response out of me, without success, finally petered out a few days ago.

As Cole releases me, I ask him, "So, what's Jameson's family like?"

"Terrifying. Why?"

"You're kidding, right?"

He gives me a contemplative look. "Not really."

Great.

"Well, I'm meeting them tonight. Jameson wants us to tell them in person."

"Jesus. So it's really official? You're going public with this, just like that?"

I show him the ring on my finger he probably didn't even notice. The jeweler's assistant returned with it just after three o'clock, security guard in tow, to slip it onto my finger. It now fits perfectly, and I still can't quite believe it's mine.

"Well, fuck." Cole yanks my hand to him and examines it. "He seriously bought this for you?"

"Thanks."

He releases my hand. "Shit. I meant—"

"I know what you meant."

"No. You don't. I just meant I never thought I'd see the day that Jamie gets engaged. To anyone. He hates marriage."

I don't know why that stings so much.

Jameson told me himself that he's not getting married. And Nicole rattled off a lot of gossip about him to me, mostly the names of famous women he's been spotted with in public. And I'm not dense. It's pretty clear my fiancé is a playboy.

Or he was, before he got engaged to me like two seconds ago.

I'd let the whispers of his past all just slide off, though. He's not with other women now, so what does it matter?

But it hits differently, hearing that he "hates marriage."

It really shouldn't.

He already told me there would be no fairy-tale wedding at the end of this engagement. In one year, we go our separate ways.

I'll be a millionaire, he'll still be a billionaire, and we'll both be single.

It's so unromantic... the glitzy diamond on my finger suddenly feels colder and weirdly cheaper than it did before.

CHAPTER 26

Jameson

"S o what's the purpose of this dinner?" Graysen inquires. "You want to break it to us that you've failed your challenge while we all have full stomachs?"

I'm dressed for dinner and waiting for Megan in the foyer outside my home office when I decide to call my oldest brother. I'm now wondering if that was a mistake.

"I used to like you, Graysen. It's a shame that's changing."

He gives a harsh sigh that says *I don't have time for this.* "It's been a tough year, little brother."

It has been. Losing Granddad, and transitioning to running the whole Vance empire without him at the helm, has been hard on all of us. It's Graysen, though, who carries most of the burden of taking over at the helm, aka working twenty-four seven.

But even he needs to eat, hence my idea to do this over dinner. It's the only way—other than starring in some scandal in the press—that I can claim his full attention for any length of time.

I force the words out because I've decided it will be better if I give him a heads-up. "I just want to share the happy news of my engagement with my beloved siblings face-to-face."

Graysen's silence is long. "Engagement?"

"Yes. I took your advice, if you could call it that." I refuse to acknowledge that he gave me an order and I followed it. "Cole Hudson's sister is now my fiancée. I wanted to prepare you beforehand. So you can back me up in front of the others."

"This is sudden."

"No more sudden than your engagement. How long did you romance Sonia before you popped the question?"

He doesn't even bother answering that because he didn't romance his fiancée at all.

Instead, he says wearily, "And how do I know you're not sleeping with her?"

"I am sleeping with her. I want it to look real for the staff. But I'm not having sex with her. You can trust me."

"Can I?" His tone reminds me that he won't be babysitting me on this. That it's up to me to deliver on this, like the man I am. The man he helped raise.

"You saw us together," I say dryly. "We have zero chemistry."

I hear his almost inaudible sigh of surrender. "I hope you know what you're doing, Jamie."

"I'm doing exactly what you said you wanted me to do. So you'd better back me up tonight. I have to go." I hang up on him as Megan appears. She pauses at the top of the stairs, meeting my eyes.

She's goddamn stunning.

The dress she's wearing is fitted, hitting just above the knee, with long sleeves and a dipping neckline. The sheen of the glittery fabric highlights every curve. I can't help wondering if she chose it because it goes so well with the ring.

She's wearing that, too.

I can see it on her finger, glittering, as she descends the stairs. The dress sparkles, flowing with the movements of her body, the silken waves of her hair looking soft and strokable.

Her sparkling amber eyes are goddamn otherworldly.

"Hi," she says, those eyes drifting over me in my charcoal-gray three-piece suit and tie. I've never felt more like a man than when she looks at me like that. The result is a shot of pure testosterone to the spine.

I swear I stand up straighter without even meaning to as I extend a hand to her.

After the slightest hesitation, she slips her hand into mine. It's small and warm, unbelievably soft.

"You look beautiful," I say roughly. *Stunning, incredible, fucking divine* would've been more accurate. But I'm trying to keep myself in check here.

Especially after staring at her over breakfast for way too long without even telling her she was falling out of her bra. Still can't believe I handled that like such an adolescent.

"Thank you. And thank you for the dress." She finishes her perusal of my suit and smiles at me, her sweet face lighting up.

My heart squeezes, because my body knows that I'm already in over my head, even if I'm too stubborn to admit it to myself.

In the limo on the way to dinner, I offer Megan a drink, but she declines, saying she's too anxious.

"I'd really like to tell you there's no need to be anxious, but I'm aware my family can be intimidating."

She laughs nervously. "Yeah, I asked Cole about them, and he didn't exactly put me at ease."

"He's not a huge fan," I admit.

"Of anyone in the Vance family?" She raises an eyebrow.

I know what she's thinking.

Cole wasn't much of a fan of me this afternoon.

He didn't tell me he was flying back from California to confront me. I came home to find him waiting in my living room, pacing, pissed that I'd gotten engaged to his sister without asking him first.

I should've known what a sore spot that would be. Maybe I chose to try to convince myself it would all be okay, because I was so fixated on getting that yes out of Megan. But I know he blames himself for failing to protect her from her ex over the years.

So, as soon as he saw me, he started yelling at me. I half expected him to take a swing at me, but he didn't. The situation was quickly defused, and we smoothed things over with a drink and a conversation that ended in a hug.

Cole couldn't be mad at me for long, so there was that. But Megan had really done the heavy lifting. Apparently, they'd already had a chat and she'd talked him down. Defended me, even, according to him.

She's already proving a loyal fiancée.

Makes me want to reward her. Wrap all that silken hair around my fist and tug her head back, seal my mouth over hers as I slide my other hand between her legs and—

I clear my throat. "He's never really clicked with any of my brothers."

"Oh."

I figure she's wondering why, and if my siblings are anything like me.

Most women I date know everything there is to know about my family before we even meet. Though it's not like she'd find much about my siblings online, even if she looked for it. Just the occasional, unsubstantiated gossip article.

But Megan Hudson isn't most women. She's so down-to-earth, it wouldn't surprise me if she's never read a celebrity gossip article in her life.

"I know you don't want to get married," she says, instead of prying about my family. "But have you ever been in a serious, longterm relationship? You already know about my one and only."

"No. Nothing serious, or longterm."

"Then I guess I'll be the first." She smiles halfway. "I mean, if you consider a fake, one-year engagement serious and longterm."

"You really don't know much about me?"

"Just what you've told me. I never looked up your relationship history online or anything." She fiddles with her new ring. "Full disclosure, though, my friend Nicole did. I guess most of what came up were all the salacious headlines about your dating life."

"That's unfortunate." I grimace. "But like I told you, that's all marketing."

She sassily raises an eyebrow. "All?"

"Most. And like I told you, much of marketing is an illusion."

"Hmm." She presses her soft lips together in exaggerated disbelief, like she's calling my bullshit.

However, I'm not bullshitting her.

I've been with a generous amount of women, sure, but I haven't screwed ninety percent of the women I've been photographed with. I may be a "playboy" and a bachelor, and I do love sex, but I'm not *that* promiscuous. The social juggling act I'd have to perform to keep that many women on the line is mind bending. I suppose it's some sort of backhanded compliment that anyone thinks I'm that much of a lothario?

But the way I see it, it's just good publicity for our brands—our hotels and resorts, our nightclubs, our liquor companies—for me to be seen in the right places with the right people, living a certain kind of life.

At least, usually it's good publicity.

But tell that to Graysen.

It's bad enough he buys into all the shit he sees about me online, as soon as he feels it's a net negative for him. Now my fiancée's falling for it? And giving me static about it?

No.

That's not how this rolls.

And I need her to know it.

We may not be fucking, but for the next year, the deal is I'm her man. That means she gets her information about me from me, not the fucking internet.

I drop my voice low. "Do you enjoy spankings, Megan?"

Her response is almost comically delayed. Then her eyes go wide. "Pardon me?"

"Spankings. Do you like it when your lover puts you over his knee and spanks you when you've sassed him? Or do you prefer that he gets down on his knees and grovels for your approval like a puppy?"

Her mouth drops open.

Then her eyes narrow, sparking amber fire. "Why, Jameson? Do *you* like spankings?"

"Giving, yes. Very much, under the right circumstances."

Her cheeks are turning pink. Much like her ass cheeks will, when I spank them. "And what would those circumstances be?"

"Maybe we'll find out. In the future."

Her whole face flushes pink. I can practically feel her pulse racing from here.

And now my cock is hard.

You're playing with fire. Stop.

"Is that a threat?"

"Absolutely not. We're getting to know one another, remember?"

"Are we? So, we're listing off our favorite kinks now? You go first."

Shit. She's a spitfire underneath all the sweetness.

My cock is pulsing and I need to defuse this bomb before I grab her by the neck and slam my mouth down on hers just so I can feel her nails scratching down my body.

"We're not talking about kinks." My voice is flooded with heat and lust that I really need to tamp down. "I was simply asking if you like your man to take control when you're using your smart mouth. Is it foreplay for you? Are you trying to dominate him? Or are you looking for a fight?"

"What if it's none of the above?"

"I assure you, it is."

She stares at me, lips parted, her chest moving as she breathes, heavily. I'm not even sure if she's more angry or turned on.

You don't want to know. Move on.

"I don't want to upset you before dinner." *Especially when I can't fix it with my mouth between your legs.* "Let's talk about something else."

"You're playing games with me."

"I don't play games with women. Every relationship has a balance of power, and we'll find ours."

She's still staring at me, floored, like she's trying to decide if she wants to slap me or suck me off first. "Yes. I suppose we will."

I look away, out the window, breaking the spell. "My family, however, are another matter. They love to play games."

She doesn't seem to know how to take that, or the rapid shifts in conversation.

"Well... my brother plays games, literally, for a living. I can handle players." There's fire on her words yet, and I wonder if she means me, and/or my family.

Still, it feels only right to warn her.

"Your brother's never played for stakes like these."

"Like what?"

"Like billions." I meet her eyes again. "We're under a lot of pressure, a lot of scrutiny from our business partners since Grandad's passing. The ones who had a long personal relationship with Granddad, especially. Our future success, or failure, will be heavily affected by the completion of current projects, ones left unfinished by Granddad. Like the Vance Bayshore resort."

"I see. That is a lot of pressure. I mean, I can only imagine."

"Then you can imagine that we're highly scandal averse, right now more than ever. Hence the engagement scenario. As Graysen predicted, I'm sure love and commitment will play much better with our business partners than a wild bachelor lifestyle. Especially an exaggerated one." I pause, giving her a chance to sass me on that point again.

Her eyes pinch a fraction like she's considering it, but she doesn't.

Good girl.

"So, enter my lovely new fiancée. Sweet, well-mannered, and down-to-earth. Not famous, but the sister of a famous hockey player who happens to be my best friend. It's the kind of thing the press and the public will eat up. As will my family, if we serve it up to them just right."

"And 'just right' would be...?"

"To follow my lead. I know how to talk to my siblings."

"Okay. I can do that." She plays with her new ring self-consciously, flashing me a look that suggests I keep the spanking talk to a minimum if I want her to behave.

"Just be yourself," I tell her, more gently, at war with myself. My instincts are to flirt with her, arouse that fire in her, and of course, fuck her. None of that is going to get me what I really need out of this situation. "We already know you made a good first impression on my brother. The only way you could ruin that tonight is if you mention anything about your life that sounds remotely scandalous."

"Like telling your family that I ran out on my whole life in Crooks Creek in the night." She swears savagely, which is incredibly cute on her. "I hate that I did that. I mean, I needed to leave. To end it. But the way I did it, it sounds like I have something to hide."

"It doesn't. You left a bad relationship. That's understandable. But you should know, my family will run a check on you. For security."

She considers that, but she doesn't seem offended. "You won't?"

I would've, in the past. If she were anyone other than Cole's sister.

"I won't. But they'll insist upon it, as will our chief of security. And they'll do it whether I agree to it or not. And they'll probably find out about your books, and maybe other things you'd prefer to keep private. They'll find out about Troy, too. About how you left him. So, it's probably better if you just tell them."

"Right. Okay."

"Is there anything else you want me to know, before this dinner? It would be better if we both know going in."

So I can defend you, I don't say.

I don't want her to worry that my family will be that ferocious in protecting me. But they will be.

It's not just me they're protecting, it's all of us. And our grandparents' legacy. None of us want to see what Granddad built go to shit on our watch.

"Well... I guess they'll find out that my pen name is my real name, then. Jessica, I mean. That's my actual first name. Megan is my middle name, but everyone's always called me Megan, even my family."

"Why?"

"I don't know. I guess I was always more of a Megan? Jessica is more like... my alter ego." She shrugs. "She's the badass I want to become. Like, she has the courage to publish my books, even when I don't."

"But you do."

She smiles a little. "That's just my inner Jessica. But like I told you, I use the pen name Jessica Rivers for privacy, because at the end of the day, there is no Jessica Rivers."

I'm not sure I agree with that. I'm looking at her right now, and she is badass, in her own way.

Her smile fades, and I realize I'm staring at her again. It's weirdly impossible not to. "I have nothing to hide, Jameson."

"Good. People can be merciless." *My family included.*

"I'm aware."

"Also... If my brother Harlan says anything horrifying please don't hold it against me. We're just related. I can't control him."

"He's rude?"

"He's an abomination. Actually, he might not even show up." *One can hope.*

Megan studies me for a moment. "I have an older brother," she says simply. "I understand."

She doesn't have a brother like any of mine, though.

Harlan does show up, and so does everyone else.

I'm not sure if this means Graysen called them all to tell them who I'd be bringing and they didn't want to miss it or if he threatened them or what, but they're all gathered in his living room in the owner's suite at the resort when we arrive.

I can feel the conversation die the split second we walk in.

Interestingly, Graysen's fiancée, Sonia, isn't here. Which can only mean he didn't invite her.

I don't know if this bodes well for me or not. Either he considers this a family affair and so important it's siblings only, or he considers it just another of my brief scandals with women and not worthy of wasting his fiancée's time on.

"This is Megan Hudson." I introduce the woman at my side immediately, before anyone can speak. Their attention, already, has converged on her. It's rare that I've brought a woman to a family dinner, and that fact really hits me now. "Colton Hudson's sister."

They all know who Cole is, of course.

I'm relieved when Savannah gets up to greet her warmly. She offers Megan a drink, showing her over to the bar, while I greet Graysen.

"Happy?" I ask him quietly.

He seems tentatively pleased, yet wary. "I'm not sure yet."

"Stick around. She's amazing," is all I tell him. Then I go to get a drink.

"Are you engaged, Megan?" I hear my sister say as I approach the bar. "That's an incredible ring."

So, Graysen didn't tell them.

"Oh. Thank you." Megan fiddles with the ring and looks to me, ready to follow my lead as I advised her to.

"Megan and I are engaged," I announce smoothly, loudly enough so everyone hears it, and all eyes converge on her again. "I've asked her to be my wife, and she said yes." I slip my arm around her waist and pull her against me.

Megan's eyes widen, but she leans into me. She puts on a pretty smile for my family, and she slips her arm around my waist, too.

There's a long, shocked silence in which I'm sure Harlan is thinking this is some twisted joke and Damian possibly wonders if

I've lost my mind since he ate lunch with me, only hours ago. Savannah just blinks at me, waiting for more of an explanation.

It's Graysen who speaks first. "Well, congratulations, you two. It's about time one of us got married."

Over dinner, my siblings gently press me on my new, seemingly serious relationship.

How did we meet? When did we meet? That kind of thing.

I know, by the way they're looking at me, that they know this whole engagement thing is bullshit.

But none of them say so.

They'll say it later, when Megan's not in the room.

Of course they know. My stance on marriage—that being, I'll never do it—is well-known by my family members.

Whenever I catch Harlan's gaze or Damian's, I can tell they're searching for cracks in my story, even when I'm not saying anything, just like the media will. The fact that I just got engaged to a woman I met two weeks ago obviously invites criticism.

I don't give a fuck.

Then Graysen and Savannah pepper Megan with casual questions about her life, her move to Vancouver, her family.

She answers them with ease, and she answers them honestly. She even admits to leaving a bad relationship behind when Savannah asks why she came to Vancouver, though she doesn't get into details and no one pushes for them.

I appreciate that everyone treats her with respect and doesn't take out their shock on her. It's not her fault they didn't know this was coming.

"How's Cole doing in the off season?" Graysen asks her, though he could ask me anytime and he never does.

"He's good, I think. He's in California for a little while and then he goes to Montana to meet with one of his special trainers. I'm not sure what they do." Megan laughs softly. "I don't try to keep up."

She sips her wine as Graysen says, "He had an exceptional season. We think his best year may still be ahead of him, despite his age."

"I almost forgot that you own the team," she says.

"We're a hockey family. None of us played, even recreationally, except Jamie. But our grandfather owned the team, so we grew up going to games."

"Your grandfather must've been such an interesting man."

"He was." For the first time in fucking ages, a slight smile etches across Graysen's features.

Then Harlan goes in for the kill, out of nowhere. "So, you two are in love?"

Of course, he doesn't believe it.

I wouldn't either, if our roles were reversed.

"I think it was love at first sight." The words slide out fast and way too easily as I turn to Megan, seated next to me.

It's too silent in here. Graysen could really put on some music or something. It's like a crypt.

I sip my wine to loosen the knot that forms in my throat as Megan stares at me. Maybe she's stunned by what I just said. But she doesn't refute it.

And I'm not taking it back.

Because the more I think about it... there was definitely *something* between us from that first moment in the street. Something that hooked into me and didn't let go.

Ever since then... everything feels different.

The whole world looks different now that I know she's in it.

Shit. Maybe I'm drinking too much wine?

"What do you love about her?"

That's Harlan again. Who else would be so fucking rude?

You can hear forks mentally drop around the table.

"Harlan." Savi reprimands him. "What is your problem?"

"It's all right. It's a fair question. And it's easy enough to answer." Megan's cheeks grow pink as I speak. "She's got a big, warm heart. She cares about people, even people she's just met. And people she's never met," I add, thinking of Romeo's wife. "She's sweet and thoughtful. She has strong core values and she lives by them. She's so goddamn beautiful. And every time she smiles, it's the best thing that happened to my day."

I stop there because she seems embarrassed and my siblings are so dead silent. But I could list Megan's good qualities all night.

It's kind of disturbing how well I already know what they are.

As we finish dinner, my siblings mercifully let it lie that I only met Megan two weeks ago.

Maybe that little speech I gave about her stunned them into silence.

Maybe they're surprised that I've become such a good actor overnight, that I had it so well rehearsed.

But I didn't rehearse a thing.

I just told the truth.

Harlan, for his part, barely says a dozen more words. But he listens, like they all do.

As dinner's being cleared away and we're having a drink, it's Damian who puts my fiancée on the spot.

"So, Megan, Jameson has told us why he loves you. Tell us, what is it you love about him?"

CHAPTER 27

Megan

On the drive home from dinner, Jameson is quiet.

Pensive.

I know I did everything he asked of me tonight. I was polite and respectful with his family. I was honest when answering their questions.

And I sold them on our fake engagement, I'm pretty sure.

There's no way, with the way we spoke about each other tonight and came across at dinner, that they can have any doubt that the world will believe our relationship is real.

There were moments when there was so much heat between us, it was downright uncomfortable. I was sure they could all feel it.

Fake engagement or not, we make a believable couple.

I'm shocked by how believable.

Maybe Jameson's shocked, too?

Maybe he's reeling, just a little, over what I said about him?

I know I am.

He's the most awe-inspiring man I've ever met. I'm halfway certain he's a secret superhero. When I look at him, I feel like he could save the world.

God. Where did that all come from?

From the place deep inside where your stubborn belief in fairy tales resides.

I'd panicked as Jameson's siblings all stared at me in the wake of those words. But we want them to support this fake engagement, right? Well, I was damn convincing.

I'd listened to his reasons for loving me, and they were utterly convincing as well.

I just can't decide if this means he's really developing some kind of feelings for me or if he's that good a liar.

I wonder if he's thinking the same thing about me right now.

The whole ride home is hot with tension, the kind I feel sizzling on my skin every time he shifts next to me. And every time I recall our conversation right here on this seat, on the way to dinner. Spankings. Kinks. Domination. He broached such subjects so casually, and then brushed it off after he set me on fire.

Have I ever felt this kind of unspoken sexual tension around a man before?

Only him.

God, I'm a fool. For Jameson Vance, apparently.

I like him.

I really like him.

I mean, I told Cole I did. But even then I didn't admit to myself how much.

Hearing him talk about me the way he did to his family... it was intoxicating. It would be way too easy to get drunk on his charms. Not just his looks and his style and his money, but the generous gifts, the thoughtful gestures, the warm words.

And the subtle implications of the scorching hot sex life we might have, sometime in the future.

The way he kissed me on the forehead and told me *Be good* before he went to lunch today, leaving me subtly turned on all damn day, wondering what would happen if I was bad.

It's like he's my dream man or something.

The office with the desk and books in it, just for me.

The flowers.

The way he genuinely seems to admire my sweetness, instead of taking advantage of it.

I keep trying to remind myself it's all fake, part of the illusion of our engagement, but I'm losing the battle with my body, which knows the man beside me and all the heat and masculine pheromones he's putting off are very real.

The air feels so charged between us in the back of the limo, I keep expecting him to reach over and grab me. Yank me to him and kiss me senseless.

I'm breathless for it.

He touched me in front of his family; a hand on my back, a brush of his fingers on my wrist at dinner.

But he doesn't touch me in the limo, or when we get home.

And he definitely doesn't kiss me good night.

As soon as we walk into his bedroom—our bedroom—Jameson disappears into his bathroom with a mumbled word about getting ready for bed.

He's avoiding me, right?

He doesn't want to touch me. *Not yet.*

Because of my brother?

Or because he just doesn't want to touch me.

I'm so tired from the whirlwind day, I don't know what to make of it. I undress in my bathroom and slip into the shower, and as I wash my hair, the warm water pouring over me, I dreamily imagine Jameson in his.

I'm buzzing with the idea of watching him again.

This time, watching him in the shower.

But no, I won't do that. I can't. He's been so generous today, and my guilt about spying on him is only growing by the hour.

That doesn't mean I'm not thinking about it constantly. Replaying it in my head.

Just remembering what I saw last night has my hands roaming over my slick body. Imagining my fingers are his...

I know I have to be smarter than this. He suggested we "get to know each other" first, before sex enters the picture, but I don't really know why. I told him he could touch me, and touching doesn't have to equal sex, yet he's not even doing that.

I know I haven't imagined the heat between us. But if he actually has no intention of touching me throughout this fake engagement—worse, if he decides to have sex with other people instead—because of my brother or whatever is holding him back...

I need to slow down and figure out how I'll deal with that.

Tell that to your body.

Too late.

I'm coming before I know it, one hand between my legs and the other pressed to the glass as I bite my lip and struggle not to make a sound.

But as soon as the pleasure fades, a strange, hollow feeling takes over.

I ache with emptiness.

I dip my face under the water, letting the warmth soothe me. I'm safe now. Safe from my past.

He can't hurt you anymore.

But I'm feeling it now, and it hurts all over again: a man withholding sex from me.

How long did I have a sexual relationship only with myself because of Troy's withholding?

I dry off with a plush towel, feeling wrung out and exhausted. I want to fall into bed and sleep. No restlessness tonight.

Just don't think about the man lying next to you or wonder if he masturbated in the shower or if he'll get up in the dead of night to do it again.

Right. Easy.

I realize I've left my nightshirt in the walk-in, so I wander in there, wrapped in the towel, the clothes I've taken off draped over one arm.

I startle when I find Jameson in the walk-in and drop the clothes.

At least I manage to hang on to the towel.

His back is to me, and I stare as he peels off his charcoal-gray dress shirt. The muscles in his tapered back flex and ripple as he moves, and my mouth goes dry.

The way his dress pants cling to his muscular ass when he bends over to pick up a cuff link he dropped is pornographic.

He told me I could change in the bathroom for privacy, but he made no promise he'd be doing that himself.

I only realize this now.

He must feel his clothes starting to incinerate under my gaze, because he turns. And before I can stutter out any words, his eyes drop—instantly skimming my body.

My skin flushes hot, and my nipples tighten.

He looks right at my pussy as if he can see it through the towel. His hungry expression makes my throat close up.

I could duck back into the bathroom.

But I don't.

The towel is too small to cover all of me, but at least it covers the private bits. My heart hammers, and I swallow hard.

The air between us is charged with electricity and a dangerous tension. The kind that could drop you into free fall if it snaps.

"I... I'm sorry," I whisper. I don't really know why.

I didn't do anything wrong.

But it's enough to startle him into tearing his gaze away. It's like we're both under some spell. Caught in the snap of electric current. "It's okay." His voice is rough and strained as he turns away. "I really should've—"

"I'll just go get dressed." I grab my nightshirt and duck back into the bathroom.

Inside, I press my back to the wall, breathing too hard. And it strikes me as my heart pounds: that as much as I want him, I'm afraid of him, too.

I'm deeply afraid of what Jameson Vance could do to my heart.

CHAPTER 28

Jameson

As soon as Megan disappears into her bathroom, I notice something on the floor of the walk-in closet.

Something she dropped.

Panties.

Just turn around and go.

I walk over and pick them up. Little lacy black panties.

What she wore to dinner tonight, under that gorgeous dress?

Put the panties down and walk away.

I bring them to my nose. I can smell her faint sex smell, and my hardening cock spasms violently.

Fuck.

She's right in the next room.

I squeeze the panties in my fist as my body goes into autopilot mode, and I stalk into my bathroom. I didn't masturbate while she was in the shower. Instead I had a long-ass argument with myself about whether or not I needed to. Or should.

I'd convinced myself that after draining myself last night, and again today after we picked out her diamond ring and she looked at me the way she did, I didn't need to. And shouldn't.

That encouraging myself to keep fantasizing about her while I did it was a slippery slope, and one I shouldn't be letting myself plummet down.

Too late.

I go straight into the room with the toilet and close myself inside, undo my belt, take out my cock, hold the panties to my face, and start jacking myself off. This isn't sex, right? She's not here. Just her pretty little panties.

It doesn't take long to get the job done.

Breathing in her faint scent, with her pretty face in my head, smiling at me... flashing me that fire in her amber eyes... it's all I can do to get her panties on the counter before my cock shudders in my hand, my body quaking as I come. I slap a hand on the counter for balance as I unload with a groan.

I keep stroking as my pulse races, squeezing out another shock of pleasure that has me biting back a growl.

When I'm finished, I realize how hard I'm panting. My breath huffs raggedly from my chest, and my heart races, blood thundering through my limbs.

I blow out a breath and hang my head, drained.

My body relaxes all at once, and I release my cock.

When I open my eyes, I glimpse the mess I've made. I blink at Megan's panties on the counter, decorated with my come.

Then I glimpse myself in the mirrored wall. My heavy cock, still half-hard, and aching dully.

Strangely, I feel no real relief.

Just like last night...

I thought it would help. It weirdly doesn't. Not as much as you'd think.

I'm still so fucking hungry for her.

Jesus.

Now that my cock is softening, I can think a little more clearly. And I can see what's happening here.

I'm losing control of myself.

I'm slipping, inch by inch, succumbing to my attraction to her. Getting up to masturbate in the middle of the night, when she could've easily heard me if she woke up. Not telling her that her nipple was in full view at breakfast for long minutes, so she wouldn't cover up, and I could glut myself on the view.

Asking her if she enjoys being spanked.

Jacking off on her panties like an overwrought animal with zero consideration of the consequences.

I try to tell myself that there will be no consequences. She doesn't know. I'm masturbating to save my sanity. To save me from fucking up and touching her.

And plummeting right off a cliff, to a place I can't come back from.

No. I can't afford that.

But every time I climax while thinking about her, it only makes me want her more.

Okay, jerking off was one thing.

Now I'm reading her book, for the sex scenes, in lieu of touching her.

It's getting pathetic.

Also, I'm avoiding her. I know she's in bed, so I draw a bath and strip down in the bathroom, sink back into the heat of the water, and open my tablet like a crack addict desperate to steal a hit.

She hasn't asked me if I'm still reading her books. I've seen her writing, though. On her ancient-looking laptop, today, before she got dressed to go to dinner.

I wonder which book she's writing now. Number four? Or is she already on five?

I'm still on book two of the three that she's published, and I'm really trying to slow down and savor it instead of gobbling it up like I did the first one.

"Just come get under the furs with me," Wolf growls. "Unless you actually want to die tonight. Or we could argue about it some more. 'Cause that's fun."

He's so snarly tonight.

"Is this some ploy to get me naked?"

"It's a ploy to keep you warm and alive."

Of course it is. Because if I'm dead when he delivers me, he won't get paid.

I want to say it just to continue the fight, try to push him to refute it, to dare to admit that he's not doing this just for the money.

That he actually cares even a drop about me.

But I bite my tongue. I sigh like he's putting me out, but I'm really shivering. "Fine. Don't look."

He shuts his eyes.

"I can't tell if you're peeking, so cover your eyes."

He throws an arm over his face.

I strip down completely. Quickly. "You better be naked under there, too."

"I didn't know you cared."

"I mean, this better not be a trick."

I slide in under the furs with him. He's lying on his side, facing me, and I feel the heat coming off his body. I glimpse his bare chest and bump against his bare legs.

I turn over so my back is to him and try to curl up, leaving a little space between us, but it's too cold this way.

So I roll over to face him. The tips of my breasts touch his chest. I don't care if he likes it or if he doesn't. "I have to go this way. You're so warm." *I bend my leg and rest my knee on top of his for balance.*

He's deathly quiet.

It unnerves me when he just stares at me in the dark.

"Is this okay?" *I ask him.*

"Not if you know what I'm thinking right now."

"What are you thinking?"

"That you have the body of a savage."

"Stop looking!"

"Too late."

I pull the fur around me, but my breasts are still touching his chest.

"*You act like a Lady, but your body is ripe. Your breasts and the flesh between your legs... like you're ready to be taken. If you were raised in the wastelands, you'd already have been fucked. A lot.*"

"*You're being vulgar again.*"

He carefully picks the loose strands of my hair from my neck and smooths them over my shoulder as he speaks. "*You think your new husband won't be vulgar? You think he'll be gentle? That he's not gonna take one look at you and claim you hard and fast?*"

A shiver runs through me as his fingers linger, grazing the line of my jaw.

"*You think he'll give one thought to your pleasure? That he'll take his time? He'll get on his knees and kiss you? Caress you? Taste you? He'll watch you, to see how you like it, because he cares? He'll make you come again and again until you're satisfied, so spent, you beg him to stop?*"

"*Stop talking to me like I'm one of your savage girls,*" I say weakly.

He runs his fingers down my neck. I shiver against him again. "*You respond like a savage girl when I touch you.*"

"*Then don't touch me.*"

"*If you prefer, I can just talk to you like I did the other night.*"

"*Don't.*"

"*Why not? You liked it.*" He runs his thumb lightly over my lip.

"*How do you know?*"

He laughs, and his breath is warm against my lips. "*Rowan, you almost brought the cave down on top of us.*"

"*Do you mean to ruin me for my husband?*" I twist my face away from his hand. "*And bring war to my homeland?*"

"*Your betrothed is a pig who doesn't deserve you,*" he growls softly.

"*Let's not talk about him if you can't be civil.*"

"*Do you think anyone is gonna talk to you about anything else once you're his bride? His possession?*"

I start to pull away, but he catches me by my hip.

He shifts to lean on his elbow, staring down at me, his eyes burning in the faint firelight. "Don't go."

"You want me to be your possession instead?" My voice quivers a little.

"I want a lot of things. Right now, I want to make you warm."

"How?"

"Let me touch you. If you don't like it, you can tell me to stop, and I'll stop. I'll stop whenever you want me to."

Well, well. Wolf; he's really a tricky bastard.

Megan had explained it like Rowan had seduced Wolf. And she did, in a way. She's definitely peppered him endlessly with questions about sex, ever since he opened that door. When they're both fully dressed.

Innocently, and sometimes not so innocently.

But they're both toying with each other pretty good by now.

"You can't fuck me," I tell him.

"I wasn't going to."

His hand claims my breast beneath the furs, and my breath catches. He strokes my nipple in gentle, teasing strokes. Then he pinches it.

I let out a little cry of pleasure without meaning to, and his eyes glaze over in a way I've never seen anyone's do.

"If I do something you don't like," he says, his voice low and husky, "or if I hurt you, tell me so. I'll stop."

I nod, unable to locate my voice.

He disappears beneath the furs.

I hesitate there.

Then I skip ahead.

I don't know why. I lap up every word of Megan's books. The knife fights, the grueling hand-to-hand battles, when Wolf nearly gets killed to save Rowan's life? The long treks through the wilderness as they grow low on food? The hunting, the hunger, the endless bickering? Every. Word.

But for some reason, I have trouble reading the sex scenes in their entirety. I just can't seem to keep from skimming faster and faster, devouring them, searching for clues about Megan, like I'm starving and her words are my only sustenance.

"Does it feel good?" he asks between licks.

It does, and I whimper.

"You'll like how it feels when you come this way, I promise." And with that, he licks me toward my peak.

I didn't know it would be like this.

I explode against the affections of his mouth before I know I'm going to, my flesh clutching at the fingers he's slipped inside me, and I cry out again and again. Because he has control, the pleasure is so intense, I don't know how to contain it.

I scream and cry and buck.

He kisses the sensitive skin of my inner thighs, watching me, as I try to catch my breath, then starts licking me again. He draws his fingers out partway and curls them forward, caressing me inside. He rocks his hand back and forth, stroking me as he takes my softest flesh in his mouth and suckles me until I explode again.

My hips lift off the ground and I cry out his name.

When I've stopped writhing, he slips his fingers out and kisses my soft, spent flesh as I shiver, the sudden cold raising goose bumps on my skin.

He draws the furs over me and I curl against his chest, stunned and panting.

"I'm sorry I called you savage" is the only thing I can think to say as his heart beats against my ear.

"I am savage."

I meet his eyes in the firelit dark. "I want to know how to make you feel that good," I whisper. "Teach me."

He softly kisses my face, but doesn't say anything.

So I reach down, my fingers drifting along his hip. He catches my hand and lifts it away. "You told me not to fuck you."

"You fucked me with your fingers."

"It's not the same, believe me."

"Maybe you should show me."

"You're not thinking clearly. You're all blissed out on come."

"So? *You can be, too.*" I reach for him again, and he grabs my hand again. This time, he presses it against his chest, and I feel the ferocious beating of his heart.

"*If you do that, I will fuck you.*"

"*Wolf,*" I whisper, "*I want you inside me.*"

His green eyes on mine are so fierce, it takes my breath away. But his words are soft. "*If we do that, I'm going to bind to you. I'll get attached.*"

He lets me go and flips over, turning his back to me.

I curl against his warmth, pressing my lips to the hair at his nape, inhaling his scent.

"*Like, how attached?*"

"*If you have to ask, you're not ready to know.*"

Well, *shit.*

I stare blankly at the tablet for a long moment, until I realize I'm not seeing the words anymore.

Steam rises from the bath. I'm coated in sweat, and my heart is pounding. My reading glasses are steaming up, and I take them off, swiping a hand over my flushed face and setting the tablet aside.

I drop my head back, and look up at the ceiling, not really seeing that either.

I'm still in some firelit cave, wrapped in furs.

I walk into the bedroom in a T-shirt and boxer briefs.

Megan's lying in bed with her lamp on. I can tell she's been politely waiting for me to come to bed, but her eyes are sleepy, her eyelids heavy, like maybe she dozed off.

"Wolf's falling in love with Rowan." My voice is unaccountably scratchy.

A soft smile transforms her face into a thing of staggering beauty. "Yup."

I walk to the bed and drop the tablet on my bedside table.

She laughs softly. "Why do you look like you just hiked a mile uphill to find there was nothing at the top?"

She's wrong.

There's such mind-bending beauty at the top, I'm mildly horrified. Because I want it so bad, yet it's out of my reach.

I can't touch it.

I can't make it mine.

Even if I could... I'm not sure I'd know how to.

"I didn't know he'd start falling so soon." I scrape a hand through my hair. "He fights her so much."

It's not soon. It's book two.

Maybe I just wasn't ready for it?

What's happening to me?

"Maybe that's why he fights her."

"And you think you're not writing a romance." I sit down heavily on the edge of the bed. It's not even that late. Eleven thirty. I feel weirdly ancient.

What's wrong with me?

"Hey, just because you skip the other three-quarters of the book to get to the sex scenes," she teases, "don't put that on me."

I give her a warning look.

"I read every word," I purr. "Jessica Rivers is my favorite author."

She laughs, exuberantly. "Liar!" Then her smile fades. "Please don't try to stroke my ego. It's not that delicate."

"I'm not lying. I don't read fiction."

She blinks at me. "You don't?"

"You live with me. Have you seen a novel anywhere?"

The bookshelves by the fireplace across the room, same as the ones in my office, are lined with nonfiction books on business, economics, politics.

"I mean, you could be reading one on your tablet," she ventures.

"I am. The ones you wrote."

She smiles so brightly, the arrow that strikes my heart isn't even as painful as I always thought it would be.

An hour later, Megan is fast asleep.

I'm watching her sleep.

Because obviously, I have it bad.

I reach over and cover her bare shoulder with the sheet that's slipped off.

She stirs in her sleep, and my reaction to the sound she makes is like a rush of pure heroin through my blood.

I mean, I've never done heroin but I can imagine. This feeling is pure, savage pleasure. It's euphoric as it floods my system, and it's startling in its intensity. It's every shade of warm there is. It's terrifying, and it's addictive.

All I want to do is melt into it and make it stay, no matter how dangerous it is.

It doesn't even matter if I touch her or not, or if I fantasize about touching her or not. That much is becoming disturbingly obvious.

It doesn't matter what I think or what I plan or what I do.

I want her.

The truth is, Megan Hudson is everything I want in a woman.

She's as cute as she is fucking beautiful.

As luscious as she is sweet.

As clever and multilayered as she is real.

How can I be falling in love with someone I've never even kissed?

Someone I had zero intention of falling in love with?

I've definitely never done that before. I've never even been in love. Never *allowed* myself to fall in love. That's never been more clear to me than right now.

And I never imagined it happening like this.

Everything is backward.

I met her, talked to her, before I knew who she was, or she knew who I was.

I hired her before I knew where her talents really lay.

I asked her to be my fiancée before I dated her.

And I started feeling things for her, long before it should've been possible to feel them.

This falling in reverse...

I've never felt anything like it.

I try to remind myself I barely know her. That I haven't known her that long.

But it doesn't make a damn difference to that fucking arrow lodged in my heart.

CHAPTER 29

I ride the elevator up to the admin floor of the Vance Bayshore resort's main tower and step into the silent foyer outside my sister's office, because of course, she's working late. When I texted her to find out where I could find her, she had her bodyguard, Peter, text me back.

I nod at him now. Formerly one of our grandfather's body-guards, Peter stands faithfully outside Savannah's door, ever watchful.

He draws the door open for me and I have to resist the urge to open it myself, to relieve him of the burden. The man looks older every time I see him. He's still sturdy, still looks like the decorated military vet he is, but his hands have started to shake sometime in recent months.

I wonder, as I walk into my sister's office, if she's even noticed.

But of course she has. She adores the man.

Peter closes the door behind me for privacy. I find Savannah hovering over a barrage of paperwork on her desk, where I imagine she spends the bulk of her days. And nights.

I don't tend to work late myself. My approach is to work as little as possible to get the job done. But tonight, instead of going to bed with Megan, I made an excuse about needing to take care of some business—which was a generous bending of the truth—and came here.

I just couldn't bring myself to get into bed with her.

I haven't gone to bed at the same time as her in almost two weeks now. Not since those first two sleepless nights.

I don't trust myself lying next to her when we're both awake. And not trusting myself is a deeply uncomfortable situation to find myself in.

It's not one I'm well acquainted with.

Worse, even, is the fear that she won't trust me. That the more I avoid her, the more she'll pick up on the vibe that I have something to hide, and the less she'll trust me.

I came to see my sister because I need to talk to someone about this fucked-up situation. And who else can I talk to? Not Cole. Not about his sister. And not my brothers; they'd just bust my balls about the challenge, and accuse me of fucking her.

And the rest of my friends... they're all "playboys," like me. Millionaires and billionaires, CEOs and hockey players and celebrities. Some married, some single, but they'd all bust my balls, too. And anyway, none of them know that my engagement is fake. I don't really want to spread that truth around.

With every day that passes, I just get more protective of Megan, and my relationship with her. And I won't risk exposing us like that.

The less people who know the truth, the better.

Savannah knows I'm coming, but she doesn't look up. She was the most reserved of all my siblings at dinner two weeks ago, when I introduced them to my fiancée, and I still haven't heard from her about it.

Meanwhile, Harlan and Damian have both dropped in on me at some inopportune moment to grill me on my obviously fake engagement.

They also asked me why I felt the need to get engaged *now*, while I'm in the midst of my challenge. I told them *that* was why— because it's helping me win the challenge by keeping other women at bay.

They were not convinced.

But then I told them Graysen insisted I get engaged, and that pretty much shut them up. News of my engagement to hockey star Cole Hudson's sister has effectively outshone other online gossip about me; my siblings have all seen the media coverage of our fairy-tale romance by now. As it turns out, *Sweet small-town girl gets twenty carat diamond ring from billionaire bachelor* makes major headlines, and public interest is ravenous for it. We already have hashtags, memes, and a lame celebrity couple name. (Megason.) And no one in the family would ever question that Graysen had decided a fake engagement for public appearances was a grand idea.

But I'm not surprised that my sister has stayed out of it. She has enough on her plate right now. I don't blame her for leaving the cleanup of my scandalous sex life to Graysen.

Her high-heeled shoes are kicked off beside her desk as I approach. Her glossy, dark hair hangs partly over her pretty face. She's wearing a long-sleeved red dress with a zipper up the front. A power dress. It hugs her generous curves, and makes her look at once strong and sensual.

I used to tell her she was fat when we were kids, when I was mad at her.

Brothers can be assholes.

Savannah not only survived us but often singlehandedly held our shit together. She picked up an unfair amount of the burden of mothering all four of us, even her older brothers, when our mother checked out.

She deserves some kind of award.

I keep telling Graysen to lighten her workload. He leans on her too much.

"Your boss never lets you go home or what?"

She makes an annoyed sound and barely glances up from the paperwork she's poring over.

I wander over to the table where a 3D model of the resort sprawls. Someone has affixed a tiny black Jolly Roger flag to the upper tower, where we're standing right now. "I see Harlan's been here."

Savannah makes another annoyed sound.

"You know, just because Graysen lives here, doesn't mean you have to."

"I don't. But I do have a grand opening to plan, and somehow my brothers keep fucking it up. Get this. Graysen insists he's bringing The Bitch, as if they'll still be together next spring, Damian insists he's bringing 'several special guests' even though I keep telling him he needs to bring *one* date for the dinner, and Harlan says he's not coming. At all. Do you believe this shit?"

"I really do. It's the reason I didn't volunteer to oversee the grand opening." I stroll over and drop into one of the chairs facing her desk. "Also, you should prepare yourself for the fact that The Bitch, as you call her, is going nowhere. She's got Graysen's balls locked down so tight, we may never see him smile again."

Savannah gives an aggrieved sigh. "Speaking of men and their sex parts. I have a question for you." She strolls over to the bar cart and starts pouring. "Can you please stop screwing every celebrity I invite to the gala?"

"You asked that so much nicer than Graysen did."

She hands me a whiskey and looks me in the eye. "Congrats again on your engagement. Does this mean you've lost the game?"

"And she cuts right to the chase. No, I haven't lost." I take a sip of whiskey. "And by the way, your team may invite the celebrities, but who serves them up to you on a silver platter?"

Savannah leans back against her desk. "You do get them buttered up nicely. I had no idea that involved so much actual buttering."

I grimace. "I haven't buttered anyone in months."

My sister laughs abruptly and grimaces right back.

"I'm not here to talk about my sex life or the game or Grand-dad's will. I need your advice. About women. Well. One woman."

She sips her drink, eyeing me. "Isn't Damian your go-to for that kind of advice?"

"I'm annoyed with him right now. You're the only one of them I can stand."

"I'm so flattered."

I force it out. "If I really like a woman but I can't be honest with her about the game, how do I get her to trust me?"

Savannah sets her drink down, considering. Then she paces over to the window and looks out into the dark night. I can't imagine what there is to see. It's gloomy out there tonight, raining hard; a rare summer downpour. Her pensive face is reflected in the watery glass.

"Is this what it's come to? You're doubting your own trustworthiness? Because of the stupid game?" Her shoulders are tight, and I can sense how she dreads her turn to play. They're probably all dreading it, and witnessing my struggle doesn't help. "Honestly, Jameson, if I needed a safe place to fall, you'd be it."

"I'm glad."

"I trust you more than I do anyone on earth. You and Peter, of course."

Of course.

"You know why you're so trustworthy?" She turns to me. "Because you're honest. You tell people what they need to hear without bullshitting them or disrespecting them, and they respect you for it."

"I'd like to think so."

"So what's this girl's problem?"

She hasn't asked me yet if we're talking about Megan. I'm not sure why.

Maybe she thinks there's someone else on the side.

I've never been that guy. But the amount of women she's seen me with, I can understand why she'd be unsure.

"It's not her fault." I choose my words carefully. I don't want my sister to dislike Megan. "Maybe I just don't know how to really connect with anyone."

Fuck, that sounds lame, when I hear myself say it.

"Since France," she ventures.

I swallow that, with difficulty. It unnerves me whenever I

discover that my siblings know me better than I think they do. But I am, after all, the youngest. They probably see all kinds of shit I don't think they see.

"Yes," I admit.

Savannah paces behind her desk and presses her hands flat to her paperwork, leaning in so she can look me straight in the eye. "Because you lead with your dick, Jamie."

"Blunt."

"But true."

"I didn't do that this time."

"Because you can't."

I sigh.

She stands back, considering. "So what *did* you do?"

"I tried to help her out. Offered her a place to stay, a job."

"So you led with your money."

Shit. She's right.

I didn't think of it that way. I'd just been so focused on helping her. For Cole's sake.

But also... for mine. Because I want her to like me.

Who am I kidding?

I want her to fucking love me.

Savannah's eyes narrow. "Is that the kind of thing this girl would go for?"

"Apparently not."

"And the kind of girl who would... Is that the kind you want to attract? Really?"

"No."

"Then what are you doing?" She sits down behind her desk. "Lead with your heart, Jamie. It's a good one."

I run my hand down my face. The whole idea of leading with my heart, putting it out there... *giving* it to someone... it's so damn uncomfortable I almost can't breathe when I think about it.

"Maybe I don't know how to do that."

"You're scared," my sister says, with compassion. "Mom and Dad damaged you more than you've ever admitted. You're afraid of giving your heart away and being hurt like they hurt each other."

I hesitate. "I think I started to, with Geneviève."

Savannah scoffs. "I warned you about that woman. She's a player and a status-climber. A user. You knew, deep down, that her heart was unavailable to you. I highly doubt she even has one."

I didn't know that. Not at first. But as soon as Savi says it, I'm not sure she's wrong. "Why would I do that?"

"Fear. You can't lead with your heart when your first priority is to protect it at all costs."

Fuck. The brutal honesty of that, the truth in it, is breathtaking.

Maybe this is why I come to Damian with these things. If you want advice on sex, power, seduction, Damian Vance is your man.

Advice from the heart, though? I know Savannah is the only one who can really give me that. And maybe that's why I've avoided talking to her about this for so damn long.

"Okay, so, how do I lead with my heart?"

"Damn, you do need help."

"Yeah? So then cough it up," I growl, "or I leave and regret asking. If I wanted my balls stomped on, I'd go talk to Harlan."

She seems to realize I'm serious and stops the ball busting. "Okay, cave man. Settle down. Yeesh. You get a crush for the first time in your life and you're untenable."

I glower at her.

"Step one, Mr. Growly, you put your dick away, which you've already done. Then you put your wallet away. And see what that leaves you to work with. What do you really care about? What does she care about? Who are you, underneath all the money? That's how you connect with her."

I absorb that.

"Here's the truth, little brother. You're the total package. And the women you sadly attract, in droves, are nothing but fame whores."

"Harsh." I swig my whiskey, washing down that painful truth.

"You know we're talking about Megan here, right? My fiancée? She is not cut from that cloth."

"I sincerely hope not."

"I think I have better judgment than that."

"You do. You just don't always use it."

I rake a hand through my hair. "I know I've been... all over the place with women. But Graysen's lost his mind. He thinks I'm out of control, just because of what he sees in the media."

"Well, you know he can't stomach a scandal. You broke a cardinal family rule." She raises an eyebrow at me. "Repeatedly. You know privacy is sacrosanct."

"Right. Ever since Mom decided it was so because her husband was cheating on her, so she cheated on him."

Savannah sighs a little. "Maybe so. But we've adapted to the times. Fame is a double-edged sword, now more than ever. We stay out of it because it's what's best for the family *and* our business."

I decide to ask her. "Did you know Graysen's the one who gave me this stupid challenge?"

"No." She gazes at me for a long moment, processing this new information. "Have you ever considered, Jamie, that maybe he's just trying to protect you?"

"From what? My raging adolescent hormones? I'm fucking thirty."

"From getting your heart broken," she says gently.

I take that in, but I don't know what to say. I never thought of it like that.

Savi gazes at me fondly. "You're so much like her, you know."

"Like who?" I say, though I have an uneasy feeling I know.

"Mom."

"I'm not like her."

"You are like her. You just don't know. You were so young—"

"You're three years older than me. Don't tell me you know Mom that much better than I do."

"Maybe I don't. But I saw them together in a way that you didn't."

That had to be true. She was fourteen when Dad died.

"You didn't see how gone for him she was," Savi says. "He had endless affairs and it still killed her when he died. He had her whole heart. She's never been the same."

"Yeah. She died right into the arms of another billionaire."

"Don't judge her too harshly. When she falls, it's forever. What if you're like her that way, too?"

Yeah. And that would be my worst fucking fear, right there.

Christ. Why did I come here?

I look away, my eyes landing on the model of the resort. I remember the day Granddad started the renovations. He gathered us all here to toast the achievement; our family now owned every property along Bayshore Drive, and the resort would be our crowning jewel, a luxury, five star destination on Vancouver's downtown waterfront. I had no idea he'd be gone by the time the resort opened, that we'd be taking over his final dream project for him. I couldn't fathom that possibility. I was nowhere near ready to let him go.

I had no idea, when I was a kid, that Mom and Dad wouldn't be here either, throughout every important event of my life since I was eleven.

It's my siblings who've been here for me, through everything. Even if I don't always see them watching my back, I know they are.

"You're so guarded," Savannah says in the silence, "you don't let the good ones in. They don't even stand a chance."

I meet her eyes. "Maybe Megan's one of the good ones."

"Maybe she is." She leans forward. "And if that's true, you need to make her your number one priority. Would you settle for a woman who didn't make you her first priority?"

"No."

"Exactly. You need to put her before the business, like Dad never did for Mom. And you need to put her before the family, like Mom never did for Dad."

"You're kidding me. Mom never put us first."

"She did. She wanted him to give up the affairs and stay in the marriage, for us. He stayed. Even when he didn't love her anymore."

I don't even know what to say to that. The idea that my dad didn't love my mom—as fucked-up as my whole childhood had been —just doesn't compute.

"Come on, Jamie. You know he didn't love her. He was all over so many other women... And she stayed for us, even when it would've been better for her to leave. Find a man who actually loved her."

"No. No, she left us."

"After Dad died."

"She replaced us with her new family."

"She did the best she could under shit circumstances, in the face of overwhelming betrayal and grief. And you need to forgive her," Savi says simply, like that's the easiest thing to do. Of course, she isn't one to hold long, painful grudges. "If for no other reason than you can move on."

"That's good advice. Why are you single again?"

"Fuck you. Get out of my office."

I smirk at my sister, behind her big desk with all the papers strewn across it. She's drowning in the resort opening, the gala, giving it everything she's got. For Granddad. For Graysen. For all of us.

Most days, I'm in awe of her. I've always admired Savannah, even when I pretended she annoyed me when we were kids.

Right now, it makes me feel like an asshole for crossing the line I did with Cole's sister.

However, I have no intention of stepping back behind the line.

"Stop staring at me and go win over that woman," Savi mutters as I get up and round the desk toward her. "She's sweet."

I stop in my tracks. "You like Megan?"

"You've done much worse." She sighs. "She's your best friend's sister, she'll make cute babies, she was polite to the family. Is that what you think I care about? All I care about is that you're happy."

"I love you, Savannah. You're the perfect girl." I lean down and kiss her on the head.

"I know."

She says it matter-of-factly, but there's that guarded look in her eyes that I know so well. It's a Vance thing. We all do it.

"Whatever you do, though," she says as I head for the door, "do not have sex with her. *Please*. You need that inheritance, Jamie. And I need you at the table."

I wave a hand at her vaguely. I've had enough lectures on that.

"I really can't handle Harlan without you," she adds in a grumble.

"He's your twin," I toss back at her. "You'd think you'd be used to him by now."

"You'd think."

As I leave the room, I give Peter a departing nod.

I know why Savannah keeps the old man around. He's one of her last living links to Granddad.

I can also see why my sister is alone, probably as easily as she can see my problems. All my siblings are unmarried, and it's not a coincidence.

I'm not the only one who doesn't know how to let people in.

CHAPTER 30

Megan

"I'm freaking out," Jameson mutters.

I tear my gaze away from the dreamy bed of fluffy white clouds below, which I've been zoning out to quite happily. We're in a private jet owned by his family, flying direct to Paris overnight.

Over the two and a half weeks we've been "engaged," we've settled into a mostly comfortable rhythm as a fake couple.

Our daily schedules mesh. He works while I write. Simple. We eat most meals together. We work out together in his home gym sometimes, with his trainer. He takes me along with him to business dinners, parties, and any other events he feels like attending, and I've met some of his friends.

We even drove down to Seattle so he could take me to a Dirty concert, and at an afterparty, he introduced me to Jesse Mayes and his wife, Katie. (Who seemed extremely surprised that Jameson got engaged. Which makes me wonder what kinds of parties—and women—they're used to seeing at his house.)

He's been attentive and supportive, making an obvious effort to ensure I'm happy, and regularly checks in to ask me how I'm doing, if I need anything, and how I feel about my book, the one I'm writing. He has fresh flowers delivered to the house for me every other day, and lavishes me with gifts and surprises, including bringing me along on this business trip to Europe.

We share a bed every night, while neither of us acknowledges the physical relationship that we don't have, and it just kind of *works*.

I haven't spied on him since that first night, I try not to think about whatever he's doing when he's in his bathroom, and I make sure I masturbate in the privacy of my bathroom instead of in bed next to him like a maniac. I face away from his side of the bed when I fall asleep, he seems to avoid coming to bed until I'm already asleep anyway, and we're making it work.

Maybe because he's so extremely nice to me, I've somehow managed to neatly look past the fact that he won't touch me. For now.

I keep telling myself it's just *for now*.

And that it will possibly change at some future date when he decides he's ready.

We'll be sleeping on this flight, waking when we arrive in Paris, and I couldn't possibly be more delighted about it. I mean, it's *Paris*.

I almost cry, *I'm freaking out, too!*

But when I look at him across the aisle, he's carefully setting his tablet aside, like if he doesn't handle it just right, it might burst into flame. His expression is nothing short of grim.

I sit up, alarmed. "What's wrong?"

"It's the end of the book and he just fucked her and now there's a cliff-hanger and they're about to arrive at the citadel," he rambles agitatedly. "He's going to leave her there, with people who will continue her bridal march and take her the rest of the way to her intended husband, to save himself."

My first thought is: *Oh, jeez. He just finished book two.*

My second thought is: *Holy mother of all that's good and holy, he's wearing glasses.*

I gape and blink, trying to wake up from the dream I'm obviously having that the most delicious man who ever lived is sitting right in front of me reading my book, and wearing glasses in which he looks so fucking hot there's no logical way I could be awake right now.

But I am. I know I am when he swipes the glasses off and rubs at his eyes with his tattooed wrist, and my ovaries groan.

How did I never catch him in the act of reading my book before? And realize that the man wore reading glasses??

I don't even know if I should be elated or fucking terrified that my fake fiancée not only checks off all the boxes on my list—I even caught him working with tools the other day, helping his handyman guy install *more* bookshelves for me!—he's destroyed the list. Incinerated it. Absolutely killed it dead in all its irrelevance.

Because he *is* the list.

And I'm a living, breathing *mind-blown* emoji.

I snap out of it, willing myself to function.

I get up and go over to him. "Aw. Come here." I take his hand and bring him to sit down on one of the cushy bench seats along the wall. I sit on the upright seat at one end of it, and he lies back.

"What happens in book three?" He starts babbling again, like he's spilling to a therapist, and I have to bite my lip to keep from giggling. "I mean, book one ended on a cliff-hanger too but they were okay. There were those two men who tried to attack Rowan in the woods but then Wolf saved her and you could've stopped right there and I'd be happy that they were together and they were safe. But then you just kept writing and now I *need* them to be okay. You know. Together."

He finishes, staring at the ceiling, like he's still reliving it all in his head.

"Jameson?"

"Yeah?" He blinks at me, like I've just yanked him back to reality.

"You know what this means, right?"

"What?"

"You're a romantic."

He groans, like it's a loathsome curse to bear. "Don't tell my brothers."

Jameson wore a three-piece suit onto the jet, but I manage to convince him to take a break from reading and get changed into his lounging clothes. He emerges from the bathroom in soft sweats and a T-shirt, looking as delectable as he does in a suit, and far more touchable.

Dear Lord.

If he really is trying to resist fucking me for my brother's sake, no wonder he avoids bedtime. It's way too intimate.

I'm already in sleep shorts and my Dirty nightshirt, a soft blanket for each of us in hand. The sky outside has darkened to a deep azure in the west as the sun melts into the horizon, and to the east, where we're headed, it's pretty black.

"Chat for a while, then sleep?" I ask hopefully, holding up the blankets like a safe buffer between us.

He holds up a bottle of wine. "Add wine to that and you read my mind."

He pours us each a glass, and we settle onto a couple of the big reclining captain's chairs near the front of the cabin. There's a small table between us where we set the bottle of German Riesling he chose, my favorite wine, in a bucket of ice that the flight attendant brings out at the tap of a button; he vanishes again into a room at the back, leaving us alone.

Locke and Rurik are back there somewhere, too. Jameson told me he never travels without at least two men.

We touch glasses and drink. "Tell me more about what we're doing in Paris?" I ask him.

"Well, we'll be enjoying your first time there."

"Ah yes, my virgin French experience." I mean that as sexually as it sounds and laugh when his eyebrow lifts slightly. His eyes darken, landing hungrily on my lips. "I may flirt more in Paris. Just to warn you. I feel like I'll be drinking a lot of wine." I swig my wine gratuitously.

"It's the French way," he says simply.

I'm not sure if he means the flirting or the wine, but I'll take plenty of both.

However, the heat in his eyes clears so quickly, I wonder if I imagined it. "And I'll be working. Though it probably won't look like it."

"What does 'work' for Jameson Vance even look like?" I inquire. He works from home while I write during the day, but I don't actually see what he does. I've only ever glimpsed him on business calls here or there.

He told me he has a corporate office in Vancouver, and I know he has an executive assistant named Annabeth who seems to work her butt off for him there, but it doesn't seem like he ever goes there.

"Whatever you do, don't ask my brothers that question," he says dryly. "My job is hard to define, if you're someone like Graysen or Harlan. As our CEO and CFO, they only see in numbers. I'm our head of marketing, but sometimes, I don't think even they know what that means. We work with a lot of celebrities, from athletes to actors, to align our luxury brands with the right ambassadors. I oversee the general direction of things, and I'm the one out there forging and maintaining a lot of the relationships that are essential to our business. So my work, when it comes down to it, is mostly envisioning our future, and social meetings."

I smile a little. "Is that code for daydreaming and parties?"

"If you ask Graysen or Harlan, it is." He raises an accusatory eyebrow. "And don't you daydream for a living?"

I groan. "I wish I were making a living from it. And if you think writing amounts to daydreaming, you're more of a dick than I took you for." I bat my eyelashes and sip my wine.

I half expect growly threats about spanking, though that hasn't happened since the one time in the limo. Unfortunately.

Instead, he frowns adorably. "You took me for a dick?"

"No. Okay, briefly. The Romeo thing, remember? The nice man you fired for no reason?"

"There was a reason," he says, so grimly, I laugh. "I'm looking at it. And by the way, when I hired him back, he said, 'I understand. I'd rather hire her than me too.' That's a direct quote, and he was dead serious."

"See?! He's such a sweetheart!" Since moving into Jameson's house, I've bonded with Romeo over our mutual obsession with plants, and spent many hours chatting over tea in the greenhouse and toiling in the gardens with him, just because I want to. "You should give him a raise."

"Don't push it. And don't call another man a sweetheart if you don't want him fired again."

Well, that was growly. And bossy.

Almost sounded like he was jealous of a little old man whom I find delightful.

Huh.

"Oh-kay. So, let's get back to your job and your brothers and why *they're* dicks. Wasn't that where this was headed?"

"Pretty much. Basically, Harlan and Graysen don't love to acknowledge that if I go golfing or yachting with a business connection, or if Damian entertains a potential business connection at one of our private clubs, that's *how* we do business. But this is why I handle the marketing and they don't. It's all about communication. Who you talk to and how you talk to them. If Harlan had my job, he'd fail miserably at it. But honestly, I'd do the same at his."

I muse on that a moment as I sip my wine. "You all seem really different. Yet similar in some ways." I search for the right word to sum up the Vance family commonality. "Self-assured? Headstrong. Am I getting it right?"

He grunts. "To put it nicely. I'd put it like this. Graysen may be the oldest and literally the boss of us, but what we really are are four alpha males and one alpha female who're constantly sinking our teeth into one another."

I smile at that imagery. "Ouch."

"Yeah. You could say that."

"So how does the littlest alpha survive in such a pack of wolves?" I tease.

He frowns at being called the littlest. At six-four, he's actually the tallest, though his brothers are all built like he is. They're all tall, muscle-toned drinks of water, and their sister is curvy and formidable in her own way.

But any way you slice it, Jameson is the baby of the family, and I can understand how much that sucks sometimes.

"Well, my superpower has always been knowing how to communicate with people. Companies spend millions to try to get the right message to the right customers, and it's tricky because different people need to be communicated with in different ways. I didn't realize I had a talent for that, so to speak, because the ability to handle each of my siblings just came naturally to me. I figured it out on my own from a young age."

I'm intrigued. "Tell me more. Like, what's the best way to approach each of your siblings? I'm terrible at knowing how to talk to all kinds of different people." Usually, I just avoid it.

And hide behind my words of fiction.

I curl my legs up under me as he tops up our wine. I could talk to him all night. We never talk this much before bed in the evenings. I'm convinced he's avoiding the intimacy of pillow talk with me because that sort of intimacy is a slippery slope to sex town. And he's never expressed any change in his stance about us not having sex.

I keep waiting for it, like a salivating, *Wanty* kitten, but it hasn't happened.

Yet.

"Well," he says, "with Graysen, you have to be serious and professional. He wants to know you're following the rules, playing inside the lines. That's very important to him."

"I could see that."

"With Damian, you have to be honest or very clever, or he'll be three steps ahead of you." He frowns slightly, like he's both impressed and annoyed by the fact. "He's a game master, like our granddad. Honestly, he's the most like Granddad of all of us."

"And what about Harlan and Savannah? They're twins, right?

Are they a lot alike?" I never would've known that they're twins, to look at them, but Jameson told me so before I met them.

He laughs abruptly. "Never let Savannah hear you say they are. They're actually not a lot alike, but they're both stubborn as hell. With Harlan, you need to talk in facts and figures, black and white. Shades of gray just annoy him. And the thing about Harlan that people don't always realize, to their detriment, is that he'll always expect the worst of you until you prove him wrong."

"So, he's a pessimist?"

"I'd say he's downright cynical."

"And Savannah's the opposite?"

"No. Not the opposite. But she's all about the feel of things. Why should she care about something? You need to get that across, quickly, or she won't have time for you."

"I guess that's understandable. She's probably a busy woman."

"That, and she grew up with four alpha brats who were always ruining her day with some mess or another. She tried to outman us for so many years, until maybe she realized she couldn't. When she stopped trying to compete with us, though, I think it left a weird void in her life. I think she's still figuring out how to deal with the hand she was dealt. Pro: she was born a billionaire. Con: she's got us to deal with, for life."

"Well, now I feel sorry for her," I tease.

"So do I," he says seriously.

"And how should one communicate with Jameson Vance? I mean, for best results?" I innocently lick wine from my lip.

His eyes track the movement of my tongue, and heat tingles across my skin. His tone is molten when he says, "All you have to do is be honest."

We stare at each other.

When did this become foreplay?

No. *Not foreplay.*

Foreplay leads to sex.

I clear my throat, and change the subject. "You have a lot of empathy for your sister."

"I do. I wouldn't want to be in her shoes."

A slow smile spreads across my face.

His wine stops halfway to his mouth. "What?"

"I was just thinking, you empathize with Rowan the same way."

He sets his wine down and drops his head back on the seat. "Fuck. I'm boycotting book three."

"No, you're not," I purr. "You're dying to know what happens next."

"I think I know." He gives me a darkly disapproving look that I'm pretty sure is meant for the male protagonist of my books. "Let me guess. Wolf fucks up."

"Maybe." I sip my wine as my heart absolutely races. It thrills me that he's responding so strongly to my books.

I didn't expect that.

But I love it.

What more could an author hope for?

I'd never pictured any of my readers looking like him, though.

"But maybe he also fucks her a lot more, so it'll be worth it?" I tease.

His eyes hit mine, all dilated pupil and ravenous need. I actually suck in a breath.

"What's the dirtiest thing that happens besides him taking her virginity?" he demands.

"Um." I almost choke on my wine. I swallow and cough a little, clearing my windpipe. "Let's see..." My mind races through dirty scene after dirty scene as I wonder if I can cough out the words. "Well. Okay. He fucks her up the ass and then licks his bloody come from her thighs afterward."

Yup. Coughed that out.

Jameson stares at me. His lips part. He's breathing soundlessly, but so deeply, his chest rises and falls with a shudder—kind of like a dragon smoldering just before it seizes the princess.

And eats her alive?

My whole body flushes. "Should I just die now?"

"That's—"

"Unsanitary."

"That wasn't even close to the direction my mind went, but okay."

I shrug. "I know it is, but I don't care. They're in the wild. It's just books."

But they're not just books to me.

And he has to have noticed that by now.

My feverish writing in every free moment I've got, curled over my laptop as I zone out everything around me. How many times has he tucked a blanket around me or left a cup of coffee next to me without a word when he finds me tucked into some corner of his house or his yard or his greenhouse like that?

"There are other scenes, too," I offer, my voice husky with the lust I'm really trying to keep at bay. "Like, ones you might find dirtier than that. I guess it's subjective. But there are reasons they're dirty. I don't think sex should just be a cheap thrill on the page. I think sex reveals character and how people feel about one another, when it's done right."

He's still staring at me. And those words hang over us.

When it's done right.

We aren't even doing it at all.

Because *him*.

Because he doesn't want to.

Not yet.

For... whatever reason.

A reason he still hasn't quite articulated to me.

"I shouldn't have asked," he says.

"It's okay."

"It was rude. The whole story is good. I'm not obsessed with the sex scenes or anything."

"Neither am I."

We stare at each other.

And finally, I crack. I laugh.

He shakes his head, and holds out his glass with a groan of surrender. "Top me up. I think I have more reading to do tonight."

I grin and top up his wine.

CHAPTER 31

Jameson

The next book starts out as badly as the last one ended.

As in Wolf is being a little shit.

"*I don't like seeing you all dressed up like that,*" I tell her.

I didn't like the dress they put on her at the citadel as soon as they found out who she was.

I don't like this silky robe either. It's something a Lady wears, and I'm not a man who'll end up with a Lady.

I'm the man who steals into her room like a thief to watch her undress.

Rowan just seems confused. "Like what?"

"Like his whore."

She doesn't get angry at that, like she should. In her eyes, I can see her sympathy for me, and it's much worse.

"I'm not to be his whore," she says softly. "I'm to be his wife."

I grit my teeth.

She hasn't met him yet, her future husband. She's barely halfway there, and she's still intending to marry him, after all we've been through. Her duty to her brothers means far more than any warmth she might have in her heart for me.

Still, she loosens her robe and slips my hand inside, places it on her breast like an invitation.

"We can't," I say, even as I squeeze her. I push her back against the wall. "I can't take one more day waiting to say goodbye."

"This isn't goodbye, Wolf." Her eyes mist with desire. She draws the robe open, and I take out my cock. I bury myself deep inside her as soon as she lets me.

I fuck her like it's the last time, because it is. I fuck her hard. I don't care if I'm hurting her anymore.

She's tearing out my heart.

But no matter how hard I fuck her, she only wants more.

"Yes, Wolf... give me everything..."

I bury my face in her neck. I pin her against the stone wall and fuck her little cunt, and when she makes all those pretty sounds of pleasure, I kiss her deep, wanting to silence her.

She tilts her hips and rubs against me in that maddening way, and I can't help it; I grind against her the way I know she wants it until she explodes, coming on me, her flesh pulsing around me, sucking me in.

I lose myself in her, coming hard, groaning against her neck.

I feel like an animal. With Rowan, I always feel this way.

"Hmph." I grumble out loud.

Megan is stretched out on the bed behind me, at the back of the cabin. Her eye catches mine, and she smirks.

It's the middle of the night, we're somewhere over the Atlantic, and I told her we should get some sleep hours ago. But here I am, reading again.

I'm not even sure why she's awake. I didn't know she was.

"How's Wolf doing tonight?" she inquires sleepily.

She knows how he is. I already told her earlier, in our therapy session. "He's a twat." Book three is no different from book two in that regard.

She narrows her eyes at me.

"I think he's saying goodbye. He's a dumbass." I close the tablet and set it safely aside. Again.

"I think you need to take another break. Sleep."

I watch her eyes close, then slip the tablet open.

A few minutes later, I'm pretty sure I startle her when I swear at her book. "*Fucking Christ.* She's going after him. After he abandoned her at the citadel like a little bitch."

Megan breathes out a soft laugh. "Don't worry. It'll be okay."

I skewer her with my gaze. "You never promised me a happy ending."

"That's true."

"Have you written the ending yet?"

"Um..."

She hasn't. I know she hasn't.

Which means she can't promise me a thing.

I wake up and find myself slumped in my seat, my tablet and glasses in my lap. Megan is sleeping soundly on the bed.

It's the dead of night.

I pick up the tablet, blink my eyes fully open and slip my glasses on, and keep reading. I've already done the calculations. If she's writing four or five books total, like she said, Rowan and Wolf are now about halfway through their story arc.

And Wolf is still being a dumb twat.

Rowan approaches on the rocky ledge above, between the trees. I see her, running toward the edge, her breasts bouncing in the tiny jacket that barely covers her.

She comes to the edge of the rock. I stand staring up at her.

"What are you bloody wearing?"

Besides the jacket, she's wearing a silky, green bustle clipped around her waist. It cascades down her backside, but covers nothing in front. She has no panties on at all, just garters dangling down her thighs.

She ran out like that, in the middle of getting fitted for her marching gown?

Because of me?

Her chest heaves. "You're leaving?"

"How am I supposed to do this with your cunt in my face?"

She jumps down from the rock, landing in front of me. I catch her so she doesn't fall. "So don't do it." *There's fire in her eyes as we grip one another's arms.*

I let go first. "Play fair, Lady Rowan."

"Fair? Like running off without a word?"

"I'm not running. I'm heading over the river before it gets too cold."

"And that's it? You just leave me behind?"

"We say goodbye now or in three days when you leave on your bridal march. What's the bloody difference?"

"The difference is you never said goodbye!"

I stare at her. "Goodbye." *I press a kiss to her forehead.*

She shakes her head. "No. Wolf. You're not leaving."

"I am. And there's nothing you can do about it."

She glares at me, starting to shake with helpless anger. She's shattering right in front of me, but what can I do?

Neither of us can change her destiny.

Or mine.

And our destinies just don't align.

"Come back with me. Now," *she demands.*

"You can't give me orders, Rowan. I'm not one of your subjects."

She steps back a bit, putting space between us. Like she's waiting for me to back down.

I don't.

She reaches down and starts petting herself, her fingers massaging in slow circles between her legs. "Fine," *she says, her voice small.* "Then walk away, if you're going."

But now it feels wrong, with her standing out here, doing that. Undressed like that. It's getting dark.

"Rowan. This is how it has to be. Don't be mad."

"I'm not mad." *Her voice is breathy, her hand moving in a delib-*

erate rhythm. "I'm just thinking you're the worst person I've ever met."

This hurts in a way I can't fathom.

I never wanted her to hate me. Maybe I knew she would, and I knew it would hurt. I just didn't know how much.

"Rowan—"

"Stop saying my name."

"Please, stop."

"Stop what?" Her fingers don't stop. Her eyelids grow heavy, her gaze burning with anger and the betrayal she must be feeling.

"I'm going now. And you have to go back to the citadel."

"Maybe I will and maybe I won't."

"What does that mean?"

"It means I'll do what I want to. You can't give me orders either."

"Fine. If you want it to be like this." I take a step away.

She stops touching herself. "You want it like this! This is your doing, not mine. Don't you ever forget that, as long as you live, Wolf!"

I'm afraid I won't. It's like there's a crack through my chest and my heart is leaking out. But I force myself to be hard. "All you're doing is reminding me why I'm doing the right thing."

She takes the delicate gold chain from around her waist and throws it at my feet. "Take it. I was going to give it to you anyway."

My fingers feel numb as I pick up the chain. It's the only jewelry she managed to keep when we fled, when the caravan was attacked.

"It's pure gold," she says bitterly. "It's worth a lot."

"I can't take it."

"Yes, you can. Don't you dare give it back. You ought to get paid something for your trouble." She starts touching herself again, and the pained look in her eyes is terrible.

"Rowan..."

"Just go if you're going to go!" Her voice hits a hysterical note, and I turn away from her distress. I don't want to see her this way. I can't take it.

I run downhill through the trees and I hear her calling behind me. "Wolf!" *Her voice is broken now, and I know she's crying.* "Wolf! Please, come back!"

I run until I'm pretty sure she can't see me, and duck behind a tree, gasping.

I can still see her on the rocks, the emerald-green of the ruffled bustle bright in the dusk. She's down on her knees, pitched forward, sobbing. She keeps stroking herself until she cries out, a sound that's racked with pain, and her body trembles and I know she's coming. "Wolf!" *She's still crying.* "Wolf, please..."

She cries a long while as the dusk grows dark.

It's not safe for her out here.

I consider that I may have to drag her back myself, tie her to the citadel gate to make her stay.

But then she gets up and scurries back up the incline, shaking. I scramble up through the trees as fast as I can, around the edge of the rocky cliff, following her. Keeping her in my sight.

I follow her all the way back to the citadel, until I see her cross through the back gate, before I head back down to the river.

I close my tablet. In the dimmed lighting of the jet's cabin, the woman sleeping alone in the bed looks so peaceful, her face serene.

Nothing like the tumult of emotions churning inside me.

My heart's beating in my throat and I'm frustrated as hell. All I want to do is grab her and kiss the shit out of her.

At this point, I'm so sure there's so much of her in Rowan—a girl who feels so completely alone in the world, so unseen for who she really is inside, by anyone but Wolf—it's driving me mad that Wolf's abandoning her.

I slip off my glasses and quietly go over to her, set my knees on either side of her body, and crawl over her on the bed. Hovering above her, I put my lips close to her ear. "Wolf is a dick. He doesn't deserve Rowan."

Megan's already awake. She started stirring when I prowled over her, probably breathing too hard. My pulse is pounding, her scent igniting some primal sense in me that makes my dick harder than it already was.

"You woke me up in the middle of the night to tell me that?" she says sleepily. Her eyes are still closed, but she's smiling.

"She's crying in the woods, half-naked, and he's fucking leaving. What would you call that?"

Her eyes crack open. "Chivalrous?"

I grunt. "He's supposed to make sure she's safe. *Himself.* Not pass her off to someone else. And he's supposed to catch her when she falls. That's what a man does."

I stare down at her until her eyes open fully and focus on mine.

"I mean, he caught her when she jumped down off the rocks. And in the trust-fall scene, remember?"

"You know that's not what I mean." My tone edges on a growl. "She made herself come while he left her, so she could bear the pain. He taught her how to have sex and now it's her only connection to him, because he *left.*"

"He knows if her new husband sees them together, it's a risk," she says patiently, like maybe I missed that part. I didn't. "By now, Wolf has heard that the man is a warlord and a notorious sadist. He's afraid of what will happen to them both."

"So he leaves her to the psychopath?!"

Megan just smiles. She seems way too amused by me right now.

"I think this author is a sadist," I growl.

She laughs.

"Let him drown in the river and write in a new hero."

"I'm already writing the next book and Wolf is very much alive."

"Still time to kill him off."

"My readers love him!"

"Then your readers are as dumb as he is."

Her mouth drops open.

I stare at those sweet, soft, open lips, and my thudding dick gets the better of me.

"*Fuck it.*"

I kiss her, hard, my mouth claiming, then dominating, then utterly consuming hers, as I tumble head over heels into her sweetness. She's soft and warm, even more luscious than I imagined she would be, and I devour her like I'm starving for her love.

Maybe because I am.

I'm so fucking hard, it's maddening as I fall, deeper and deeper into her, ravaging her mouth.

So hard...

And yet I can't fuck her.

That fact, which I can never escape, crashes over me like cold water.

I pull back, tearing myself away when it really hits me how passionately she's kissing me back. We were eating each other's faces off and she was moaning softly, pleadingly, her hips riding up into mine.

My cock, pressed between us, thuds with the drive to bury myself in her.

Megan blinks up at me, panting. "What? What's wrong?"

"I shouldn't have done that."

"Why not?"

I swallow, my pulse pounding in my throat as we stare at each other.

"I know you were kidding," she says softly, "about my readers."

I was. Her readers aren't dumb, obviously. I can barely turn the pages fast enough to feed my hunger for every word. I love the world she's created, and no, I don't just read it for the sex. But fuck, it makes me hard.

"Your books are great. I'm invested." I push back, detaching myself from her. Somehow, my hips magnetized to hers and her legs became entangled with mine while we kissed.

My head is spinning with the force of the conflicting signals as I battle with myself, doing the exact last thing my body wants me to do, when I settle beside her on my back. I take a breath to calm my pounding heart.

She laughs a little, like she's struggling to catch her breath. "I noticed. And thank you." Her eyes meet mine, shining with affection, and gratitude I don't deserve. "It feels so good when you say that."

"It's true."

It's also just words.

I feel like that dumb twat Wolf.

Maybe things will change, but right now, he isn't being the man Rowan needs.

I'm failing similarly with Megan.

There's an uncomfortable parallel there.

"I think I see myself in Wolf, actually." I stare at the softly glowing ceiling of the jet, avoiding her eyes. "That's a testament to how good you are."

"Thank you. But I wouldn't say you're much like him."

"We're both cowards."

There's a long silence, the hum of the jet the only sound.

"Why would you say that?"

"He makes decisions based on fear."

"So he should risk losing everything, including his life, for love?"

"Yes."

It's maddening how easily that answer falls out of my mouth.

I want to punch myself in the face.

"Maybe he should." Megan's voice is small, pensive. "But maybe he hasn't arrived at that conclusion yet."

Yeah. Dumb.

"Like I said." I tug the blanket that's wrapped around her hips and spread it out, covering us both with it. "He's a twat."

She snickers softly.

Then she shifts, and I feel the warmth of her body, closer to me. "Can we please snuggle?" she whispers.

That she even has to ask is so fucking wrong, it kills me a little.

"Of course." My voice is gruff and tight, and I swear to myself that I'm not going to kiss her again. Or grope her. Or roll on top of her and grind her into the mattress.

I don't move at all.

I suck back the soft scent of her hair as she curls against me and slips her arm around my waist, resting her head on my shoulder.

Then I feel her relax against me, and I wrap my arm over hers, trying to relax. My cock is still thudding.

There's no way I can sleep like this.

"What about *her* life?" she says after a moment. "Should he risk her life for love?"

I grumble into her hair. "He should find a way to save them both. That's what a true hero does."

"Maybe he will."

"Maybe I still think you should write in a new hero."

"Maybe this one will surprise you, Jameson."

Yeah. I fucking hope so.

CHAPTER 32

Megan

P aris is, as I assumed it would be, ridiculously amazing.

As our limo slides through the streets of the central *arrondissements*, I can picture the city in partial ruins, the beautiful historic buildings reclaimed by nature, green foliage climbing up the crumbled walls in some distant, postapocalyptic future.

Because that's just how my twisted mind works.

In the here and now, though, I can't get over the intricate artistry of the buildings in pale pinks and blues and creams, block after block, the history that seems to whisper from every ornate old door and window we pass.

"Canada is so *young*," I marvel. "I can't get over the old buildings."

"Wait until we get to Berlin," Jameson says. "It's quite different. Paris wasn't destroyed in World War II, so the old buildings are very much intact, whereas much of Berlin has been rebuilt."

My eyes go wide as I envision it.

"It fascinates you, doesn't it?" He tips his chin up and studies me. "That intersection between the past and the future."

"How did you know?" I breathe, like I'm an addict and he just shot me up with my favorite drug.

His lips quirk. "I'm reading your books, remember? The desolate landscape littered with relics of the past, where people struggle to survive in the distant future? If you weren't interested in the way the two time periods touch each other, you could've set your story somewhere else."

"I could've."

"What interests you so much about that juxtaposition?"

"Hmm." I've never been asked this before. Mainly because I've rarely chatted with anyone about my books.

Suddenly, I feel shy.

"I guess it makes everything feel like it doesn't belong together. The world is at odds with itself, and with the people in it. As humans, the hero and heroine of the book are trespassers in nature, and we get to see that, in those relics left behind, and in the way the natural world reclaims itself when humanity fails. Wolf and Rowan adapt and survive, but they're always on the razor's edge of survival. It's not guaranteed." I hesitate. "Maybe I like not knowing how it will end. And I like readers not knowing how it will end, but still rooting for a happy ending, as improbable as it may seem. I think... I long for a happy ending in a world where there shouldn't be one."

Jameson's furrowed gaze is locked on to mine. "Then write that happy ending."

"Maybe I will..."

I gaze out the window.

We're circling the Arc de Triomphe now, where it seems that six or more unmarked lanes of traffic are weaving through one another. I can't believe we're not hitting any other vehicles, but maybe it's always been this way.

Things often stay the same, until one day, they break.

"Maybe I just can't envision it yet."

I make Jameson be an absolute shameless tourist with me, and have the limo drop us off at the foot of the Eiffel Tower. I'm thrilled to discover there's a freaking carousel right there, across the street.

Naturally, I insist he ride it with me while Locke takes commemorative photos of us.

"That's so going on your Instagram," I tell him as I send the best one to Clara. In the photo, Jameson is riding on a white horse. While wearing a three-piece suit.

He probably expected to be in the air-conditioned limo and/or fine restaurants all day.

Then I make him wait with me until it's our turn to have an old French man on the sidewalk draw a caricature portrait of us.

He's so talented. In the finished sketch, Jameson and I are seated at a French café. True to life, he's wearing his suit, but the artist drew a blue beret on his head that isn't there.

"I love this so much," I gush. "I'm putting it up in your living room."

"Our living room," he corrects me.

I can't believe he doesn't even argue with me about it.

I give it to Locke so he can secure it in the limo for safekeeping. "Please make sure this gets home to Vancouver," I tell him.

"I'll protect it with my life," he replies gravely.

I like Locke. A lot.

Jameson refuses to stand in the hours-long line to go up the Eiffel Tower, but by then, the big digital displays announce that the lift to the top is closed. "This happens a lot," he grumbles, promising me, in the same breath, to take me up in a helicopter anytime I want to see the world from above. I get the feeling he gives a hard pass to most things that regular mortals are willing to line up for. Maybe he's never had to line up for anything.

I'm starving anyway. We've been surviving so far off *pâtisserie* from street vendors.

"Please tell me it's time to go to dinner," I practically beg as we walk back to the limo. "I really need a meal."

"And how about some French wine? The good stuff."

"Now you're speaking my language."

"Oh, yeah?" Jameson lifts an eyebrow, and as we settle into the limo, he says, "*Alors allons te saouler, ma douce.*"

My jaw drops as my ovaries moan. That was way too sexy for broad daylight. I suddenly feel like I'm in some dark, sweaty corner at the Moulin Rouge while he growls French filth in my ears.

"What was that?" I sound pathetically breathless. "You speak French?"

"Don't you?"

"What, because I'm Canadian? I only took it up to tenth grade because they forced me to. I know, like, colors, the days of the week, and weather conditions. I can't actually understand a word of what anyone says around here. Well, other than the English-speaking tourists."

His lips curl in amusement. Then his eyes drift to my mouth, half-lidded.

"*Tu es la plus belle femme de tout Paris.*"

"Stop that."

"You are the most beautiful woman in all of Paris."

That was what he said to me. I'm pretty sure. I type it into Google Translate when we stop back at the hotel to get dressed for dinner, and he says it again.

I *feel* beautiful as I float out of our hotel suite on Jameson's arm an hour later, wearing the short black-with-silver-sequins Balmain dress that he surprised me with. And the lovely, silky French lingerie underneath.

In the lobby on our way out to the limo, a photographer is waiting, at the ready to take "candid" photos of us—making sure to heavily feature *the ring*.

Jameson's PR team has arranged for photos to be taken of us many times already, both formally and, like tonight, informally; those photos have all been released to the press, and it's strange to me what a giant deal the media has been making about the engagement ring, of all things. As if the price tag on the ring a man gives a woman is directly proportionate to his feelings for her. As if a poor man can't love a woman as much as a rich man can?

Regardless, our romance, starring *the ring*, has gone viral.

Or so I've heard from Jameson. And my brother, and Nicole. And everyone else I know, who are suddenly flooding my inboxes.

Troy included. Unfortunately.

After glimpsing his first explosive text about it—*I can't believe you'd betray me like this*—I stopped looking at them, instead swiping them away, unread.

The idea that I've "betrayed" him is his delusion, not mine.

And after checking out the first online post or two about the engagement, I stopped looking at those, too.

That version of Jameson and Megan is just a story.

I should know, since I write fiction.

When we arrive at the elegant restaurant, one entire side has been booked out for Jameson's meeting/party with his French connections. There are about a dozen people in the room mingling over drinks, and the crowd gradually doubles as we make our way around.

When I'm introduced to a sophisticated, middle-aged Frenchman named Jean-Charles, Jameson casually mentions that the man is a fellow billionaire, that he and his family own a number of French hotels, including the one we're staying at while in Paris, and that he's codeveloping a resort with the Vances on the Côte d'Azur.

He also mentions, belatedly, that Jean-Charles is his stepfather.

I can't put my finger on what it is that bothers me about this abrupt introduction, exactly, but it throws me a little off-kilter that Jameson didn't tell me beforehand that we were visiting his stepfather in Paris.

I feel put on the spot.

Or maybe it's Jean-Charles who's being put on the spot?

Because he seems equally surprised to be meeting me, when Jameson tells him "This is my fiancée, Megan."

Being a gentleman, though, he recovers quickly.

"Congratulations," Jean-Charles says warmly. "I heard the happy news."

Which means that Jameson didn't reach out to tell him himself? I have no idea how to navigate this situation, since Jameson never even told me he has a stepfather. I'm not even sure if this man is currently married to his mother or what.

I really should've researched his family a little more. Or at least asked.

But how could I know Jameson would spring a situation like this on me?

Luckily, Jean-Charles seems very pleased to meet me. While we're engaged in conversation with the charismatic Frenchman, Jameson eventually touches me on the back, excuses himself, and goes to speak with a trio of very attractive women.

To say it's distracting would be a gross understatement.

Soon enough, I excuse myself from the conversation with Jean-Charles and several of his business associates, and head for the ladies' room to get a breather.

As I dab cool water on my throat and take a breath, my heart pounds viciously. I'm insanely bothered, just seeing my fiancé talk to those beautiful French women.

I feel it in the pit of my stomach, the discomfort of that no-sex barrier he's put up between us.

He's working, I tell myself. I can't expect him to hold my hand all night. And they're just talking.

But I can't help wondering if he would actually have sex with someone else, and *not* talk to me about it beforehand like he said he would.

Troy did.

And I didn't know.

We lived in a tiny town where everyone knew everyone, and I didn't know. Not until I walked in on it and saw it for myself. Even then, for several dark hours afterward, it was hard to believe.

I didn't want to believe it.

Would I see it now if it was happening right under my nose?

Jameson is in and out of the house for "meetings" all the time while I'm writing. How would I even know what he's really doing? Nicole hasn't exactly sent me any Google alerts about him being spotted with another woman, but why would he be?

If he was cheating, he'd be careful about it. Keep it private.

Cheating. Ha. It's not cheating if you're not in a real relationship anyway.

I try to wash down my discomfort with wine.

God, I hate this.

Not knowing how he really feels about me and where I stand with him...

Other than being his fake partner.

Is that truly all he sees me as? And will ever see me as?

Am I really letting myself start to feel for another man who won't treat me right?

And do I really believe that Jameson Vance is going to be celibate for a whole year while he's fake engaged to me? And never touch another woman?

No. I don't believe that.

And the more days that pass without him broaching the subject of *us* having sex, the more I'm starting to fear that he's going to decide to do it with someone else instead.

And if he does, what will I say?

I like you, please don't sleep with someone else?

I already told him that he could touch me.

I told him, like a dumbass, that I wanted "first dibs" on his attention.

The truth is, if he chooses someone else instead... I already know it will crush me.

If I thought Paris was exhilarating in the daytime, the city truly comes alive at night. Jameson and I have to navigate around the crowds spilling out of the bustling sidewalk cafés and bars.

We're strolling back to the hotel along the narrow sidewalks, with Locke and Rurik at our heels, when I ask him, "Can we hold hands?"

He hesitates, but when I offer him my hand, he slips his into mine. I soften almost instantly, melting into our connection. No matter how on edge I felt at dinner, it puts me at ease to touch him.

"It really is romantic here, isn't it?" I marvel over it as I try to absorb every sight and sound, the wisps of music, and the rich scents of food and coffee on the night air. "It's in the air. I can *feel* it. I've never felt anything like it."

"It is." Jameson's voice is low, his tone reserved.

He's been pretty quiet since we left the restaurant. Even so, my heart thumps a brutal rhythm, the one that tortures me whenever he's this close to me, my skin pulsing where we touch. Sex feels imminent.

But I know it's not.

And because there's nothing I can do to indulge these romantic urges with the man at my side, the man I'm engaged to, but who won't have sex with me, I change the subject.

"You didn't tell me your stepdad would be there tonight. I didn't even know you have a stepdad, or that he lives in France. You could've warned me, so I could mentally prepare."

His stepfather was very nice to me, and he was clearly happy to see Jameson, but we both know what I mean by that. The man is a parental figure of Jameson's, and here we are, engaged out of nowhere. Honestly, I would've worn a slightly less sexy dress if I knew this was meet-the-stepdad night.

"Did you need a warning?" Jameson sounds amused.

"Yes! This hemline should be a few inches lower and I would've toned down the glitter eye shadow, for one."

"That's two."

Yup. He finds this funny.

"You should've told me! I sweated right through this dress when he noticed the ring."

He squeezes my hand, which makes me purr inwardly, and forgive him instantly.

"I didn't see the point in causing you any stress over something that might not even happen. I wasn't totally sure he'd make it tonight."

"Well, I appreciate your intentions. But I would rather have had the heads-up."

"Okay. Lesson learned. Next time, I'll give you a heads-up."

"Are we going to see him again while we're in Paris?"

"No. I need to be in Berlin tomorrow. That's why I really came. We have another potential partner there, a very historic beer company. Prepare to drink much beer."

"I'm prepared," I say gravely. "But seriously, you come all the way to France and you don't want to spend more time with your stepdad? Is he married to your mom?"

He looks at me sidelong. "I forget that you don't have the internet."

"Funny. I just don't creep on people. I prefer to use the web for writing research, and leave it at that."

"You're an anomaly, Jessica Rivers."

"Thank you." It gives me a little thrill, actually, when he calls me Jessica. Maybe because no one else does, and it feels like our little secret.

"Yes, Jean-Charles Moreau is married to my mother. They live just outside of Paris."

I consider that. "And you're not going to see her while you're here?"

"She could've come tonight."

I try to read between the lines of that brief response. "But she didn't. Because... you two aren't on good terms?"

"We are. More or less. But she doesn't take much interest in business, her husband's or the family's, and this was a business dinner."

I don't buy that excuse. "But her youngest son was here. Her baby. All the way from across the globe."

"Correct."

"And she didn't make time? Or didn't want to come? Help me out here."

"I wish I could. But I can't really explain Rachel Vance-Moreau to you. As far as I've ever known, her life, moment to moment, is driven by her emotional state. If she has a bad day, she might disappear and not resurface for months."

He seems so undisturbed by that. But how can that be?

I know what it's like to have an absent parent. Which means I know how confusing and damaging and downright painful it is. Especially if that kind of behavior was present when he was young.

"That doesn't upset you?"

"I'm used to it now, and I know not to set expectations. So I don't end up disappointed. But when I was a kid, I can tell you, it upset me."

It's upsetting to me, just hearing about it. A young Jameson, hurt by his mother's emotional abandonment.

But the fact that he's sharing this with me makes me hungry to hear more.

"Did she do that a lot? Disappear on you, when you were a kid?"

"Yes. Unfortunately."

"That must've been very hard."

"It was. Back then, it made life turbulent. We lived in a huge house, bigger than the one I live in now, and most of the time, my mom would be locked up in her room and I couldn't even go see her if she wasn't in the mood for it. And I never knew what set her bad moods off. When you're a kid with a parent that emotionally unstable, you blame yourself. I naturally assumed I was the reason my mom didn't want to see me."

I consider that. And I know, of course, that he wasn't the reason. Any more than I was the reason my dad couldn't love me.

"What was the reason?"

"I don't know for sure. But years later..." He hesitates. "Well, I guess I was deemed old enough to be let in on all the family secrets. The family truths."

I wait, wondering if he'll let me in on these truths. "Go on," I prompt, when he pauses too long and I worry he might not tell me. "Please."

"Are you sure you want to know these things?" He glances at me, his handsome face a myriad of colors from the lights of a bustling café across the street.

"Yes."

"Well, the truth is, my dad had a lot of affairs. He cheated on my mom repeatedly, throughout their marriage."

"Oh. That's... " I don't finish the sentence.

Obviously, it was a lot of things, none of them good.

"Yeah. I always wondered, what kind of marriage is that? I mean, she ended up cheating on him, too, apparently. With Jean-Charles. She had five children with my dad, and he wasn't faithful. She had no job. Her whole life was our family, until it wasn't. And then she disconnected from us, so easily, when there was a time when we were her whole world. But maybe I reminded her too much of him. Maybe we all did. Who knows."

"And what about your dad? Was he around at all?"

"He was, but he worked a lot. And he had all those affairs to manage," he adds dryly. "But he died when I was eleven."

"Oh. I'm so sorry." I don't know what else to say.

Damn, that was young to lose a parent.

"It's all right."

"Was he sick?" I probe when Jameson doesn't offer more.

"No. It was a helicopter accident. Sudden and unexpected. The whole family was devastated by it. Mom never recovered, I don't think. She remarried quickly and moved to France to live with Jean-Charles and his children from a previous marriage. She brought me, Savannah, and Harlan with her. But at that point, any interest she'd had in mothering us was abandoned in pursuit of doting on her new husband and his kids, maybe in hopes that he wouldn't cheat. We spent the rest of our teenage years in prestigious boarding schools around Europe."

"Wow. What was that like?"

"Lonely," he says, which is not what I expected him to say. "Savi and Harlan and I didn't even go to the same schools all the time, since there was a three-year age difference. So I was on my own for most of my teens. I hated it here, honestly. Being an outsider. Those were the worst years of my life, when they could've been some of the best. I begged Graysen to fly me home, like every time I talked to him."

"And did he?"

"Eventually. When I was seventeen, as soon as I finished school. He and Damian had become Granddad's business partners by then, stepping into our dad's shoes. It was my brothers who told me all about the affairs Dad had and why Mom probably was the way she was."

"I see."

"At least it made all the pieces fit together. Suddenly I understood why Mom was so damn eager to start over in a new marriage. And why she was so paranoid and untrusting, and so uncomfortable with being in the public eye. She had a lot to hide. Her husband had all those affairs, and she still stood by him, but she didn't want the world to know how he'd betrayed her. Or how, in the end, she'd betrayed him, too. I think it was her worst fear, that she might be humiliated like that in public. That everyone might find out her great love story was a lie. I think that's also why she likes living in France. They have such strict privacy laws here."

"I suppose that does explain some of her behavior," I say carefully. "But it still must've been hard for you to learn all those things about your parents."

"It was. I was pretty angry about it. I even had a brief rebellious streak." Jameson cocks an eyebrow at me. "Which mostly amounted to a few tattoos."

"Such a rebel," I tease. "Thank you for telling me all that. I know it can't be easy."

"It's just the truth. My family's really not as pretty as they want to look."

"I understand. My family's not always pretty either."

He snickers. "Tell that to Cole."

I laugh.

Neither of us says anything more until we reach the end of the block. I can see our hotel up ahead, and I already regret that our walk is coming to an end. As we cross the street, still holding hands, I tell him, "I just realized why I may be having such a hard time envisioning a happy ending for my book series."

"Yeah?"

I take a breath. "I've never seen a happy ending play out in real life."

He considers that for a moment, then admits, "Neither have I."

CHAPTER 33

W hen we arrive back at our hotel suite, I release Megan's hand.

She wanders around the room, checking out the view from the windows. Seeing her struggle with what to do with herself, alone with me in this hotel room, is about as depressing as watching her struggle with how to touch me in the restaurant.

I've become accustomed to avoiding her touch while restraining myself from touching her at the same time. It happened very quickly, adjusting to this delicate dance. I hate that I've put up this barrier to force distance between us. But obviously, I had to.

Getting closer to her in any way just makes this whole situation harder.

I feel raw enough about the things I told her as we walked hand in hand through the streets of Paris. Because they were painfully true.

And I keep thinking about what she said in the limo today. *I long for a happy ending in a world where there shouldn't be one.*

Like I told her, I've never witnessed a happy ending in real life. Those are things in movies and books and fairy tales. My grandparents' marriage, my parents' marriage, Graysen's engagement, and now even my own; they're all lies.

But I don't want to live a lie.

I spent my teenage years grieving my father's untimely death, only to find out that he'd betrayed us. It wasn't just Mom he betrayed with his affairs. It was our whole sense of family. He'd lied to us about who we were to each other, and it broke my heart.

That was when I got the dagger tattoo over my heart: when I swore to myself that I would never lie to those I love like that.

I do love. I love my family, fiercely.

And of course, I want to be loved.

Maybe much more than I've always feared falling in love, I want it. Badly.

I want to be the kind of man who leads with his heart, like Savannah advised me to. But how can I connect with Megan in the ways that matter, when what matters to me most is honesty, and I can't be fully honest with her, because of the stupid challenge?

This fucking challenge that's taking over my life.

"Did you enjoy yourself at dinner?" I loosen my tie, struggling for something safe to talk about as the nightly tension that always surrounds getting ready for bed presses in.

"I did." She looks at me from where she stands by the open doors to the balcony, the long curtains billowing in. The sparkly dress shimmers over her curves, the skirt showing the exact right amount of her legs to appear seductive, to make a man hunger for what he can't see.

My chest feels tight, my cock so swollen... I'm half-hard already, just looking at her across the room. I turn away. "I barely got a word with you. You were so popular with the men at the table."

She doesn't say anything as I pour us each a glass of the Cristal I had delivered for us just before we got here. I hand her a crystal coupe of champagne.

"Thank you." She touches her glass lightly to mine, and we both take a sip.

As we stand here in silence, my senses flood with the awareness of her. I always feel her when she's near, my attraction to her overwhelming me. And all the way here, holding hands in the streets, her soft, warm touch sent rivulets of lust streaming up my veins, heady and intoxicating. I can still feel it.

I crave touching her like that, skin to skin.

I can't believe how erotic it is, just holding her hand, or brushing against her in public. It feels like I've been starving for her for long, aching years. So much longer than I've actually known her.

"Do you want to shower? Or take a bath?" I put my champagne down to unbutton the collar of my shirt, and go over to where my open suitcase is spread on a luggage rack, avoiding that look in her eyes.

"You can go first," she says softly. "I'll just enjoy the view."

I look at her like she's zapped me with an electric current. My pulse beats in my cock like a ticking bomb about to go off. I couldn't be harder if she dropped her dress right now.

I know, when she smiles wryly, that I've mistaken her meaning. "The view from the balcony," she clarifies.

Heat floods me as her cheeks grow pink.

I head stiffly into the bathroom, and start running her a bath. Maybe I want to do nice things for her to make up for what's missing. And somehow, it's getting more difficult to read her, to know what she wants, to figure out how to make her happy, instead of easier.

No. That's not true.

She wants sex, asshole.

She wants you to take her in your arms and kiss her.

You've seen the way she looks at you.

You've read her books...

She wants you to be her goddamn hero.

She told my siblings I was some kind of superhero. I think half of her believes it. And the other half desperately wants it to be true.

I drag my hands over my face. I feel like a fucking fraud.

The idea of sleeping next to her in the hotel bed...

My heart is racing just thinking about it.

At home, I've taken to hanging out in the living room when she goes to bed, passing out on the couch. I set an alarm to wake me before she gets up in the morning so I can slip in next to her.

Because going to bed with her at night, and sleeping next to her, is impossible.

I'm way too aroused for that.

You'd think I'd be jerking off on the hour.

Instead, I've stopped masturbating at all. When I realized there was no way I could do it without picturing her, and picturing her while I did it was only making it harder to resist touching her, I decided it would be a better idea to stick with cold showers and abstinence.

Just avoid sex of any kind, all together, until the challenge ends.

Stupid.

In the hotel room, what excuse do I have to avoid sleeping in the bed with her?

I'll have to sleep with her. And maybe I won't get a minute of sleep because I'll be picturing her in that glittering dress, looking at me over dinner all night like she wanted me to be her dessert.

Thirteen more days.

I walk back into the room, and when I tell her that her bath is ready, she looks sweetly surprised.

"Come here." I hold out my hand to her.

She comes to me and slips her hand into mine, and I lead her into the bathroom, where the tub is nearly full.

"Take your time," I tell her, and leave her alone.

While Megan has her bath, I pace the length of the hotel suite. I'd be suspicious as hell about me, if I were her. My evasive answers. The fact that I barely touch her.

I wasn't lying about the way my business associates were all over her at dinner. In Vancouver or Paris, it's all the same. Men stare at her. Doors are opened for her. She could have her pick of men, if she wanted it.

I live with her, and I've barely even kissed her.

And when I did, on the jet... I jerked away from her as if I realized I was allergic to her halfway through.

At this rate, she'll start thinking I'm nuts.

Or secretly gay.

Or fucking someone else.

And lying to her about whichever of the above.

I blow out a breath, flopping back on the couch.

Faintly, I hear the water in the bath slosh, and my head immediately goes to her stripping off that dress. I picture her naked in there, the water sliding over her luscious curves as she washes herself.

This is killing me. I'm fairly sure it's starting to kill her, too.

I lie sprawled on the couch, listening to the faint sounds of her bathing, going out of my mind.

Eventually, I pick up my phone and stare at it for a moment, debating. Then I call one of my brothers before I can stop myself.

It's getting that desperate.

I hold the phone to my ear, bury my other hand in my hair and squeeze. While I wait for him to pick up, the look on Megan's face when she asked me if we could hold hands tortures me. So hopeful, and yet devoid of hope at the same time.

She was afraid I was going to say no. And yet she'd had the courage to ask me anyway.

"Aren't you in Paris?" is my brother's greeting. I can hear the amusement in Damian's voice. "It's after midnight there."

"Can I watch her touch herself?" I keep my voice low, so she won't hear me. My tone is desperate, like a dying man begging for water. "If I don't touch myself at the same time or get any gratification from it?"

Damian gives a low chuckle. "Tell me you'd get no gratification from it. I want to hear you lie to me for the first time in your life."

I groan as I claw my hand through my hair.

"Are you grasping for some loophole because you already screwed up?"

"No."

"Did you have sex with your fiancée? Or someone else? How bad is it? Be honest, Jamie. I won't even tell the others."

I believe him. Damian has never been one to play by the rules. I doubt he'd seriously want me to lose my inheritance over the rules of this game. And what does he really care if I cheat? He doesn't, probably.

But I have nothing to hide.

"I promise you, I haven't had sex with her." As those words come out of my mouth, the bathroom door opens and my eyes meet Megan's.

She stops abruptly in the doorway. She heard those last words.

"I have to go." I hang up on Damian and sit up.

Megan steps out of the bathroom, wrapped in a hotel robe. Her hair is twisted up, not wet.

"You're finished your bath?" I state the obvious. "You want another drink? Or should we get some sleep?"

She blinks at me. "When I said I was going to enjoy the view," she says hesitantly, "if I'd actually meant that I wanted to enjoy the view of *you* in the shower, would you have said yes?"

I clear my throat, which suddenly has an entire day-old croissant jammed in it. "Uh... I don't think that's a good idea right now."

And now she's probably thinking there's something wrong with me. If I don't even want her to see me naked in the shower, what am I hiding? Some ghastly rash? A tiny dick?

"Why not?"

Fuck me.

I lean forward, resting my elbows on my knees. "Megan." I swipe my hand through my hair. "We just need to wait a bit."

"Until you're comfortable," she says softly.

I don't answer that, just grit my teeth. Because I've never been able to come up with an answer for this. Unless I make up a lie, I have no reason to delay putting my hands all over her body. Even telling her that I won't touch her because of Cole would be a lie at this point.

So I just say nothing.

"Are you into me that way? Physically?"

Shit. I've really fucked this up.

"Megan... of course I am."

"So, if you were ready for something to happen between us... it would happen?"

"Yes. If you wanted it to."

She studies me for a long minute, like she isn't sure if she believes me.

It fucking slays me.

"Tell me the truth, okay?" She glances at the phone in my hand and takes a little breath. "Was that a woman?"

"No." I stand and slip my phone into my pocket, closing the distance between us, wanting to reassure her.

"I heard you. You were telling someone on the phone that you haven't had sex with me." Before I can respond, she adds quietly, "How do I know you're not going to sleep with someone else?"

Fuck. How can I assure her that if I could have sex with anyone, it would be her?

Not being able to tell her *why* I can't is becoming a worse problem than I ever anticipated.

"I'm not sleeping with anyone else," I try to reassure her. "Other than what you've seen when we've been socializing publicly and I'm with you, I'm not even spending time with any other women, personally or professionally, right now." *Thanks to Graysen basically ordering me to stay away from womankind.*

She gives a short, weary sigh. "It was my brother on the phone, wasn't it? He's still having a hard time with this. And you're trying to cover for him."

My mouth opens and shuts as I struggle with what to say to her. I decide to go with the truth, while avoiding actually answering the first part of her question. "Whatever your brother thinks about this, about us, even if he's having a hard time with it, that's not our responsibility either. We both care about Cole. But he doesn't get to choose your partner or mine."

Megan's tension seems to dissolve as she takes that in. I only feel worse when my evasive answer puts her at ease.

She's trusting me, even when I'm not being fully trustworthy.

"I agree." She glances over at the Cristal on ice. "Why don't we finish that champagne? I'm in love with the balcony. We can see the Eiffel Tower from here. It's all lit up."

I know that. That's why I picked this room. For her. "I'll meet you out there."

"Okay." She gives me a small smile that I don't deserve and steps out onto the balcony.

I refill our glasses for us, my chest constricting with the fear that all this evading the truth—*lying; I'm lying to her, at least by omission* —is going to kill our relationship before it even gets started.

Thirteen days.

I just have to usher us around this landmine that I can't acknowledge for thirteen more days. Then I won't have to work around this ridiculous secret anymore.

I can finally have sex with my fiancée without my life blowing up. And everything will fall into place.

CHAPTER 34

Megan

"How does this song never get old?!"

I'm drunk on champagne. Oh yes, I am. Very fine, very French champagne. All my worries have been drowned in heavenly bubbly and music. "Like, it still sounds as good today as it probably did when it came out in the eighties!" I blather on.

Jameson lies on his back on our grand hotel bed in his lounge pants and a T-shirt, freshly showered, legs crossed at the ankles, his bare toes twitching a little and a soft smile on his face as he watches me dance around in my Dirty nightshirt. To INXS's "Need You Tonight."

I'm also dramatically lip-syncing the words, tousling my hair and slithering around the bed as I fake serenade him.

"Are you still sticking with this story that Dirty is your favorite band?" he inquires. "Or is that just the cool answer?"

I stop dancing. "What's your favorite band?" I demand, realizing that I have no idea. He puts on music a lot, but it's always different stuff. When we work out, he puts on driving heavy metal, but I think that's just for the adrenaline.

Now that I think about it, he seems like a mood listener.

I usually listen to music in my earbuds so I don't bother people around me. Maybe he truly has no idea what I listen to.

"If I said Dirty," he muses, "would you believe me?"

"Hmmm. You promised me you wouldn't lie to me. So, yes."

"I do love Dirty. But I'm also partial to the music of Harry Styles and Maroon 5."

My jaw drops. "Does my brother know this about you?"

"Very few people know this about me. And yes, your brother would be one of them." He shrugs a shoulder. "I like musical sunshine." He frowns adorably, like the reason for that is just occurring to him. Maybe he's drunk, too? "I don't think I naturally produce a lot of sunshine myself. I need outside infusions." He gazes at me for a long moment, like I'm pure sunshine beaming down on him right now.

"That's weird. Because when I met you, I thought you were about as blinding as the sun."

He blinks at me. "What?"

"You're right, though. You're more of a sunny day in a storm. You know, like when the sun breaks through the dark clouds, and it's epic?"

Now he looks more confused. No, drunk. He definitely looks drunk.

"Never mind." I shake my head, feeling woozy, and giggle. "So, shiny male pop stars are your jam, huh?"

"Don't hold it against me, okay?"

"Why would I hold it against you?" I'm so excited about this revelation, it's making my head spin. "My favorite-*favorite* bands, besides Dirty, are System of a Down and the Jonas Brothers."

"Really?"

I crawl onto the bed and up his legs, telling him soberly, "I like metal and boy bands."

"Are you serious?"

"Very." I plant my knees on either side of his hips, my hands beside his shoulders, hovering over him. "I like anything with a lot of dick in it."

His eyebrows go up.

"Metal is major big-dick energy," I explain. "And boy bands make me want to dance. And both of them make me horny."

His eyelids drift lower as I dip down, putting my mouth to his ear, and murmur hotly, with one-hundred-percent sincerity, "I'm a closet freak."

Clearly, I've had too much to drink.

I don't care. Because that's what bubbly does. It makes you not care that it's getting you smashed.

Jameson's mouth drifts open.

I smile and settle back, sitting on his pelvis. Something quite firm jabs at my butt.

He's hard.

Heat thrills through me.

Emboldened, I drift my fingertips over the conservative neckline of my nightshirt. "Megan on the outside..." I drift a finger down the bare outer curve of my breast, revealed through the gaping armhole. "Jessica on the inside."

His eyes glaze over with heat as he watches me.

I press my hands flat to his chest and lean on him. "Do you like that?" I'm panting, my pulse speeding up.

He finally figures out how to work his mouth again and utters, "I think you're cut off."

The words make no sense to me. "What?"

"No more champagne for you," he says slowly, so I can follow.

"I don't need more champagne," I say, just as slowly. "I need to make out with you." I lean down and kiss him, just like that.

With a whole lot of tongue.

He kisses me back. For a long, wet, hot minute that takes my breath away.

Then he takes my face in his hands and gently lifts me away from his lips. He's panting slightly.

I'm panting a lot.

His hazy blue eyes hold mine. Or maybe it's my vision that's hazy.

"I don't want you to do anything you wouldn't do," he murmurs, "just because of alcohol."

"I didn't drink that much. I want to do this." I try to kiss him again, but he holds me away.

"Sweetheart. You're bubbling."

I giggle. He's still holding my face just above him like I'm some wriggling puppy about to lick him.

I sigh and hiccup at the same time. "I kind of hate tonight. It was weirdly emotional. Can't we start over?"

He softens as we gaze at each other. "Of course."

"Except I love that you told me those things about your family and your tattoos. And the champagne, that was good. Can I keep those?"

"If you want to."

"And I love the view from the balcony. You chose it for me, didn't you? Because I'm a virgin in Paris."

A tiny groan lodges in his throat. "Don't say things like that."

"Like what?"

"Sex words."

"Did I?" I purr.

"Yes. Don't. It's bad enough reading your books."

"Why?"

He swallows, hard.

I love these rare moments when we get our flirt on and his desire for me burns through whatever pretense of respectability and manners he keeps trying to uphold all the damn time, like I'm the freaking crown princess and he doesn't want to sully me with his dirty thoughts.

"I just..." He stares at me.

I stare right back.

"We shouldn't." His thumb traces my cheekbone like he's hypnotized by the features of my face. "We can't..."

None of those words make any sense to me.

The music has switched to a song by Amy Shark called "Adore" that I freaking adore, and holy Christ... it's making lust pound through my body.

He's making lust pound through my body.

His hands are hot on my face, his whole body is hot and hard beneath mine, and I slither against him slowly, grinding my hips. I can feel how hard he is when my pelvis drags against his, my pussy rubbing against the thick, unyielding ridge of his penis.

I can feel my heartbeat between my legs and in the base of my throat.

He's long, and the swollen tip of his cock feels plump and soft as I nudge against it.

God, I want to lick it.

I realize I've muttered something to that effect when he makes a growling sound, low in his throat. I can't even tell if it's more pleasure or pain. Or just the effort of his never-ending restraint starting to suffocate him.

Whatever it is, I like it.

"Please kiss me again," I breathe, and then we are kissing, deep and wet, and I'm swimming in the song, in the champagne, in the heat of his hands on my face.

"Tell me what you meant," he whispers between all the lush, hot kisses. "About that freak thing..."

"*You know.* I want to do so many things with you." Maybe his restraint makes me feel safe to say it, but I feel no shame or hesitation.

"What things?" His voice is low and hungry, a restrained whisper.

"All kinds." I shift my hips, dragging myself against his hard length again. "You asked if I like spankings. My answer is yes. In theory. But I've never been spanked before. I've never been manhandled or had my hair pulled or been choked, but I'd let you do all those things and more." I catch his mouth again and kiss the horny hell out of him as the space between us vanishes, our clothes growing hot and damp as we strain together.

He kisses me and kisses me, but he never ventures away from my mouth. He never touches my breasts, even though they're readily available through the gaping holes of my shirt.

His strong hands slide down my back to my ass, grip my cheeks, but don't venture under my nightshirt, much less under my panties.

His cock strains, hard as steel against the softness of my pussy, but he doesn't grind against me.

And just as things are getting so hot I know I could drive myself to orgasm by dry humping his massive dick through our sweaty clothes... he lifts me and sets me gently aside, detaching me fully from his body with a growl.

Somehow, he's sitting on the edge of the bed, and we aren't touching anymore. Because he made it that way without my consent. He's that strong.

I pant, splayed on the bed like a broken doll, disoriented and way too drunk. My pulse pounds so hard through my veins, I'm shaking. My pussy throbs with the incessant need to fuck.

Doesn't he feel the same need?

Even a tenth of it?

Seriously, I could come on a tenth of it. If he just let me rub against him a little more...

He clears his throat as he leans in and presses a kiss to my forehead. My clit jerks when I feel his pulse in his lips against my skin.

That's how hard up I am.

His hair is a mess as he breathes over me, his blue eyes two pools of frustrated desire as they lock with mine, and I swoon. "God, Jameson. I—"

"I'm gonna go for a walk," he interrupts me. "With Locke."

I catch his wrist before he can get up. "Why?"

"Because I can't sleep right now."

Like I can?

His erection is preventing him from relaxing, from sleeping next to me, is that it? And he still won't screw me? Let us undress each other? Just kiss and touch and see where it leads...?

Why?

Because of my brother? Some silly bro code?

Really?

"Rurik will be stationed outside the door while I'm gone. You're safe here." He gets to his feet. "We'll be leaving for Berlin after breakfast. Try to get some sleep."

He kisses the palm of my hand, then leaves me there—still panting, still drunk—without another glance.

CHAPTER 35

At midnight tonight, I can have sex.

Fuck, that's weird.

It's the final day of my challenge. I made it. And I'm really trying not to acknowledge that this forced time-out from my active sex life has actually somehow made me appreciate sex—namely, the sex I'm very likely about to have with my fiancée—all the more.

Like way, way more.

All I want to do is savor it, savor her, and not think about my oldest brother and how fucking pissed and weirdly grateful I've been feeling toward him lately.

Fuck you, Graysen.

Seriously.

The best thing I figure I can do is take Megan somewhere private and amazing, where we can be totally alone, and show her how I really feel about her. Because barely touching her for weeks on end is not it.

I've never thought of sex as being a way to show feelings. Sex isn't about feelings.

At least, it never was for me before.

Now, as I look at her, on the flight over the water from

Vancouver to Vancouver Island on the helicopter I promised I'd take her on, her face lighting up in awe at the view below, I can't imagine sex, or anything else I do with Megan, being separated out. It's all blending into one pulsing mass of feelings. Spending time with her, getting to know her, and soon, touching her freely... it's all about feelings.

It's actually occurred to me what a fucking shame it would've been if I'd met her outside of this challenge, very possibly screwed her early on, and then did the usual: moved on. If I didn't even take the time to get to know her, but had sex with her soon after meeting her, like so many other women... "we" would already be a thing of the past, and I'd probably never even know what I'd missed out on.

Worse, knowing she was Cole's sister, I might've even gone out of my way to avoid her after we had our little fling, so as not to complicate things. Again, never knowing that I was missing out on the loveliest woman I'd ever meet.

But that's not to say that this entire "fake" relationship has been a smooth ride.

It's been over a week since we arrived home from our Europe trip, and ever since that night in Paris, things between us have been strained as I continue to struggle with maintaining my distance, while still keeping up with work, and trying to make sure Megan's happy, even with this careful boundary between us.

I can't wait to tear it right down. Obliterate it. The distance, the boundary, the line I had to draw between us. I want to unleash everything I've ever had to hold back, to keep myself from losing control with her.

I want to sweep her away and make it up to her for days on end. Naked.

So, I've decided to bring her to the island, to a resort my family owns here. It's got a fantastic restaurant, a world-class spa, and it's surrounded by lush rain forest.

But most importantly, the VIP suite is ultra-private. It's the perfect place to hole away with a lover.

As soon as we arrive and get settled into the suite, I show her the pool on the huge private patio, and the incredible, peaceful view into the mossy green trees of the forest that border it.

Then a romantic dinner for two is served for us on the patio.

We take our time eating, then take a dip in the pool, enjoying the fresh air off the forest and the view of the stars as the night grows dark around us.

At eleven o'clock, we're lingering in the hot tub when I lean in and kiss her, obviously taking her by surprise. I've managed to avoid kissing her, or being kissed by her again, since Paris, which has been one of the most ridiculous and difficult things I've ever had to do.

She hesitates when my lips touch hers, but then she kisses me back. I indulge in the luscious heat of her mouth, kissing her soft and slow for long minutes in the steaming water, before I break away, suggesting we shower off and have some wine by the fire.

She seems delighted by this.

The energy between us, as usual, is heated and electric, and clearly neither of us has sleep in mind anytime soon.

At eleven fifty, I pour us a glass of wine and we sit down to drink in front of the fireplace in the suite, in our bathrobes, with the fire burning low. It's cooler here than it is in the city, wrapped inside the shelter of the forest.

I can tell Megan loves it here.

Or maybe she especially loves being here alone with me.

She's happy tonight, and it makes my chest burn.

At midnight, I set my wineglass down and get to my feet. I take off my watch and set it aside. I've been checking it all night, and she's probably wondering if I'm distracted about some business thing.

I plan to give her all my attention, for the next seven days.

As much of it as she can handle.

I've booked us here for a whole week, but if she wonders why, she hasn't outright asked. Maybe she assumes I brought her here so she could write in peace. And that's part of it. A very small part.

I lock eyes with her and tell her, "Come here, Megan." My voice is low and demanding, and it sends a shiver up my back when her eyes go wide in response.

They go soft and glassy, too.

Maybe she can sense the lust pouring off me.

She sets her wine aside. Then she gets to her feet and hesitantly comes over to me.

I reach for her, slipping my hand around the small of her back, and draw her to me. My hard cock, trapped between us, flexes hungrily.

She makes a soft sound of surprise. Or maybe pleasure.

I slip my other hand into her hair and squeeze a little, tipping her head back. She dangles there, leaning into me.

I told her when she accepted my proposal that I wouldn't be throwing her any curveballs. I don't intend to.

I'll make sure this one lands as gently as possible.

I tell her "I want you."

After a slight hitch in her breath, she says, "I've been yours for weeks, Jameson."

I drift my lips over hers, not quite kissing her. "I want you to know what you're getting into first. We agreed to discuss this beforehand. So, here's what's going to happen. I'm going to slip off your robe and eat your pussy. Then I'm going to fuck you. I'll try to be as gentle as I can, but that might be a struggle right now."

I lick my lip, giving her a moment to absorb that, and she swallows, her body soft and willing against mine.

"Then I'm going to let you sleep. Then I'm going to fuck you again. Much harder. I'm going to fuck you a lot, in every position I can think of, as long as you'll let me. And I'm going to make you come so much that just the thought of sex, any time it comes into your mind, will make you long for sex with me."

That's my goal, anyway. And I'm pretty determined to make it happen.

My heart thuds a broken rhythm when I utter, "Tell me you want that," desperate to hear it.

"Yes," she whispers fervently. "I want that."

I want her so fucking badly, by the time I slam my mouth down on hers, I'm shaking with the effort to hold back.

CHAPTER 36

Megan

WOW.

I've never seen someone crank up the *I'm going to fuck you now* vibes so hard and so fast.

It's like a horny switch was flipped.

Jameson kisses me deep and slow, like he's waiting for my response to catch up, tightening his hand in my hair when I take too long to kiss him back just as passionately. I'm still halfway in shock. My hand grips his robe, and I can feel his heartbeat thudding where we touch.

When he breaks away, I sag against him, wanting more.

"If we do this," he tells me devoutly, "it changes everything. There's no going back."

"I know that."

He shakes his head slightly, like he's not sure I do, though.

"I'm very hungry, Megan." His thumb strokes the side of my neck. "You haven't even glimpsed my appetite yet. And I've never wanted anyone so badly. I want to make you come until you can't come anymore."

My heart pounds, ferocious now, against his.

I'm a little dazed, to say the least, from the abrupt change. The way he's talking to me. And touching me. So different from how he usually avoids touching me, to put it mildly.

But I quickly surrender.

"Please," I say softly.

And I swear I see something snap in his eyes.

He releases my hair. Then he unties my robe and slips it off my shoulders, letting it fall. I'm naked underneath.

I stand bared to him in the firelight as he drinks me in.

He tears off his own robe and tosses it aside.

I watch, practically panting already, as he goes down on his knees in front of me. It throws me so much, I'm not even sure what to do.

However, Jameson knows exactly what to do. And say.

He breathes hotly on my pussy. "Fuck, I've wanted this for so long..."

"Oh god." I tremble, burying my fingers in his hair. "Can I... can I sit down?"

"No." He wraps his hands around me, cupping my ass cheeks and squeezing my flesh. He inhales my scent as my grip tightens in his hair. "You're a queen." He looks up into my eyes. "You stand, and I worship you."

I make a little peep of shock when he licks my clit.

Then he kisses my pussy.

I can't seem to process what's happening, right in front of my eyes.

He told me exactly what he was going to do, but maybe I was too shocked to believe it. Or to fully absorb it.

But we're naked now, and Jameson Vance, my fake fiancé, is down on his knees in front of me, his strong hands gripping my ass, pulling me to him as he feeds himself my pussy.

I'm very hungry, Megan.

My legs quiver as he suckles on my clit, and all my blood, all my awareness, races to the place where his mouth meets my body. It's such a rush, I almost fall over.

You haven't even glimpsed my appetite yet.

My knees threaten to buckle as his tongue lashes my flesh, over and again. My heart pounds so fiercely, it rattles my bones when I feel him groan, his mouth working feverishly between my legs.

I'm fucking shaking.

My whole body is on fire. My senses all snap to attention, to bask in every sensation as he lavishes me with pleasure. My fingers dig and twist into his hair, gripping him so I don't fall right over.

But he's holding me, and I know he won't let me fall.

He's too strong. Too sure of what he wants.

This.

My pleasure.

He makes out with my pussy like he's in love with it and it tried to run away from him. Then he suckles my clit like it's the sweetest thing he's ever wrapped his lips around. His touch is alternately brutal in its intensity and so devout, so sweet, so patiently indulgent, it makes me tremble and sweat with the mounting ecstasy.

The pressure gathers between my thighs, coaxed toward a dazzling pinnacle by his mouth.

I'm almost there...

Already.

He sucks my clit harder, making me gasp, then lavishes me with long, loving strokes of his tongue.

Then he sucks again.

Then he flickers the tip of his tongue gently over my clit, over and over, like he's savoring the taste, and mutters, "Megan," in a broken voice. And when he suckles again, greedily, the ecstasy screams through me in a burst of white light.

No. *I'm* screaming.

I'm coming, hard.

The contractions rack my core, and I jerk, but his grip on my ass tightens, steadying me. My hips buck as the convulsions shudder through me, making me grind against him, and he moans his pleasure.

Delicious heat floods my shaking limbs with liquid sugar.

I can't believe this is happening.

I can't believe I stay on my feet.

But I'm a slave to the magic he's unleashed in my core.

We both are.

Just as the contractions are beginning to fade, he hungrily coaxes out another climax, like waves crashing over one another. I'm crying out again, I'm swearing, and I jerk myself shamelessly against his mouth as he groans his approval.

He's latched onto me, sucking, that exquisite tongue stoking the fire.

I'm burning, and he's the sun.

I'm a castle in hot sand, built up and smashed down again in the crashing waves.

I cling to him as he drinks me in.

And when my knees finally give out, he catches me as I fall.

CHAPTER 37

Jameson

Megan melts into my arms as I pick her up and take her to the bed.

I lay her down on her back and lower myself over her. She's limp with pleasure and gazing at me like I'm superhuman.

It makes my cock so hard, it jerks with hunger, and I groan.

Have I ever seen anything so goddamn beautiful?

"Spread for me, sweetheart," I order gruffly.

She does.

Like the sweet, perfect lover she is.

I shove into her.

She cries out, a pleasured gasp, as she takes me. She's slick and hot from her orgasm, and I fucking shiver as I slide through her come.

A growl of pleasure rumbles up from my chest as I start fucking her, deep and fast. I hold her hips in place with one hand so my strokes are smooth and sure, my thrusts controlled in their intensity as I drive into her.

I told her I'd try to be gentle.

But she's moaning and grabbing at my ass like she's loving it. Pulling me in... as if there's any possible way I could fuck her any deeper.

I can't.

She took me to her limits in the first few thrusts.

But she wants me deeper...

She wants me pounding against her clit and driving her open, filling her with heat until she shatters, coming again.

We both want that.

She's so fucking gorgeous beneath me. I take her lush mouth in a deep kiss. Her hands are all over me, squeezing and pulling me close.

I want to make it last.

I want to make us both wait for it.

I want to possess her again and again, feeling her from the inside for hours on end.

But I'm already so close. And so is she.

I can feel it.

Her skin is flushed, and she's panting, her chest moving against mine.

I slow the pace of my hips as I hold back my climax.

I want her to come again first.

I lower my mouth to her breast and suck her pink nipple into my mouth. It's flushed and firm, and I suckle, growling with the effort to maintain my control.

She tastes so fucking sweet. Like love. Like everything good I've ever denied myself, right here beneath me, for the taking.

I want to make her see stars.

I want to pour myself into her.

I'm way too fucking close.

My hand finds her throat and grabs her jaw just before I get there. I hold her tight, looking into her eyes.

"Megan. Baby. Come for me." My voice is harsh, broken, and she bucks beneath me, her hips meeting mine, over and again.

She whimpers.

"That's it. Good girl."

I feel her tighten around me. Her pussy squeezes, then ripples around me as her orgasm hits and she cries out.

I kiss her again, deep and slow.

I keep thrusting, slow and hard, savoring her sweet convulsions. I'm so bent on making sure she gets off, my own orgasm slips away.

Momentarily.

When she comes down, panting softly, her hips slowing right down, I nuzzle her breasts. I bite her nipple softly, making her moan. Then I bite her neck.

She cries out, bucking into me, loving it.

I can't hold back anymore.

My hand tightens around her throat as I fuck her, driving into her faster and faster. "Can you come again?" I demand. "Right now?"

She nods, clutching at my ass with her hands, squeezing. Her hips move frantically against mine. Her eyelids drift.

"Jameson..."

"Yeah. Say my name while I fuck you, Megan."

She breathes my name.

My balls pull up tight.

"I'm gonna come. Come with me, baby. Come for me again."

I grind into her as I pump, and her back arches. She screams as she comes, her core convulsing in pleasure at the same time I explode.

I shove into her, letting go.

She grabs my face and pulls me down, kissing me while I come, and I close my eyes, tumbling through the dark with her.

I've never felt anything so fucking breathtaking as her mouth sucking me hungrily as I jerk into her, filling her with my come. I growl into our kiss, undone, and come away panting when it's finished.

She's panting beneath me.

We stare at each other, and then she smiles.

I smile back.

"That was..." *Intense. Mind-blowing. Fucking terrifying, actually.* "So hot," I breathe.

Megan blinks up at me in a daze. "I knew it would be," she says dreamily. "What took you so long?"

I knew it, too.

I also knew, the moment I slid inside her and another arrow slid into my heart...

For me, this is real.

I have no intention of faking anything anymore.

CHAPTER 38

Megan

I lie curled against Jameson's body, my face tucked into his neck, his heavy arm around me as he sleeps. His pulse beats lazily against mine everywhere we touch.

I take some pride in the fact that maybe I exhausted him?

I just had the hottest and most satisfying sex of my life. With my fake fiancé.

I should really sleep, but I just keep drifting in this heady haze of satisfaction and the lingering excitement.

Not only did he screw my brains out, he cuddled me afterward.

And kissed me for what felt like hours before he finally fell asleep.

Wait.

Does this mean it's not fake anymore?

When he brought me to this resort, I'd expected more of the same as what I experienced in Europe: accompanying him to business dinners and frustrating nights lying next to him in our hotel bed.

Since Europe, there's been an uncomfortable rift between us. I was afraid when I withdrew from him—feeling like I needed to, to protect my heart—that I was only worsening that rift. But it bothered me deeply when he continued to withhold sex.

For no known reason.

But tonight... something has changed.

I don't know what it is.

I'm just grateful for it.

Jameson blew me away, not just with the sex, but with taking care of me the way he did.

But when we had sex... the line between fake and real became blurred in all the steam.

And the multiple orgasms.

Troy was never patient enough to give me multiples. The sad truth was our sex life revolved around my admiration of him.

That has never been more obvious to me than it has been tonight, experiencing another man making love to me.

In that department, Jameson is clearly a giver.

And yes, he's a romantic.

He made me come until I physically couldn't do it anymore and he had to peel me off the bed, quite literally, and tuck me in under the covers.

I hadn't come with a man in so long, I'd almost forgotten what it was like.

But then again... it was never like *that* before Jameson anyway.

In the morning, I wake in Jameson's arms.

The first thing he does when I look at him is smile sleepily.

I trace the dagger tattoo on his chest with my finger for a while as we just lie there, entangled in peaceful silence.

Then I say, "Tell me about this. Why so bloody?" I quirk a smile, touching the tattooed drops of blood with my fingertip.

His expression grows serious. "I got the dagger after I found out about my dad's infidelities, to remind me that even the ones you love can betray you. Maybe I thought if I documented my wounds, then I wouldn't have to carry them inside."

"And did that work?"

He laughs under his breath. "No. It turns out it doesn't really work that way."

I trace the drops of blood again, dripping from the tip of the dagger tattoo. "One of these looked raw when we met, like it was a newer tattoo."

"It was. The first drop of blood was for my mom, because of how Dad hurt her. I never wanted to forget that. I was an angry teenager, and I didn't want to idealize him in my mind over time as I grieved for him. Because that's what happens after you lose someone, right? I didn't want to forget the harm he'd done and how he hurt us. It was important to me to remember."

"And the second drop? The new one?"

He kind of groans. "I got it recently, after Granddad died. It's for my grandmother. I only found out when my granddad was dying that he'd had an affair, too. And I didn't want to forget that either. He'd lied to all of us for years, and I didn't want to make him into a hero in my mind. He was like another father to me after Dad died. But he was far from perfect."

I take this all in, then offer, "That's really brave, Jameson, choosing to remember those things. Marking them on your body so you won't forget. Most people would probably rather forget."

"It's not brave. I just don't want to repeat the same mistakes. I never want to forget how their betrayal felt. I wasn't even the one married to them, and it hurt me."

I consider that, and how much we have in common in that regard. I know what it feels like to be cheated on.

I lay my head on his chest, listening to the beat of his heart, until he starts to get up and I moan in protest. He just smiles and drags me into the shower, where he makes the effort incredibly worth my while when he soaps my body, slowly and throughly, with his big hands.

Then he wraps my legs around his waist and fucks me up against the wall.

Hard.

It's heaven and the most delectable hell at once as we moan and slap together in the heat, driving into each other so hard, it almost hurts.

I still can't get enough.

He makes me come three times before he finally releases into me with a groan, his face buried in my neck.

I guess we'll talk later about the fact that we haven't talked about condoms yet. Or the pill.

I'm on the pill, and I'm not worried.

He's barely pulled out when he gives me the most regretful face I've ever seen and tells me he has a few calls to make after breakfast.

I laugh, I'm so happy and sated, and he seems so adorably sad.

He gives me a warning slap on the ass that's far too delicious to be chastising and tells me to behave.

Oh. Is this a thing now?

I can't even hide my grin.

"I think I'd rather misbehave," I say, and I love the way his eyes darken.

"If I could get it up right now," he says warningly, "I'd be fucking you senseless for that."

I don't think I've ever smiled so hard in my life.

We eat our amazing gourmet breakfast on the patio.

As soon as I'm finished eating my last bite, my fiancé beckons me to him with a crook of his finger.

He pats his lap as I come to him.

I sit down in his lap and wrap my arms around his neck. "I'm going to get these pesky calls out of the way," he tells me, his hand on my neck, his thumb drifting over my pulse. "You enjoy the pool. Then I'm going to enjoy you again."

"Sounds like a plan," I say breathlessly.

Then I kiss him, long and slow, until he groans. He gives my ass a deep squeeze and gives me the gruff order: "Be good." Then he removes me from his body.

So much for working only when he wants to. While that's usually the case, I've learned that if his siblings expect him to be on a call, even he can't get out of it.

I grin.

"Why do you look so happy?" he grouches.

"I just never knew until now that teasing you would be so much fun."

He glowers.

"What?" I say innocently. "It's true." Now that he's showing me how much he wants me... letting himself *have* me... "I like seeing you get all worked up."

When he reaches for me, I think he's going to try to spank me again, but he turns me by the hips. I'm now facing a line of hooks along the wall, where luxurious robes hang.

"Bikini," he orders. Then he slaps me on the ass.

Tingles spread through my body, but I give him a dirty look over my shoulder.

I go to pluck the bikini down, and I hear him follow; it's dangling from one of the hooks. It's a terra-cotta color, with little white flowers on it.

"Do you like it?" His hot breath teases my skin, and he presses a kiss to that sensitive spot where my shoulder meets my neck. One night and one morning of passionate sex and he's already sussed out so many of my hot buttons, it's insane.

I try to keep my cool. "It's cute." I hold it up. There isn't much of it; it's mostly string. It's definitely skimpier than the one I brought.

"It reminded me of the sundress you wore the day I met you. You know, in the street."

I laugh a little. "Oh. I'd hoped we'd forgotten about that by now."

He turns me by the hips to face him. "Why?"

"Because, I was such a mess. That wasn't exactly a good day for me, Jameson."

A wounded expression flashes over his face, and I automatically encircle his neck with my arms, pressing my body against him. I love that I can touch him so freely now. It's like a drug. Addictive and dangerous.

I know he'll be impossible to quit.

I try not to think about it.

"Except meeting you, of course," I clarify. "That was the highlight of my day."

"Liar."

"I'm not lying. That day was an emotional roller coaster for me. I was shell-shocked by meeting you in the street. I didn't even know what hit me. But when Cole introduced us by your pool..." I sigh dramatically, as if I'm laying it on thick when I'm really not. "It was love at first sight."

His lips quirk. "That was the second time you met me."

"Yeah. But it was the first time I was calm enough to actually see you fully. And baby, you are a sight." I reach up to kiss him, and his mouth melts into mine with a low groan. His tongue laps hungrily against mine, and when I moan, sagging into him, he growls and pulls away.

"Phone calls. Let me just take care of these. You change into that skimpy thing and meet me in the pool."

"Okay." I nip his bottom lip with my teeth, and he swats my ass yet again as I turn away.

I could really get used to this version of Jameson. Like stalker-hoarder obsessed with this version.

I wonder if he's planning to stick around...

Because I definitely want to keep him.

Dangerous.

I go change in the dressing area by the showers, and when I emerge, Jameson is pacing in the little sunroom off the patio, on a call.

"Fucking seriously, Harlan," he growls, as I wander past him, heading for the pool. "You need to bring someone. It's a formal event." He makes a grab for me, but I dance just out of reach, then linger at the edge of the room, eavesdropping. "Every seat at the gala dinner will be accounted for. Savannah expects you to—no, look, you're just making stress for Savi. Just muster up a plus one and make sure she's presentable." He hangs up on his brother.

Then he throws me a look that tells me I'd better get my ass in the pool or he'll be fucking me while he makes his next call.

I seriously consider sticking around for that, but then he says, "Hey, Savannah," and since he's talking to his sister, I decide to behave.

I go slip into the pool. I can hear him on the phone in the sunroom, where he watches me. I can't hear the words as I glide through the warm water, but I can hear the timbre of his voice, low and controlled.

His business voice.

It's even sexier than it used to be.

Everything about him is sexier now.

It's kind of frightening, actually.

When he finally steps out of the sunroom a while later, I'm pondering this conundrum—that I'm getting scarily attached to my fiancé, and I'm really not sure if I should.

He's changed into swim trunks, though, and my thoughts are instantly hijacked by the view.

Long, lean torso sculpted with muscles.

Yes, please.

And that gorgeous face...

Those light-blue eyes, burning with hunger.

I swim to the shallow end and walk up the wide steps, smoothing back my wet hair. I move slowly, letting him enjoy the view of the bikini he picked out for me. I'm soaking wet and barely covered, which is clearly how he wanted it.

He bought the top of the string bikini a generous two sizes too small, which I know was no mistake. His stylists have all my sizing. The fabric of the unlined triangle top covers my nipples and a little more, but I'm spilling out.

As I walk toward him, my breasts jiggling lewdly, his cock stands at attention. Thickening in his swim trunks, it flexes when my gaze falls to it.

Appetite, indeed.

He holds two flutes of champagne, but sets them down on a table as I approach.

Then he reclines onto a lounge chair, admiring me, his hard-on shamelessly evident.

"Hi."

"Hi. Why don't you be a good girl and get on my dick," he greets me. His voice is soft and indulgent, like a stroke across my skin.

I stand just out of reach, dripping, my nipples hard through the pasted-on fabric. "Oh? Is your business all finished?"

"Yes. Come here."

"Anything wrong? You seem stressed," I tease, not coming here at all.

"It's fine. Just the usual nightmare of renovating a resort. We've got seven months left, and Graysen's heading steadily toward his heart attack."

"Hmm. Maybe he needs to get laid more."

He laughs shortly. "Yeah. I'd say." He reaches, trying to grab me. "Now give it here."

Sadly, "it" is just out of reach. "I thought we were swimming."

"Plans change."

"Are you objectifying me, Mr. Vance?"

His gaze roams over me hotly. "I have every intention of objectifying you every chance I get, wife."

A shiver runs down my back at that word.

Wife.

A thrilling, delicious shiver.

He only referred to me as his wife one other time; when he told his siblings he'd asked me to be his wife and I'd said yes.

But that was all fake.

What is it now?

"You haven't earned the right to call me that yet," I say, still teasing, and watching his eyes darken dangerously.

"Show me what belongs to me before I put you over my knee and spank you for that."

I pull the string, loosening my top slowly, teasing him as I peel it off. While my body buzzes with the adrenaline blast.

The truth is, I'd love a good spanking.

He squeezes his hard length, letting the head pop out the top of his swim trunks. Giving me a show, too.

Have I seriously found a man to play with? A man this hot?

Could he really be this much fun?

Heaven, thank you for letting me in.

The head of his cock is wet with precome, and I lick my lip.

"Do you like what you see?" I ask him.

"When you emerged from the water with that wet bikini clinging to you, I could've come in my shorts."

"Wow. What a waste."

"Now show me that pussy."

"So bossy..."

The truth is, I love it.

I love dirty talk.

I peel off the bottom of my bikini just as slowly as I stripped off the top. Making him wait for what he wants.

Maybe this is payback.

Just a little.

For all the time he made me wait...

When I stand in front of him naked, I say, "No one can see us, right?"

"Now you ask."

I giggle, glancing around.

"We're alone. Get that gorgeous body over here," he purrs.

I drift closer, standing next to his lounge chair. His eyes gleam at me. A lion without a cage.

Where has he been hiding all this ferocious hunger, all this time?

And why?

"Take off my swim trunks."

I peel them down and off as he shifts his hips to let me.

When he's naked, I know my appreciation of what I see gets him hot. My desire for him turns him on. It's obvious.

But his desire for me is equal, and it takes my breath away how badly I needed this.

I forgot what this was like.

Being *wanted*.

His cock strains lewdly, wanting me.

My mouth drops open as he grabs my wrist and suddenly pulls me down, drawing me over his lap. Before I know it, he's got me face down, spread over him with my ass up. In spanking position.

His hand spreads over my ass cheek, hot and possessive, squeezing, and tingles run through me. *Oh god, is this happening?*

Thank you.

He strokes his hand over my ass, massaging gently. "Teasing me is so naughty of you, Megan. Don't you agree?"

I shudder in surrender and make a desperate mewling sound.

"That's my good girl." Jameson's voice is low and soothing, choked up with lust. "You're so lovely, even when you misbehave." Then he slaps me on the ass.

The sting and the sweet burn of pleasure hum through me, making my toes curl.

He squeezes my cheek again, digging his fingers into the tenderly stinging flesh. "Good?"

"*Yes.*"

"That's my girl," he murmurs lovingly, then slaps my other cheek, and squeezes there, too.

Suddenly, I'm choked up.

He proceeds to spank me, over and over again, so thoroughly and with just the right amount of pressure to make my whole body sing. I arch, gasping. "So beautiful," he purrs. "So perfect, Megan."

I pant, my head spinning, as he runs his hand over both cheeks, soothing the tingling flesh.

"Now come sit on me, baby." His voice is throaty with longing now. "You're torturing me."

I'm torturing *him?*

I clear my throat a little, trying to keep playing. "Poor baby," I coo. "Do you need pussy?"

"I need *your* pussy," he growls, and spanks my ass again. "Give it to me, or I'm coming to take it."

I consider my options on that.

Admittedly, they're pretty win/win.

Then I decide.

I take my time, pushing myself up, then kneeling over him and sliding into place in his lap. When my knees are settled on either side of his thighs, he spreads his legs, forcing me to spread wider for him.

"I feel like we're being watched. It's so bright and open here."

"We're not," he says firmly. "I'd never allow that to happen. This is mine." He grabs a breast and a tender ass cheek and squeezes. "I would never let the world have you like this." He yanks me closer and sucks a nipple into his mouth, teasing me a little, before adding darkly, "And my staff know better than to disturb me when I'm pleasuring my wife."

My wife.

Jesus, that sends an unbelievable thrill through me, like an electric current to my ovaries.

Jameson jerks my hips forward and down, impaling me on his cock so suddenly, I'm not fully prepared for it. I cry out. My hands land on his chest, steadying me.

"Yes," he murmurs. He yanks me down farther, hard, filling me completely.

The flood of heat flushes through me fast, and my body reacts, knowing what to do. I start riding him in a quick, almost frantic rhythm, hungry for him, as he murmurs sweet encouragements between the kisses he lavishes on my breasts.

And at the same time, he slaps my ass.

I reach behind myself, where his swollen ball sac is nestled under my ass. I'm grinding on it and he's already coated in my slick juices and his own precome. I squeeze gently, and his balls throb, telling me the sweet pressure is probably driving him insane.

His hand falters, losing the rhythm as he spanks me, and I know I'm winning the little battle for control.

"So big," I purr. "My man is so loaded."

His eyes flash with something deep and dark and heady, and overflowing with lust.

I struggle to retain my composure longer than he does. I can feel him stirring, restless with the urge to come already.

Or maybe he's just fighting the urge to flip us over, throw me down, and drive into me without mercy, punishing me further for teasing him.

He grits his teeth and growls something in his throat that's not quite words as I tease his balls, stroking, then squeezing with my slick fingers until I feel the answering throb. Over and over.

He groans hoarsely.

"You feel so full and needy," I gasp out.

It's me who's needy, desperate to climax with him again.

"It's all for you," he grits out, grabbing my breasts to shove them together and stroking his long, hot tongue between them. "Tell me to come."

"Yeah? Do you need to come?"

He growls again, swallowing back his answer to that. He seems to know only two words now. "Fuck, Megan. *Fuck.*"

"Yeah," I breathe. "Fill me up, Jamie."

I lean forward a bit, inviting him to chase, my breasts bouncing in his face as he rams his hips up, driving into me repeatedly.

"You feel so good," I gush.

I'm turned into this purely sexual being every time he's inside me.

I know nothing but the want of pleasing him.

The want of exploding in quivering, shaking fireworks with him as my heart bursts open.

When he lets go, it's with a loud groan as he buries his face between my breasts, his hands gripping my ass. His cock jerks, pouring his heat into me. His fingers dig into my flesh—and one of them touches my asshole.

I whimper without meaning to, and he pushes his finger into me.

My whole body is a rush of conflicting sensations as that probing finger drives deep.

I come as he whispers sweet things about how perfect I am against my throat.

I shake, my back arching, a scream of relief tearing from my throat as he rocks into me and the waves of orgasm crash through me.

Afterwards, he wraps his arms around me.

"Megan," he gasps as we settle, pressed together, heavy and hot, panting.

"Did you really book us here for a week?" I whisper shakily as it hits me that he brought me here for *this*, and I get a little choked up again.

"Of course I did." His hands slide into my hair and cup my head. "Give me your mouth."

Our lips collide in a hot, ravenous kiss that goes on and on as his heartbeat and mine blur into one. All my cautions to myself are flying out the windows of this runaway train.

Because maybe *this* was all I was waiting for, all along: for him to express his affection for me.

I've been so starved for it, I gobble it up.

In the midst of all this smoldering heat, though, I feel a twinge of fear. Troy used to withhold affection until I was starving for it, too. Until I just learned to go without.

And over the years, part of me shriveled up inside.

My heart. My heart and my capacity to trust, and even to love, shriveled up.

And now Jameson is bringing it back to pulsating life.

But if he lavishes me with affection like this and then takes it away, puts up that silent barrier between us again... I know it's going to hurt like hell.

"I need to fuck you again," he murmurs against my neck, and I suppress the euphoric giggle that bubbles up my throat.

"Are you always this insatiable?"

He hasn't even pulled out yet.

"For you... *Yes*." He lightly bites my throat, making me shiver. Then he looks into my eyes, sending my heart to the moon when he utters, "You'll just have to get used to my appetite if you're going to be my wife."

Then he kisses me so deep and so long, my chest starts to burn.

And I know if he actually asked me to be his wife... to stay... to make this thing between us real...

I'd say yes.

CHAPTER 39

Megan

The night after we arrive back in the city, Jameson takes me up Vance Tower for dinner.

At fifty-six floors, it's the third-tallest building in downtown Vancouver, and the restaurant at the top boasts the most epic three-hundred-and-sixty-degree views over the city, the mountains, and the waters beyond.

It's called Gravity Lounge. It's a private club with a costly annual membership, valet service, a private elevator, a fixed dinner menu, and a strict dress code. You don't get in without a membership.

Or an invitation from the owners.

Luckily, I'm with one of the owners.

To top it all off, there's a great DJ playing sultry music, sparkling chandelier lighting, and stylish people mingling by the bar and dining at the cozy tables. This is the high life, and somehow I'm a VIP.

I'm flying on pure lust, adrenaline, and happiness as Jameson and I dine at our private table in a dark nook, with its unobstructed view of the sparkling city through the wall of windows next to us. I feel like I've been high for a week.

When the waitress clears away our dinner plates and Jameson

orders us a second bottle of wine, the only thing I want to do almost as much as I want to climb into his lap and ride him right here is just stare at him in wonder.

He catches me staring and smiles at me before lifting his wine-glass to his lips.

I take a sip of my Syrah, my heart pounding.

I'm falling.

Hard.

There's no doubt in my mind about it.

If I questioned it before... any questions I had in my heart had all been answered when Jameson Vance slammed his dick into me and started calling me "my wife."

You'll have to get used to my appetite if you're going to be my wife.

Yes.

Yes, I could get used to it.

I've gotten very used to it this week already, and now I'm addicted, thank you very much.

He leans in across the intimate table and speaks low in my ear. "Don't look now, but my brother's here."

I lean closer to him. "Which one?"

He nods to someone over my shoulder, someone I can't see. I don't look, because he told me not to.

"Damian. Quick gossip for you." He twirls a lock of my hair around his finger as he speaks in my ear, his breath heating my neck. "Damian oversees our hospitality assets. Luxury hotels, restaurants, bars... you know all that. But his pride and joy is a private sex club he started up himself. Don't tell him I told you. Pretend you don't know."

I gape at him.

Sex club?

Jameson smirks at me as he sits back in his seat. I can see he finds the idea as *what the fuck* as I do.

Have you been there?? I mouth at him.

No, he mouths back. With a look of horror that tells me he thinks the idea of going to a sex club owned by his brother is right up there with incest on his list of turnoffs.

"I have so many questions," I say out loud, then bury my face in my wineglass.

"Save them. He's coming over."

A moment later, he reaches up to shake hands with his brother as Damian Vance stands over our table.

I swallow wine and smile up at him, shaking his hand when he reaches for mine. Damian briefly kisses the back of my hand, a move that not many men could pull off so authoritatively. He wears a sharp suit of such a deep blue, it's almost black, his wavy dark hair swept back. He's the epitome of dark, dangerous, and elegantly mysterious.

His eyes sparkle at me as he takes one of the empty seats at our small table, and I realize Jameson has invited him to sit down with us.

My head is still pulsing with those two words. *Sex. Club.*

Jameson hides his smirk behind his wineglass. He's amused by my shock.

Jerk! I mouth at him discreetly.

His eyes narrow with a heated look that tells me I'll be getting a spanking for that later.

We share a round of pleasantries, and Damian asks about our trip to the island. Jameson tells him how relaxing it was, and I fill my face with wine.

Yeah. Relaxing.

If multiple rounds a day of doggy style, girl on top, reverse cowgirl, intense-eye-contact missionary, throaty blow jobs, and endless cunnilingus could be considered relaxing.

It was. Occasionally. Briefly.

Until we both got aroused and started fucking again.

Jameson pulls his phone from his jacket pocket. He glances at it, and I realize I've been screwing him in my head while he chats with his brother.

"It's Savannah. I should take this." He gets up and leans to kiss me on the forehead. "I'll hit the men's room on my way back," he tells me as he cups the back of my head. "Order dessert if you like while I'm gone."

Then he kisses me on the mouth, unexpectedly, and I melt.

As he walks away, I wave at him with my fingers, ogling his butt.

Then I remember his brother is still sitting at the table with me.

In fact, he's watching me.

I smile at Damian, and sip my wine.

He smiles, much more slowly than I do, never taking those cunning eyes off me. Yeah, he just caught me staring at his brother's ass.

But hey, he owns a sex club, right? He knows what's up.

And now my face is probably fuchsia.

"So," I say, "hospitality. That must be an interesting line of work."

"Yes. Playing host to people is always interesting. But hospitality goes two ways. Making sure people who are welcome feel welcome. And making sure those who are unwelcome... don't stick around."

Well, that felt ominous.

I can't help thinking that when he said that while staring at me, he's talking about... me?

"I see."

Point-blank, he asks me, "Are you after my brother's money, Megan?"

"Of course," I say, leaning my chin on my palm and not missing a beat. If he can be an ass, so can I. "Why else would I be with him? Clearly, he has nothing else to offer."

A slow smile spreads across Damian's handsome face. It's annoying, really, how handsome he is.

Then he laughs. Somehow, I've charmed him. This man is twisted or something.

He's a game master. I remember now; that was what Jameson said about him.

"You're surprising, Megan Hudson."

"You don't like me," I venture.

"You're a beautiful girl. And you seem very sweet. But you're a stranger to me." He tips his head in the direction Jameson disappeared. "To him, too."

"We're still getting to know each other, that's true. It's been... a whirlwind romance." I sit back and study Jameson's brother as he studies me. "Maybe you'll get to know me, too."

"I know your brother," he says lightly. "I know things you probably wouldn't want to know. We used to have problems with him at some of the bars we own. Did Cole tell you that?"

"I know all about my brother's struggles. He knows he's made mistakes. And he's worked hard to get his life and career back on track."

"Maybe you do know." He cocks his head thoughtfully. "But that was all back before he and my brother decided they were best friends, wasn't it."

I don't know what he's implying, other than that he distrusts Cole, just like he distrusts me.

"And do you know why they became best friends?" I ask him, sadly desperate for intel, still a little curious about how Cole and Jameson got so close.

"Trust," he says simply. "Cole told Jameson something no one else did."

"And that was...?"

"That the woman Jamie was seeing was cheating on him."

I didn't know that.

But it explained a lot. Like the deep loyalty Jameson felt for my brother.

Which just makes me wonder about the loyalty of the man in front of me...

"You knew, but you didn't tell him?"

"I didn't know. But apparently, others did know. Others who didn't tell. Friends of Jameson's, who are no longer friends of Jameson's." His expression is merciless, as if I'm the woman who cheated on his brother. "She slept with one of his friends, you see. That's who the affair was with."

Oh. *Shit.*

I'm not sure if I should be bothered that Jameson never told me about this, when I told him Troy cheated on me. But obviously, it affected him. Maybe he didn't like to talk about it?

"Jamie values honesty and trust, maybe more than anything," his brother concludes.

I believe that. But I wonder if the same goes for the man in front of me.

"Would you have told him if you knew?" I ask him.

Damian chuckles humorlessly under his breath. "Yes. I'd tell him. And then I'd go have a nice chat with his 'friend.'"

Wow.

I take a long swig, finishing my wine. Then I watch as Jameson's older brother reaches for the bottle of Syrah and refills my glass for me. He wears a pinky ring with a black stone, etched with some kind of insignia.

This guy gives off Mafia kingpin vibes or something. I get the distinct impression that by "have a nice chat with" he actually meant "do physical damage to."

"You're interesting, Damian," I tell him.

"And by 'interesting,' you mean...?"

"Not much like Jameson."

"We may seem different, but my little brother is more like me than you might care to know. Men like us..." He peruses me slowly. "We don't settle."

"Meaning?"

"You'll need to be interesting yourself if you expect him to keep you."

Keep me.

Like I'm an object.

Is that how he sees women?

I know he's looking out for his younger brother, his family, their fortune. And I can't even refute what he's said. From his point of view, I am using his brother for money. I said yes to his proposal for the security he'd promised me in return.

At least, that was how it started out.

"Tell me again." He leans in, like we're sharing a secret. "What is it you love about my brother?"

That's so easy for me to answer at this point, my throat squeezes as I speak. Maybe I wish it weren't so easy. "His heart. His generosity. He's always been good to me. Respected me."

"In what way?"

"You doubt that? Maybe you don't know him very well."

"Oh, I know him very well."

"He wouldn't touch me. Not for weeks, until he knew I was ready."

I don't know why I tell him that. Maybe I just want him to understand.

To know that there's something real between Jameson and me.

For a man who owns a sex club, the fact that his brother abstained from having sex with me in the beginning of our relationship must surely have meaning.

Maybe he'll even understand why Jameson did it better than I do.

But he says, "Is that what you've convinced yourself to believe? He did it for you? If you think you know him, you haven't looked hard enough yet." He rises to his feet, buttoning his jacket. "Jamie might share his wealth, but he won't give it up. Not even for you. Have a nice evening, Megan."

What the hell did that mean?

Give it up?

I watch him walk away, my heart in my throat.

And he warned me that Harlan was the cynical one.

The conversation with Jameson's brother leaves me ill at ease.

I pass on dessert, and as soon as Jameson and I are heading home in his car, I tell him, "I don't think Damian likes me."

"Did he say something?" He draws closer to me on the seat. I keep staring out the window. "He's just being protective, I'm sure. He doesn't know you yet."

"He doesn't like Cole either."

He sighs. "Damian holds killer grudges. It's one of his less charming personality traits."

"You'd think he'd be grateful to Cole."

When I look at Jameson, he seems worried, like I'm mad at him. But I'm not.

"He told me that Cole told you a woman you were seeing was cheating on you. With one of your friends."

He takes a deep, inaudible breath, and I can tell it's not one of his favorite topics. "Yes. That's true."

"You could've told me."

"It didn't occur to me to tell you. It's not something I think about, much less enjoy talking about."

"Why do I feel like there are other things you're not telling me?"

He slides his hand over mine and squeezes it.

"I'll tell you anything. I didn't know you wanted to know more about my previous relationships."

I look away, out the window. "I really don't."

I know it.

I know it in my gut. And in my heart.

Jameson isn't being fully honest with me.

About what, I don't know.

But his brother sure seems to think he's keeping something from me.

If you think you know him, you haven't looked hard enough yet.

Damian hinted at it, maybe to try to scare me away.

Maybe to see how I'd react.

To see if I'm really wife material, if I care enough about his brother to probe deeper, or if I'll just let it slide.

As we get ready for bed, I wonder if I'm freaking crazy to let myself fall in love again.

And with a man like Jameson. So wealthy, so glamorous, so unlike me.

And so damn soon.

I didn't even have a month of alone time between the end of my last relationship and this one.

My chest feels tender and raw where Jameson's breathed the life back into my hope for a happy ending.

It's so fresh, this hope.

I don't want to suffer another broken heart so soon.

But Jameson's heart was broken, too, by his parents, and maybe by former lovers.

Maybe he's guarding his heart, too.

"Why don't you want to get married?" I ask him when I emerge from the walk-in to find him in bed, waiting for me. He's sitting up against the headboard, watching me.

"Come here."

I come around and slide into my side. When I settle down onto the pillow, he slides down to face me.

His expression is serious when he says, "My parents' marriage wasn't good. I think... ultimately, I never wanted that."

"And that's the only type of marriage you can imagine?" I challenge. Because can't he picture us together in the future, still enjoying the hell out of each other?

And if not, why not?

"I haven't really tried to picture another type of marriage," he says carefully. "I just decided long ago it wasn't for me."

"And that's it?"

Surely he can't pretend that he never called me *my wife* in the heat of the moment, or that it meant nothing at all. He's done it several times now.

He swallows. I can feel his hesitation. Now that this is a serious topic of conversation and we're not flirting, it's hard for him to address it. But why?

What is he afraid of?

He said he makes decisions based on fear; that he's like Wolf that way. But I've been living with him for a while now, and I don't see that in his daily actions.

And really, am I that scary? I'm actually ridiculously loyal, and he must've gleaned that by now. I'm hardly the type of girl who cheats. He must realize that. He knows what happened in my last relationship.

"What is this about?" he asks gently, and strokes my cheek. "Something's bothering you."

I sigh. The man can make me melt with nothing but a look or the slightest touch. "I'm feeling guilty," I admit. "Damian thinks I'm engaged to you for your money. And I am. I don't feel good about it. And I don't want you to hate me for it."

Jameson gathers me to his body and holds me close, making my heart speed up. I'm wearing my soft nightshirt but he's naked, and his skin feels so right against mine. "A lot of people are always going to think that, Megan. It doesn't matter. I know you care about me."

"I do."

"There's nothing to feel guilty about. You and I are the only ones in this engagement. And we both went into it honestly."

"Right."

"We agreed to the terms."

"Yeah. One year, for two million dollars."

"And then you get that fresh new start you wanted."

Silence stretches as my heart pounds and I know, for me, that fresh new start includes him. In my fantasies, at least.

But does his vision of the future include me?

I still don't know.

"Why did you really say yes to my proposal?" He's studying me as I study him. "At that point, I was pretty sure you didn't think too highly of me. I can't imagine you saying yes to someone you couldn't stand or respect, for any amount of money."

"Because you won me over with the new suitcase. And what you did for Romeo. And reading my books. And..." I laugh softly and roll my eyes a little, knowing this part is some part ridiculous. "Because it's the Summer of Yes."

His brows draw together.

"At least, it is for me. You know, like when you say yes to everything. Like Jim Carrey in that movie."

"Yeah, I'm familiar with the concept."

"You look confused."

"Just confused about why a rational person would do such a thing."

I laugh again, then sigh. "So maybe I don't let life and opportunity pass me by, by always saying no?"

He twirls a lock of my hair around his finger. "You know... many of the most successful people in the world advise the opposite."

"What opposite?"

"That it's best to say no. That your level of success is directly related to how often you say no."

"That makes no sense."

"It makes perfect sense. If you say no to everything you're asked, you only do what you actually intended to do. Not what the world dangles in your way. Those are usually called distractions."

I ponder that for a moment. "So instead of saying yes..."

"You should say no."

"I see," I say, thinking: *That is the most unromantic thing I've ever heard.* "But what about romance?" I ask him. Because isn't he the romantic? "Adventure? Twists of fate? Thrills? Magic? The unexpected?"

His expression is oddly sad, and now I can feel his fear. "Pretty words for things that just distract you from what you really want."

My heart slams in my chest as I make myself ask the question. "And what is it *you* really want?"

"I thought it was obvious by now." He lays his hand on the side of my face, his thumb brushing my lip. "You."

CHAPTER 40

I n the early morning, after we make love slowly in the faint
dawn light, we lie in bed in each other's arms. I play with
Megan's soft hair.

I don't want to say anything. I don't want any of my fears, or
Megan's, to ruin this.

I know they're going to.

I can feel it in every ferocious beat of my pulse when we're close,
my heart straining under the pressure of all those goddamn arrows
she's lodged in there with her sweetness.

Last night, she asked me about marriage. And yes, I've been
thinking about marriage. Looking at it in a much different way since
she accepted my proposal.

Thinking about what it would be like if she were my wife.

But I didn't have the balls to tell her that. Not when I wasn't
prepared to follow through.

It wouldn't be fair to mess with her head.

More than she needs some promise of a fairy-tale marriage, she
needs a stable man. And that's the kind of man I need to be
for her.

I won't make her any promises unless I know I can keep them.

She stares at me so long, her head nestled next to mine on the pillow, I finally break. I brush my thumb over her soft cheek. "What are you thinking about?"

"Why were you holding back before?"

I know what she's asking, and why. She's concerned about why I changed so suddenly. From avoiding her touch to fucking her like my life depends on it.

Who wouldn't be?

She wants to know what my reason was for delaying our sexual connection, which is obviously intense and electric.

If we could stay in bed and fuck all day, I'm sure we would.

But she already told me she's spending the day with her friend Nicole today.

Maybe she needs room to breathe before this ravenous connection between us swallows her whole.

I know I'm being consumed by it.

I don't even know what to tell her anymore.

"Was it really about my brother?" she says softly.

She's never asked me that so directly before.

But just because I've completed my challenge doesn't mean I'm off the hook.

I roll onto my back and stare at the ceiling. I still can't tell her about the game, even now that my part in it is done.

My siblings know; the ninety days are up, and I swore to them all that I completed the challenge. There would be no women—Megan included—popping up to claim I'd fucked them during those ninety days. And if they did, they were fucking lying.

And I didn't tell Megan about the game.

I didn't break the rules.

We'll be meeting up again soon to draw the next name from the box.

The pressure will shift to someone else.

But for now, for me, even though my challenge is complete and I'm free to have sex with Megan, the game is still causing problems.

"No," I admit. "Not entirely."

"Was there ever someone else? While we were together?"

I look at her, and she holds my gaze like she's still worried there might be something *that* bad that I'm not be telling her.

I roll close to her, prop up on my elbow, and look deep into her eyes. "No. I told you, I'm not that guy."

"Then what is it? What are you not telling me?"

"It's really not important. It's..." I sigh raggedly. "It's done."

Megan stares at me.

It's the first time I've admitted that there *is* something I'm keeping from her, and she didn't miss it. It wasn't a slip-up or a mistake. I had to tell her something.

I have to give her as much of the truth as I can.

"How can you say that?" Her voice is soft and small. "I told you honesty is important to me, and you said the same. I've felt it, all along, that there's something you're not saying, Jameson."

"There is." I exhale, suddenly feeling exhausted from the weight of this thing I've had to carry, and keep concealed from her. "You're not wrong."

"Then tell me."

I shake my head, slowly. "I wish I could."

She shakes her head, too, not understanding.

I've answered her questions as honestly as I can. But I can tell I've damaged her trust.

She needs more from me. More of the truth.

And she deserves it.

I struggle with what to tell her.

"All I can tell you... is that I can't tell you."

I can see her struggle to believe me. "What if that's not enough?"

I take her hand in mine and hold tight. "It has to be."

Over breakfast on the balcony, Megan's quiet.

"You're mad," I say gently. "Let's talk about it."

"I'm not mad. I'm hurt. And confused about why you're not being fully honest with me."

"About this one thing, I can't be. I wish I could." I try to put all my feeling about it into my words, so she knows this isn't easy for me.

It's fucking torture.

If I thought it sucked to not be able to fuck her, not being able to tell her why I couldn't is much fucking worse.

She sighs and rubs her forehead. "I haven't been totally honest either. The first night I slept here with you, I followed you to your bathroom and watched you masturbate. I loved it," she says, sounding apologetic. "But I'm sorry I didn't tell you."

My cock stirs at this new information, and I lick my lip. "Why didn't you tell me?"

"Because you seemed so distant, sexually. You said we weren't going to have sex. I had no idea how you'd take it. That should've been enough to stop me, I know. But once you started... I couldn't look away." She groans a little. "I wasn't kidding that I'm a voyeur. And I don't know if I became one because I was with such a self-obsessed narcissist for so long that I developed this almost fetishistic craving for watching because sometimes it was all I was allowed to do, or if he picked me because he knew..." She blows out a breath, and I get to my feet, going over to her and kneeling down in front of her.

She meets my eyes, and I can see the residual pain there. "He knew I'd crave him, adore him, admire him, and never be strong enough to leave."

I grind my molars, struggling to ignore the flames of jealousy that lick my insides when she talks about him like that. "You did leave."

She shakes her head. "I wanted you from the moment I met you." She sounds so sad when she says that, like it's some great tragedy.

I slide my arms around her waist. "I wanted you from the moment I met you, too."

"How am I supposed to believe that? You barely even kissed me. You avoided touching me, all the time. *Why?*"

I swallow the growl of frustration in my throat. It's not for her.

It's for this whole fucked-up secret I have to keep.

"I can't tell you why. All I can tell you is that I wanted to, Megan. I wanted *you*, so badly. That first night, when you say you watched me masturbate... you must've *seen* how badly I wanted you."

She doesn't say anything. She tears up, and my chest aches until I can't draw a full breathe.

No matter how I try to convince her, I know she's crushed that I won't tell her everything, that I'm still holding something back—even after she just shared something so vulnerable.

"I was honest with you," she breathes. "And you won't reciprocate."

"I'll tell you anything you want to know."

"Except that."

Yeah.

Except that.

I walk straight into Graysen's office as soon as I arrive. His home office, which is the whole main living area of the owner's suite at the Vance Bayshore resort, because all Graysen Vance does in life is work.

I stalk across the grand room, right up to his desk in front of the big windows, which are dimmed out so he can see his computer screens. He's at his keyboard, typing.

His secretary gets up from her desk along the side wall and hurries the hell out.

I'm pretty sure it's Graysen she's afraid of, not me—as worked up as I am right now—and she doesn't want to be here to witness whatever's about to go down between brothers. My impotent rage must be crackling off the walls.

Graysen looks up, cool and incredulous. He lifts an eyebrow.

He says nothing.

"I'm going to lose her." I slap my hands down on his desk and lean in. "You wanted me to get engaged. Well, you got what you wanted. You got your celebrity love story. The whole 'Prince Charming and Cinderella' romance, the engagement ring, all the leaked photos. It's the hottest thing in the headlines right now. And I'm going to lose her because of Granddad's stupid game and this lie he's making me uphold."

"It's not like Granddad knows what's happening in your life right now," he says dryly.

"My inability to tell her the truth will just drive her away."

He considers that for maybe two seconds, then says evenly, "You'll manage it."

"She's not some business to be *managed*." I push off the desk, clawing a hand through my hair. "You knew Granddad best. He had to have left me a loophole here."

My brother studies me, sitting back in his chair. "He left us to play the game. That's how he wanted it. And his only part in it is what he left us in black and white."

I start pacing in front of his desk. "So there's no way around it." I wonder if I look as unraveled as I feel. I run a hand down the front of my shirt. I'm pretty sure I buttoned it straight.

"I'd tell her for you myself," he says, "but the rule is clear. None of us can talk about it."

"So no one can tell her. Ever." My voice cracks.

Then I stop dead. Savannah's voice is suddenly in my head.

Have you ever considered, Jamie, that maybe he's just trying to protect you? From getting your heart broken.

I point at Graysen accusingly. "You knew this would happen. You know that I'm all soft and fucking broken inside, and when I fall it'll be forever. And you *knew* this would happen."

My brother's eyebrow raises. "I knew that what would happen, Jamie?"

I can't even say it. Can't admit how I feel about her out loud.

Maybe he didn't know. Maybe I'm just going crazy with the

thought of losing her, and want someone else to blame for the mess of shit I'm feeling.

He watches me pace as I unravel some more.

"I had an interesting chat with Damian last night," he says after a moment. "He said he pressed Megan on her loyalty."

I turn to stare at him. Damian did what now? *When?*

When I was in the men's room at Gravity?

"He could sense that the situation was getting real for you," Graysen says. "We all can."

I stare at my brother for a long, painful minute as he stares back calmly. *Situation.* When did my love life and my engagement become a situation?

This is Megan we're talking about.

My *life*.

And very possibly my future wife.

"So," he says, "are you telling me it's real?"

Rivers of blood pound through my ears and my heart strains in my rib cage under the pressure of all those arrows. It feels like a dam about to blow in there. There are way too many fucking holes.

"Are you sure it's as real for her as it is for you?" he presses.

I turn and walk out without answering him.

Fuck him.

I pull out my phone and dial Megan, because she's the only one I need to talk to. My family doesn't have answers. Granddad fucked me with this game, and even he can't take it back. The man is gone and I'm fucking falling in love with my fiancée, and if Megan is ever going to trust me enough to love me, I'll have to make that happen myself.

Somehow.

She's been at Nicole's all damn day, though.

I *need* her.

I just have to see her tonight, convince her somehow that I'm trustworthy. That we can just bury this stupid little secret that doesn't mean anything anyway, put it in the past, and forget about it.

But when I hear her voice, I feel like I've dropped off a cliff.

"Jameson?"

Her voice sounds so small. She sniffles, and somehow I know, I fucking *know* she's far away.

Fear creeps up my throat, threatening to strangle me.

"Megan?" I stop midstride, alarm spiking my adrenaline. "What's wrong?" I hear a soft sob. "Where are you? Are you with Nicole or Rurik? I was just about to come pick you up."

She sighs and says sadly, "I'm in Crooks Creek. I'm sorry. I had to leave." She sobs again. "This was such a mistake."

With her next words, the thudding dam in my chest fucking breaks under the weight of all my mistakes. "Troy called."

CHAPTER 41

The flight to the Winnipeg airport and the almost two-hour
drive to Crooks Creek is fucking murder.

As in I spend most of the time talking myself down
from murdering Troy Duchamp the moment I meet him.

It was a weirdly hard decision, getting on the plane. Every
instinct I had told me to go after Megan, and fast. But I was torn.

What if she didn't want me to? What if going after her just
made it worse?

What if I broke her ex-boyfriend's face and she hated me for it?

What if, in some small part of her, she was still in love with him?

I'm my panic, I'd called every one of my brothers, even Harlan,
and gotten a roundup of the world's worst advice.

Graysen: *Tell her she needs to be back in two days. And stay
away from cameras.*

Damian: *Just let her go, and see if she comes back.*

Harlan: *If she doesn't stay put like she's told, just tie her to
the bed.*

Yeah, thanks.

But then I called Cole and he nailed it.

*Call me the second you know she's okay, and if he's not in a coma
yet, I'll come put him in one.*

That sounded like a plan to me.

I know Troy has been calling Megan, messaging her, trying to reach her ever since she left him. Trying to guilt her into coming back to him. More so, ever since our love story hit the media.

I know everything there is to know about the piece of shit.

The day I first proposed to Megan, I'd ordered a complete background check on him. And I'd kept tabs on him ever since, because I knew he wasn't done with her.

Narcissists don't give up easily if they still think they can suck some more attention out of you.

It's called *narcissistic supply*, and Megan was his for a decade.

He won't give her up, unless he's found someone else to fulfill his needs as well as she can.

Clearly, he hasn't yet.

That part is understandable. Megan would be impossible to replace.

But he'll move on soon enough.

It's a common practice of narcissists to keep other potential sources of supply in the wings, primed and ready, just in case.

Like whoever he'd cheated on her with.

I know this because I read up on narcissism and even consulted with a top expert in the field after I found out Megan had been manipulated by and emotionally abused by one for years. I also know she was raised by a struggling single mom, abandoned by a narcissistic father who loved only the prospect of his son's success and invested nothing in his daughter's life other than the meager support payments he was required to cough up. Cole told me enough to make me despise the man, when I've never even met him.

But her ex-boyfriend is worse.

He'd preyed on her goodness, her vulnerability, her need to be loved. He'd taken advantage of the kind, giving person she was, for years.

The fact that he'd somehow gotten his hooks into her today, convinced her with whatever lies that she needed to race home, was unconscionable.

The man was garbage.

He had her so upset that she'd somehow given Rurik, who drove her to Nicole's and was waiting for her outside, the slip. And hopped on a plane to rush here.

For him.

He probably told her he was dying or something.

The fucking con artist.

She must know this guy is Mr. Wrong. Mr. Fucked-in-the-Head.

She'd never go back to him, would she?

When Locke pulls our rented car up in front of Megan's mom's house, I'm out the door so fast, Rurik has to run to follow me.

There's a truck outside, and I know it's Troy's.

"I just want you to leave, Troy! How many times do I have to say it?"

I hear Megan yelling from inside the house, and the rage that crashes through me is blinding as I push my way inside. I barely know how I got there.

What if he put his hands on her?

"Calm," I hear Locke mutter from somewhere behind me. He and Rurik are both on my heels.

We all pile into the living room to find Megan and her ex-boyfriend facing off. I'm so fucking relieved to see they're not touching. That they stand several feet apart, and Megan isn't crying.

She's just telling him to leave.

They both look at us in shock. The dog sitting at Megan's feet startles, pops to its feet, and starts barking at Megan's ex.

Megan gives the dog a hand signal and says calmly, "Quiet," and the dog stops barking. "Now sit." The dog sits.

"Megan." I stand there, panting, and her attention moves from the dog to me. Warmth explodes in my chest when our eyes connect.

"Who the fuck is this?" Troy demands.

"Jameson," she breathes.

When I force myself to look at her ex, his face is going pale, and I can tell he knows exactly who this is.

I take stock. He's thinner than me, dressed in a plaid shirt and work jeans, kind of ruggedly handsome in a blue-collar sort of way, and I hate him instantly.

No, I hated him the moment Cole first told me about him. Even before I loved Megan.

"We're kind of in the middle of something, man." His voice wavers a little as he takes in the men behind me.

"No. You aren't." I seethe. "Megan just asked you to leave. So. You back away from my wife and get the fuck out of her mother's house. I'll give you thirty seconds to comply. Then I beat your ass."

I'm already yanking off my tie, and he looks scared. But also outraged.

His ego deplores this.

"You want to make it a fair fight," I tell him, "I'll have the other guys step outside while I stomp your head in."

It still wouldn't be a fair fight. I have fifty pounds and a few inches on him.

He glares at me like he'd prefer I go flush my head down a toilet, but swallows.

Then he glares at Megan again.

"Don't look at her. Don't say another fucking word. Just start walking. Or should I tell her about the other women you slept with behind her back?"

After a long, tense thirteen seconds—I count, mostly to keep my cool—he finally starts walking, stiffly, like he's on death row and this is the end.

Maybe it's the way Locke and Rurik are watching him from the doorway.

He passes between them in silence. The dog pops to its feet again, watching Troy go, anxious.

"I'll be right back," I tell Megan, my adrenaline still pumping.

I vaguely notice her mouth is open, but she doesn't say anything.

Locke gives me a warning look as I follow Troy outside. In the driveway, I grab him by the back of his shirt and spin him around, pushing him up against his truck.

"Listen, asshole," I growl in his face, low enough so only he can hear. "You don't speak to her again. You don't reach out to her in any way. You're done with her now, just like she was done with you when she left you. You try to contact her again, I send a lawyer to deal with you next time and you will not like my terms."

I shove him away from me like the trash he is and take a step back before the urge to hit him becomes too strong to resist.

I won't risk that. I don't think Megan would want me to.

"Now, get in the truck you bought with the money you stole from her, you piece of shit, and get the fuck off this property before I have you arrested."

He tears open the door and climbs in. "Fuck you, man," he grumbles before he slams the door. Then he backs out of the driveway and tears up the street.

Fucking coward.

Locke squeezes my shoulder.

"How did I do?" I mutter.

Then I fold forward, hands on my knees. It's strangely exhausting fighting back the urge to strangle someone to death for hours on end.

Who knew.

"Not bad," Locke says. "I would've run him over accidentally with the truck myself. But we all have our methods."

He's trying to ease the tension, so I grunt a laugh.

When I finally catch my breath, I realize Megan is standing in the entrance of the house, watching, the dog at her feet. The dog starts barking again, at me this time. Megan turns and disappears into the dark of the living room with the dog, and the dog quiets again.

I follow her inside and catch her arm, turning her to face me. "Are you okay? He didn't touch you, did he?"

"No. It was never like that. He never hit me or anything. He just... wants something he can't have."

I suck in a breath through my teeth. "He won't be back. He won't bother you again. He's not that brave. If he does... He knows I'll come after him."

She hesitates. "Thank you."

"You don't have to thank me. It's my job. I'm your man."

She stares at me, tears shining. "I feel terrible."

"Megan." I pull her into me, her head to my chest, and hold her tight. "I'm sorry I said that thing about the other women..."

"Is it true?"

I hesitate. I can't stand to hurt her. But I can't let him hurt her either.

And I can't lie to her.

"Yes."

"How do you know?"

"Background check. And surveillance. I'm sorry I didn't tell you. I needed to know if he posed a real danger to you."

She squeezes me tighter. "He doesn't. Not anymore."

The relief that floods me is heady. I feel dizzy. There's so much adrenaline thudding through me, my cock is half-hard.

I take a deep breath and try to calm down. I don't want my pounding heart to scare her.

I need to be her rock.

Her hero.

She peeks over my shoulder toward the two men who linger on the front porch. "Is Rurik in trouble?"

I sigh. "Baby. Why did you run off? You could've asked me for help. You should've asked me."

"It was a mistake. I should never have come. I knew that as soon as I got here." She sucks in a deep breath. "I knew he was lying over the phone."

I tip her head up and look into her eyes.

"I've been ignoring his calls. I haven't said a word to him since I left. Because the only way you can get rid of a narcissist is to cut them off. Stop feeding their bottomless need for attention. I know that." She laughs humorlessly. "My dad taught me that. He was the same way with my mom. She eventually had to just end it cold to make it stop. And eventually... he moved on to someone else."

"Baby... I'm sorry." It's the only thing I can think to say.

She deserves a better father than the one she got.

She breathes a soft, sad sound of surrender. "I got a call today from an unknown number, and I shouldn't have answered it. Ever since our relationship went public, I get a lot of random calls. But this one was from a Manitoba area code and I just thought, what if it's someone I know? And once he got me on the phone... He started laying into me about how wrong it was, what I did to him. That I had to come back. That I'd never find anyone like him. He actually tried to convince me that he was the best thing that ever happened to me."

I can't help it. I snarl in disgust.

She peers up at me. "Did you just snarl?"

"I think I did."

"Well, don't worry. I didn't fall for it. I knew he was just trying to manipulate me, to get what he wants, which is more of my attention. So... I snuck out the back of Nicole's building so Rurik wouldn't know I left and went to the airport and waited for a flight on standby. I kept thinking what I was doing was ridiculous. That I wasn't even going to get a flight. That I should just call you and tell you what was going on. But... I had this killer urge to come back here and face him. I feel like I ran out on him like a coward. And I had to tell him, to his face, that it's over."

"But that didn't really work."

"No. Because all that did was give him *me* to argue with. He'll never stop believing he can convince me. Best thing I can do is just walk away, and never give him any part of me, ever again."

I want to kiss her so badly right now. But I don't know if she wants me to. She seems so sad.

"Come home with me, Megan," I say instead, my voice husky with relief and affection.

"I can't. Not tonight. The least I can do is spend the night with Mom. I came all this way, and she hasn't even met my fiancé." Her lips quirk.

"Shit. You're right." I'd met her mom, Donna, over video call twice now, but that was it. "Where is she?"

"At work. She'll be home any minute, though." She puts her hands on my waist and tugs my hips against her. "Stay here? With me? We can have dinner with Mom."

"You want me to?" My pulse thuds, slow and hot, as I absorb that.

She sighs. "I want *you*. But not the way things are. Basically, what you told me this morning is that there's a limit on our relationship, you've set it, and I just have to accept it, no questions asked. But I've been there before. With Troy. And it wasn't good."

I cup her face and tell her devoutly, "There are no limits on what I would do for you, Megan."

She softens. "Me, too."

Oh, fuck.

My heart.

I'm just about to kiss her, when a few feet behind her, the dog stands up and whines softly. Watching me, alert and uncertain. I pause. "And who's this?"

Megan looks over at the dog. "This is Daisy. It's okay, girl. *Sit.*"

The dog sits, still staring at me.

"And Daisy would be...?"

"My dog."

When I raise an eyebrow at her, Megan looks a bit sheepish.

"She's one of the reasons I felt so guilty about leaving. Mom's been taking care of her for me while I get settled. She's a three-year-old Lappie. A Finnish Lapphund. They're herding dogs. You can say hi. She's not aggressive. She just hates Troy right now."

That makes two of us.

I'm already crouching down and holding out my hand so the dog can smell me, which she does. She kind of has the coloring of a husky, but she's much smaller and fluffier, with a puffy tail that curls up over her back. "She's adorable."

"You like dogs?"

"I love dogs. I used to have one."

"Really?"

"She died, a few years ago." Daisy noses into my hand and lets me pat her head, then moves in cautiously so I can pet the rest of her. I give her a gentle rub-down and tell her how pretty she is.

While I'm shamelessly kissing up to her dog, I gaze up at Megan. "Please don't be mad at me. We'll work it out. I promise."

She glances at my bodyguards just outside, flanking the door. "You rushed in with the cavalry to save me. How can I be mad?"

"You can't," I agree.

She watches me snuggling her dog in my shirt and tie, and the corner of her mouth tips up. "Do you ever just want to be normal, Jameson Vance? I mean like not wealthy?"

Huh? "Why would I want that?"

She can't even hold back her smile at my total confusion. "Go put on a pair of jeans and a T-shirt. I'm taking you out on the town tonight."

"This town?"

"Yes. Your best friend's hometown. My hometown."

"I didn't bring any jeans."

"Well, what do you have that's casual?"

"Uh, I threw some sweats in my bag in case I had a chance to work out. You know... after I rushed in with the cavalry and saved you."

"Why am I not surprised?" She laughs softly. "So wear those."

I get to my feet, eying her cotton eyelet dress. It's cute, white and summery. "Won't I be underdressed?"

She pats my chest. "Oh, Jameson. You have no idea where you are."

CHAPTER 42

I drop off my things in Megan's old bedroom, which is now a guest room/sewing room/junk storage, and get changed as requested.

Then we have dinner with her mom, who is weirdly not much at all like Megan, other than kind, and somehow a lot like Cole. Donna seems delighted to meet me in person, thrilled that I'm engaged to her daughter, and I'm not sure she even cares about my money.

The fact that I'm Cole's best friend seems to have more currency with her. He must've said good things about me.

I'll have to thank him.

She also doesn't seem to have a clue about my arrangement with Megan. Which means, presumably, she thinks her daughter really fell in love with me, just like that.

I wonder if Megan told her it was love at first sight.

The entire time we eat, Daisy sits at my feet, staring up at me, like she's deciding how much she likes me, while I sneak her food. I'm not above trying to win her loyalty with treats.

After dinner, we do the dishes together, me and Megan, while her mom plays Neil Young on her ancient stereo and Megan tells her all about our trip to Europe. Daisy sits at Megan's feet while still staring at me.

When we say good night to Donna and leave the house, Daisy comes with us, happily trotting along at Megan's side, on her leash. I follow Megan's lead as we walk along the sad little roads past the sad little houses, Locke and Rurik trailing behind. The sky is dark and the mosquitos have come out, buzzing around my ears.

How is it dusty and yet muggy in the air at the same time? It's hot and swampy, claustrophobic, even though the sky above us is wide open. There are no mountains, no massive, ancient green trees.

I already hate it here.

No wonder Cole and Megan left.

"Well, this is it," Megan announces.

I look around the dreary landscape. It's flat in every direction. The buildings sag, depressed and starved of funds. I can hear music playing faintly somewhere.

"Uh, what are we talking about?"

"You, Jameson Vance, are in for a real treat." She waves a hand at some sad commercial buildings that are maybe some kind of storage facility and whatever else. A library? There's a faded sign with a book on it. "Ta-da! Bet you didn't know this one-horse town has a bar!"

In the direction she's indicating, the same direction the faint music seems to be coming from, there's an old building with a faded old sign that I can't read in the dark. And a small, harsh spotlight shining over the door. I blink at the side wall, which faces a dumpster. "There's a painting of Cole on the side of the building."

"Yes, there is."

We cross the street, where there's zero traffic. We've seen no one on the short walk here from her mom's house.

Near the bottom of the weathered and faded wall mural with the admittedly terrible likeness of Cole, words are painted by a sloppy hand.

Colton Hudson

Right Winger - Dallas Heat

The Heat was Cole's college hockey team.

"Why don't they list his other teams?"

Megan shrugs. "No budget to update it? The guy who painted it doesn't live here anymore? Someone complained about it? It's a small town with no money, Jameson. Things move slower than molasses, and they generally don't get updated or repaired. They just drift into obsolescence."

"Oh."

We continue past Cole's wall of glory—which I take a photo of and am definitely going to send to him with some kind of amusing remark later—and reach the shabby entrance of the bar.

As I draw open the weather-ravaged door beneath the spotlight, I recognize the song that pours out into the night. It's "Boots or Hearts" by The Tragically Hip. A song I only know because I grew up in Canada and, you know, radio.

"You know you're in Canada when..." I remark.

Megan snickers. "Let's get a beer, eh?"

I take Daisy's leash and hand it off to Rurik, so we can head into the bar with Locke; surprise contorts Rurik's features for an instant before they resettle into a scowl. I know he loves dogs. He used to walk Sunny for me all the time, voluntarily.

"What year is this?" I inquire as we step inside the time warp. Not only is the music from decades past, so is literally everything else. Ancient pool tables that have never been upgraded. Glowing Molson Canadian beer signs that are just plain old rather than retro cool.

You can smell the decades of spilled liquor that's seeped into the floors and the cigarette smoke embedded in the walls from like twenty years ago, before they banned smoking inside public places here.

"Come on now," Megan says. "There's nothing wrong with living in the past. We love the past here in Crooks Creek." She takes my hand and leads me toward the bar. I try to ignore the way it sticks in my gut like a shard of rusty metal when she says "we." Like she still lives here. Or will again, inevitably.

Instead, I focus on the relic television sets that hang precariously over the bar, playing commercials and some old movie. There's hockey paraphernalia everywhere, though that, too, is outdated. Some of it might even be so old, it now has value. "My granddad would've loved this place."

"Really?"

"He started out in bars. His very first business was a small bar he bought in Vancouver, when he was twenty-eight. Kind of a dive."

"Huh. I turn twenty-eight next year. So you're saying... I could still launch my empire?" She smiles at me as we lean on the bar.

I smile back easily. "You have to start somewhere. I'm sure your fiancé would spot you some seed money."

"I do like seed." The filthy expression she flashes tells me she's not referring to plants.

And now I'm hard.

In sweats. In public.

I turn my hips toward the bar.

She frowns thoughtfully. "So how did he take a dive bar and turn it into billions?"

"Decades of hard work. In the eighties, he owned a chain of upscale sports bars that he revamped and from there it expanded to restaurants, hotels, a winery, alcohol brands. He went from buying and selling to developing. Buying Vancouver's hockey team wasn't even his biggest acquisition but it was his biggest dream. My dad branched us out into luxury resorts and condo developments, and the rest is history."

The bartender finally comes over; some regular has been hogging his attention.

"Gentlemen first," Megan announces, smiling at me again. "What would you like, Jamie? I'm buying, and don't even think of arguing with me. I'm your host here."

I frown, but relent. It's cuter than cute when she calls me Jamie.

It takes mere seconds to peruse the entire beer selection in the dirty little fridges behind the bar. "I'll have a Grasshopper." The bartender grabs my bottle of Big Rock wheat ale from the fridge and opens it while I tell Megan, "And you'll have a bottled beer as well."

She lifts an eyebrow. "Will I?"

"You will."

There's a silent standoff that lasts about five seconds while she debates whether I'm seriously telling her what to drink.

I am. With good reason.

Then she orders a Moosehead and opens a tab. We clink the necks of our beer bottles and take a swig as we wander to find a table. She finds a booth to her liking on the side of the dance floor. The place is maybe half-full, and other than a few people who say a casual hello to Megan, no one comes over to us.

They're definitely checking us out, though.

I suppose the local girl who disappeared in the night, leaving her job and her home and her boyfriend behind, made some waves. And returning with her new billionaire fiancé weeks later... definite gossip material.

By morning, maybe the whole town will know about that little scene in her mom's driveway.

Maybe they already do.

Locke is also collecting stares where he sits at the bar, sipping his soda water.

Rurik will hang out just outside, keeping an eye on the entrance. At least I know that whatever happens tonight, Troy Duchamp won't be wandering in.

"Hey, Jameson," Megan says happily as we lean on our table, facing each other. It's sticky. A waitress came by as soon as we chose it and dragged a dirty, wet rag over it that didn't help. "Why are we drinking beer from the bottle? I've only seen you drink beer when you were looking to partner with the beer company. You know, in Germany."

"Because we're not risking anything on tap or by the glass. The glassware doesn't look sanitized, and no way do they clean those keg lines properly."

Her nose scrunches. "Ew. I never thought of that."

"Think of it. Beer on tap is always a risk. You want to be sure you're in a place that cleans their lines properly. Every two weeks, they need to be flushed with a cleaning solution. Many places do not." I sip my beer, smirking a little as she absorbs that with horrified fascination.

"I'm never drinking beer from the keg again."

"I know. Don't even get me started on the lime wedges they leave out on the bar. Bartenders touch cash all night. Do you know how dirty paper money is? And the credit card machine? And then they dip their fingers in that bin of lime wedges and put one on your glass, and you're supposed to squeeze it into your drink? Fuck, no."

"I had no idea you were such a germaphobe."

"It's not a phobia. Just common sense and self-respect."

"Even if we put aside that the alcohol probably kills the germs anyway—"

"Maybe."

"—you are ruining bar nights for me."

"Then I've succeeded."

"You don't want me going to bars?"

"No. I want you home on my dick, where you belong."

She laughs and smacks my arm like I'm kidding.

"So," I say, ogling her perky cleavage in her little cotton eyelet dress for the dozenth time. "Who do we know here?"

For the next many songs, Megan points out every person in the bar she recognizes, which is all of them, and spills gossip on the ones she knows gossip on, which is most of them. Now and then, the waitress who looks, sounds, and smells like she's been a pack-a-day smoker since 1973 comes by our table, bringing more beer, which Megan puts on her tab.

We hold hands and play with each other's fingers while we talk.

Then we dance slowly to Kings of Leon, "I Want You," like no one's watching. They are.

We dance right by our table, pressed together, eyes closed. At least, her eyes are closed. I'm cheating and watching her the whole time.

When a faster song comes on, Megan pulls back and hands me my bottle of Grasshopper off the table. "Drink," she says, a soft smile on her lips. "Locke will watch your back."

Another hour later, I've had too much to drink and I'm passionately pep talking her on why she can never move back to this place, having lost all chill and every filter I've got. I may use the phrase "worst mistake you could ever make" at least three times.

Megan seems amused as she listens patiently, sipping from her bottle of Moosehead.

"What if Frodo never left the Shire? What if Luke never left the farm?"

The situation is getting dire.

I've trapped Megan in the booth with my body, both of us on the same seat. I can't be sure how much time has passed except that they don't clear your table throughout the night in this place, just keep bringing more beer, and there's an army of bottles on the table. A few old friends of hers joined us for a while, but have long since wandered off when I turned out to be a complete buzz kill and Megan hog. "Can you imagine that?"

Megan rolls her eyes at me, but laughs. "I had no idea you were such a closet nerd. You've been holding back, Jameson."

"Okay, okay." I gesture wide with my beer, slopping it. "Maybe in those two examples the answer is that the known world might've literally ended, but still. What if Megan Hudson never left Crooks Creek? What kind of travesty would that be?"

She seems to be considering the answer to that, or just watching me try very hard to sip my beer like I'm not having trouble finding my mouth. I am. I'm drunk, and we both know it.

"It would be a fairly major travesty," she admits. "For me."

"Right?! And I don't mean because you never would've met me."

She blinks at me innocently. "But meeting you was the best thing that happened to me when I left the Shire."

"Really? Thank you."

She puts her drink down. "Are you really likening me to a hobbit? Am I that short?"

I ponder her tits, then her succulent lips. "You're a luscious woodland fairy."

"Nerd," she teases.

"Why aren't you as drunk as me?"

"I don't know. Maybe because that." She sweeps her hand over the empty Big Rock bottles. Which is when I notice there are only three green Moosehead bottles in the crowd of them.

I squint at her.

She smiles wide.

I lean, or maybe fall, into her so suddenly, my lips hit her teeth. She laughs, and I take advantage of her open mouth to invade her personal space, delving my tongue into her warmth.

I moan involuntarily and her fingers curl into my shirt, her mouth meeting the demands of mine as well as she can, as I eat her mouth, deep and sloppy.

When I finally break the wet suction, she turns her head a fraction so I can't do it again. "Everyone's looking at us."

"I don't care."

I grab her head and kiss her again. I'm mad for her. Ravenous for any scrap of her I can get.

And I'm pissed at myself for not being the man she deserves.

I know I'm hurting her by keeping this fucking secret, not telling her the full truth. I can never tell her about the damn game I had to play.

But I can't let it kill us. Even if the light in her eyes dies just a little bit more every time we circle around it.

She knows it's there, unspoken between us, a shadow that can never be washed away with light.

I'll just have to find so many ways to make her love me, she'll forget about it.

Yeah, that will work.

She pulls away, taking a deep, shuddering breath. She blinks at me, her eyes glassy. Arousal and alcohol.

Maybe she is drunk.

"I know I'm not really what you want, Jameson."

"What?" I cling to her dress as she clings to my shirt.

"I know I'm not enough for you. I know you won't change your stance on marriage for me. I'm not in your vision of your future. If I were... you'd tell me everything. You'd open up."

"What are you talking about? *I* was never what *you* wanted. I was just a distraction along the way."

She shakes her head. "What?"

I dig my hands into her hair, holding her face close to mine. "What you wanted was to start your life over. *Your* life. And you wanted to be able to count on your brother for once, even though you didn't want to admit it—"

"That's not—"

"It's true. And you got that. Along with some help from me. But the rest of it... I didn't offer you a new life. I offered you a distraction from the life you wanted."

She draws back a bit, absorbing that, as her words from the night I proposed to her ring in my head.

You're a terrible distraction, Jameson Vance.

"Well, tell me," she says. "What is the life I really wanted?"

"You tell me."

I blow out a breath and let her go, dragging a hand through my hair. I need to stop drinking. My gaze sweeps across the empty bottles; they have no answers inside.

"The thing is," I tell her, "maybe I've distracted you so thoroughly that you've forgotten."

CHAPTER 43

Jameson

We walk the few blocks back to her mom's house in silence. My head thuds with the slow beat of "I Want You." And everything I said to Megan in the bar seems distant, obscured through a descending fog, adrift on a body of water just beyond my peripheral vision.

"I just want you to be happy."

My words, out of nowhere, seem small and unimportant in the muggy night air. Mosquitos prick at me, and I'm constantly brushing them away, smacking my arms and neck. They don't seem to bother Megan.

I read somewhere that they're more attracted to some people's blood than others.

Just more scientific evidence that Megan Hudson is a perfect specimen.

I stare at her long and hard, aching for some response.

Finally, she speaks. "You talk to me like you know me better than I know myself. Like you know what's best for me and I don't."

"I don't know what's best for you. But I know you. You won't be happy if you keep sacrificing what you want for a man. Any man. You've sacrificed for *years*. I know how much you gave up." I wave a hand vaguely at the crappy little town she spent her life in—for a man who did shit-all for her.

He didn't love her.

He didn't put her first.

"But you don't really know me." Her face scrunches a little, thoughtfully. "Do you?"

That's cute. She's asking, like she doesn't actually know.

I try to think of something definitive to prove that I do know her. I know her better than I've ever known any woman, even my sister, and I'm close with my sister.

"I know you wish we lived in the house across the street."

She looks at me. "What?"

"The house with the big gate diagonally across from mine. The one with the huge, flowering cherry tree in front. You sigh every time we drive past it."

"I do not." She chews thoughtfully on her lip. "Well, just imagine how ridiculously beautiful it is when it blooms in spring."

It is. I've seen it. "You take a picture every time you see a rainbow."

"You got that from Instagram," she says, unimpressed.

"You've donated an uncomfortably high percentage of your life's earnings to the little animal shelter at the veterinarian's office here in Crooks Creek. You desperately want to bring Daisy out west with you, but you haven't yet because you're afraid you're too unsettled. And you haven't asked me if she can come live with us because you're afraid it will be an imposition or something."

"How do you know that?"

"Because you sigh whenever you see a puppy, too."

She narrows her eyes at me. "I meant the money thing."

"You pretend your favorite song is 'Sweet Caroline' but it's actually 'Bibbidi-Bobbidi-Boo.'"

Her jaw drops.

I shrug. "You sing them both under your breath when you're getting ready to start the day and stuff. You're a Pisces, born on February twenty-ninth on a leap year. Every year that isn't a leap year, you stay up to midnight on February twenty-eighth to celebrate your birthday in the moment between eleven fifty-nine and twelve o'clock, where February twenty-ninth should be. When you were a kid, your brother told you your birthday didn't come at all on the years there was no February twenty-ninth, so you didn't get any older, and it drove you crazy."

"Hey. You got that from Cole."

"You pretend you like plants better than people, but deep down, you desperately want a few people in your life who you can trust with your life, you want to be a mom one day sooner than later, and you want a Prince Charming. You're a hard-core romantic. You don't realize that you've been writing an epic love story for four damn novels already, but you not only believe in happily ever afters, you want one so badly, sometimes you wake up in the night and it's the first thing on your mind... the fear that you won't have one."

We've completely stopped walking as I talk, and she draws a shaky breath.

"How do you know that last part? That's scary."

"Because I have the same fear."

My heart beats hard and fast as we stare at each other.

Megan twists her lip between her teeth. "That's stupid." The insects are louder than her voice, creaking and buzzing in the overgrown weeds of the ditches around us. "Why would someone like you have that fear?"

"I could ask you that same question."

"How did you find out all those things?"

"A combo of drilling Cole for information and my keen observational skills when I want something."

"Stop talking and kiss me."

I kiss her.

But two seconds after I've lapped my tongue over hers, a mosquito pricks my neck. I slap it. "*Fuck*. Mosquitos can fuck off and die."

"They're part of the ecosystem. They have a purpose."

"No. They don't. If we could lose one entire species and be better as a planet, it's mosquitos."

"Humans," she says, at the same moment I say mosquitos.

She cracks a smile.

I smile back, as much as I can as the bloodthirsty little fuckers prick my ankles. "Please. If you like me even a little bit, get me out of this hellhole dust-bowl swamp and into some mosquito netting or something."

She laughs easily and takes me by the hand, tugging me toward her mom's place.

We break into a jog.

"Christ, how can anyone live in this province? It's goddamn biblical—" My complaint is cut off by Megan's mouth slamming into mine as we step into the house. She pushes me back against the door, and our collective weight slams it shut.

"Shh," I whisper, even as I start pulling up her dress with impatience.

She giggles. "Mom can't hear a thing when she's sleeping," she whispers. "She snores too loud."

"Huh." My mind flashes forward to a distant future wherein an older Megan snores in bed.

"You're wondering if I'm gonna snore when I'm older," she accuses.

I shrug, making up my mind. "I could live with it." I kiss her again and steer her blindly into the kitchen. "Where am I fucking you? Bent over the arm of the couch? Kitchen table?" I peel her dress off over her head and toss it aside. "Bathroom floor?"

"He is *such* a romantic. In my bedroom." She pulls me in that direction. And as soon as we get through the door, she shuts it behind us.

In the moonlight that glows through the window, I tear off her bra and panties. I'd love to sweep her up in my arms, carry her to the bed, and have my way with her, but I'm a bit too drunk to pull it off.

Instead, she helps me get undressed, and when we're both naked, I just kind of fall on her, pinning her to the bed and kneading her soft flesh with my greedy hands as I probably squish the breath out of her.

She's panting as we make out, her hips rolling against me. My cock is deliriously hard as I grind against her, wanting in.

"Your dog's watching us," I tell her between kisses. Daisy is curled on a blanket on the floor, staring.

"It's okay. She's a voyeur like me."

I groan as she sucks on my neck.

"Guide me inside you." My voice is thick with lust. "And please tell me you locked the door, because if Donna throws it open and comes face-to-face with a plumbing shot, I will never get over it."

"It's locked." She bites my lip as she grips my dick and angles it, pushing the head into her soft, wet opening. Then she kisses me, hot and soft, making my balls ache.

"Your cunt's a little slice of heaven," I groan as I sink into her.

"Jameson. You're so…"

She never finishes that sentence as she digs her fingers deep into my ass muscles and pulls me deeper, panting hungrily.

We fuck slow and wet and desperate, grinding into each other like we want to merge our souls.

I collapse back on the bed with a satisfied sigh. I just came, dizzy with lust for her, when the convulsions of Megan's orgasm racked her body so hard, it yanked me right over with her.

Mutual perfection.

Now my lungs feel shaky. My stomach presses up into my ribs. This unease I've carried with me ever since I found out Megan had flown home has only intensified.

Maybe it's all the beer.

Maybe it's the singular, unsettling fear that I'm losing her and there's nothing I can do about it.

That she'll choose another life over me and the one I can give her.

That at the end of our fake engagement, one year from when we started, she'll set off on that new life she wanted when she left this place. I've given her the means to do it. She won't need me anymore.

The panic of it pounds into my brain with every beat of blood through my veins now, the truth purified by alcohol.

Daisy's head rests on her paws, and she's still watching me, those pale-blue eyes assessing sleepily. Still deciding if I'm a good idea or not.

"What would make your life complete?" I ask Megan in the silence.

Next to me, she shifts, drawing a blanket up over our cooling bodies.

"I don't know. I wish I could figure that out, but I just haven't been able to do that yet."

We lie in the near-dark, her breathing gradually settling back to normal. I'm still breathing like I'm floating on some raft in a swamp and a creature from the depths is lurking, bumping at my boat. I'm afraid I'm about to capsize, and I don't know how to find the shore.

Without her, I don't know what the shore even looks like anymore or why I'd want to get there.

I feel adrift. Poised to drown.

"Sometimes, it takes a while," she adds with a sigh.

Like when you weren't born into the life of a billionaire, with everything laid out for you so nicely, she doesn't say. But I know what she means.

I wasn't just given everything in life, like some people probably think. But at the end of the day... I kind of was. Even so, I've always wanted *more.* I've always been driven.

But right now... I have no motivation. For once in my life, I don't want anything but the woman lying next to me.

I lie here, half panting and really absorbing that truth into the marrow of my bones, even as the room vaguely spins.

So this is love.

"I thought my life was complete before I met you," I muse out loud.

It's the wrong thing to say. I know that when Megan sucks in a breath.

I turn my head to find her staring at me.

"I meant—*Shit.* I'm drunk. My life was complete *except* in the relationship department." I drag my hand down my face. "Obviously. Remember what I said about my fear of no happily ever after?"

Her eyebrows pull together. "So you don't think there's any way you could have one with me?"

"No, I *fear* I won't have one with you. But that's up to you."

"It's up to you, too."

"No. It's really up to you."

She stares at me for an infinite minute. "This is a dumb drunk argument that's going nowhere."

"No. It's going somewhere."

She frowns.

The woman is so fucking adorable when she's annoyed with me. Like a kitten in a bad mood.

I roll on top of her and kiss her little frown. Twice. Three times. Both corners, then the middle.

"*You're* going somewhere," I clarify. "With or without me. Can't you see that? You don't need me, Megan." I say all this while I crush her with my body, trapping her. Because I'm so damn scared she'll say, *You know what, you're right. See ya.*

"I never said I did." Her face softens and her frown melts away. "I said I want you."

I shake my head slowly, smoothing her hair back from her face and looking deep into her gorgeous amber eyes in the moonlight. "I want to give you back the opportunity I took away," I tell her solemnly. Because at this point, fucking millions or even billions aside, I know it's the best thing I can ever give her. The most important thing.

And I don't want to wait until a year's up to do it.

I need to know. Now. Is she in or is she out?

"What opportunity?"

"To decide the life you want."

"What, this life? You seriously think I'd come back here?"

I force the words out. "I don't know."

"And you'd let me do that? I thought you wanted me out of Crooks Creek," she says softly. "You know, Frodo?"

"I do."

"I thought... maybe... you loved me," she says, even softer.

I do. Jesus Christ, I do.

But for a long minute I can't answer. My heart is beating too hard, way up in the knot in my throat.

I take a deep breath, gathering my words. In the thudding silence, I can really feel how drunk I am. So drunk, I can't be expected to make sense, maybe.

But I know this much is true.

"I'm saying this because I love you. Imagine you never met me, Megan. What is the life you want?"

She stares up into my eyes as we breathe together.

Then she says the best thing she could ever say to me. Something so good, I never actually imagined her saying it.

"No, Jameson," she breathes. "I don't want to imagine a life without you."

CHAPTER 44

Megan

"You're kidding me." Nicole literally shoves popcorn in her mouth as she listens raptly to my retelling of how Jameson came to Crooks Creek and served up my ex-boyfriend's ass to him on a platter. "He did that?"

"He did that. Then he screwed me in my old bedroom and all the way home on his private plane."

"I'm in lust. You know, vicariously."

I sigh. "I'm in love."

"God."

We both stuff our mouths with popcorn and chew for a long minute. That's the first time, since I realized it was true, that I said those words out loud.

And I realized it quite a while ago, really.

We're lying out by Jameson's pool. Daisy is stretched out in the shade beneath my lounge chair, dozing. When we left my mom's house in Crooks Creek, Jameson picked her up and carried her out to the car with us without even mentioning it to me. She flew home with us on the jet, and that was that.

Jameson himself should be home any minute. When his sister asked him to come down to the Vance Bayshore resort, where she's working, to have dinner with her tonight, I basically ordered him to go.

Both Jameson and Daisy have been glued to me for the last few days, ever since we got back from Crooks Creek, as if they're both afraid of losing me.

But I'm not going anywhere.

Because: love.

I've never had it like this before.

I'm not about to let it go without a fight.

Nicole drops her head back on her lounger. "Well, I'm happy for you. If you're sure it's the real deal..."

"It is. How could I not love a man who comes racing to my hometown, for me, and tries to save me like a damn superhero? He also makes love to me like his very existence depends on getting me off. And *he reads my books*. And enjoys them. If that's not love..."

Daisy suddenly gets up, barks happily, stretches, and trots off into the house. I know that means Jameson is home.

"Shit. Are there any more of him?" Nicole moans. "I really need one of those."

"Well, technically, he's got three unmarried brothers, so..."

"So you'll hook me up?" Her eyes go big and pleading.

"Well..." I snicker. "I don't know. Even if I could. I mean, Harlan just seems... dangerous. And Damian is... intensely intimidating. And possibly perverted. And Graysen is... well, he just seems above the world. He's engaged, but I don't know how any mere woman could actually win that man's attention for life..."

I drift off. Because unfortunately, Nicole's eyes have glazed over more hotly with each successive description. Which means that my words, meant to deter her, are doing the opposite.

Oops.

"There's my beautiful wife." Jameson's husky voice sends a warm shiver through me.

I glance over my shoulder to find him strolling toward me, Daisy following. His sleeves are rolled up, and he loosens his tie as he approaches.

"He's calling you that?" Nicole stage-whispers. "Already?"

"Yes. It's a whole obsession," I stage-whisper back. To Jameson, I say "Hi, stud. Enjoy dinner?"

He makes a yummy growling sound as his eyes ravage my body in my pink bikini, telling me that I'm more delicious to him than whatever he just ate.

He leans in for a kiss. I make it quick since Nicole is here and all. "It's still warm out here," I murmur breathlessly. "Why don't you take off that suit and put on your swim trunks?"

He kisses me again, then bites my lip. "I was thinking I'd just take everything off. And we can skinny-dip."

I stare into his blue eyes, hypnotized by that vision. We haven't done that in his pool yet.

Stupid, really.

"Uh, guys? I'm right here."

I clear my throat, and Jameson straightens.

"Sorry," I tell Nicole.

"That's okay." She sets her empty glass aside and gets to her feet. "You guys have all your naked fun. I should go anyway. I'm working tonight."

"I'll walk you out." I get up and pull on a robe over my bikini.

After I see her off at the front door, I'm making my way back to the pool when I find Jameson in the living room. He's still wearing his shirt and tie and his dress slacks, with bare feet. And he's looking at the floor as he claws his hands though his hair.

My dog sits at his feet, gazing up at him with such adoration, it makes my heart skip a beat.

But I can feel the tension in his body from here. His expression when our eyes meet makes me stop in my tracks.

"Jameson. What's wrong?"

"Megan." He breathes out heavily. "I have a confession to make."

My heart cracks at the pain in his eyes. Whatever this is, it isn't good.

I drift closer.

"I should've just manned up and told you sooner. You know, that thing I told you that I can't tell you..."

"You don't have to tell me," I say quickly. Because I can see how it's weighing on him. "If it will hurt you..."

He closes the space between us, slips a hand around my waist and tugs me to him, and buries his other hand in my hair, cupping my head. "The only thing that hurts me is lying to you. Keeping the truth from you."

A terrible ache presses against my ribs, from the inside out. I can feel his pain.

What else can I tell him but the truth?

"I love you, Jameson."

He closes his eyes and hangs his head.

"You're kinda scaring me, though."

When he lifts his head, his expression is fierce with devotion. He pushes his other hand into my hair, holding my head with both hands.

"Don't be scared. I only want to protect you," he says devoutly. "Protect *us*. Between us, my only regret is the only lie I ever told you. The reason why I couldn't be with you like you deserved. Couldn't make love to you. The truth is, I'm not allowed to talk about it. At all. Even now."

I take that in, fear tingling up my spine. "Why?"

He sighs wearily. "It could've made me lose everything. Including you. I think I get now why my brother chose it for me," he adds, almost to himself.

"I don't understand."

He takes a breath. "The thing is, if I told you, I stood to lose everything I have. And I still will. But I've thought about it a fuck of a lot." He pauses, and if you can see a person's heart through their eyes, I'm looking into Jameson's right now. He's laying it wide open for me.

He looks deep into my eyes, searching for a long moment. And the heat and the urgency, the frustration and desire, the pure love I feel from him takes my breath away. Then he says, "Fuck it," like he's uttering an oath, and kisses me, hard.

He kisses me so deeply and so long, I'm bent backwards over the arm he slides around my waist.

When we come up for air, I feel dazed, but he's still locked onto me like his life depends on it. "I *will* tell you," he swears to me, "if you want me to. If that's what it takes to earn your trust and your love."

"I do love you."

He takes my hand and presses it to his chest, shaking his head. "I swore to myself when I got the dagger tattoo over my heart that I would never lie to anyone I love, betray them, the way my parents did to each other. And I love you, Megan."

"I know you do." I take a breath, shoring up my courage, even as my insides quiver with dread. I do know. I can feel his love. "But I don't want you to lose everything. So... *No.* Whatever it is... you can't tell me. I won't let you."

He shakes his head. "You're so brave, it's ridiculous."

"Or so stupid," I say quietly. "Because if you don't tell me, that means there will always be this secret between us."

He takes a deep breath. "Not if you'd allow someone else to tell you."

"What do you mean?"

"This secret... Only my siblings are allowed to know. But there's one other person who knows about it. I ran into her at the resort tonight, and it hit me. That I could ask her to tell you. She was... how do I put this? The love of my grandfather's life, I suppose."

"But your grandmother is deceased," I say, confused.

"She is. And it pains me to tell you this because I don't want you to think I take after my grandfather this way. But I mentioned to you that he cheated on my grandmother. It was even worse than that. In truth, he had a lifetime affair with his secretary. Her name is Valerie, and she's here, right now. My siblings are bound to not tell this secret, ever. So Valerie is the only one who can."

"So... you want me... to let some woman I've never met, your grandfather's mistress, tell me the secret you've been keeping from me?"

"Uh... yeah. When you lay it out like that, it sounds terrible. And I should probably just have Locke drive her home now."

"Are you kidding me? Send her in."

"Really?" Jameson seems stunned. "You want to hear her out?"

"Seriously? I want all her stories. Go get her. I'm putting on tea."

Finally, his shock dissolves. A faint smirk quirks his lips. "Actually, knowing Valerie, she'd prefer a brandy."

"Brandy, coming right up." I hurry behind the bar to get the woman a drink, sifting through bottles. "Where is she?"

"She's in my office."

"Well, let's not leave the woman waiting."

I sit in my little office, off Jameson's office, where I said yes to his proposal. My head's kind of throbbing with all the information Valerie just gave me.

She's just left. Clara came to walk her out.

Valerie was polite with me, very formal, and not at all what I might've pictured.

She wasn't beautiful in that way that told you she'd been a stunning-looking woman in her youth. She was rather plain and straightforward. Neatly dressed in a modest skirt and blouse with a cardigan.

The great love of billionaire Stoddard Vance's life... was fascinating.

I'd seen pictures of his wife. She was beautiful. She was the mother of his two sons, the grandmother of his five grandchildren. What was it about his secretary that had captured his heart? Was it just that they were in such close proximity, that he relied on her day to day, and they'd formed a bond?

No. It had to be more than that. Jameson told me just before he introduced us that his granddad had left Valerie a billion-dollar portion of his estate.

I hear the office door open and get to my feet, walking to meet Jameson when I see him step in and close the door. We meet in the middle of his office, in front of the elegant sofa I flung mud all over.

"She told you?" he asks. I can see his tension.

I take his hands. "She told me everything. About the game, and your challenge." I squeeze his hands. "And you can relax. All it did was make me like you more."

"God." He exhales with relief.

I raise an eyebrow. "Though I now know why you warned me about your family."

Jameson puts his hand on the side of my neck, his thumb running over my jaw. "Yeah."

"I can't believe one of your siblings did that to you."

"It was Graysen."

"Really? *Why?*"

His thumb caresses my jaw. "I really didn't understand why, until I fell for you. But I'm pretty sure he thinks I'm too much like our mom."

That surprises me. "In what way?"

He sort of rolls his eyes. "Emotional. Moody. Capable of falling in love way too hard, and never coming back from it."

I soften, and I don't know what to say. Because truly, that sounds exactly like the Jameson I know.

"He thought the way my love life was headed," he adds, "I'd end up with a broken heart. And maybe end up sullying the family name in the process. But in short, he was worried about me. He called me several times while we were in Crooks Creek to check on me. And you. He likes you, Megan. And he likes you for me. I think my whole family's glad we're engaged. They're just cautious about outsiders. And like me, they're slow to trust. But I trust you. And I'll never hold anything back from you ever again, I promise you that."

"I believe you."

"You do?"

"Yes. Because I know you, Jameson." I gaze at him adoringly. "There's this thing in romance writing called a cinnamon roll hero. That's you. I just want to keep peeling back your layers and licking the sugar I find inside."

Now his eyebrow creeps up.

"You're a romantic," I go on, "and an honest person, even though you know how to create an illusion and make people believe what you want them to. You believe in happily ever after, and you want one, with someone like me. Someone you can trust." I try to do that thing he did in Crooks Creek, where he listed off all those things he knew about me that I didn't even know he'd noticed. "You clearly love dogs, but maybe you felt guilty when your dog died because you weren't home enough and you thought you weren't ready to be a dog dad, so you didn't let yourself get a new one even though you have a ton of love to give. You live in this giant house alone with that big guest wing, because you hate being alone and lonely, and you want all your friends to be welcome, all the time. This challenge was extra hard on you because you thought it put a rift between you and other people, but in the end, it just brought you so much closer to me, and maybe to Graysen, too, than you ever imagined it could."

"You're scaring me right now. I didn't know you were a mind reader."

"I'm not. I've just learned how to read you. And I have more."

"Shit..."

"You like to pretend you're in control of your time, but in reality, you're so devoted to your family and your business, you work more than you'll ever admit. You actually love working with your hands, and helping your handyman whenever you can around the house. You like simple things, like local food and watching the sunset over the water from your patio and daydreaming about the future, and shooting hoops and drinking whiskey. And you love hockey. That's part of why you admire Cole. Because you wanted to be a hockey player when you grew up, and you were angry that your mom moved you to France and you didn't get to play anymore. And you've struggled to forgive her for abandoning you for her new life. You've been single and alone for so long, because you're scared to fall in love and end up like your parents. But more than anything, you want a family of your own, to try to make up for your lonely childhood."

"Jesus," is all he says.

"And maybe you resent Graysen for knowing you better than you know yourself, because you never thought he understood you like that. You think you're different, but you're not that different. You may be years apart, but you grew up in the same home. You just processed your pain differently. You cope differently. But maybe he knew the exact challenge you needed to face. Even if it seemed nonsensical at first."

"Yeah." This time, he sounds defeated. "Fuck, I kind of love him for that."

I laugh a little. "Maybe a challenge isn't so bad. Maybe the people around you, those who know you best and love you through it all, *should* challenge you. If you're not being challenged, you're not really growing, right?"

His lips quirk. "Sure. There are probably better ways to go about it."

"Not if you're a game master."

He smiles. I can tell he appreciates that I can see the cunning in what his grandfather set out to do.

"Do you feel like you grew from this challenge?"

"Hell, yes. I feel like everything I've been through, every moment of my life was orchestrated to get me here. To you."

He goes down on one knee, so suddenly, I don't see it coming.

"Um. What's happening?"

He swallows, looking up into my eyes. "Sit down, Megan."

I almost crumple. He guides me to sit down right in front of him, on the edge of the sofa.

He takes my hands in his. "I tried to prove my love to you publicly, to please my brother. The flashy ring. The press. And I didn't fully understand why *you* didn't believe it. But then I realized, you thought I was lying to you, because you thought I was also lying to the world about how I feel about you. When all that time, I should've been proving to you that it was real—right here, between the two of us."

"Jameson..." I sigh softly, happily.

"The truth is, I didn't lie to anyone. Everything I said from the start, everything I told my family about why I love you, is true. I meant every word of it."

Hot, happy tears threaten to spill, and I try to blink them back. "Then kiss me already."

He kisses me, pushing me back on the sofa, giving me his weight until I'm swimming in the heat between us. Falling, like I always do in his arms.

Falling into him.

Falling *with* him.

He kisses his way down my chest and smooths a hand up my thigh beneath my robe. He presses a warm, possessive hand to my pussy, then tugs my bikini aside, and I arch my back, wanting his touch.

Wanting him inside.

"I don't have sex on this couch," he murmurs between my breasts, even as his fingers slide into me.

I move my hips into his touch, gasping. "You do now."

"I love you, Megan." His rough-velvet voice is devout. His fingers are determined as they work inside me, his thumb circling around my clit, coaxing me to the edge.

"Jameson..." I gasp, relaxing into the rising pleasure that he's orchestrating, so perfectly.

He lowers himself between my legs, and his tongue joins his thumb in urging me toward climax. I revel in it, in how much he wants to please me, in the warm and hungry affections of his mouth as he licks and sucks while moaning in pleasure.

And when I finally shatter, my core contracting in ecstasy, he says, "Marry me."

Our eyes lock. My heart thuds as my body arches, the shivers of orgasm still pulsing through my body, his fingers moving slowly inside me.

When I stop moving and lie panting, he says, "I want you to be my wife, Megan. And I don't need a fucking year to decide."

A tear slides down my temple. And as soon as I catch my breath, I give him the only answer I can.

"Yes."

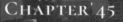

CHAPTER 45

Jameson

L ater that evening, I emerge from the shower to find Megan lying on our bed, waiting for me. She's wearing my shirt, the one I wore today, unbuttoned, and she's naked underneath.

So beautiful.

She smiles at me sleepily, but there's no way we're going to sleep yet.

I climb over her and peel the shirt open, baring her beautiful tits and pussy to me completely. I'm already getting all kinds of ideas about how I'm going to make her come again.

After I made her come on my no-sex sofa, I fucked her on it, then had Chef make us a celebratory dinner.

Then we called our families to tell them the news: that we're getting married, for real, and will be setting a wedding date soon.

I know my family approves of Megan. Even Harlan, as much as he can bother approving of such a thing. He's been in a black mood the last few days, ever since we all met to draw the next name from Granddad's cigar box, and his name was chosen.

But when is Harlan ever in a good mood?

As for Graysen, I told him we're having dinner soon, just the two of us, and he seemed pleased. It's not like Graysen and I to spend much one-on-one time, but maybe that's my fault more than it is his. And my soon-to-be-married status seems to have checked off an item on his to-do list, so at least he's off my back about that.

My part in the game is over.

All there is left to do is enjoy planning a life with my bride.

And if she thinks we're done celebrating, she really doesn't know me as well as she thinks she does.

I slide my fingers inside her, watching how her eyes glaze over with pleasure. I take my time coaxing out another luscious orgasm, two fingers plunging deep inside her and my lips wrapped around her sweet little clit. I stroke and suck as she grinds her hips into me, and when she goes off, it's with an ecstatic cry and a deep shudder, her cunt pulsing around my fingers and her hands grabbing at my hair.

When I release her clit, she sighs and relaxes against the bed.

"Best engagement celebration ever," she says shakily.

I slide my fingers out of her. "We're just getting started, sweetheart."

She laughs softly. As if I'm fucking kidding.

"Baby, I can't help it if I'm obsessed with romancing you. It's biological. You knew what you were getting into." I yank off the towel that's still barely clinging to my hips and toss it aside. It's getting hot in here. "You're the one who told me I was a romantic when I wanted to chuck my tablet, and your twat hero, Wolf, out of the jet on that flight to France."

Her eyebrow arches. "And clearly, I wasn't wrong."

"Good thing for both of us, you've assured me that Wolf has stepped up and become the alpha Rowan needs him to be. Which means I'm willing to read the final two books, and see if he comes through."

"Lucky me."

I grab her thighs and spread her legs wide around my hips, making her gasp. I bite her throat lightly. "Did you really think I'd find you lying in bed wearing my shirt and not demand to fuck you?"

She gives me a sultry look. "I would never."

"Oh. You knew. Because you're my little tease." I slide my fingers inside her again, and I pulse them against her flesh.

Two can tease.

I'm not nearly done with her. She just agreed to marry me. My idea of doing our engagement right this time is making up for all the fucking we should've done the first time.

Her pussy spasms in response to my touch, and she moans, still hungry.

My beautiful, insatiable girl.

"Jamie," she gushes.

There's something about that sweet way she says my name that makes my heart clench and all the arrows lodged in it quiver. Only my family and closest friends have ever called me Jamie. To the outside world, I'm Jameson Vance, untouchable billionaire, a member of the ultraprivate Vance family.

But when Megan says my name, it feels like we're family already. And it turns me on.

"I want in you," I growl.

"You are in me."

I slip my fingers out and caress her sensitive little asshole with my fingertip. Her breath hitches, but she doesn't protest or pull away. I already know she likes it when I use my fingers here.

And I hate to bring up her fucking lowlife of an ex at a time like this, but I suddenly need to know. Right now.

"Did he fuck you here?"

If he did, I'll make it my mission to fuck her better.

"No," she breathes. And the hit of primal, alpha possessiveness that surges through my veins is like a fucking superdrug.

I know I can love her better. That's no question.

I know I can fuck her better, too.

But to fuck her first and last... I don't even know until she says no to that question and heat expands in my chest how badly I want to own every single part of her.

For life.

And the fact that he never did that... that she's never been possessed that way by any other man...

I'm so fucking hard, it almost hurts.

I tease her little asshole with my fingertip, stroking softly, and my cock jerks with anticipation. Megan shivers, her tits bouncing as she wriggles, her nipples hard and flushed.

"God. Everything's so sensitive. So... *fuck*."

"You like that."

"I like everything." Her expression softens from hunger to adoration. "Everything *you* do, I mean."

Another surge of alpha male satisfaction and lust hit me with those words. I massage her little hole, and her muscles tremble in response, slipping open for me. But I don't push inside.

"I *want* everything," I tell her, my voice gruff with longing. "No barriers between us."

"Yes."

"Do you want me here?"

"I want you everywhere."

"It'll hurt."

"I don't care."

"Damn."

She laughs softly. "What?"

I drift my hand over one of her breasts and gently squeeze, making her shiver. "I need something." I get up, and disappear into the bathroom, then reemerge with a bottle of lube.

"Oh," she breathes.

I stalk toward her, the urgency building. Every time we fuck, I want Megan just that little bit more.

It's crazy, heady shit.

I put the lube on the nightstand and grab her under the knees, turning her as I tug her toward me, so I can fuck her while standing next to the bed.

My cock is hard as rock, and I give it a few solid strokes as I stand over her. "Spread your legs. Lift up your knees for me."

She spreads wide, lifting her knees out to the side, so I can get at all of her.

I grab the lube and squeeze out a generous amount of the cool liquid, letting it pour over her already slick pussy and coat her little asshole.

Then I smear it all over my cock.

I toss the bottle aside.

I lean over her, lining up my cock, watching for any sign of fear. I don't see any. Only love and longing as acute and overwhelming as what I feel for her.

I grip her hip with one hand to hold her in place. I can feel her panting little breaths. My own breathing is already rough and uneven.

I was so afraid that I'd lose her. If I didn't ever tell her about the challenge... Or if what Valerie told her ended us, drove her away...

But she's right here, opening herself for me in ways she never has for another man.

With such trust...

It tears me open, makes me want to lay everything I am at her feet.

I push, but her body resists me. We're both so slick, I could force myself right in, easily. But I won't do that.

She needs to be in this with me.

"Relax, baby," I soothe her, drifting my thumb over her clit. "When I'm inside you, I'm going to make you come so fucking hard, I promise you'll like it."

She laughs nervously. "I believe you."

"Then relax for me, Megan."

I caress her clit until I feel her open. I immediately push in, and she gasps. My cockhead settles into place, and she squeezes me.

"Fuck," I breathe. "I need to be deeper. I want all of you."

She nods, exhales, and the second I feel her relax, I shove all the way in.

She cries out, tensing, but I'm already in.

She wriggles, impaled on my hard length as I lock my hips, holding still, letting her adjust to the feeling.

From my side of it, it's pure goddamn heaven. Tight and hot.

But this isn't about me. This is about *us*.

"Good? Bad?"

"Full," she gasps.

"My good girl." I rub her clit. "You like that cock inside you."

"Y-yes."

"You're so perfect."

She moans in response.

"You're mine."

"Yes," she sighs and shudders. Like she's surrendering to the inevitability of it.

My heart burns with the sting of a fresh new onslaught of arrows, and I know I'd give up anything for this.

For us.

It was an inevitability I'd felt overtaking me, long ago.

We were made for each other. And now we're bound to each other. Sex is just a physical expression of what we already feel, already know to be true.

"You're mine," I tell her again, pinching her clit in a gentle rhythm now, "and I'm yours."

She shudders. "Yes."

"Your tight ass is mine, just like this pretty, hungry little cunt of yours and this greedy little clit, and those bouncy, juicy tits and all the rest of you. You were made to get me off."

She breathes out, a sound between a laugh and a sigh. "Only you could make that sound filthy and romantic at the same time."

I leave my thumb on her clit and push two fingers into her cunt, filling her more completely. Her eyes haze with pleasure.

"I'm not going to move," I tell her, lavishing her clit with my thumb, fucking her in a slow rhythm with my fingers so she gets my meaning. My cock is staying put, right where it is, filling her ass to the hilt.

My hand will take care of her. I just want to own her like this, get her used to the feeling.

No barriers.

No more lines.

Nothing is off-limits between us.

"Just let me give you pleasure. When you climax, I'm going to feel it. Your ass is going to milk my cock."

"Oh god." She shudders. Her nipples are swollen, red, and I know they must be aching. I lean in and suckle them, one, then the other, and she moans in ecstasy at my touch.

There's nothing more to say.

I told her what I wanted, and her orgasm is inevitable.

I reach up and wrap my free hand around her throat, squeezing lightly. I wrap my mouth around one nipple and suck hard, and after a few deep, luxurious pulls, her cunt jerks. I fuck her with my fingers a little faster, rubbing my thumb over her clit while I suck... and then she's coming for me.

I feel it all over.

Her tits shake as her body quivers. Her clit pulses under the pad of my massaging thumb. Her pussy spasms on my fingers, slick and soaked.

And the tight heat of her ass, gripping my cock like a slippery, silken fist, jerks, then squeezes. I groan as she milks me, the deep clenches urging me to climax.

I sink my teeth into the soft flesh around her nipple as I come, struggling not to move my hips as my cock strains and I pour everything that's in me into her with a long groan.

She seems to like the feeling and stirs, gasping, her silken heat rippling around me in response to each jerking spurt. She moans, her hands buried in my hair as I press my face between her breasts, my cock pulsing inside her.

We lie like that until the tremors fade, and we catch our breath, stroking each other's skin.

I lift my head and kiss her breasts, suckle her pretty nipples, and kiss my way slowly up her throat. I take her mouth in a sweet but deep kiss that makes her stir beneath me.

Then I press my face into her neck. I sigh against her skin, my whole body shuddering with contentment.

I can't get up.

This feeling is too exquisite.

I just hope the orgasm made it worth any discomfort for her. That she really doesn't care if I caused her some pain.

That she trusted me enough, let me go there, let me have that control, just makes me feel more attached to her. She must feel the way my heart is pounding against her, so fucking strong, so fucking fragile.

She must know it: that she owns me completely.

"I love you so goddamn much," I tell her, still buried deep.

"I know, Jamie," she whispers. "I'm yours."

Megan

Six months later...

I let my bridal gown slide gently to the floor around me and step out of it. Jameson unzipped the back for me, and now I'm alone in the large closet/dressing room.

I'm almost shaking with anticipation, but trying to stay calm.

Just breathe. This is the best part.

I feel like I'm floating somewhere over the mountains.

I just married Jameson. My dream man.

We celebrated our wedding with three hundred of our friends, family members, and some of his most important business contacts; it was the first event held at the Vance Bayshore resort, a private event, one month before the official grand opening.

I can't imagine a better place to start off our marriage than right here. Jameson said tonight, when he gave a toast, that his Granddad would've been thrilled to know one of his grandchildren's weddings was the first celebration at the resort.

The wedding was grand and beautiful and exciting, like our life together.

But now it's getting late, and the rest of our night will be quiet and private and close, like the space between our hearts.

As soon as he walked me up to our VIP suite after the reception, the grandest suite at the resort, and carried me over the threshold, my groom gave me my wedding gift.

He got me a publishing offer for my books. From a major publishing house.

It was just an offer, from a very interested party. But it was mine to negotiate if I wanted it.

When he told me, Jameson seemed worried that I'd be mad he talked to a literary agent without telling me, had them pitch my book series to the publisher, but I really wasn't. I knew him so well, I knew why he did it.

For me. Because I would've hesitated to do it for myself.

Because he believes in me, sometimes far sooner than I believe in myself.

"Your stories are too good to be read by only a few thousand people," he told me devoutly. "You just need distribution, that's all."

I cried.

And I couldn't be more grateful to him.

No matter what comes of the offer... his belief in me is the most meaningful gift he could ever give me.

I stand in front of the mirror and peel off the lingerie I wore with my bridal dress. It was a perfect fit to go under the classy, elegant gown.

But it's time now to get into the *other* lingerie. Because obviously, I had to have two.

Megan on the outside.

Jessica on the inside...

I take the second set of lingerie off its hanger and carefully slip it on and into place. It's expensive, delicate. Comfortable, even though it's so damn skimpy.

Jameson spent a lot of money on it, even though he hasn't seen it yet.

My man loves to indulge me. I know that the fact I don't ask for much turns him on, makes him want to spoil me.

He's a giver in every way.

I've never met anyone who cared so much about my happiness from one moment to the next. Sex, luxuries, his touch, his time, anything he can give to put a smile on my face, to lavish me with pleasure, to make sure I feel loved, safe, and adored, he'll do it.

Jameson Vance is a virile alpha with a romantic heart. I consider myself unbelievably lucky to be the woman who owns that heart.

It's not a position I take lightly.

I want to do for him what he does for me. Always.

When I emerge from the dressing room, he's sitting on the edge of the bed in his groom's suit, with his tie loosened and only the jacket removed. He knows how I love him in a suit.

That's probably the only reason he's not naked yet.

Our eyes meet, and a shock of awareness runs down my spine.

Mine, that look seems to say.

God, I adore him.

I miss him, too, and I know he misses me. I've been so busy lately. Not only with prewedding preparations, but I've found myself so inspired, I'm finally writing my final Wolf-and-Rowan book.

With a happy ending.

Jameson's expression relays not only how much he misses me, but how hungry he is for me.

I'm sure mine relays how damn hot I feel in what I'm wearing for him. I see that he agrees when his gaze rakes down my body.

The lingerie is white, and there's not much of it. The sheer bra has tiny bows above my nipples. The matching panties have a tiny bow above my clit.

My husband spreads his thighs and adjusts his hips as he takes me in. His cock hardens, straining inside his slacks.

I know how much he loves it when he gets to undress me himself, or watch me undress.

"You look fucking gorgeous." His voice is rough with longing, sending a thrill through me. "Come here, baby. I want my wife."

But I don't go to him.

As he drinks me in, I slip a finger over the central seam of the right bra cup. It runs down from the little bow, right over my nipple, and as I touch it, the seam parts, exposing my nipple.

Jameson's eyes darken with lust.

I do the same to the panties, sliding my finger from the little bow down the central seam a bit, parting it to give him a glimpse of my pink flesh.

His cock flexes hungrily, drawing my attention.

My hands fall away, ending the little peep show as I walk toward him.

Even at this distance, he worships my body, like I'm offering him a gift and he's savoring it. My breasts jiggle with each step, the sheer bra hiding little more than nothing and offering little support. The panties are pretty much a wisp of floss.

And knowing those easy-access slits are there, even though they've slipped closed... I know I'm being a tease.

I love to stoke Jameson's desire until he's ravenous for me.

He lets me get away with it, just a little bit.

He reaches for me as I get close, but I hold back, just out of reach. "No touching the bride until the official honeymoon," I tease.

"You better be fucking kidding me."

I laugh. When I drift closer, he grabs me by the waist and the ass and drags me between his legs.

"I'll have you know I didn't wear this under my dress all day," I say sweetly, my fingertips walking up his tie. "I think my groom should get something special, just for him, on our wedding night."

I wrap his tie around my hand, pulling him toward me even as I lean into him, sliding a knee onto the bed beside him.

"I hope you like the peekaboo vibe..." I kiss him, lightly. He growls softly, warningly, and my lips tease his. "My dress was so classic and elegant. Fit for your queen. I love it when you call me your good girl. And I wanted to be your queen on our wedding day."

"You are my queen."

I kiss him again, deeper this time, my tongue lapping luxuriously against his as desire rises through me, hot and intoxicating. His taste. His masculine scent...

"But underneath it all, on our wedding night," I whisper against his mouth, "I want to be your slut, Jameson."

He swallows. "Oh, *fuck.*"

I kiss him, sinking against him. His fingers dig into my ass, pulling me close. And as soon as the balance of my weight tips into him, he lifts me off my feet, flips us over, and pins me beneath him on the bed.

I'm already breathless as that move sends a shock of heat to my core.

"I don't think I like that word directed at my wife." His voice is hot and bleeding with the desire he feels for me. He rams his rock-hard length against my soft pussy, making me gasp. "But when you just said it... it made me so fucking hard."

He sucks on my throat, then kisses his way down my chest.

"Good," I whisper. "Make me your slut."

He groans. "Megan... Jessica... I feel like I got two women in one."

I raise an eyebrow. "And are two women always better than one?"

"Only if both of them are you."

Such a good answer.

"I love it when you fuck me with your suit on. It makes me feel like I'm your bad girl."

He groans again as he licks my skin. "When you say dirty words, it drives me crazy."

"Mmm. Use the holes, Jameson. That's what they're for. Suck on my tits and fuck me."

His eyes flash as they seize mine.

He yanks open his belt and rips down his zipper with such force, the bed shakes. He tears his underwear out of the way and his cock springs out, hard and heavy. Grabbing himself impatiently, he angles between my thighs, nudging the tip of his cock into the slit in my panties... then into my slit.

I gasp and he groans with relief as he pushes, sinking his cock-head into me. Just a couple of inches.

I'm wet, the little wisp of sheer thong drenched in my desire for him.

But he pauses as I wriggle beneath him, trying to take him deeper. He pants over me with restrained need and a look so possessive, it takes my breath away.

His lips are already swollen from my kisses, and I revel in the tumult of feeling that smashes through me. Hunger and adoration. Satisfaction and longing, like nothing I've ever felt in my life.

Jameson grips my jaw with his hand. "You're shaking," he murmurs.

I manage a whispered "I love you."

"I love you, too," he says roughly.

"You're my hero."

"Stop it. You'll make me come too fast."

I laugh breathlessly. "Tell me you love Wolf, too. I know you do. He won you over."

"Don't push it. I'm holding out until I read the ending."

I smile.

"Actually, I'm working on convincing the author to let me read it before she publishes it. I like happy endings." He drifts his lips over mine. "No. I love them."

Then he shoves into me, and we stop talking. There's nothing more that needs to be said.

Because we already have our happy ending.

THANK YOU FOR READING!

Need more of Jameson and Megan's happily ever after?
Get the free *Charming Deception* bonus epilogue at
jainediamond.com/bonus-content
or scan the QR code:

Don't miss Harlan's book, *Darling Obsession*,
the next book in the Bayshore Billionaires series!
Scan the QR code to see it on Amazon:

NOTE TO READERS & ACKNOWLEDGMENTS

WOW. Looking back at where I started out on my writing and publishing journey, it feels incredible to be writing these words: this is my twentieth published book. It's the eighteenth book in the "Dirtyverse" book world, which all started with rock star Jesse Mayes and sweet Katie Bloom; if you haven't read their book yet, you can pick up *Dirty Like Me* and head down the Dirtyverse rabbit hole. It's loaded with fun, feels and steam in here!

Veering off on this new branch in the Dirtyverse and introducing a whole new family was both thrilling and a little nerve-racking. I haven't introduced a brand new hero *and* heroine in a book since, well, eighteen books ago! I hope you're as intrigued as I am by Jameson's siblings and hungry for their stories, because they are coming! And of course, there's Megan's sibling, too; you may notice I've been introducing hot hockey players, bikers, bodyguards, and others all along the way. Eventually, all the stories of the Dirtyverse will intertwine.

To everyone who supports my work and helps me continue to grow as an author... A big thank you to Valentine and the incredible team at Valentine PR; with all your help I feel like I have a book-loving army at my back. To my PA and Queen of Fandom, Alyssa Giselbach, thank you for keeping the readers' groups Jaine Diamond's VIPs and Jaine Diamond's Spoiler Room such fun places to be, and for all the pics of Christian Hogue, which gave me major Jameson vibes. Thank you to editor Linda Ingmanson for meeting my tight deadlines with zero panic. Thank you to narrators Lee Samuels and Victoria Connolly, and Samara and the team at Brick Shop Audio, for bringing Jameson and Megan to life!

The biggest, squishiest thank you, as always, goes to Mr. Diamond, my partner in love and publishing. Thank you for keeping me fed while I forget everything outside the author cave, understanding all my crazy, and loving me for it.

And a massive, heartfelt THANK YOU to YOU, for reading this book!

If you've enjoyed Jameson and Megan's story, please consider posting a review and telling your friends about this book; your ongoing support means the world to me.

With love and immense gratitude,
Jaine

PLAYLIST

Find links to the full playlist on Spotify and Apple Music at
jainediamond.com/charming-deception
or scan the QR code:

Too Sweet — Hozier
Thunderclouds (feat. Sia, Diplo & Labrinth) — LSD
I Said Hi — Amy Shark
Plans — Birds of Tokyo
Only Love Matters — The Black Keys
Stir Fry — Migos
Adore You — Harry Styles
Game — Doja Cat

Overdrive — Post Malone
Chills — june
Lost — Maroon 5
Uh Huh — Julia Michaels
Watermelon Sugar — Harry Styles
Forever (feat. Post Malone & Clever) — Justin Bieber
Dreams (Piano Version) — Lissie
You're the Best Thing About Me (Acoustic Version) — U2
DELIRIUM — Elley Duhé
Need You Tonight — INXS
Adore — Amy Shark
TALK! — Elley Duhé
So Am I (feat. Damian Marley & Skrillex) — Ty Dolla $ign
It's All So Incredibly Loud — Glass Animals
You'll Pay — The Black Keys
Boots Or Hearts — The Tragically Hip
I Want You — Kings of Leon
Lights Up — Harry Styles
How Deep Is Your Love — Calvin Harris, Disciples
Nobody's Love — Maroon 5
Espresso — Sabrina Carpenter (BONUS EPILOGUE SONG)

ABOUT THE AUTHOR

Jaine Diamond is a Top 5 international bestselling author. She writes contemporary romance featuring badass, swoon-worthy heroes endowed with massive hearts, strong heroines armed with sweetness and sass, and explosive, page-turning chemistry.

She lives on the beautiful west coast of Canada with her real-life romantic hero and daughter, where she reads, writes and makes extensive playlists for her books while binge drinking tea.

For the most up-to-date list of Jaine's published books
and reading order please go to: jainediamond.com/books

Get the Diamond Club Newsletter at jainediamond.com for
new release info, insider updates, giveaways and bonus content.

Join the private readers' group to connect with Jaine
and other readers: facebook.com/groups/jainediamondsVIPs

- goodreads.com/jainediamond
- bookbub.com/authors/jaine-diamond
- instagram.com/jainediamond
- tiktok.com/@jainediamond
- facebook.com/JaineDiamond